9,50 $ 950
c 5-0
7/88

The Brick People

Alejandro Morales

Arte Publico Press
Houston, Texas

This book is made possible through a grant from the National Endowment for the Arts, a federal agency.

Arte Publico Press
University of Houston
Houston, Texas 77004

Morales, Alejandro, 1944–
   The brick people

   1. Simons Brick Factory—Fiction 2. California
—History—Fiction. I. Title
PS3563.0759B7 1988   863   88–10409
ISBN 0–934770–91–3

Copyright © 1988 Alejandro Morales
Printed in the United States of America

The Brick People

For
Delfino Morales Martínez and Juana Contreras Ramírez

The world dissolves when someone
ceases to dream, to remember, to
write.

Fuentes, *Terra Nostra*

Chapter 1

From the east where time began, the wind blew hard through the canyons and cold off the snowy mountains as Rosendo Guerrero waited in the early grey morning for Joseph Simons to emerge from his office. The morning brought back memories to Rosendo of his mother and father who were murdered by a deranged Frenchman who believed that the Emperor Maximilian was imprisoned near the Guerreros' home. He was thirteen when the demented man broke into his home, demanding to know the whereabouts of Emperor Maximilian, a man whom neither Rosendo nor his parents had ever heard about. The crazed man shot wildly at the Guerrero family: father, mother and five children of whom Rosendo was the eldest. His brothers and sisters did not scream but watched and turned into small brown rocks. Within the room filled with the the screams and hand defenses of his father and mother attempting to stop the bullets with torn voice and bloody hands, and the insistent questioning and firing of the Frenchman, Rosendo overcame fear and leaped out through the doorway to survive in the blackness of the North.

For many days, perhaps weeks, there was only blackness before his eyes. He kept advancing on the Flint Knife of the Northern axis of the ancient Aztec coordinates his parents had taught him. He could not go toward the Red Reed axis of the East, nor to the White House of the West, nor dare to look back at the Blue Rabbit of the South. At this time these colors and images were hidden deep in his mind. Traveling through the pure blackness for seven years, Rosendo followed the brilliantly sharp Flint Knife that opened a path to the North. Rosendo arrived in Los Angeles to realize that most of his young adult life had been spent journeying to a place that he knew nothing about. He had followed a directional mandala that his parents had inculcated in his psyche.

At the Simons Brickyard in Pasadena in 1892, he now traced the directional mandala in the soft red earth. The morning was one of complete loneliness as he finished the last oval figure of the mandala, which consisted of a center and four ovals interrelated in a continuous unwinding, infinite spiral of energy, time and space. The figure symbolized Rosendo's perception of the cosmos. It represented the pattern Rosendo would follow to construct the buildings on the six acres where the brickyard evolved.

The men had worked for two hours. They had started early and would soon finish a complete order of bricks for a small house to be built on Fair

Oaks near the intersection of Glenarm. The Simons Brickyard had achieved the capacity to produce fifty thousand bricks per day. The constant demand for brick projected a lucrative future for the brick business. Joseph Simons, the owner, had given Rosendo the authority to hire and fire the workers. At this time the yard had forty men, interviewed and selected by Rosendo. Most of the men hired were from Guanajuato, Rosendo's home state.

Rosendo tossed away the stick with which he had traced the figure on the clay. He looked at the door of the office from which the patron would emerge. He waited and observed the men at work. He, Rosendo Guerrero, did not labor; he directed and ordered. He, the privileged foreman, felt powerful. Physically he feared no one. He respected Joseph's business capabilities and the abilities of the labor organizers who mounted strikes against men like Joseph. Rosendo's job was to keep the Mexicans producing constantly and remaining content with what they had, as well as function as sheriff of the town of Simons. Thus far no trouble had arisen and Rosendo did not expect any.

Bricks were in demand and production continued to expand daily. Although Joseph knew a great deal about the production of brick, it was Rosendo who had taught him about clay and formulas for the preparation of mud, information which Rosendo had acquired from John V. Simons, Joseph's cousin. Joseph listened carefully and experimented to improve his company's products. For the first year and a half he labored side by side with Rosendo and the workers. He built molds, trays, and long-drying racks; mixed, poured and formed red mud into bricks; dried and stacked the bricks into monolithic kilns for firing. Joseph acquired knowledge and business sense from Rosendo, whom he recognized as a business mentor.

Inside the office as he prepared for the day, Joseph remembered the strange story he had heard the first time he met Rosendo. The waiter had offered the menu, but Joseph was not concerned with breakfast. Waiting for his coffee and reviewing some financial statements, he noticed a painting of a man and woman on the wall.

"Who is that woman?" Joseph asked the waiter as he poured the coffee.

"That's doña Eulalia. She used to own lots of land around here. People say she still roams and haunts the countryside, especially the road that leads up to this hotel." The waiter casually glanced over at the painting.

"How old is she there?" Joseph queried as he studied her dress.

"That's the mystery of la doña. Nobody knows her real age. In 1836 or so, according to some kind of census, she was said to have been fifty-seven. Then eight years later she gave her age as forty. When she lost her land it's written that she was one hundred and fifty-five years old. And finally when she died in 1878, the doctor said he saw documents that would make her, on her dying day, one hundred and seventy. Some people think she is still alive."

"Absolutely astonishing," Joseph said.

"What's more astonishing is what happened to her," the waiter replied.

Doña Eulalia Perez de Guillen married Juan Marine and became a guiding force in their life. Together they petitioned for a parcel of land known as El Rincon de San Pascual. Doña Eulalia had been active in the affairs of Mission San Gabriel where she attended to the Indian women, teaching them personal Christian hygiene and how to look after the infirm and dying. She grew to love the land which she and her husband developed. As a symbol of her love she planted an oak near the beginning of the road that leads to the Raymond Hotel in Pasadena. Her husband was present when she gently placed the tree into the earthen womb that she had dug and formed with her hands.

"Juan, I am this oak. It will grow as certain as my love for you and the land. The day they chop it down I will die and I'll become an insect of the land."

Doña Eulalia and her husband covered the tree with earth, watered it, and placed several large rocks and a wooden cross around it for protection. They mounted their horses and moved on to their house on the other side of El Rincon de San Pascual.

She kept nurturing her oak tree and it sprouted three main branches— her sons. Soon after the birth of their third child, Juan Marine suddenly fell ill. He lasted seven days in bed. He lost hair, could not eat and his skin turned reddish as if it were burned. During his agony he stated that he had seen strange objects coming from the sky which had surrounded him and left. The three sons became terrified of their father, and the people who saw him were convinced that he was bewitched and that the family had been cursed. Immediately after the death of Juan Marine, proceedings were initiated to take El Rincon de San Pascual from the Marine family.

Over the years, doña Eulalia fought each petition which threatened her legal right to the land. Throughout these long psychological battles she continued to care for her oak tree that grew stronger. One day upon her return from watering the tree she discovered that her three sons had abandoned her. They indicated in a note that they had lost interest in the fourteen-thousand acre ranch and that they preferred to seek their fortune in the city. The letter was not signed. Of course doña Eulalia could not believe that her sons were capable of such an unexpected action.

She began to search for her sons. She traveled to Los Angeles and inquired in all the outlying communities. She sent messages to the newspapers and asked at the various churches and missions. As she ventured further away, it became obvious that she was under surveillance, and the fear that her home was in danger was born in her heart.

On a Sunday she had gone to early Mass and then to Los Angeles to inquire about passage on a ship to San Francisco. When she returned home, certain that her decision to go to San Francisco was the correct one and convinced that surely her sons had gone to that mighty city, she found her house ransacked. Doors, windows and furniture had been broken. The criminals had taken everything of value. Food and every article of clothing were gone. Doña Eulalia realized that she had absolutely nothing but the clothes on her back and her oak tree.

Shocked by the devastated house, she ran through the rooms and glanced out at the world through each window. Suddenly she understood that the oak tree was in danger, and bolted out of the house and ran in the direction of the tree. She struggled to keep breathing. Falling and ripping her dress and undergarments, she advanced. Crawling, she moved forward, thinking that under no conditions would she ever give up. Her arms and legs felt like rocks, her mouth was dry, and yet she continued to get closer to the tree. She knew that they had been watching her for some time and were probably observing her now. Soon she would arrive at the place.

Doña Eulalia stumbled on one of the rocks guarding the oak and fell before a large wound in the earth. With the last illumination of the sun she noticed the stripped root system and further on the fallen tree. They had chopped it down and cut the tree into four main pieces. The trunk was in front and perpendicular to her; the three principal branches were cut where they joined the tree trunk and then placed like a head and two arms forming the symbol of a man.

"¡Mi familia! ¡Mi vida!" Doña Eulalia's scream tore into the coming night.

There on the ground she saw her husband and three sons and beyond them was the cross that she and her husband had placed so many years ago for the protection of the tree. On her knees she grabbed fistfuls of earth and rubbed it on her body. She ripped at her dress exposing her flesh to the elements of nature. She faced the pit and allowed herself to fall forward.

Three weeks passed before a local farmer and his family discovered the remains of doña Eulalia's clothes in the pit. The farmer went for the authorities in Pasadena. Hundreds of people from the town returned to see the clothes of the tragic doña who had been reported missing by neighbors the day after she discovered the severed tree. No one was willing to touch the clothes. Finally one of the local roughnecks jumped into the hole and grabbed the dress and threw it out at his friends whose faces suddenly communicated terror. The man in the pit looked at his feet and saw hundreds of indescribably large brown insects. The insects began to crawl onto his pant legs. Many people were paralyzed. Others ran screaming that the doña had turned into millions of insects. Horror choked the people as they watched the insects overtake them, spread out and cover El Rincon de San Pascual.

"Absolutely astonishing," Joseph repeated.

"Yes," the waiter agreed. "It's unbelievable that she turned into millions of brown insects, and yet people saw it happen. She understood the earth in a special way and possessed powers of the earth. She is the soil and those insects are her."

Shaking his head in disbelief, Joseph put his coffee cup down and walked outside to the front of the hotel. He strained his eyes to see but in the distance there was no sign of horses, wagon or driver. Irritated, he checked his watch—eight-thirty—and remembered that John's reply had indicated eight o'clock. He returned to the hotel dining room and ordered more coffee. No telling when the wagon would arrive. Hours passed and by ten-thirty he had had enough. He decided to go looking for the wagon. At the moment he rose to go to the room to leave his luggage, a ruckus broke out in the lobby. Joseph moved nearer to see what had occurred. The reception clerk shouted at a dark man wearing grey woolen trousers, a white shirt, black vest and a grey wool cap who stood calmly in front of the counter.

"You can't be here! If you have something to sell, go to the back entrance. No Mexicans or niggers are allowed! Get out!"

In his compact and strong stature, the dark man projected the image of power. The clerk's aggressive insults failed to perturb him. He expressed no fear as he stood his ground. From under his vest he slowly and deliberately pulled out an envelope addressed to Joseph Simons and handed it to the belligerent man. The clerk turned to find Joseph by the dining room entrance. Joseph sensed that this was the wagon driver and was relieved that he had arrived. He was not angry at the driver but at the clerk. The Mexican works for John but could easily work for me, he thought as he was handed the envelope. The driver turned and walked out the main hotel entrance.

"Mr. Simons, I . . ."

Joseph raised his hand indicating that he did not want an explanation from the clerk. The Mexican was not much older than Joseph, but his face and demeanor revealed waves of experience. Outside tending to the horses he waited for his orders. With a growing smile Joseph pushed the door open to see the unexpected. To his surprise John had sent a team of four large horses pulling two wagons. The horses were of obvious excellent stock and the wagons were new, the best and the biggest of their kind. The driver studied Joseph for a moment and stepped up onto the seat. Joseph nodded yes. The Mexican nodded yes. Joseph and Rosendo drove four horses and two wagons down Fair Oaks toward Glenarm Street. As they paced along confidently, men and women scrutinized them. Rosendo had turned out to be an excellent carpenter, handyman and shrewd business-man, a key factor in the success of Joseph's brick company.

Rosendo glanced at the office door and shook his head in disgust when a man interrupted.

"Don Rosendo!" the large man who moved parallel with him called from a distance. Rosendo waved.

"Some friends would like to speak with you. They are interested in a little job. If you would please, don Rosendo."

Rosendo stopped at the barn where workers laughed and prepared horses, mules, wagons and tools for the day's deliveries. The man who made the request stood twelve feet away and waited for an answer.

"Why, of course. Tell them to be here tomorrow at eight in the morning for an interview. At exactly eight," Rosendo spoke sternly, eye-to-eye.

The man lowered his sight to the ground. "Thank you, don Rosendo. Thank you."

"You're very welcome. Now back to work," Rosendo said, motioning the man to the pits where he would put in a twelve-hour shift digging red clay. Rosendo turned his attention to the barn and to his surprise he saw Joseph guiding a favorite horse saddled and prepared to be ridden. Joseph let go of the reins and approached Rosendo.

"I want ten more men hired. Remember, no Chinamen."

"Yes, we have a lot of work." Rosendo crossed his arms.

"Within a year I'll double the crew," Joseph smiled.

"The ten men you want to hire, where will they sleep?" Rosendo asked cautiously.

"They can sleep in the barn or share the bachelors' quarters. You don't expect them to complain, do you?" Joseph laughed.

Rosendo shook his head but with eyes, mouth and hands communicated that to prevent their leaving, the men should have something better.

"I'll order wood to build cottages. Meanwhile they can live in tents. You suggested a place for the cottages. Where?" Joseph waited.

Rosendo stepped out in front of Joseph for a better view of the place in question. "The west side of the yard. In the White House of the West."

Rosendo made statements that Joseph could not comprehend; however, he respected the meaning and importance Rosendo gave to them. There was always an abstruse logic which Rosendo brought to the surface. Joseph had a high regard for Rosendo's linguistic ability. Since the time that they had met, Rosendo had spoken English well.

"Why the west side? Aren't we going to dig there?" Joseph asked.

"No. The pit in the south is rich. For many years we will get clay out of it. We will dig towards the north from the furthest point in the south. Towards the center of the yard. From the center we will gradually go down, deeper. The deepest point will be the furthest away from the center. We have houses on the east now and we should build more on the west separating the workmen. We will have two sources of energy, two sources of labor. The brick works and the new machines will be on the north side of the center, on the north side of the east-west axis. The office is located at the center. From there you can observe the world you create." Rosendo seemed satisfied.

"I'm convinced, Rosendo. But you know I want you to move into the office. It will be the foreman's quarters."

Rosendo welcomed the change and opportunity to be at the center of the evolving directional mandala.

On that grey morning of changes, Joseph had an appointment at a Pasadena bank to finalize the purchase of two stiff-mud brickmaking machines. The parts had been delivered and in the afternoon the mechanics would assemble the apparatus. Joseph planned to observe the arming of the technological beasts. Rosendo would also be present to learn their operation. On schedule was a trip to the property on California Street which Joseph had bought to build several homes for his family. The houses would be constructed with Simons brick, of course.

"Rosendo, I want you to hand-pick the best brick, the best material for my house. Start on that today. I'll see you in the afternoon with the mechanics."

Joseph grabbed the reins, mounted the horse and galloped out from the center of his company, following the north-south axis to the outside world.

Rosendo marched through the yard, watching the men to make sure that the production was maintained at approximately fifty thousand bricks per day.

With the installation of the new machines, the digging in the clay pit became more intensified and in six months the Mexicans had gouged out of the earth twice as much clay as Joseph and Rosendo had estimated for that period of time. An immense red hole began to form, a wound located in an unnoticeable place on the earth's precious skin. Rosendo hired more Mexicans who fell into the pit as laborers who dug, molded, and created the material that built small to large pyramids.

Joseph, satisfied with the progress of his company, valued the Mexican worker and, in his opinion, endeavored in every way possible to keep his peons happy. Above all he did not want outside labor voices heard inside the brickyard. There were labor movements in the country that inspired unmeetable demands and lethal strikes. If his workers demanded fewer hours and more money, the company's economic progress would be greatly retarded. In different parts of the world social movements threatened to destroy established world powers. Brown men nibbled away at portions of the British and Spanish colonies. In the United States, unionism became stronger and urged labor to fight for fair pay and improved working conditions. Unions and radical socialists compared the situation of exploited workers in Latin America, Africa and Asia to laborers in the United States and urged the people to guard against unjust treatment. Joseph, aware of what could happen if extreme idealists infiltrated his workers, did whatever was necessary to keep their spirits high, without damaging the company's profits.

In the afternoon Joseph chose to ride alongside Rosendo as he made his rounds through the directional mandala of the brickyard. As they neared the ridge of the pit, several workers ran excitedly toward them.

"Don Rosendo! Difuntos! We have discovered thousands of cadavers!"

Rosendo heard the cries with a puzzled expression which soon turned to a serious look.

"I won't enter the hole anymore! It's sacred ground!"

"I'm afraid the dead saw me!"

"We might awaken them!"

Joseph steadied the horse and waited for an explanation from Rosendo who searched beyond the men toward the pit.

"The men have found a burial ground. Probably Indian," Rosendo said as he moved away from the screaming men. Abruptly he turned the horse.

"Calmense! If you're afraid, go to work in the drying racks! Cowards! The dead won't harm you; they only scare you!" he shouted.

Rosendo daggered the workers' pride. He had questioned their machismo. They were not cowards, but they had been frightened, shocked into running like children away from what under normal circumstances would be considered simply a corpse in the natural process of decomposition. They had been taught to respect the dead and not violate their right to peaceful rest. Four men followed Rosendo as he advanced to the pit. One remained behind and walked slowly away to the center of the yard. Joseph recognized the contorted expression of terror on the man's face as he left.

By the time the group arrived, the work had stopped at the pit. The men, in a red field of clay, circled and stared down into several deep cavities in the earth. Silence dominated the area. A slight breeze passed from the north to the south as Rosendo and Joseph dismounted and moved into the nearest circle. Both men studied the grave and noticed a strange logic to its whole. In the center was a clothed and preserved body. Contrary to what the observers expected, the body had not decayed. Around the mummified remains, almost in a perfect arrangement, parts of other bodies reached out from the clay wall to touch the body at the center. Joseph saw a hand, an arm, a foot, a leg, and buttocks extending to the center. None of the cadavers was dismembered, but they were contorted in an exaggerated way to emphasize a specific part of the human body.

Joseph turned away, yet curiosity made him join another circle of men staring at the human remains. He moved to another and then another. To his surprise most of the mummified bodies, clothed in Chinese garments with hair and beards arranged in the Chinese tradition, looked up through Asiatic eyes. Ten holes had been filled with corpses. Joseph understood about the land being a sacred burial ground for the Indians, but why hundreds, perhaps thousands, of Chinese were buried there was beyond his comprehension.

"Massacre, massacre," Rosendo repeated, with a disgusted, angry tone.

The many accounts of the massacre had rendered the infamous occurrence a blurry memory in the community's conscience. Most people believed that the Chinese were apt to spin tales against the Anglo Americans and that the story of the massacre was a legend brought from China. Few people were convinced that the massacre had taken place. But Joseph and Rosendo peered down at hundreds of Chinese bodies with bullet holes, stab wounds and crushed craniums. Bodies piled four and five deep comprised the proof that a horrendous massacre had occurred in the recent past.

Joseph and Rosendo ordered the men to continue digging and to place the remains in a pyramid at the center of the main pit. Some of the workers simply refused and left. The majority, motivated by pity, morbid curiosity or the desire to give some kind of acceptable ritual burial, stayed to exhume the victims so that their souls would sleep in harmony with God. While the pyramid of flesh grew, the bodies began to dance in Joseph's mind.

The blood had flowed from a feud between two Chinese fraternal organizations. The battle had resulted from a forbidden love affair between two young people whose parents belonged to rival Tongs. The Nun Yong Tong accused members of the Hing Chow Tong of stealing one of their women. The father refused to allow his daughter to wed, under any circumstances, a man from the Hing Chow Tong. It so happened that Chang, the young man deeply in love with Kim, arranged a meeting with his beloved in the garden of Antonio Francisco Coronel's residence on the Calle de los Negros. On the day of the meeting Kim was followed to the garden by members of her Tong. There the lovers were surprised. Fearing for her life, Kim ran away with Chang to the main residence of his Tong.

Against the Chinese tradition of complete obedience, Chang took his lover and ran away to hide somewhere in the city of Los Angeles. That evening, sporadic shooting broke out between the Tongs, both clans convinced that the other had caused a serious affront to the honor of their family. As more members of the Tongs gathered throughout the night, the gunfire became more constant. The residents of the Calle de los Negros called for the police.

In the early morning hours Officer George Bilderraine arrived as the Chinese waited on the street. Seemingly unafraid, Bilderraine positioned himself in the center of the street between the two feuding Tongs and called for a ceasefire. As he pronounced the last word of his order, shots rang out and one Chinese fell. Bilderraine followed the gunman into an adobe building which was on the Coronel property at the corner of Arcadia and Los Angeles streets. Approximately one-half hour later, shots sounded from within the Coronel compound, and soon after Bilderraine walked out to the street and fell fatally wounded. Worried about Bilderraine, the Chinese screamed and cried for help. At that moment a passing businessman went to Bilderraine's side. As he tried to move the wounded man to a safe place, he was killed along with three bystanders: a Chinese man and woman and a Mexican child who had been observing from a buckboard tied in front of the hardware store. When the child's father and mother emerged from the store and discovered their son, more cursing and screaming began, accompanied by indiscriminate shooting into the crowd of Chinese. The father was restrained by friends and was taken away with his wife and dead son.

As the morning progressed, more Chinese appeared with guns and more townspeople, Mexican and Anglo, reached for their arms. The word of the killings spread to the outskirts of the city. Crowds, mostly men, gathered at different points around the central plaza and on streets leading to the Calle de los Negros. On Los Angeles Street another mob, composed of the lowest elements of the population who wanted only to murder, fight, loot and rape, prepared to advance toward the entrance to the Calle de los Negros. By late afternoon whiskey and wine circulated abundantly and freely; now nothing could hold back the monstrous specter of violence and bloodshed.

The Chinese block was on Sanchez Street behind the Coronel adobe, where the Chinese had businesses and restaurants. The street, a gathering place for most of the Chinese in Los Angeles, was the safest cultural zone for them. As the night advanced, the Chinese gathered in the buildings on Sanchez Street as well as in the Coronel compound. In the early evening Sheriff James F. Burns came on the scene, deputized several citizens, and with a few city police surrounded the area where the Chinese were concentrated, especially the Coronel building where Sheriff Burns believed the leaders of the Chinese uprising were holding out. The sheriff moved to face the uneasy crowd.

"Alright, now hear me out! When mornin' comes I'll arrest those Chinese murderers and rioters." The sheriff pointed to the Coronel building as he spoke.

"I'm in charge here," he continued. "Now I want you to disperse and go home. I've posted a guard. None of those Chinese are gonna get out. Now I'm gonna get some more help and when I get back I expect all of you good citizens to be gone. Marshal MacGowan will be in charge. He has orders to shoot anyone who tries to escape or anyone who tries to take those Chinks."

The sheriff looked at the marshal and made his way through the crowd, disappearing in the darkness beyond the torches. Marshal MacGowan positioned himself in front of the Coronel building and waited. The crowd broke up into smaller groups which grew larger by the minute and more unruly with each bottle of whiskey consumed. The mob began to yell insults and threats and throw bottles into where the Chinese were corralled. Many began to shoot toward the firmament. Several shots were fired into the Coronel building. The Chinese screamed for the mob to stop. The response was laughter. Marshal MacGowan ordered the rabble to disperse but his voice was drowned out by laughter, screams and shots. The uncommon sounds in the night danced madly in the minds of the besieged Chinese. Suddenly fear transformed into panic and several Chinese made a wild attempt to escape. As they ran out into the street, two men were felled by gunfire and two others were caught by Marshal MacGowan, but the mob instantly overwhelmed him and took the two terrified men.

"String 'em up!"

"Hang the Chinks!"

"Hang the yellow bastards!" the crazed, drunken throng shouted as they dragged the Chinese up Temple Street to the nearest corral where on the highest crossbeam both hapless men were lynched.

While the bodies twisted and kicked against the effects of the noose, attempts were made to close in on the Chinese barricaded in the Coronel building. An enormous legion guided by the frenzy of irrationality, hatred and alcohol broke windows, shattered doors and hacked through the roof to shoot at the horror-stricken prey inside. The Chinese had no alternative but to run for their lives, now measured by the distance covered from the place where they hid to the place where they died. Immersed in chaotic fury the mob did not discriminate between man, woman or child. Slanted eyes were condemned to death. The Chinese who fled to the streets were shot; others were hanged from the nearest makeshift gallows: a prairie wagon with conveniently high frames, sturdy high awning bars, and tall solid corral wood beams. As the night progressed, Chinese bodies were to be seen hanged or kicked and dragged through the streets of Los Angeles.

Many Chinese ran to the homes of their employers for safety. Others hoped for refuge in the residence of city officials. Some Chinese found refuge; many were turned away, for the majority of the doors were never opened, not even to acknowledge them before their death. The madness of the night had no exceptions. The violence increased, spreading out from the plaza area. The mob intended to find and kill all the Chinese in town and began to search homes where Chinese were employed.

Early that night the family of don Roberto Londres had taken in as many Chinese as the house allowed. The incensed rabble axed through the door, smashed windows, looted, beat members of the Londres family and captured twenty-five Chinese. The males were brutally beaten and three younger women were separated to a bedroom and repeatedly raped. One of the murderers who reviewed the women with eyes and hands suddenly recognized a female face which he had seen at the beginning of the massacre. The woman stood next to a young man who protected her. The enraged vigilante confronted the couple.

"You're the cause of it!"

The scream echoed into the silence that dominated the Londres living room where the couple embraced.

"You're the Chinese whore the Tongs wanted! You're the ones who caused the killin' of my kin folk!" The enraged man knocked Kim down, followed her to the floor, and struck her again before Chang tore him off his lover's body.

The mob dragged the young Chinese couple outside.

"Strip them!"

"Bring horses, eight horses!"

"Kill the Chinese whore and her Chink prick!"

They were clubbed to the earth. Their bodies glimmered from the perspiration of fear. On the ground they turned to find each other's eyes and held their gaze while men kicked him, felt her and commented on the exposed genitalia. The lovers held their gaze until they were separated to create space for the horses to stand at the side of the four points of each body. The few cries of protest were immediately shouted down. Savage strangers tied ropes to the horses and secured them to the arms and legs of each body. They wrapped wire to prevent slippage of the ropes from the human limbs. Tightly as a razor the wire pierced the skin; blood streamed from the lovers' arms and legs onto the earth. The riders steadied the horses and waited for the crowd's command which, imperceptible to the lovers, at one stroke violently smacked into the silence as an inhuman cry: "Pull!"

The horses, controlled by the executioner who had given the signal with a red handkerchief, moved slowly away from the bodies. The rope became taut and pulled straight on the limbs. From Chang and Kim came not a tear from their bolted eyes, nor a cry from their clinched throats, but only a strange, painful smile from their lovers' lips. The executioner halted the horses and the bodies dropped to the ground. The enchanted crowd continued insulting while more whiskey and wine circulated. After some consultation with the riders the executioner gave the signal again and the horses moved apart faster and pulled harder. The loud popping of bones from sockets and muscles and tendons ripping made the observers grimace with pain. The mob demanded that the horses pull even harder but the bodies still held together.

After twenty minutes the executioner changed the direction of the horses so that those tied to the arms pulled toward the head and those connected to the legs pulled toward the arms. Twice the bodies were assaulted but to no avail. The broken persons remained whole. The mob demanded more horses, and two more for each body were attached to the thighs, which totaled six beasts for each body. While the horses were being positioned, the lovers shook and quivered on the ground as if cold. On the third try the horses burst apart to be stopped by each whole of blood, flesh and bone. The mob became impatient and threatened the executioner who whipped the horses apart, stretching the human bodies to the limit, but still Chang and Kim remained one. At a signal the bodies dropped again. The heads bobbed; the lower jaw on one moved as if trying to speak; the woman's tongue extended from her mouth as if mocking the executioner.

The two riders dismounted and each went to a body, drew out a knife and cut deep incisions inside the thighs next to the genitalia. The same bone-deep incisions were made at the armpits. The riders, skilled at dismembering cattle, were swift and expert with the knife. They mounted, the executioner gave the order and the horses broke into a gallop. At the point when the maximum tension was reached, an other wordly scream came from the mob. At that instant the horses carried off four different thighs and three separate arms. One horse had ripped off only the hand of the woman. In the middle of the street lay two human trunks: an arm and the head on one, and only the head on the other. The executioner returned, cut the ropes, left the human members by the side of the torsos and disappeared. No one came close to the bodies. For hours into the early morning the mob, slowly sobering, filed by the remains.

The killing continued after Sheriff Burns returned with help. He organized a law-and-order group and attempted to dissuade bands of looters, rapists and murderers. In each case only after the criminals had done their evil deed did they disband. When morning broke, the streets were abandoned except for the hundreds of dead Chinese. After consultation with two judges and other political leaders, Sheriff Burns ordered the collect ion of the cadavers at the plaza in the Calle de los Negros. By noon the dead were gathered and piled onto wagons. Tarps were placed over the carnage. Sheriff Burns then indicated to the drivers that the bodies should be transported outside of Los Angeles to a burial site in Pasadena. The sheriff promised that justice would take its course.

Several men were brought to trial before a jury with Judge Ygnacio Sepulveda presiding. Some men were convicted—to be freed within six months. In spite of the unimaginable crimes that occurred, little punishment followed. The City of Los Angeles had shown little concern for the Chinese even at the most brutal moments during the massacre. The entire city fell into a state of historical amnesia. Few people talked about the massacre, and it soon became a Chinese legend or myth, a story about the Chinese populace being torn apart and devoured by giant beasts of the night.

Joseph notified the authorities of the discovery. The reply was a simple "Burn the remains," a statement made by an unidentified messenger who rode off as suddenly as he had arrived.

There were now five large heaps of bodies in the central pit. A strong stench of death reeked in the air. The workers kept digging and extricating more cadavers. As the mounds grew, so did the flowers that the women were bringing to surround the heaps of bone and leathered flesh. From a distance sobbing women with playful children gathered to pray the rosary. They mourned for the unknown dead, for the loss that had never been recognized. Joseph and Rosendo watched and periodically expressed disbelief as to what was happening, what they were directing.

Earlier they had discussed the possibility of abandoning the site and beginning another pit on the west side of the yard, but the best clay was located under their feet and Joseph refused to alter the master plan that Rosendo had envisioned and explained. Joseph was prepared to eliminate anything from the past that might halt the successful progress of the plant.

The bodies would be exhumed and cremated. Joseph would follow the orders given to him by the messenger. He ordered Rosendo to bring in straw, logs and fuel. Rosendo organized some of the men to prepare the bodies for the burning. As men placed logs and fuel on the heaps of cadavers, the women brought more flowers and covered the faces of the dead with beautiful, colored embroidered doilies, quilts, mantillas, aprons and tablecloths. When finished, the crematoriums appeared to be multichromatic mountains of flowers.

As night enveloped the scene, Joseph asked for volunteers to keep the fires burning throughout the night and if necessary through the next day. The cadavers had to be eradicated, reduced to grey ashes. Rosendo selected ten young men to accompany him during the vigil. Joseph went to his horse and gave orders to torch the bodies. The flames rose rapidly. An explosive hissing sound competed with the chorus of women praying the rosary. Gradually the stench gave way to the burning smell of wood, bones and leathered flesh. All night and part of the next day Rosendo put wood on the fire. By the late afternoon Joseph Simons got his wish. The only physical evidence left of the dead were five mounds of ash, blown away that evening by a strong warm wind that came from the east and flew to the sea.

Chapter 2

Joseph held the reins of his horse as he looked down, from the highest hill behind his property, toward the intersection of Colorado Street and Raymond Avenue where his business had gotten its first big break, a major long-standing contract with the City of Pasadena. As the city grew and prospered, more people moved in, built houses, raised families, and traveled daily in and out of town. Because of the traffic, the streets were worn.

Joseph recalled the day when Rosendo had rushed into the office, excited, as if he had received the good news from God, that the bottom had fallen out of Colorado Street at the intersection of Raymond. The rain had weakened the substructure which had buckled under the weight of the pavement. With Rosendo's urging, Joseph went to the City Council and requested permission to put down a square of brick that would cover the intersection of Colorado and Fair Oaks, the busiest intersection in town, to demonstrate the superiority of the Simons product over any other material being considered by the City Council. The experiment was an overwhelming success; however, before the Council could come to a vote and an agreement, the dry months came on fast. Extraordinarily hot weather flattened and hardened the thoroughfares. Only Joseph knew that the streets would have to be fixed on a more permanent basis.

Time proved him correct; the next winter brought about the collapse of several streets and unbearable mud. By late winter the conditions had grown worse, promoting the City Council to award the Simons Brickyard a long-term open contract to repair the Pasadena streets at the first symptom of deteriorations. Joseph was proud that the City Council had approved a program of preventive maintenance introduced by him and developed by Rosendo.

Joseph remembered that year as he walked along the hilltop. He proudly studied what he had created: a successful brick company in the Los Angeles area. He looked at the dwellings of the new workers who numbered about one hundred, not including their large families. He saw the office that would become Rosendo's house as soon as the homes that Joseph built were completed. Only the landscape and gardens remained to be done.

In the full-blooming shrubs in front of the house with three chimneys which Laura Bolin Simons had chosen as her wedding gift from Joseph three years ago, newly hatched birds hungrily chirped while the parents scrambled and darted noisily in and out of the nest bringing food and protecting their charges. The day was hot in the middle of July. A Mexican workman from the brickyard irrigated the trees, shrubs, and flowers in the garden. The workman chuckled and was amazed at the commotion the birds made.

"¿Pues qué alborote traen?" The workman laughed, whistled and continued watering.

At nine that morning, Joseph's father had gone to the yard to tell him that Laura had commenced labor and that by late afternoon, according to Dr. McProssler, she would give birth. A quiet excitement prevailed throughout the house. Joseph could hear the voice of his brother Orin Elmer who encouraged everyone not to worry—that Laura was an exceptionally strong woman and that this child would be the first of many. Everyone wished he would be silent but none dared tell him to be quiet and take away his excitement and happiness. Orin Elmer was a sensitive person whom no member of the family wanted to hurt. As the midwife made several trips to the kitchen and the doctor had not come out of the bedroom for an hour or so, Orin Elmer's talking became more incessant and hurried. The two soon-to-be grandfathers left Orin Elmer in the living room to wait and talk to himself.

On the porch, Joseph raised his sight from the photographs as he waited for news of his wife. He wiped his brow, loosened his tie and again studied the photograph of his parents and brothers which had been taken in 1898 when Theodore Roosevelt marched right up San Juan Hill. Even now, three years after the war, Teddy and the Rough Riders impressed him still.

Of the photographs that had been taken at the wedding, one daguerreotype especially captured Joseph's mind. The image, composed of his father, mother, two brothers and himself, had been taken at his house in the middle of an argument that was interrupted by the arrival of the photographer. In Joseph's opinion the discussion was never resolved and had lingered in his mind ever since. Joseph picked up the photograph and carefully peered at the faces.

Joseph's father and mother were seated next to each other. They were extremely close with their hands almost touching. Ruben Simons, in a black suit and bow-tie, smiled out at his observing son Joseph who stood at his right, as proud of his achievements and family as he knew his father was of him. An invisible line of power went from mother to father to

Joseph, the first son to have survived. Between his parents stood the slim, fragile, delicate Orin Elmer, twenty-eight at the time. Joseph remembered how nervous Orin Elmer became as the photographer prepared to take the shot. Afraid to ruin the photo, he fidgeted with his tie and collar, and buttoned and unbuttoned his suit. When the photographer snapped the shot, Orin Elmer was caught unprepared. His eyes and mouth appeared limp as if at that instant he discovered that he had failed to look strong and intelligent. Orin Elmer drew the energy of love and protection from the center of the family. The photograph had captured Joseph's mother, in a simple blue dress with white collar, turning slightly toward Orin Elmer as if to calm him at the moment of the flash. Positioned behind and to the left of her stood her youngest son Walter Robey who, with a swaggering independent aura, boldly looked straight into the camera and smiled through the photograph and time. With his fingertips, Joseph caringly went over his brother's image.

Walter had not yet arrived from the yard. His work and dedication to the business could not be criticized; nonetheless, Joseph found fault with Walter's arrogant, almost lordly manner of blustering influence on the family and the future of the brick company. Their ways of accomplishing objectives were different; they stood philosophically at opposite poles, as in the photograph. Between them was their family, which was perhaps the only entity that kept them together other than their desire for monetary growth.

Joseph overheard his father talking about building more homes like the ones they lived in today. With that sentence Joseph remembered the unresolved argument at the time the photograph was taken. Walter considered the house which he occupied to be his, but Joseph had built the three homes for his children. Joseph was the legal owner and the homes were destined for his sons and daughters. The understanding with his parents had been that once they were settled, they would build their own homes. Joseph and Laura's first child was to inherit the house in which Walter lived. Walter rejected the idea. He was convinced that an agreement had been made with the family before he came to California that he would eventually buy the property and house he now lived in—the house he had already spent money on for paint, furniture, and improvements. Granted, the Simons family could and would construct new homes, but this particular house was special to Walter. It was his first home in California and he wanted it for his bride, whenever the time came for him to marry.

The argument was never resolved, Joseph thought, as he gathered the photographs and placed them in individual envelopes in a wooden album inside a lovely lacquered wooden box decorated with painted white roses.

Joseph closed the lid. The cry of a newborn infant suddenly filled the silent house, and cries of jubilation followed. Joseph still held on tightly to the box of wedding day memories as his eyes teared and he smiled at the two new grandfathers who congratulated him. Orin Elmer ran in from the living room.

"Did you hear it? Joseph! Did you hear it?" Orin Elmer, drowned in joy, repeated the utterance throughout the house.

Joseph walked into the living room to find his mother holding the newborn. A smile of love and protection for the infant and the father reigned on her face.

"Your son James," she said, looking at Joseph. "That's what Laura called him."

"Yes, we decided on James a long time ago," he said. Pride for Laura and his son James overwhelmed him as he touched the child's forehead.

"He's a strong boy," Joseph's mother whispered. "I must take him to Laura." She walked away with her eyes consumed in tears.

"Mother!" Joseph raised his voice as she entered Laura's bedroom. "What's wrong with Laura?" Joseph yelled as he moved toward the doctor who raised his hands to stop him.

"She is fine," Dr. McProssler sternly replied. "There was a problem, but Laura is all right!"

Dr. McProssler took Joseph by the arm and guided him outside to the porch. The doctor ordered brandy and was joined by Laura's mother who called her husband to her side. The four sat at the table where moments ago Joseph had studied the photographs of his wedding which were not stored in the beautiful lacquer box. Joseph stared into the glass of brandy poured for him by his father-in-law, James Bolin. Something had marred the perfect birth of his beautiful son James. For some reason he was led out of the house and not to Laura's room. Mother and child were fine. They would both survive but yet something drastically wrong had occurred. Joseph knew that in a few seconds one of these three people would tell him. Dr. McProssler and the Bolins looked at each other, desperately, silently urging the other to speak up.

"Joseph," Mrs. Bolin broke the tension. "Laura had difficult labor. She lost a lot of blood. She was never in any real danger." Mrs. Bolin turned to the doctor.

"Yes, that's right, never in any danger. But after the birth and the placenta, Joseph, the uterus was contorted. I don't know why; perhaps the muscles were extremely weak. I can't explain it." Dr. McProssler paused, looking into the lingering afternoon.

"Laura will not bear any more children," he continued. "I'm sorry,

Joseph. I must attend to her now. You can go to her in a while. Recovery will be slow, but she will be fine."

Dr. McProssler had nothing else to say. Mr. Bolin, visibly shocked, followed after him and went to Laura's room. Joseph contemplated the bush where the birds chirped in their nest.

"I'm sorry, Joseph. I had no idea. She was always a strong child," Mrs. Bolin said. "If I knew I would have told you before you were married. Laura feels that you will think that she betrayed you. I'm sure she didn't know! It's nature's way . . . God's will. Don't hold it against her!"

Tears ran down her face. She, like her daughter, was disappointed, perhaps even more. Mrs. Bolin stood and waited. Joseph said nothing.

Mrs. Bolin left her son-in-law alone, staring at the lacquer box and listening to the chirping birds in the late afternoon. Joseph could hear the life, the world around him. In this time of joy, Joseph was overcome with a feeling of great loss. He had experienced a type of multiple death in his heart, and in his mind an eradication of images that represented his sons and daughters. He and Laura had lost them. There would be only one heir to their properties—their only son, James Bolin Simons. Unpredictable waves of anger and hatred toward those he loved came upon him.

If James is to be the only child she can give me, he will be the best! Damn you, Laura!. . .

The afternoon gave way to the oncoming darkness. From the house came smells of food, a light beaming out to the porch, people laughing, the world returning to normal. Everyone rallied around the newborn child and the mother, but to Joseph the birth marked the death of his family.

"Dinner will be ready soon. Doctor McProssler is still with Laura," Orin Elmer said.

The door closed and Joseph was alone again. From the west a glimmer of sunlight struggled to be seen. A light shone in the Bolin house down the street.

"Back to normal," Joseph commented to himself.

The sound of approaching horses and a wagon carried faintly through the darkness.

"Whoa! Here we are. Gracias, Rosendo. See you tomorrow. I hope it's not as hot," Walter Robey Simons said as he pushed open the gate.

"Please give my congratulations to Mr. and Mrs. Simons," Rosendo called out as he maneuvered the horses and wagon around and prepared to return to the black Flint Knife Gate of the Simons Brickyard.

Walter, excited to meet the newborn child and congratulate the parents, was about to enter the house when he noticed his brother.

"Congratulations! Boy or girl?" he asked.

"Boy," Joseph answered softly.

Walter forced Joseph to stand and embrace him. "Well done, brother. God bless you with many more!" he declared. "Let's go see Laura."

"No, the doctor is with her," Joseph said. Both men fell into an uncomfortable silence.

"What's the boy's name?"

"James," Joseph answered.

"James Bolin Simons," Walter pronounced with pride. "The doctor is still with her? Is Laura all right?"

"She is fine. She will be fine. Don't worry!" Joseph stated angrily. He revealed his emotions, but before Walter could ask anything else, Dr. McProssler emerged from the house.

"Laura wants to see you."

For an instant Joseph peered into his younger brother's eyes. His lips were pursed, his brow crushed down on his eyes. An unidentifiable emotion made Joseph turn violently away and retreat into the house.

Dr. McProssler placed his hand on Walter's shoulder. Dumbfounded by his brother's reaction, Walter turned to the doctor.

"What happened?"

"You must not worry about it," Joseph was saying to Laura when the midwife brought James and placed him next to his mother's breast. As the baby's mouth searched for the nipple, Laura reached for Joseph's hand.

"Please forgive me," she said, hoping tears would not come, but they did and she sobbed as her son nursed.

"Don't cry, Laura. The important thing is that you and the baby are well," Joseph said, trying to reassure her.

"But I can't have any more children, any more beautiful babies like this one! Don't you see, I have failed you!"

"Laura, please don't say that. Look to me who loves you dearly and look to your child.!"

"What child? This child marks my disappointment. I feel no joy feeding it. I don't feel anything for this child. It is a stranger to me!" Laura declared in a stern tone. "I will nurse him like a beast and watch him devour me."

"Laura, calm yourself!"

"This child represents the end of my motherliness!" Laura said bitterly.

"Laura, I love you. You're going to be fine. Don't fret anymore. You need time to recover."

Joseph watched Laura nurse their baby. In a few minutes both mother and child slept soundly. He went for the midwife, who took James and placed him in the crib. Joseph watched over the woman and infant he loved, while the midwife busied herself folding diapers, sheets and night-gowns.

"You missed dinner, Mr. Simons?" she asked.

"Laura's taking it hard," Joseph said.

"It will take her a while to return to normal, physically and mentally as well. It's quite a shock, sir." The midwife carried a stack of diapers and placed them in the closet. "Why don't you go out and get some food. I'll be here with them. Come along now, sir."

She walked Joseph to the door. He smiled at his wife and son and suddenly felt good inside. Upon opening the door he was startled by the cry of his son and a large brown insect scurrying joyfully across the floor toward where he heard his family in the dining room.

Chapter 3

The idea had come to Walter late one night when he heard Rosendo speaking with four men who had recently arrived from Mexico. During the past three years Walter had become close to Rosendo. Both were about the same age and had immediately taken to each other. Walter, willing to be guided and taught by Rosendo, had learned the business rapidly and was able to understand the nature of the internal structures of the yard as well as the psychological and physical condition of the workers. Walter had studied the Mexicans in an attempt to identify what made them happy and angry and what their limits of endurance were. He wanted to know how far he could push them.

Two of the four men Rosendo was talking to complained that they had been chased off their land in Mexico by Rurales who supported the hacienda owners. Another man cursed the foreign-owned railroad companies that took what land lay in the paths of their steel tracks. The fourth person who spoke under the lights of Rosendo's office revealed himself to be a boy of about thirteen or fourteen years who described the manner in which his family lived like slaves on the great Teraza hacienda in the northern state of Chihuahua.

Walter, attempting to understand as much as he could of the boy's story, quietly joined the group. While the youth spoke, Walter stood at his side and watched the light dance on his shiny cheek. From the boy's eyes a sheer gleam of desperation, hatred and intelligence sparkled with every gesture and word he said. Walter moved closer. He struggled to understand every word. The boy had fled slavery, and because of his escape from the hacienda his family would suffer horrible consequences. The boy could not return, for if he did it meant death. Walter remembered the boy's last sentence.

"My parents, brothers, and sisters? I assume they're dead."

When the boy finished, a cold silence fell under the light bulb swarmed with insects. The four men humbly and politely answered Rosendo's questions. Only the aggressive and confident boy dared look into Rosendo's eyes when he spoke.

"Don Rosendo, with all respect and humility we ask for the opportunity to serve you," the boy said.

Rosendo caught a glimpse of Walter who stood with an emotionless face. It was Rosendo's decision. He knew what was needed.

"Gentlemen, at this moment there is nothing to offer you. If you want, return at the beginning of next month. Perhaps then there will be work," he said.

The four men communicated with looks and stepped back and bowed as they thanked Rosendo for his time.

"You are welcome, gentlemen, you are welcome."

The men disappeared into the night as Rosendo entered the office and left Walter alone under the light. For days after, Walter thought of those men. He could not forget how the boy glanced at him and how in that minute portion of time the boy's facial muscles tensed, became contorted with fear and hatred. The mask over the boy's face was caused by Walter's breaking the circle of communication among countrymen. Because of whom and what he represented, Walter experienced the emotional weight of the boy's hatred. When Walter spoke to Rosendo about these feelings, Rosendo urged him to travel to Mexico to find out what was happening and where his employees originated.

Walter consulted with a travel agent in Pasadena who lacked information about Mexico but suggested that he travel by boat from New Orleans to Veracruz and overland to Mexico City where he could visit the haciendas near the city. Walter rejected the plan. He wanted to travel from northern Mexico to the central plateau, not as a tourist but as a businessman investigating the advantages of investiture in United States interests in Mexico. His objective was to explore for brickyard sites. Walter wanted his own brickyard, and the possibility of producing brick in Mexico and shipping to the United States could be profitable.

Walter's second objective was to learn about Mexicans, to discover why that boy's face was transformed into such a threatening mask when he saw Walter. The boy's face, even more than his own great desire for economic independence and success, pushed him south.

The travel agent had spoken to an acquaintance who was aware of the financial status of the Simons family and who had worked with them since Joseph's arrival in Pasadena. Walter listened as the travel agent's acquaintance, Mr. Riley, explained what, in his opinion, the political and economic situations were in Mexico. Mr. Riley spoke about Porfirio Diaz.

"For the last thirty years, Mexico has been pacified under Diaz. He's been a good president who understands the importance of foreign investment in his country. And you, Mr. Simons, are doing the correct thing investigating the economic advantages in Mexico. Labor, of course, is a prime concern. For example, if you were to establish a brickyard in Mexico your labor cost would be practically non-existent. Transportation costs would be higher, but with United States railroad interests there, I am sure you could arrange a workable solution."

Mr. Riley carefully moved three crystal bottles of perfume from the left to the right side of his oak desk. He sat back, tapped his fingertips together, and formed a pulsating temple above his chest. He flexed his fingers as he spoke.

"Mr. Simons, there are excellent examples of Americans whose investments have been richly rewarded by President Diaz. Allow me to cite a few. President Diaz gave Louis Huller thousands of acres in Baja California, and Colonel Greene got thousands of acres of copper-rich land in Cananea. He sold rubber-rich lands in southern Mexico for peanuts to Rockefeller and thousands of acres of forest in the Mexican States of Morelos and Mexico to a group of paper-producing American companies in Northern California," Riley said as Walter's gaze followed a cockroach scurrying under the table.

"President Diaz has modified Mexican mining codes for the benefit of American investors such as Huntington, Fitzer and the metallurgical monopoly held by the Guggenheims," Riley continued. "The president has also made certain economic concessions to Ambassador Thompson in order to organize the United States Banking Company and the Pan American Railroad. These concessions have also been beneficial to American oil intersts. President Diaz is a true friend of the American businessman, and of course his country and his people are benefiting greatly from our investments. I am sure that you can be successful in Mexico."

Mr. Riley leaned forward, smiled and spoke softer. Walter moved closer to the banker.

"Mr. Simons, I have made arrangements for you to travel with a group of American businessmen who are interested in Mexico. Some of the men already have major investments or are owners of large parcels of land. This trip has been organized by a William Randolph Hearst who is the proud owner of a three million hectare ranch in the state of Chihuahua. Mr. Hearst and his friends are encouraging American investment. I have spoken to Mr. Hearst's secretary about your company and your financial concerns. He has extended an invitation. What should I tell him?" Mr. Riley asked.

"Yes. Tell Mr. Hearst yes." Walter did not hesitate.

"Splendid, Mr. Simons. In a few days I will give you the details of the trip."

The conductor's announcement had brought silence and a sense of relief in the entertainment coach where Walter and two other gentlemen sat drinking an early afternoon cocktail. In a matter of an hour or less the train they had been on for a week would arrive at the Hearst ranch located north of the city of Chihuahua in Chihuahua, Mexico.

The Hearst party consisted of seven men from California. They had been very cooperative and patient throughout the crossing of the desert. The train had all the conveniences the guests could want: excellent food, drink, comfortable pullman car, dining and bar car and a special entertainment car where several of the men had spent most of their time. Three women worked and slept in that car. The women were there to sing, dance and perform at the gentlemen's command. Nonetheless every passenger waited eagerly to arrive at his destination, to get off the train, to walk on the earth, to sleep in a stable bed and be free of the constant noise of the locomotive and the iron wheels rolling forever over iron rails.

The train slowed and finally stopped. From the windows of the cars the men discovered the white fences of the Rancho Mexicana USA. As the men boarded carriages that would carry them the four miles to the ranch house, Mr. Hearst explained that the name meant that the ranch was on Mexican land but was all American.

On the road to the main house Walter noticed the peasants' dark faces. The people seemed dirty, unwashed. The children never smiled; they simply stared forever into space. Upon arrival at the main house, Mexican women waited to serve them in every way the Hearst guests desired. The house, a beautiful white adobe structure with a red tile roof, had a squared U-shaped floor plan which gave every room access to the central garden.

That evening, after he slept for two hours, a woman about thirty years old with shiny black hair and black eyes prepared a bath for Walter. He was told that dinner would be served at ten, and hors d'oeuvres and cocktails would begin at nine. Walter went out to explore the garden. Upon doing so he concluded that the house servants were the most beautiful of the Mexican stock on the hacienda. The women were striking and the men were handsome. His idea was confirmed when he entered the dining area to find well-trained handsome male and female servants. Some even understood and spoke Engish. These people appeared healthy, intelligent and happy. Walter remembered the faces of the workers outside the house. There were many more, hundreds, perhaps thousands, who worked on the vast ranch.

The guests sat at a large table filled sumptuously with the best native foods produced on the ranch. The business conversation continued into the early morning as well as the eating and drinking. They discussed the possibility of acquiring land adjacent to the Hearst property, of exporting goods to the United States, of expanding the railroad lines into the mountains, of the possibility of gold. Walter listened and at times contributed some commentary on the benefits of producing brick in Mexico; however, as the early morning hours grew darker he looked out the large window facing the land. He felt thousands of protruding eyes peering through to the table, to the food, and thousands of hands reaching toward the meat. He heard the distinct cry of a child, the scream of a woman and the laughter of a man. Musicians played and women danced. No one noticed the other; the men did what they did and the women did what they were compelled to do.

When Walter shut the door he was outside in the cold black morning. Unafraid, he walked out to the land. He thought he heard the child's cry again. Time did away with time as Walter advanced up a hill. The light of the stars allowed him to determine the crest as he struggled to reach the summit.

Suddenly at the top a man appeared. Walter stood his ground and watched the man come down the hill. The man, ragged, filthy, and smelly, carried long moist pieces of putrid intestines. He saw Walter and stopped defensively, protecting his food. Suddenly the man bit savagely into a section of the intestine which burst, streaming liquid onto Walter's face. The man showed his teeth, a deformed face, and as he ate horrible noises came from his mouth. He was not human. What moved toward the bottom of the hill into the darkness, crusted with earth and scales on its back, was an enormous insect. Walter was not afraid. He continued walking to the top.

Before him about twenty insects of all sizes swarmed over a horse's rotten carcass. The animal smelled. To one side burned a fire where the creatures barely cooked the portions of rotten flesh ripped from the stiff horse. A female insect noticed Walter. She wailed as if she had confronted death. She and the others ran from the fire. Some stayed to guard the carcass. A child stepped into the horse's open abdominal cavity and hid. Still other creatures ran off, dragging pieces of meat. Made visible and framed by the light of the stars, the vision screamed through Walter's eyes: a mutilated rotten horse, broken legs, glittering white bones piercing through hide, bloody chest and abdomen gaping open, and centered in death an inhuman child, an insect that sucked and bathed itself with putrefaction. At its mutilated limbs four large insects guarded the carcass. All the senses of Walter's humanity provided proof that the image, intensely sharp and clear, was concrete. The darkness slowly retreated to the first invading light of morning.

Suddenly heavy hooves pounded the earth. Horsemen brutally smashed what Walter saw. Screams and shots pierced the surrounding space Walter occupied. The insects started to run but the horsemen easily overtook them and split their backs with bullets and machetes. The creatures fell into violent spasms, the last struggle before internal physical stillness. A horseman made sure no one got near Walter. While protecting the shocked gringo, the horseman periodically insulted the insects and encouraged his men to search out and kill more creatures.

"Punish them! Who gave you permission to consume that dead horse! Damn fucking lazy animals! Now you will pay for it!"

The killing continued until the sun revealed itself. This was the signal to stop. With ropes the horsemen pulled away the carcass with the child still sitting in the midst of the gaping wound. They dragged off the dead and disappeared over a distant hill. A man brought a horse to Walter and escorted him back to his room.

In the afternoon Walter went to the dining room and asked for Mr. Hearst. The servant woman said that Mr. Hearst was unavailable until evening. Walter walked to the garden and found two men from the group and invited them out for a walk. He took them to where the killings had occurred. Not a trace of anything could be found. He inquired about screams or shots in the early morning. Negative was the answer. A group of peasants returned from laboring in the field.

"¿Muertos?" Walter asked.

The quintessence of hungry, fearful, ill, illiterate dehumanized beings indicated they had seen, heard, smelled nothing. The group stared at Walter and his two companions and seemed to float away. The peasants multiplied, and as they passed they bowed their heads. The horsemen who escorted the workers tipped their hats, smiled and saluted the visitors to the Rancho Mexicana USA. The head horseman, whom Walter recognized as the leader of the murderers, motioned to the visitors that they should return to the house. Astonished that no one would confirm the occurrence of such a hideous act, Walter arrived pensive at the house. Mr. Hearst waited under the patio.

"Mr. Simons, the mayordomo has told me that you asked about the killing of a horse last night."

"No, about the killing of people," Walter said coldly.

"Two horse thieves died last night. Thieves must be punished. President Diaz's policy of 'pan o palo,' bread or the club, is adhered to the letter. We give the workers on the ranch 'pan,' food. My mayordomo takes good care of our people, but there are always some unruly elements that must be dealt with effectively and swiftly. If we did not have a firm hand we would lose the possibility of high productivity. And you know that President Diaz wants his people to be productive," Hearst concluded.

"But I saw hungry women and children horribly slaughtered," Walter declared angrily.

"Now, now, Mr. Simons. The mayordomo reported that his men caught two thieves in the act of butchering a stolen horse. He told me that he found you out there wandering alone. He suggested that you were drugged, perhaps from too much drink. Tequila makes you perceive happenings in an exaggerated way. It causes bad dreams," Hearst said seriously. "You must forget your nightmares because you know that they are only dreams, Mr. Simons."

Hearst now directed his conversation to the men gathered for a work session. "Come, let's have a bite to eat and after I will explain where we will travel next."

Hearst put his hand on Walter's shoulder. "Will you join us, please?" he asked.

Walter disappointedly followed William Randolph Hearst into the dining room, where he would be served by beautiful Mexican maidens.

Hearst cut short the group's stay at the Rancho Mexicana USA and took them directly to the Teraza family's hacienda where for four days the group observed the workings of the hacienda system. One of the Teraza sons acted as their official host. He made the stay pleasant and allowed the businessmen to explore freely the hacienda. The peasants' faces reminded Walter of his father's description of the hollow, hungry faces of enslaved British miners, factory workers young and old, men, women and children denied their humanity and forced to live like beasts. Walter found similarities in the effects produced by the enclosure of the English commons and the Mexican hacienda. Both the English enclosure system and the Mexican hacienda created a destitute and economically uprooted population.

From what he observed, Walter reasoned that in Mexico the situation grew critical. He had seen hundreds, thousands of peasants without land or food. He concluded that millions lived as virtual slaves on the large haciendas. Some haciendas were so huge that no one, not even the owners, knew the real extent of their holdings. The owners rarely lived on their properties. Instead they lived in large beautiful homes in Mexico City where they used whatever political power they possessed to enlarge their estates rather than make them more productive. Walter understood that the owners wanted to exploit labor more and the soil less, that they refused to invest in machinery for they preferred to work their cheap labor to death rather than pay for machine maintenance.

One evening Walter asked the Teraza son the whereabouts of his parents. The young man answered calmly that his parents were either in London, Paris or the Riviera and that they seldom came to the hacienda. The hacendados, a privileged, luxuried class, courteous, sensual and decadent, with nothing to live for except pleasure, Walter discovered, were usually the favorite families of President Diaz.

As Walter rode through the peon villages he saw that the conditions of the Terazas' workers were at best repulsive. Slavery was the only word that described their situation. The Terazas provided a larger than normal tienda de raya where the peasants made all their purchases after getting paid on Saturday night. A man and his family lived on six to eight cents a day and the men earned about fifty cents a week. They did not pay for rent or firewood and seldom bought any clothing.

For several days Walter had watched the men return from the fields and report to the bookkeeper who sat behind a large table on the porch of the mayordomo's house. They waited for the mayordomo to call out their name. Each man answered when called. It took several hours to register one thousand or more names. On one occasion a hacienda horseman beat a man for not taking off his hat in the presence of the mayordomo. After the beating, the victim thanked the mayordomo for the punishment. The peasants waited quietly, respectfully, hats in hand and bowed politely as they filed past the mayordomo's desk.

From the Teraza hacienda the group visited some estates in the state of Jalisco. All the haciendas were relatively similar. Beans and corn were the basic foods in the workers' diet. They used strong chile to help digest food. Pulque was consumed to soothe the effects of the chili. This combination of foods represented an unending vicious, painful and fatal circle which plagued the peasants with intestinal disorders. The lack of water for bathing and general hygiene contributed to attacks of amoebic dysentery, typhoid, and hepatitis.

Walter would have liked to help these people but he didn't dare. He was amazed at their ability to survive. He was not offended at the fact that they were dirty but gave them credit for being as clean as they were. He did not consider them lazy or weak but understood why they were continuously ill and was surprised that any were ever well. He did not believe that the Mexicans loved to get drunk but that they could not bear to remain sober in the conditions in which they existed. He recognized that liquor was the mayordomo's tool to suppress the worker. Ironically alcohol represented perhaps the only escape the peasants had from the misery that was their life. In the haciendas an overwhelming feeling of hopelessness prevailed. Walter saw the Mexican peasants as people who were born and died without hope. Death seemed always to be present, waiting and lurking. The hacienda was a place of death. The hacienda, thought Walter, was a metaphor for Mexico.

As he moved south Walter realized that the tienda de raya was the mechanism that enslaved the peon to the hacienda. He saw that the peon paid with special metal disks that could only be exchanged in the hacienda, or he was given lite credit at the tienda de raya. The debt that the worker accumulated could never be paid. Corrupt administrators charged whatever they liked for the basic commodities needed to live. As a rule the worker went deeper into debt. In most cases the peon was born into debt because children inherited their parents' obligations. In any case Walter learned that a child would acquire a debt on the day he was baptized to cover the cost of the priest, liquor and food for the fiesta. The child's first clothes were bought on credit at the tienda de raya against his future earnings. When the peon was old enough to marry, the money for the wedding was borrowed. The lives of men, women and children were manipulated by the continuous mechanisms of enslavement which were initiated at birth. It became clear to Walter that what he saw of peasant life was the destiny of just about all of Mexico's population.

The majority of people in Mexico had no rights or freedom, and the only justice they knew was dispensed by the patron or his mayordomo. The Hacienda justice was backed by President Diaz's Federal Rurales. These men had the final word and they, like the hacendados, treated the peons worse than animals since animals had more value and were more expensive to replace. The peon was helpless to protect his family against the Rurales or hacendados. If a man dared to defend his wife, daughter or son his efforts were usually fatal.

On one hacienda in the state of Guanajuato the mayordomo who guided Walter through the estate came upon a peon family. While Walter observed, the mayordomo ordered the young daughter to follow him into the field where, in the presence of the parents, he raped the girl who was no more than fourteen years old. After the mayordomo finished, the parents thanked him for his kind attention. As the mayordomo and Walter rode away, the mother and father ran to comfort the naked child. The mayordomo noticed Walter's interest and asked him if he wanted her. Walter almost answered yes. He had been disgusted by everything he had seen except with the idea of absolute power that the hacendados had over the peons. Walter felt that power was needed to help the people, but in Mexico the abuse of power was the way of life.

One morning Walter found himself drinking tequila in a village of about three thousand people located on the Amor family hacienda in the state of Morelos. Hearst considered the hacienda one of the best administered in Mexico. The Amor family had a paternalistic attitude toward their peons and believed in exercising relatively fair treatment. The peons of the Amor hacienda paid no rent and were lent the land on which they built houses. The peasants had the privilege of farming a portion of land for themselves, and in return were obligated to work for the hacienda whenever called upon. Like the other haciendas a priest came to celebrate Mass, to baptize children, to marry couples, to confess sinners, and to perform burial services. Different from other haciendas was the nun that came once a week to teach the children of the village. This was the only hacienda which Walter visited that offered some kind of minimal educational program for the children. The Amors added a doctor to their hacienda staff who treated the workers twice a month. The family believed that they were obligated by God, not President Diaz, to look after the spiritual and physical needs of their peons. The Amors considered themselves gods who held the power of life or death over their peons. On the Amor hacienda the peons were often subjected to the violent wrathful hand of God.

Hearst, a personal friend of the Amor family, had decided to bypass Mexico City and go directly to their hacienda where the Hearst party was well received and stayed for two days. It was the twentieth of December when the group left the Amor estate and traveled two days to Quiseo de Abasolo in the state of Guanajuato where Hearst had made reservations at a favorite resting place, the ancient Caldera Sulfur Baths. The travelers would spend the Christmas holidays at the Residencia Caldera, the best hotel in the area.

On the afternoon of the twenty-second, Walter stepped off the train in Iraputo, Guanajuato. The party boarded a carriage directly to the Hotel Real de Minas. The excitement of Christmas pervaded the spirit of the city. The streets were decorated with colored lights and piñatas of the Three Wise Kings, and nativity scenes were displayed in the windows of businesses and houses. Red, green and white danced everywhere and intensified as they neared the plaza. The cathedral next to the hotel was ablaze with lights. In the square the children played while a choir of young girls directed by nuns sang Christmas songs.

Upon entering the hotel lobby, Walter studied the activity of the vendors and the townspeople. For a moment he forgot what he had witnessed during the past weeks. These people were among the few fortunate who could laugh and enjoy the Christmas festivities. But still, contrary to the good feelings of the holidays, underneath the facade of contentment lay an undefinable tension, an uneasiness that the fiestas could end violently and unexpectedly.

Three large luxurious carriges drove to the front of the hotel. In an hour or two they would depart for the Residencia Caldera. They had time to wash and have a drink. While Hearst and Walter enjoyed a light drink, three Rurales entered the hotel.

"Señor Hearst, llego la escolta," the waiter announced.

"Why do we need them?" Walter asked.

"There has been trouble in the silver mines near Guanajuato. A strike and then a workers' rebellion. Peons were killed," Hearst said softly, only to Walter.

"How does that affect us?" Walter asked nervously.

"There is a renegade band of peons who are attacking travelers on the open roads. I was told there was an attack on the road to Quiseo de Abasolo a few days ago. That's why I asked for the escort. Those damn bandits won't dare come near the Rurales," Hearst said confidently and walked over to the Rurales.

The early evening had turned cold during the two-hour trip to Quiseo de Abasolo. As they passed the agricultural fields Walter recalled that Quiseo de Abasolo was Rosendo Guerrero's hometown. Walter's thoughts wandered from Mexico to the United States, from these fields to the fields surrounding Pasadena, to his family preparing for Christmas, to James and how fortunate they were. Shacks with smoke rising from them dominated the landscape. Tenant farm families prepared for the cold night. The shacks seemed abandoned and alone.

To avoid being a slow moving target and to arrive at the Residencia Caldera as soon as possible, the Rurales insisted on maintaining a fast pace. Heavily armed with two pistols each, machetes on both sides of their fine horses and two new Mauser rifles inserted in leather holsters, the Rurales constituted awesome, unconscionable elite lethal weapons who worshipped President Porfirio Diaz. The Rurales were conditioned to kill anyone who resisted their commands. They were accustomed to shoot first and not ask questions or be questioned. Hated and feared by the peasants as well as by many hacendados and their administrators, the Rurales dominated the countryside and demanded the highest privileges. Everyone worked to remain on the Rurales' good side.

As the carriages approached Quiseo de Abasolo,the town became aware that three Rurales accompanied the visitors. Family activity immediately intensified. Parents hid their young daughters and women prepared what food they had. They cleaned their sleeping areas and the men made sure that some alcoholic beverage was available. This preparation was conducted in the poorest shack, the richest house and the best hotel in the community. The residents had to be prepared to satisfy the Rurales' request. A bocadito, traguito, un lugar para dormir and the most dreaded una compañera were the demands most often made to the population. If the man of the house was not at work he stood before his shack, hat in hand, and bowed when the Rurales passed. Even in the night the people knew when the Rurales were near. In the country, peasants were concerned for one another and communicated rapidly by word of mouth when danger threatened.

At the Residencia Caldera the Rurales were the first to be received. Their horses were immediately taken to the meson where they were brushed and fed. Hearst thanked the men and gave them each an envelope. The Rurales entered the Residencia and were welcomed by the proprietor. Behind the cockeyed trio followed the Hearst party. The proprietor pulled aside a heavy curtain to a dining room where a large table with food and tequila had been prepared. Three young women in white cotton dresses tied at the waist ran to embrace the three men. The proprietor and the Hearst party watched for an instant while the couples kissed and the Rurales helped themselves to handfuls of women's bodies. Upon observing, the proprietor's eyes drooped and the tip of his tongue penetrated slightly through his lecherous smile. Suddenly he remembered his other guests who watched the enthralling young women being caressed. Abruptly the curtain closed.

"Bienvenido, señor Hearst. Bienvenidos, señores."

The proprietor ordered servants to unload the luggage and show the guests to their rooms.

"If you'd like to go to the mineral baths, they are very hot. Perfect for tonight," the proprietor smiled.

Walter followed the servant. From behind the curtain laughter and guitar music could be heard. He imagined the soft brown skin of the women.

"The mineral baths, señor?" the servant asked.

"No, hasta mañana," Walter answered and closed the door.

He pulled off the sheets and fell into bed. At about two in the morning he awoke perspiring. He went to the watercloset to urinate. The music and the laughter of the women were louder. Walter made out the voices of some of the men of his group. He walked out of the room and followed the porch to the sulfur baths where he found five of his countrymen and two Rurales with five unclad women bathing and drinking. Off to one side the musicians continued to play. Near them in a hammock was the third Rural being caressed by one of the three white cotton-dressed women whose dress was off the shoulders, exposing her brown breast. She smiled.

"Come in! The water is great!" one of the men shouted.

Walter searched for an exit but realized he could neither move physically nor respond mentally. He was trapped. If he joined them, he would be one of them. Unknowingly he moved toward the woman who had smiled at him. She went to Walter, held his arm and walked to his room. The men in the pool approved of what was happening. Some clapped, others cheered him on, and some yelled "bravo!" Walter could feel the woman's warm breast against his forearm. Her skin was soft, her flesh beautifully heavy and intensely alive. The woman entered first. He closed the door and capitulated to a Mexican woman.

On the morning of December 24, 1901, accompanied by one Rural and the woman he had made love to the night before, Walter left the Residencia Caldera to explore the countryside around the town of Quiseo de Abasolo. As they made their way around the small plaza to connect to the road leading out of town, they passed the church decorated with paper flowers and a large stage mounted in the church courtyard. He had learned that in Quiseo de Abasalo as well as in other small towns in the area, the townsfolk celebrated Christmas by staging elaborate and ornamented pageants and plays telling of the birth of Christ.

Alongside the stage Walter noticed the priest scolding five peasants, two of whom knelt. Walter and the woman brought their horses to a stop while the Rural rode on. The priest shook his hands vehemently, screamed, and in a rage untied the braid and crucifix around his waist and viciously beat the kneeling men about the head and back until blood was profuse. He then made the sign of the cross and muttered over the battered men while the other three stood, hats in hand and heads down. Walter's horse stepped forward. The woman grabbed the reins, turned the animal around and made it break for the road out of the plaza.

They galloped for about an hour through barren and cultivated fields, passing small clusters of shacks and two colorful cemeteries. The woman halted her horse and dismounted. She looked out over a plain and pointed to a trail that, according to the Residencia Caldera clerk, would take them to a small ranch which was known for its natural wells and hard working families. The clerk had also said that near the ranch was a small adobe and brick factory which Walter wanted to visit. He stared angrily at the woman.

"Don't spook the horse ever again!" Walter yelled. He knew she would understand the tone of voice.

"And you what? You were frightened. Right?" The woman stood her ground and watched Walter's face.

"Vamos, la ladrillera," Walter said calmly.

"Watch out, gringo, or I will lose you." The woman smiled, mounted and moved ahead.

The woman demonstrated superior horse-handling abilities. She was unlike the peasant women he had encountered on the trip. She never told him her name. They communicated by sight, sound and movement. In the opinion of the populace this woman was considered as una mala mujer, yet there was a respect for her abilities and declaration of total freedom which she manifested in thought and action. The night Walter first met her he did not perceive her as a beautiful woman, but as she lay sleeping with the morning sun illuminating her face he discovered her beautiful full-tressed hair, fine eyebrows, long black lashes, strong delicately defined nose, sensual demarcated lips and smooth graceful cheeks. He remembered that when she arose her brownness danced in his eyes, mind and heart. They would both break away soon, but for now they traveled ambiguously related.

In the early afternoon they arrived at the brickyard. The Rural had gone on ahead and had been waiting. As Walter and the woman approached, the smell of burned wood and rotting flesh came and went. The trail turned and followed the circumference of a large boulder. When they reached the other side, Walter and the woman found the brickyard, houses, and shacks destroyed. The stench was now unbearable.

"What happened?" Walter cried out, shocked by the devastation and death that confronted him.

Not visibly upset, the woman shook her head and stared at the corpses as if she had seen death many times before.

"It's getting late for us," the Rural said, bringing his horse alongside Walter and the woman.

"Let's go to Rancho Ojos de Agua for food and a drink. We will spend la Noche Buena in Quiseo," the woman told the Rural.

The Rural and the woman observed Walter who did not respond, but instead fought off the swarm of flies that now blackened his clothes and covered his face. As they galloped away from the putrefaction, the flies subsided. Nausea flooded Walter's stomach and mouth. For the first time during his trip through Mexico he felt he needed a drink of strong liquor.

The Rural, the woman and Walter stayed over in Rancho Ojos de Agua for two hours. Bowls of posole, tortillas and two bottles of tequila were ordered. The majority of the men of the rancho were in the cantina celebrating la Noche Buena while in the houses the women prepared the Christmas Eve meal. The peasants were especially excited, for in the Rancho Ojos de Agua a woman was with child about to give birth. The men drank and wagered on whether she would give birth to a manchild or a womanchild.

The Rural sat unemotionally staring through the open door into the cool night. The woman went and sat by the comal for warmth. She opened her coat slightly to allow the gun holstered below her left breast to swing out and rest on her left thigh. The gun handle was only a blink away from her right hand. Walter drank another small glass of tequila. Strangely, fear began to leave his heart. The quick glances that seemed to come from between the peasants' eyebrows were no longer evil, or cunning, or fearful to Walter. He moved freely from the table to the counter and ordered another bottle of tequila for the Rural who sat like a stone. Men returned, excited with reports as to the condition of the woman giving birth. Walter had captured her name, Milagros, from an old woman who made tortillas and pozole at the comal and predicted how far away the birth was from what the men reported to her. At about eight-thirty a young man walked in and went to the old woman.

"Within twenty minutes, son," she said, her face beaming with joy.

Everyone in the cantina cheered and clapped.

Walter, inebriated, followed the young man outside. Not far from the cantina was a natural well that gave the rancho its name.

"Damian!" Walter heard the young man call to another who contemplated the gurgling water. "Let's go home. It's time!"

Directly across the cantina on the other side of the well both men approached a small adobe thatched-roof house. A warm light came from within. Several women waited outside in case the mother and her assistants required help. Walter had understood that this child was to be the couple's first-born. He had deduced that the man called Damian was the father-to-be and that Milagros labored with the cosmos inside her body to bring forth life.

While Walter waited, music and poetry pushed out the noise from the cantina and the murmurings of the men and women who guarded the expectant mother's door. Down a rocky path, not far from Damian and Milagros' home, was a church. The music and poetry grew louder. A procession of men, women and children who wore colorful costumes and carried shepherds' staffs advanced down the path leading to the plaza. Walter perceived a religious play whose actors were the townspeople.

Periodically the company would stop and someone would step forward and recite a verse. Devils who tempted the spectators and spoke of the delights of sin, old hermits who prayed for the salvation of the townspeople, angels who sanctified the crowd, two jesters who tumbled and made the townsfolk laugh, shepherds who walked solemnly with staff in hand, and pilgrims who encouraged the spectators to join the procession constituted a chorus of El Rancho Ojos de Agua.

When the people came upon the house where the child was to be born, the procession stopped and faced Damian, the relatives, and the neighbors who accompanied him in his wait. After he congratulated Damian, the leader signaled to the players, from whom stepped forth a shepherd and an angel who recited a poem of celebration.

Before pronouncing the last verses, the angel began to lead the procession to the center of the plaza facing the cantina. Walter had forgotten about the Rural and the woman. His concern was for the woman who was about to give birth. He recalled Laura and James, and worried about complications. A doctor was constantly at Laura's side, but the Mexican woman Milagros had only relatives and neighbors. There were no doctors who would come to the Rancho Ojo de Agua.

A fire burned in front of the expectant parents' house. Men gathered to warm their hands and speak about the land, the animals, the weather and the tragedies which occurred throughout Mexico. The men compared the violence to a disease brought about by decades of injustice and hunger. Walter comprehended some of the conversation.

"We can't stand much more. Something is going to happen."

"La violencia."

"We're miserable and we have nothing."

"Damian, this will be your first-born. You almost hit it on the twenty-third. It would have been nice for your birthday. Well, what can you give your first-born child?"

"The strikes, the massacres, the bandits."

"Many are leaving."

"Damian, you have relatives in Los Unites."

"This situation will explode."

"It will be charged to the general and his government."

"Be careful, friends. Strong ears are lurking about."

Damian realized that Walter was listening intently. He looked beyond Walter and observed the Rural and the woman guide a horses toward the gringo. As the three visitors mounted and passed the workers, the wail of a newborn infant came from Damian's house. At that instant a child had entered his creator's earthly garden of delights.

Chapter 4

In the short time Walter had been away, Joseph and Rosendo saw the company grow. Rosendo had hired twenty-five more men, built more houses for the workers' families, installed two more machines, sped up excavation of the pit which grew deeper and larger, and increased daily production of brick. Walter found Joseph and Rosendo satisfied as the Simons Brick Company prospered. Nonetheless, there was one urgent situation which Joseph immediately discussed with Walter upon his return. Convinced that within a few years the Pasadena yard would not be able to handle the growing demand for brick, Joseph wanted to purchase a portion of land in Rancho Laguna owned by Harriet W. Strong. The land, which contained perfect red earth for brick, became an obsession for him. Rosendo had seen the area and he too thought that it was superb for the establishment of a yard much bigger than the Pasadena enterprise.

When Rosendo took Walter to visit the land, Walter touched the red earth and was impressed by the consistency of the clay found in the area. Many of the surrounding properties were agricultural, farmed by Japanese and Anglo-American tenant farmers. Mexicans commuted from colonias near the center of Los Angeles to work in these fields. As Walter let the soil fall from his hand he knew that here he and his brother would build a brickyard. Walter contemplated the immensity of the place, the unlimited possibilities, the millions of brick they could produce and the hundreds, thousands of men who would work for him. Here they will be happy, he thought as he grabbed another handful of red earth. Hundreds of people fell from his hand. Rosendo looked toward the four points of the directional mandala and planned the layout of the brickyard.

At about three that spring day they came upon a well, one of the natural artesian wells that Harriet W. Strong was so impressed with. Rumors indicated that she had bought the land to develop an artesian well water system to serve Los Angeles. She believed the water could be bottled and sold as naturally purified medicinal water. Mrs. Strong had planned to build a series of dams and sell irrigation rights to the local farmers, but during the short time she owned the land the plans were abandoned, for she had more formal interests that demanded her attention. Finally she decided to sell her part of the Rancho Laguna to the Bartolo Water Works. She hoped that the company would continue with the projects she had planned.

Walter and Rosendo rode back to Pasadena with a strong sense that the land they had surveyed was to be a great force in their future plans. Walter wanted the land and promised himself that he would have it. He asked Joseph to send a letter to Harriet W. Strong and to the Bartolo family expressing their interest in purchasing the land.

The Bartolo Water Works Company had had various skirmishes concerning water rights with farmers and the city of Montebello, California. But not until after the death of Mr. Bartolo, who was shot by an assassin, did the Bartolo family decide to sell. Previous to the murder of Mr. Bartolo, several pitched battles had occurred between the Bartolo family's employees and the tenant farmers, some of whom had died. A series of attempts on the lives of several Bartolo family members followed. The county coroner recorded the cause of Mr. Bartolo's death as a result of an uncurable disease known as violent vengeance. The consequences of this horrible sickness could be fatal to the entire Bartolo family.

Immediately after the murder, a family representative sought advice from Mrs. Strong. She suggested that the Bartolos sell the property. She mentioned that the Simons brothers from Pasadena were interested. The preliminary discussions began and proved to be successful. Finally the Bartolo and the Simons family reached acceptable terms. It was decided that the final documents and deeds should be signed officially at the Theodore Roosevelt campaign picnic to be held at the Pio Pico residence on September 16, 1904, Mexican Independence Day.

Joseph, Orin Elmer and Walter arrived at the Pio Pico mansion, were served the "Whole Ox Barbecue a la Mexicana" and were introduced to people who had lived on or near the mansion and who had personally known don and doña Pio Pico. Hundreds of people wandered about the run-down mansion. Some peered through the windows; others tugged at the permanently shut doors and kicked them in frustration. Political dignitaries circulated through the crowd asking the people to support Roosevelt. Flags and banners were carried and agitated up high by Anglo-American youths. One by one the speakers passed onto the platform spouting a river of words which at the time meant little or nothing to the Simons brothers.

The day was hot and the guests perspired easily. The strong odor of the human male and female animal mixed with the aroma of barbecued beef gave the picnic a sensual, spice-filled spirit. The picnic continued into the night when a small band arrived to perform for the group who were now quite animated. Joseph, Orin Elmer and Walter waited. From among the Support Teddy commotion appeared a woman guiding an old woman who was escorted by two men. The female guide was Mrs. Strong, whom Joseph recognized. After the appropriate introductions Mrs. Strong led the party to a long room in whose center was located a long, narrow, black table and six black chairs.

While the five men positioned themselves around the table, Mrs. Strong helped the old woman sit. As Mrs. Strong took her seat, a man dressed in a black formal suit entered and placed several notebooks on the table. The contracts were read and agreed upon. They had been drafted to satisfy all parties present. Doña Santa Bartolo signed first, followed by the two men who had accompanied her. Joseph and Orin Elmer, in that order, also signed the documents. Outside the music and song continued along with cheers for Theodore Roosevelt. The signing was over; there was nothing left to say. The Simons brothers observed silently as doña Santa Bartolo struggled to rise. The two men assisted her and moved toward the door. As she passed through the doorway she grabbed the door jamb for support. She stood motionless for several moments. In those seconds Joseph and Walter noticed that on the lace at the bottom of her full dress were two large brown insects. As she released herself from the door, one insect fell to the ground and followed her out, dodging the eight feet that stepped forward into the celebration.

For the Simons brothers there was no need to stay at the Pio Pico mansion. The three thanked the hostess, mounted their horses and rode to Pasadena. The brothers rode in silence, each one lost in himself and in his specific dreams and fantasies. They felt proud of their accomplishment. They had purchased close to three hundred acres of prime brick-making land. Their dream of establishing the biggest brick company in Southern California was on the edge of becoming reality. After long hours they arrived at Glenarm Street.

"Walter, tell Rosendo to start moving men and equipment to Rancho Laguna. We need to start building right away," Joseph said.

"Where do we start?" Walter asked, giving his horse to Orin Elmer.

"At the end of Vail Street there's a little road, Rivera Road. On the corner of Vail and Rivera by the railroad tracks is where we will build our main office," Joseph declared. He smiled at Walter and went into the house.

Walter walked alone. Far off he heard the faint sound of gunshots in celebration of September 16. It was an important day for the Simons family. As he opened the door to his house he noticed that the volleys had multiplied. The shooting continued into the early morning.

It was Walter who carefully directed the moving of equipment from the Pasadena plant to the Rancho Laguna building site. In six months Walter, Rosendo, and a new man, Gonzalo Pedroza, transported the equipment and materials needed to set up one machine to produce brick for the company buildings. Walter modeled the plant and town after Rosendo's directional red mandala, the successful design for the Pasadena brickyard. Rosendo's plan, along with what Walter learned about the hacienda system in Mexico, projected his dream for the future. Walter spent hours late into the stillness of many nights designing and drawing buildings, plotting and mapping the grounds for the brickyard. With him he always had his favorite map: a simple sketch of his initial idea. It showed the north and west axis of the mandala extending out from the center of his company and his "Simons Town," as he whispered to someone not present. His loneliness packed itself with the excitement of the beginning of the construction of the first building of the brick company.

The rains began early, in October of 1904, became stronger toward year's end, and continued into March of 1905—a bad six months which found materials and equipment deposited on the corner of Rivera Road and Vail Street. The rain, mud and the disposition of the men and mules made the move happen slowly, at times crawlingly, dangerously and costly. But April passed and the red mud dried.

Three men observed the area where the Simons Brickyard Office would rise. Walter pulled out his map and a drawing of the structure. He showed Rosendo and Gonzalo Pedroza the L-shape of the building and where he planned the doors. Nearby stood a crew of twenty-five men waiting for the order to begin digging. Here at the new yard Gonzalo was crew chief and foreman. He hired and fired the men and answered only to two men: Rosendo Guerrero, his mentor, and Walter Robey Simons, his patron. Gonzalo's crew accomplished the job well, did what they were told and never criticized the foreman. He demanded respect and insisted that the workers address him always as "mister."

Gonzalo Pedroza's place of birth remained a mystery to both him and his parents who had given birth to eighteen children. They had forgotten exactly when and where their son had entered the world. Gonzalo didn't know whether he was younger or older than his brothers and sisters, but he understood that he was stronger than any of them. He depended on strength and brutality to achieve what he desired. This pattern of life, his innate knowledge of how men and women react to fear, and his intelligence made him extremely effective as a foreman.

Gonzalo had worked well in the Pasadena brickyard for several years when he entered in Rosendo Guerrero's favor. When he heard talk of the new yard to be constructed in Rancho Laguna he volunteered to lead the work crew. Rosendo brought him on as foreman. During the initial months of organization Gonzalo stayed alone on the site to guard materials and equipment. Periodically, on weekends, he would ride to Pasadena to visit his wife, Pascuala, and return with supplies that sustained him through the lonely nights. He had constructed a one-room dwelling in which a bed, a table, a chair, a lamp, a string of nails in the wall and one square mirror made existence bearable. Square mirrors obsessed him because his jaw and face square like a Simons brick, never suited a round mirror. No matter the size of the mirror, immense or minute, his face was forever too large. In spite of these unique facial characteristics and his short stature, Gonzalo Pedroza perceived himself as an extremely desirable man.

That morning in May he looked into his nine-by-nine mirror, put his salivated tongue to his thumb and index finger, sharpened and curled the ends of his thick black moustache, slicked his hair back, slipped his hat on and walked out of his wooden cubicle. The twenty-five-man crew had arrived before Rosendo and Walter. Gonzalo ordered them to set up six tents: five sleeping tents and one large mess tent. He prepared coffee and observed the crew. By seven Rosendo and Walter dismounted from their horses and served themselves a cup of coffee. Walter waved the crew closer and explained where they would dig the foundation. When he finished he looked at Gonzalo, who stepped toward the crew, and the construction began.

The crew transported thousands of bricks for the construction and installed machine number one which began to produce the day the building began. Walter believed in always having more than enough materials as well as producing a surplus for future sales. He also planned to trade brick and labor for the other building materials he needed. The company store and pool hall were the first structures to rise from the red soil. Walter planned a company store which would supply the basic living commodities that his workers might need. A post office would be situated in one corner along with Walter's personal office. As Walter perused several postal application forms, he noticed that his post office required a name. He did not hesitate one instant when he wrote "Simons, California" into the identification space. He smiled as he surveyed his workers, his property.

May ended with the furnishing of the office and the building of counters, stands, and wall cases inside the general store. As the months passed, Walter's dream took physical shape. Other dwellings were also started during the raising of the general store. The bunk house, blacksmith shop, and amusement hall, all of brick, were completed one after the other through the months preceding October, 1905. Gonzalo's crew built twelve drying racks next to machine number one, and as the production of brick increased two large kilns were formed along Rivera Road. In September Walter ordered the building of a large supply room, a machine shop and a handball court. By this time Gonzalo's hard-working crew numbered fifty-three, all from the Mexican state of Guanajuato.

By year's end, Walter gave orders to add twenty-five more men to the crew. Gonzalo now directed approximately one hundred men. The company and town grew. Caught in the exuberance of the re-elected President Theodore Roosevelt's Square Deal, Walter decided to build individual family dwellings for the workers. By mid-December twenty-five four-room wooden houses had been completed on Vail about one mile from the general store. Gonzalo chose the best house and was the first to bring his wife. Later that week he gave permission to his best and most dedicated workers, nineteen men, to indicate privately to him the house they desired. A few days after, Gonzalo made his choices and distributed the homes. There were no complaints; everyone seemed satisfied.

The first Christmas in Simons, California was celebrated with a spirit of mutual caring among the workers. In the middle of December a severe cold spell struck and continued through Christmas day. Gonzalo had ordered ten wood-burning stoves which arrived three days before Christmas. The ten families that did not get the stoves went to Gonzalo and politely requested that he make some kind of arrangement to hurry up the delivery.

"Who do you think I am—Christ?" Gonzalo answered the woman who came to him.

The next day he gathered the men whose families had shivered in the night. Out of steel barrels they constructed ten makeshift temporary stoves which they installed in their homes. By Christmas Eve morning everyone in Simons had heat.

On Christmas Eve, the last day of the Posadas, the Mexican families of Simons gathered at the general store. The women had worked through the day meticulously preparing the holiday delicacies: tamales, buñelos, menudo, flan, sweet breads and candy. Chocolate, café de olla and different liquors were in abundance. The brown faces felicitously escorted San Jose and the Virgen Maria to the entrance of the general store where inside Walter, Joseph, Laura, James Simons, Rosendo Guerrero and Gonzalo Pedroza waited to bid welcome to the Holy Couple. When the request for shelter was made, the door opened and the innkeepers who waited inside looked out to hundreds of candles carried by the workers and their families. The candles flickered in the cold blackness of the starry night as they waited for the response from the innkeeper. Rosendo and Gonzalo led the singing of the responsorial. So off-key were their voices that the crowd applauded loudly to hide the laughter. With a grin and nod of thank you, Walter stepped forward and invited his workers to come in and share food, drink, song and happiness. In the warm social atmosphere, the people ate, drank and sang. Children ran and played amongst the crowd, and laughter and cries floated through the aroma of delicious food. Periodically the men and women glanced over to assure themselves that the patron and his family enjoyed the festivities. Near the Simons family were the two foremen, but few workers said hello or wished them a Merry Christmas. About an hour into the celebration Gonzalo asked for silence. Rosendo stepped forward.

"I present to you Mr. Walter Simons, the patron," Rosendo said, projecting his powerful voice to the back of the room. The crowd became silent and listened to Walter's words as Rosendo translated them.

"I have a few announcements, but first let me wish you, on behalf of my brother Joseph, his wife Laura, their son James and my father and mother and the rest of my family a very Merry Christmas. Although we will have to leave shortly, we are very happy to be here with you this evening."

Rosendo led the workers in applause and continued to translate what Walter said.

"Now the announcements. As you are aware we have only one machine here at Simons. However, I believe that this yard will someday produce millions of brick and the sooner we install another machine the sooner we'll get started on reaching that goal. So we plan to set up machine number two a few days after the New Year. We will begin to build more houses for all of you with families. I am also aware of the need for a priest and church here and for a school for your children. I intend to resolve those needs. You probably already know that we have a post office here. You can receive and mail your letters from here. You don't have to leave our town for anything. In January the general store will be open for business. You will be able to buy groceries and anything else you might need. If we don't carry what you need we'll get it for you. A doctor will come once a month to see any worker or member of his family who is ailing. If you have any problems please talk with your foreman, Gonzalo Pedroza. If any legal matters come up, any enforcement problems, Gonzalo is the legally designated law enforcer in Simons. Gonzalo, would you please step forward."

Gonzalo moved to the front of the crowd where Walter pinned a silver star to his lapel and handed over a holstered pistol and belt which he hung around his waist. Walter shook his sheriff's hand and walked away. After the translation Walter and family exited, followed by Rosendo. With badge and pistol, Gonzalo now stood alone by the table where the women again served food. The music and drinking began and as the night passed on to Christmas morning the workers and their families paid their respects to Gonzalo Pedroza.

From that moment Simons, California, was complete for growth. Joseph was still the administrator of the family investments. Nonetheless, since the dispute over the ownership of the houses in Pasadena, two clear and powerful forces had emerged in the family. As cooperation in the business intensified, an alienation based on driving personal competition grew between the two brothers. Although Joseph, Walter, Orin Elmer and the immediate family owned the Simons Brick Company, only Joseph and Walter administered the economics and expansion plans. Joseph concentrated his energies on the Pasadena yard and considered investing in cousin John Simons' Los Angeles yard and possibly starting another in Santa Monica. Likewise, Walter was completely involved in the expansion of the yard and town he founded in Simons. He considered the Simons project his personal toy yard and the town and people who worked and lived there his dolls who existed only for his enjoyment and waited for his bidding.

By the middle of February, 1906 a second water tank had been installed and the fifty new houses had running water. Machine number two was in full operation and Gonzalo had hired twenty-five more men, again all from the state of Guanajuato. His crew now numbered seventy-five. Twenty of the newly hired men were married. Not once did Gonzalo have to discipline or remind the men of the fast work pace demanded by the patron. Bricks had to be produced to fill the orders from Montebello, Whittier and Los Angeles. Walter, determined to meet small and large invoices, urged his foreman to keep the men working fourteen-hour days. The workers started at five in the morning, had a half-hour lunch at twelve and left at seven in the evening.

During these long days Gonzalo constantly watched over the production. As he observed the men work, he often indicated disapproval with a slow movement of his square head. One evening as Gonzalo walked by one of the large two-story brick kilns burning in the early cool night, he noticed a recently hired man sitting near a fire opening. The man stared, sitting motionless, into the light of the burning gas piped through the kiln. Gonzalo moved toward him.

"Well, get to work!" Gonzalo yelled.

The man turned his back to the light. He held a pad of paper with his left hand and a pencil with his right. Gonzalo recognized Epifanio Trejo who had been employed for two weeks. Epifanio and his family came directly to Simons from El Barral, a small rancho in Guanajuato, Mexico. Startled, Epifanio did not answer.

"What are you doing?" Gonzalo insisted.

"I'm writing," Epifanio answered nervously, as if he had been caught not working on company time. Nonetheless, he looked directly into the eyes of Gonzalo Pedroza.

"You are writing?" Gonzalo, surprised and angered, interrogated Epifanio. "Why are you writing when you should be watching the burning of the kiln?"

"My shift is over now, Meester Gonzalo. We don't have lamps in the house. I get up and return home in the dark. We don't have candles either so with the light of the burning gas I write letters." Epifanio's eyes confronted the foreman's.

"Tell me, who is so important to risk your job by writing letters?"

Gonzalo's words felt hot and Epifanio moved away from the fire.

"I repeat, it is not my turn to work. I write to my relatives in Mexico. I write to my brother-in-law Malaquias de Leon," Epifanio explained cautiously.

"It's true, your shift is over. Well, tell your brother-in-law to come to Simons, that we need more workers," Gonzalo said as he walked away from the kiln and Epifanio Trejo. Suddenly he stopped.

"Finish your letter. And tell your wife to come by the store tomorrow for some lamps and oil. I'll give you a good price so you tell her to charge it to your account," Gonzalo said as he moved from the light into the dark, starry night.

The same stars that had shone over the Los Angeles night dominated the morning when Walter brought William Melone to the Simons Brick Company. Hurriedly and excitedly Walter opened the door to the office. He was accompanied by Laura Simons, who had come to prepare the letters that Walter was to dictate to government officials about the burning city of San Francisco which had been struck by a massive earthquake the day before. The devastation was complete and fires continued to ravage the city. At one o'clock in the morning Walter had received a telegram from several city officials in San Francisco requesting that he prepare his brickmaking business to work around the clock to produce material for the rebuilding of the city. Walter did not know the extent of the damage;

however, from the opening phrase of the telegram, " San Francisco wiped out, burning," he understood that a disaster had occurred in the north. He realized that a great city was being destroyed and he and his company were to participate in the reconstruction.

Walter sent William Melone for Gonzalo. Upon their return to the office, Walter explained to Gonzalo that William was assigned the job of general superintendent. Gonzalo now had someone to answer to, and all decisions regarding hiring, firing and housing had to be cleared through William. That morning they made plans to install three more machines and to expand the brickyard in four directions.

"By the end of May we should have eighty thousand pallets and a capacity of one hundred thousand bricks per day," Walter said to William and Gonzalo. "We will increase our labor force to one hundred men or more. Gonzalo, you have done a good job of hiring. Hire twenty-five more, but clear them with Mr. Melone. Start working twenty-four-hour shifts. Not only the kiln tenders but the rest of the production has to proceed day and night until we have a large surplus. I want to outproduce the other yards."

Gonzalo walked through the red dust of the mandala, acknowledging the men who built the racks and drying pallets, those who prepared the red clay, those who watered the wet, long, rectangular cake, those who watched the machine cut the brick, those who placed the brick on pallets to dry, those who loaded the brick on wagons, and those who pitched five or six bricks at a time to other men who stacked the thousands of bricks into gigantic blocks. Gonzalo stood between machine number one and two and ordered the men to gather before him.

"Starting at seven in the morning there will be two shifts: two twelve-hour shifts. The patron and the new superintendent, William Melone, want you to kow that last night a disaster took place in San Francisco. The patron received a telegram notifying him that an earthquake destroyed the city, and that it is up to us to produce the brick to reconstruct the city. That is why we must work twenty-four hours. The men on my right take the first shift and those on the left take the second. Now form two groups," Gonzalo ordered.

"We will have fewer men on the machines. We must work harder! Well, what do you say?" he asked, knowing the response. They had only one choice and none of the men wanted to leave.

"We are not afraid of hard work!" a worker yelled from the back of the group.

"That's right! We'll give the patron all the brick he wants!" a slim man yelled and coughed.

"Very well, the first shift starts at seven, the second at seven at night."

Gonzalo walked through the one hundred men who discussed the earthquake. He had not gotten to know any of the men well, although he knew most by first name. He was strictly a foreman to them and not much else. He was never invited to their homes, but at times he would socialize by having a drink or playing cards. Gonzalo Pedroza, man of authority, was alone. He recognized Epifanio Trejo who listened intently, along with five other men, to Galindo Correaga, one of the older men of the crew. Galindo was speaking about one of his seven daughters who was nick-named El Eco.

"Didn't you hear the dogs barking, howling last night? My daughter El Eco heard them and she started in also. She was in a deep sleep when she began to describe what she saw." Garlindo Correaga captured the attention of Gonzalo and the others who moved closer to hear about El Eco's vision.

"The child got up from bed. She fell to the floor and her body contorted. She spoke in English and Spanish. She felt an enormous weight on her body and said it was tons of bricks, that a whole building had fallen on her. She saw the city destroyed before her eyes. She suffered great pain which caused her to see everything clearly. Her vision penetrated the earth itself. She witnessed fire consuming the city and she heard the screams of children who burned. The earth moved, El Eco told us, the earth shook. And then she stared at the earth and told us of a plumed serpent so large, so great, that it could not fit in our mind, but she saw it all. That serpent was an energy that twisted and turned within the earth, causing great tremors. El Eco said that a part of the great serpent ran throughout the state, north and south. For a long time she did not move or speak and then it was as if she had died.

"Oh God, I said, and then she began to cry and all the children came into the room. And there we were, all of us, crying because El Eco had gone. Suddenly her body twisted violently as if it were burning and slowly she became tranquil. But before she slept peacefully she told us that the great serpent would twist and turn until we as a people would have the necessary children to reconstruct a homeland here in this place."

Galindo Correaga spoke his words with a smile. The silence which followed was broken by a man who tried to understand.

"Your daughter is crazy. Take her to the hospital," the man said and walked away.

"That is enough stories; earthquakes are earthquakes and nothing more. You act like a bunch of superstitious Indians! Now get to work!" Gonzalo shouted.

"I believe El Eco is right. In space there exist energies that come from great distances, that cause these disasters and that communicate through imbalanced people like El Eco." Epifanio Trejo spoke with Atilano Castro in front of an enormous fired kiln.

"It is God on earth," Epifanio concluded.

The sun lay low in the Southern California sky. Its light spread across the two hundred-and-fifty acre Simons Brickyard, making the earth of the mandala redder than natural. From where Gonzalo advanced to the general store, children played and mothers worked at homemaking as he passed. The images of a great plumed snake and his calling the workers superstitious Indians aroused latent emotions deep in his mind. Gonzalo and Pascuala, childless, lived comfortably in Simons, but still the deep feelings of their history rushed forth to identify and remind them where they were and who possessed the power. Gonzalo walked with hard fists, contemplating the loss of power to William Melone. A pyramid appeared in the structures of his reason and he saw himself as the third man from the top. Before this, he had answered only to Mr. Simons, but now he would have to deal with Mr. Melone who had the power to fire and throw him out of Simons. To survive and maintain his position, he had to please William Melone at all cost.

Roberto Lacan was the first person Gonzalo saw upon entering the general store. He had given Roberto the job of managing the general store. Roberto, who could read, write and knew basic mathematics, explained the system of credit for the workers set up by Walter Simons. Roberto, a twenty-two-year-old from Guanajuato, had left his studies in Mexico City because of political harassment. He had supported Francisco I. Madero and the Flores Magon brothers as did his father, mother and brothers, all of whom paid with their lives for the relationship. Roberto and two sisters were the only ones to survive the punishment of the Rurales in Guanajuato and the federales in Mexico City. In Mexico, as the political and economic situation deteriorated, thousands of Mexicans exited the country for the United States.

The exclusive few who came to Simons discovered a bucolic peace and a perfect isolation from the turmoils of the world.

Roberto was hired with the approval of Walter Simons on the condition that he keep quiet about his family and that he not stir in the workers any desire to return to Mexico. He agreed and told Gonzalo that it would be difficult to convince any Mexican living in Simons to return to the living conditions of the mother country.

As William walked through the general store, he noted the supplies that were needed and listened to Roberto's suggestions explained in broken English. William noticed Gonzalo's silent presence.

"How did they take the news?" William asked as he set pen and paper down on the counter. "Very well," Gonzalo answered.

"No complaints?" William smiled.

"No." Gonzalo watched Roberto move behind the counter.

"Good, now let's work them," William said enthusiastically. "Gonzalo, the store looks real good. Smart move hiring Roberto. I'll see you here at seven sharp. You're doing excellent work, Gonzalo."

William glanced at Roberto but ignored him. He took Gonzalo by the arm.

"Good work," William whispered maliciously, and left Gonzalo and Roberto alone in an immense silence.

The square face of Gonzalo had never felt the wine as warm and kind as on that evening in the middle of June in 1906. It would be a warm summer, he thought, as his house on Vail became larger. He wondered about how objects, like a house, get smaller as you move away from them and how they grow as you approach them. He stopped at the front of the house. The lamps were lit. Pascuala did not like being in a dark house; consequently, she lit every lantern every night.

Gonzalo's house was one of the three best in Simons. It had three bedrooms instead of two, a large kitchen, living room and a very large service porch. He checked the street and saw that he was alone. He pulled from his inside coat pocket a small square mirror. Looking into it, he tugged at his moustache and pushed his hair in place. He shined his badge, unbuckled the gunbelt, and slung the holstered pistol over his shoulder. Pascuala came to mind. Three years they were married and still their love had not engendered a child. Children were important to both. Pascuala, like Gonzalo, came from a large family whose women were proud, strong mothers of many sons and daughters. He opened the door and walked through the living room to the kitchen. Pascuala had prepared dinner as usual. The house was in perfect order. She heated tortillas on the hornilla on the stove.

"Buenas noches, Gonzalo. I'm glad you arrived early," Pascuala said with a strong, encouraging tone of happiness.

"Gracias." Gonzalo, spiritually uplifted by her happy attitude, sat and she served while he ate.

"Do you have plenty of wood?" he asked, puzzled by her mood.

"There is enough. We have plenty of everything, thanks to you, Gonzalo." She wrapped three tortillas in the basket on the table. "This morning when I went for water I ran into Mrs. Narvarte, Mariquita Carrillo and Dolores Correaga. They told me that more machines were going to be installed."

That's right, two more. There will be six by the end of the month," he answered, reaching for another tortilla.

"Good, more people will come," she said softly. "Gonzalo, we also spoke about other things." She went and sat at his side.

"I told them that the past few days I have not felt well in the morning, that I got sick to my stomach. Mrs. Correaga asked me embarrassing questions. They were necessary questions. Then she asked permission to touch my stomach and breasts. The three women laughed. But I allowed them to because they had told me before that I might be with child and they wanted to confirm it. And it happened that Mrs. Correaga concluded that without a doubt I am pregnant. They embraced and congratulated me. They told me I could count on them when the time came. It might be in November. Forgive me, Gonzalo. I don't know if they are gossipers." Pascuala's lips cradled into a slight smile.

Gonzalo, amazed at the wondrous news, reached for her hand.

After dinner Gonzalo and Pascuala strolled through the back garden of their house.

"That's why you're so thin, woman, because you are pregnant. Look at the night; it is beautiful, filled with stars and the soft wind, warm like your arms. Let's stroll through the fields."

Gonzalo led Pascuala past the barn, through a road leading to the agricultural fields planted by Japanese farmers. They embraced and kissed, and while they enjoyed the warm balmy Southern California evening they discussed the future.

As usual Walter had discussed business with Joseph throughout the half-hour walk in the warm, windy, mid-June evening in Pasadena. They returned to Joseph's house on California Street where Joseph and Laura had been receiving guests since seven-thirty that evening. It was a grand celebration and many people came from throughout Southern California to wish Reuben and Melissa Simons, patriarch and matriarch of the Simons family, a happy forty-sixth wedding anniversary. Reuben Simons, seventy, and Melissa, sixty-nine, had made many friends through their church activities and their sons' growing business. That evening they were the life of the party and the center of attention. By eleven-thirty most of the guests had left except for ten couples, close Pasadena friends who sat speaking with Reuben and Melissa.

Joseph and Walter had left the party to discuss several financial emergencies that had come up at what Joseph called Walter's yard. They left the party in order not to disturb the guests nor embarrass their parents in case they shouted during the discussion. Ever since the San Francisco earthquake, Joseph and Walter had been at constant odds. Neither one could make a suggestion to the other without causing friction. However, tonight they both agreed to what needed to be done to solve the immediate needs at Simons Town. More mules, hay to feed them, and wagons were needed. Joseph offered to transfer the animals and whatever else was necessary to keep Walter's yard producing enough brick to fill the orders from Northern and Southern California. The success of Walter's yard was money in Joseph's pocket, for it was he who controlled the financial matters in the Simons Brick Company.

Outside, Rosendo looked into the gay sounds and lights of the Simons' home. He was in charge of organizing the furniture for the dinner in the garden. He had been invited to enjoy the evening with the family, but he preferred to stay outside in the garden. He ate and drank by himself on the furthest table from the center. Joseph smiled at his faithful worker. He was convinced that the Mexican Rosendo would be loyal for life. Walter watched as Rosendo gave his boss a complimentary abrazo.

"Thank you for allowing me to stay. Please congratulate your father and mother again for me. Good night, Joseph. Buenas noches, Walter." Rosendo moved away, turned, waved good-bye and disappeared into California Street.

"He hasn't married yet, has he?" Walter asked, opening the gate of the fence covered with bougainvillaes.

"No, he has not," Joseph replied, stepping up onto the porch. "Why is that so strange? You're not married, either."

"What does he do?" Walter asked, not sure of what he was searching for or what he wanted to know.

"He reads a lot. Anything he can get his hands on, in English, Spanish and French," Joseph said.

"What about women?" Walter asked.

"I think he goes into Los Angeles for that. Sometimes he rides south to Santa Ana. But for the past several years he's been reading. He asked permission to use the library in town and that's where he spends his time off." Joseph reached for the front door.

"Strange. I think that's strange." Walter was bothered by Rosendo's pastime activity.

The brothers observed their parents discussing and laughing with friends. Joseph opened his watch and smiled.

"It's getting very late for him," Joseph said.

"Let them enjoy it. How has he been?" Walter asked.

"Sometimes good, other times he can't get out of bed. But tonight he seems to be as strong as any of us," Joseph said as he looked at the twenty or so grey-haired heads on aged bodies sitting deep in sofas and couches. Laura came to Joseph's side.

"Well, they seem to be having a wonderful evening," she said, taking Joseph by the arm. "Before I forget, we received a nasty letter from the Montebello City Council complaining that they don't want your Mexican workers shopping in their stores. In fact they don't want the brickyard anywhere near their town."

"Too late to complain now. We're there to stay," Walter said with a tinge of annoyance in his voice.

"That's right, you're there to stay," Joseph said.

Laura and Joseph joined their parents. Walter, puzzled by his brother's last remark, did not follow but instead went to the dining room for a drink. His eyes watered. His vision blurred. Tired, he thought, and downed a whiskey.

Walter had felt two people present, a man and a woman, but had not paid attention. Only after the whiskey did he hear the voices clearly and recognize his brother Orin Elmer who sat at the table talking excitedly. Never had Walter seen his brother so content and proud. Orin Elmer's conversation was with a woman in an intensely blue dress. From her shoulders hung a deep blue shawl knotted on the left side of her heart. The neckline plunged to the initial rise of her breasts and sealed the rest of her, revealing nothing, and yet for Walter everything in his imagination. A pearl necklace marked the initiation and merging of a graceful and powerful neck. She pushed her delicate, soft brown hair away from the left side of her face.

Excitement, warmth, comfort, heat and a wetness in two parallel vertical furrows appeared above her nose. She placed the middle finger of her right hand there and moved her fingers across her eyebrow, never ceasing to observe Walter.

Orin Elmer, startled by the presence of something, someone unknown standing at his back, stood, turned and discovered his brother.

"Oh, come sit with us," Orin Elmer said nervously. "I was getting ready to retire. I, oh, I have been talking with Miss Sarah Patenkin, Mr. and Mrs. Patenkin's daughter. They opened the new drugstore in town."

Emotionless, Walter expressed nothing on his face. He watched her in a way that probably would have made any woman uncomfortable. He made his brother more nervous and Sarah curious. Orin Elmer left the room, his words faded and forgotten. Sarah remained at the table. At that moment they were the only people in the world. Voices gradually re-entered the magic space.

"How do you do? I'm Sarah Patenkin," she said confidently.

She smiled and went to the doorway leading to the living room. The guests were gathering their coats and leaving.

"I think I know everything about you, Walter," Sarah said on the verge of laughter.

Walter sensed the friendly silliness and relaxed. He understood he was in the presence of the first woman he could love and consider for marriage. He took her arm and led her to the living room. He announced to his parents and hers that they would wait for them on the porch. Walter found it curious that the Patenkins were the last to leave, but too soon they were riding in their carriage toward downtown Pasadena.

As Walter walked home under a blanket of stars exposed by the warm winds, his mind filled with the images of his two most important concerns: the Simons Brickyard, which Joseph had identified as Walter's yard, and Sarah Patenkin, the beautiful woman who already knew everything about him. Surrounded by the sounds of early morning life, he listened to the rustling of animals resting and struggling.

Chapter 5

The earth had opened twice during the night. In the morning the village of El Barral discovered that five houses and families had vanished. By mid-day, water rose from small cracks in the earth. The news spread that other families and villagers had been lost to the underground movement of the great serpent that bore through the earth. Malaquias de Leon's hut on top of the hill would not be touched by the rising water, but the fields were ruined and the crop lost. To the north enormous thunderclouds formed. It would rain by late afternoon and thunder and lightning would terrorize animals and people.

Malaquias almost cursed the sun on that twenty-second of June, 1906. The rainy season promised to be long and overwhelming, he thought while walking to the entrance of the house where inside Lorenza Trejo de Leon lay tense, in pain, split open by the act of giving birth to their second child. He reached in his pockets and found a few coins and a letter. Lorenza's moans were more constant. It would be over soon, he hoped. Their first-born, Paquita, now one-and-a-half years old, would soon cry. She would be hungry and Lorenza would nurse and comfort the child. This time there was no midwife to help in the delivery. Overnight the moving earth and floods had isolated the de Leon family. People dared not venture out of their homes for fear of being swallowed up, swept away by water or burned by lightning.

Malaquias peered into the house. Lorenza lay quietly waiting for the next contraction. Paquita sat in a corner with a wooden doll purchased in Quiseo de Abasolo after her birth. The great thunder and curtains of water would soon be upon them. Malaquias could do nothing now but wait. The forces of nature were rushing toward them. The family would survive or perish together. He squatted outside the entrance beneath the last warm rays of the sun which were now being swallowed faster by the clouds darkening the earth. The rain was less than an hour away. The thunder was louder. He stood his ground and stared out at the vast living land before him.

Angrily he felt his cousin's letter. Trabajo was the word that kept jumping from cell to cell in his brain. Here he worked and got nothing. He could never count on water. It was either too little or too much. How he hated and loved this land. He could never save enough money for the family to leave, but someday he would go to find work and buy land and after he was settled he would send for his wife and children, he dreamed as the sky darkened. Faraway a hazy red light floated where the sky meets the earth. Above him the sky was deep grey with black water tumors that would soon burst. He thought of Lorenza, lying there inside praying that it would be over quickly.

Malaquias felt the wind pick up strength. The light on the horizon became a line of white. The house, Lorenza, their daughter, the child to be born and he were encased in a moist blackness. Through the monstrous clouds, silent streaks of light traveled downward. At any moment the lights would be upon them and would announce their presence with unimaginable thunder, and tons and tons of water would fall upon him and the persons he loved. The wind was stronger and it began to sprinkle kind little droplets. Now surrounded by lightning working its way down through the tonnage of water, Malaquias knew there was nowhere to go except inside his house and hope that it would be able to withstand the weight. From inside, a scream broke the song of the droplets. Instantly the sky shattered and responded with intense, painful thunder.

Malaquias crawled inside the house and watched Lorenza struggle to give birth. At Lorenza's right side sat their Paquita silently waiting to clutch a breast. A massive contraction seized Lorenza. Malaquias placed a towel between her legs. Outside, the water curtain shifted and moved toward the hut. The earth rumbled and shook. In seconds the curtain would fall on them. Lightning bolts illuminated the sky; loud thunder crashed nearby.

Malaquias moved the candle closer and saw that between Lorenza's legs an infant squirmed. As he picked the babe up to give to Lorenza, a massive lightning bolt struck just outside the opening of the house. Lorenza's body tensed up and their first-born clung to her mother and the newborn infant. Lorenza screamed with every bolt that crashed to the earth. The curtain fell on all four: the newborn with umbilical cord still attached screamed, searching for a breast; the first-born hung on to her mother and her new sister while Malaquias tried desperately to embrace the three of them with his arms and chest.

Amidst nature's energies and noise Malaquias peered into Lorenza's bright eyes. She never knew whether she heard laughter or crying, or whether it was water or tears that trickled from Malaquias' eyes. She held her children, Paquita, her first born, and Nana, her new baby, warm and safe in her arms. With Malaquias there to protect them, Lorenza was convinced that the house would stand against the fury of Tlaloc, the rain energy's soul.

Dark, brown, round head, large black eyes, high-ridged wide-nostril nose, thin lips, wide mouth, large white teeth, large protruding ears: the ten-year-old boy's face smiled as he turned to tell his friend to get ready for the photograph that Mr. J. R. Allen, Walter Robey Simons' personal photographer, was about to shoot. The boys giggled at the attention they got from the "gringos" from Montebello Unified School District who had come to register the workers' children and set up a school for them only. The two boys stood in the front row of twelve; on a bench behind them posed eight girls and four boys, and above them seven boys and two girls looked down at the camera. All of the boys wore overalls and white long-sleeve shirts buttoned up to the collar. Caps in hand pointed down to their bare feet. White was the color for the girls' dresses. The clean, innocent faces shone with excitement and fear that filtered through their hearts.

After the photograph was taken the children stepped down and stood in line with their parents to register. Four groups of thirty-three children would make up the first classes at the Vail Elementary School. The classes were organized according to age. In the first group the children were from seven to ten years old; the second class had children from ten to twelve; the third class consisted of the thirteen and fourteen-year-olds and the fourth class was made up of youngsters from fifteen to sixteen.

As the children moved through the line the parents were asked for their child's birth or baptismal certificate. None had the former and few had the latter. The school officials took down the information given by the parents and allowed the roster to be approved as official. From eight in the morning to three in the afternoon the children were registered. While the mothers talked with friends, the children stayed to play. At one o'clock an impromptu ceremony was announced when Walter and Sarah Simons, Jonathan and Clarissa Vail and Miss Betty Haylock, the teacher and administrator, arrived to officially open the academic year and the school.

J. R. Allen maneuvered his black box into position to capture forever the momentous occasion. Miss Haylock met the children and carried on a one-way conversation with the mothers who nodded and answered yes to her statements and questions. She told them to sit in front of the benches and to listen to what Mr. Simons was going to tell them.

Walter watched the faces of the young mothers who attempted to understand and do what Miss Haylock ordered. Suddenly he thought of the people he had seen on his Mexican trip. His people would have everything. They would not turn against him. Never would they despise him, nor would they ever wish him dead. He studied those sharp Indian faces and in their eyes recognized thousands of years of history. Walter feared the children. He would give them a school, a church, a clinic, everything, and create a paradise in which his workers would depend totally on him, so much so that the rising unrest in Mexico would not affect him or his people. They would never leave, he thought.

Miss Haylock escorted the Simonses and the Vails to the benches in front of the children and mothers. She handed Walter a list of names.

"Mr. Simons, these are some of the children who have registered for your school. Would you please call out their names?" she asked in a very proper manner and handed Walter the official first roster.

"Bartolome Becerra, Alberto Caballero, Nicolas Ortiz, Andrew Ortiz, Henry Ortiz, Joe Rodriguez, Albert Ponce, Fernan Alarcon, Bernard Alarcon, Carmelita Ortiz, John Cano, Leopoldo Martinez, Rita Juarez. . ."

The audience clapped and the children made funny faces as Walter recited and transformed the list into the book of Genesis. Suddenly, to everyone's astonishment, Walter blurted out loud: "This is the beginning!"

The children and parents applauded their patron's enthusiasm.

"Let me just say that this is a very important day for all of us. For you children it's the beginning of a great opportunity to learn. To learn a new language, to learn new names for all the things you now know. For you mothers and fathers it's the beginning of dedicating yourselves to helping your children advance. For Miss Betty Haylock it's a beginning as your teacher and administrator. There will be other teachers who will soon come, but she will be the person in charge of the school and your education. The people who made this beginning possible are Mr. and Mrs. Jonathan Vail, who donated this land for your school. Soon we will construct beautiful school buildings out of brick for all of you," Walter declared.

Sarah came to stand by him as the children, mothers, school officials, Mr. and Mrs. Vail and Miss Haylock applauded and cheered the patron's promises.

"Those of you who have already registered, please line up for a tour of the classrooms. Please, let's not dally now." Miss Haylock motioned with her hands and the Mexicans got in line.

The tour began with Miss Haylock's stopping each child at the entrance of each classroom. Her strong hands grabbed the head of every student to rigorously examine first the mouth and teeth, second the ears and nose, third the eyes, and fourth the hair, scalp and neck. There was no doubt that Miss Haylock was also the school nurse. As the children walked through, they argued.

"I want that desk," a ten-year-old said.

"No! That one is mine!"

"But I'm taller!" a thirteen-year-old girl insisted.

"Let's not argue. Please! I will decide who gets a desk and who doesn't," Miss Haylock shouted after realizing why the children were upset.

One small child grabbed at the two hands that pinched his cheeks and forced his mouth to open. Miss Haylock studied the boy's angered posture.

"Now don't get upset; this is for your own good." She pushed the boy forward and reached for the next child.

Her words sounded familiar but did not settle fittingly, snugly into the niches of understanding in the child's brain. He still had the sensation of being shoved on his shoulders, and his cheeks hurt. He turned, rubbed his cheeks and left ear, and watched Miss Haylock grab at the other children as they entered the classroom. He heard sounds but moved through the room not grasping their signification. Some words he heard as hollow and empty; others were perforated and spelled out a foreign feeling. He understood none wholly. The words spoken by Miss Haylock were occidental and not appropriate for the ancient Mexican teachings he inherited and felt at this moment. The boy's mother followed the others, and in the furthest recesses of his mind a sensation of pain slowly emerged.

That September day in 1907 the children of Simons began their American education.

From the evening when Walter had met Sarah at the party honoring his father and mother, Reuben Simons had relentlessly deteriorated. Three years had passed without anyone ever seeing a smile on Reuben's face. In the last year he often started to strangle when he lay on his back; consequently his life was now spent sitting in a chair. His life became constant non-action rest. He had lost physical control of body functions and his mind had hardened to senility and regressed to infancy. His wife Melissa alone struggled with him, refusing help. She had declared to her sons and written to her daughters that it was undignified for her husband to be seen unclad by anyone else but her. Nonetheless, as Reuben's condition worsened, his body became heavier until finally she could not budge him.

Reuben was gradually transfigured into brittle rock. He recognized no one. He blurted nonsensical words and phrases, seemingly conversing to whoever stood before him. He elucidated flashbacks, and he verbalized in clear and beautiful descriptions the places, people and situations of his past.

Once in a great while, in stances of clarity, he recognized the people who loved him. He would call their name, but before a dialogue could be established he was gone. He would surface in infancy where he entertained himself with wooden beads, blocks and dolls. When dinner was brought to him he would gulp it down with his hands. No matter what the food was, he would use only his hands. He ate as if he had no fill and was capable of probably eating himself to death. The brain did not receive the message of fullness or hunger. He ate automatically when food was placed in front of him. Reuben Simons had been transformed into a helpless infant, at the mercy of all human beings. He had no function and members of his family wished him a speedy death to save him from the horrible and humiliating agonies of decrepitude.

Joseph, who had been with him during his last moments, sat in the parlor of his parents' home waiting for the guests to pass through and express the socially expected words of condolence. On a couch next to him sat his mother and Orin Elmer who was the most visibly shaken by his father's passing. Standing at the window watching the visitors come and go was Walter who that afternoon had said nothing to any of the family members. A sense of resignation and relief reigned over the persons in the room. In a few hours the elaborate coffin would be taken to the Christian's Presbyterian Cemetery in Pasadena to be lowered into a pit, covered with earth, and separated from the world of the living. Next to the coffin sat Laura, nine-year-old James, and Sarah, waiting for the men from the cemetery to take the coffin. Outside, when the coffin was being lifted onto the wagon Orin Elmer screamed and sobbed.

"Why must they bury him so deep!" Orin Elmer repeated on the way to the cemetery.

As the family entourage arrived at the gravesite, Melissa Simons broke down, praying out loud and crying for the beloved one. There was no preacher to say the last words. The family and friends said goodbye in their own private way.

"Reuben, I'm so afraid of being alone!" Melissa called to the coffin as it was being lowered.

Mr. and Mrs. Bolin went to Melissa and led her away. The women of the family followed. The three Simons brothers stood around the mouth of the grave.

"Sarah is pregnant," Walter announced, facing Joseph.

"My God, Father would have been so happy. Another grandchild soon to arrive," Joseph said, extending his open hand.

"I hope you two will stop fighting. Do it for him!" Orin Elmer dropped a carnation into the pit.

"Let's go home." Joseph guided Orin Elmer to the wagon. Walter remained by the grave.

"Come on, Walter," Orin Elmer insisted from the top of the wagon.

"No, I want to stay. I'll walk," Walter said as the wagon pulled away.

Moments later two Mexicans came and began to shovel dirt down into the pit. The dirt clods thudded on the coffin. The Mexicans padded down the soil of the mound they had shaped.

"A nice cool bed," Walter said softly.

"Si, patron, bonita cama," one of the Mexicans repeated while the other pulled out a cigarette and lit up, then offered one to Walter who took it and waited until the other took one.

Walter lit the man's cigarette and then his own and walked away, leaving footprints and ashes on his father's grave.

The night was magic. Voices from forty years past came to him and danced as he looked out from the window of his second nuptial chamber in the National Palace, searching for the long brilliant tail of light traveling through the clear night of the western sky. Was the world really going to end? Not according to his consultants. The Golden Age would never end. Halley's Comet was a sign of everlasting power that represented another one hundred years of reign for the Coming Man.

He had ruled with a strong hand guiding his people to the promised land, a land of tranquility, for until now there had been peace in his country for twenty-five years. His enemies accused him of being an irresponsible despot and those voices began to speak against him. But he would pay them back; he would be glad to return the favor. To pay his opponents the respect they deserved he had organized his urban Bravi, a private army that he could count on to destroy any person or organization who dared to challenge his authority.

The Bravi did away with whatever don Porfirio Diaz deemed an obstacle to his government. He controlled the Bravi by offering it a free hand to obtain all the human blood it needed to satisfy its unquenchable thirst. He was a master at offering bread and the club. In the provinces he set up the national police, the Rurales, who decided life or death for the peasants. Their murders went unquestioned for thirty years. Don Porfirio Diaz gave bread to the Bravi, Rurales, army, bureaucrats, foreigners and the Catholic Church, and to the common Mexican in the cities or the countryside he reserved the club which he used mercilessly.

He thought of himself as the father of all Mexicans. In his dreams he held and stroked his fatherly, enormous penis which he lay throughout the land. He had given birth to railroad lines that stretched north and south, to the silver, gold, copper, lead, zinc mines, to the coffee, sugar, banana, and henequen plantations and to the exportation of Mexico's natural resources. Porfirian sperm impregnated the country with foreign economic interest which exploited Mexicans and Mexico. The United States, England, France, Germany and other countries positioned their economic virgins for don Porfirio's rich penis. He gave them everything they desired and in return they gave him simple sensual pleasure. In don Porfirio Diaz's logic, Mexico was not getting fucked but was the one doing the fucking. He smiled and patted himself on the back for what he considered one of his greatest accomplishments.

The people who surrounded the great barbarian began to believe in his immortality and so they decided that the city in which a forever god dwelled must be clean of filth and human hideousness. The capital was cleaned up and modernized. Electric lights illuminated the boulevards and glimmered and sparkled on the new streetcars that circulated through the city's main thoroughfare. On orders of don Porfirio, large marble edifices were built for the god to behold. To house his selected entertainment he constructed the fabulous Palace of Fine Arts. The building was as foreign as the way of life don Porfirio modeled. The only authentic element of Mexico at the time was the enslaved masses considered no better than beasts. The aristocracy praised the dictatorship for it brought in a golden age, the neofeudal system on the haciendas and the Rurales to keep the peace.

If any peon or poor Mexican complained of the aristocracy's considerations, the Rurales arrested him, and when the Mexican attempted to escape he or she was shot, according to la ley de fuga. Indians, the majority of Mexicans, were don Porfirio Diaz's predilectable targets. Yaquis and Mayas he enslaved and slaughtered by the thousands. His generals boasted that in his delight to kill Indians he was matched only by the best American cavalry.

It was also his wish that the Indians and leperos who begged on the Paseo de la Reforma an other elegant avenues and boulevards of the capital be kept away permanently. The thousands of dismembered bodies that were later discovered along the country roads and open fields outside Mexico City were explained as leprous corpses that fell apart because of the disease. The rich accepted without question the official explanation and the poor had no choice but to bury the remains. Don Porfirio's immortality grew on the mountains of the bodies of dead Mexicans in the cities and in the country.

On an occasional Sunday he would parade in an elegant carriage drawn by beautiful, high-stepping coursers down the Paseo de la Reforma to the magnificent home of one of his trusted cientificos. There they would chat about the latest French style, the best French schools that their sons and daughters attended. The women compared the *dernier cri* and commented on the absolutely inferior quality of the Spanish mantilla. Throughout the conversation the aristocrats injected a French word or two. How they lamented the horrible barbarism of their country. How they prided themselves for collecting French objects. How they bragged and pointed proudly to the imported French artifacts which decorated the entire house and with a sense of accomplishment, told don Porfirio Diaz: "¡En esta su casa no hay nada mexicano!"

Within his circumference don Porfirio saw nothing but white faces at the parties he attended. At his meetings with his chosen and faithful government administrators there stared back at him only white silent faces . . . Era verdad, no hay nada mexicano en Mexico . . . he thought as he circulated through the crowds of praising international well-wishers. Don Porfirio carried his penis in his left hand and his beautiful wife doña Carmen Rubio on his right arm. But for the very poor, Mexico had become the mother of foreigners and the stepmother of Mexicans. Three times a week don Porfirio held audience for international dignitaries who came to shower the immortal one with gushes of flattery and foreign decorations, which he loved. For don Porfirio Diaz's people, international interest offered systematic exploitation and slow death.

The man who was born into a poor mestizo family, who was an illiterate guerrillero, who fought and stopped the French in the rugged mountains of Oaxaca, who suddenly found himself the immortal dictator of Mexico, who, as he gained power and strength in political office, married—after his first wife died under mysterious circumstances—doña Carmen Rubio, a young, beautiful and forceful creole woman, gradually underwent a metamorphosis. He began to turn white.

This strange phenomenon was first noticed when a French painter, commissioned by doña Carmen, unveiled a portrait of don Porfirio at a public audience which the immortal one gave once a year. His consagrados, his caballada, high ranking Bravi, Rurales, and the illustrious científicos were present. Immediately after the revealing of the portrait a murmur overtook the great hall at the Palace of Fine Arts, followed by thunderous applause. When don Porfirio and doña Carmen Diaz stood in front of the portrait they saw his exact image, except that the face was that of a white man. Don Porfirio and doña Carmen agreed that they were white. The dictator called for a mirror and reviewed his mestizo face and arms. Of course he was white, and when he raised his white arms above his head the applause came again. From that moment, don Porfirio and every member of his family and all other people who wanted his favor began to use a white talc to whiten their faces. A sickly pale shine was the look of the time.

Don Porfirio kept searching the evening sky for the white tail of Halley's Comet. He realized that his detractors would say that the white of his face was caused by fear and cowardice. He touched his face with the fingers of both hands and slowly pulled them down and contemplated the contrasting white smudges on the fingertips with the dark of his wrinkled hands.

Far to the north Malaquias de Leon wiped the mud off his dark face. He had been forced, like many others, to pass through a large area of mud which led to the international boundary. Malaquias cleaned his bags and clothes, for he had taken a head-first fall into the slime. Malaquias spat out mud as he crossed the border into the United States. He saw Halley's Comet and walked away from it to Simons, California.

Chapter 6

In the distance appeared white, red and purple smudges to the left of the tracks. Nana de Leon pushed her face against the glass so she would not lose the colors from her sight. She glanced over to her Uncle Mario, a whitish spot on her left cheek and nose, and implored him silently to open the window. Beautiful brick buildings with red tile roofs grew in her vision. Her sister Paquita climbed on Nana's shoulder and looked at a man waiting alone at the Simons depot. Now the white, red and purple areas had turned into flowers that decorated the oblong depot located in front of the general store. Nana could see people going in and out of the other nearby buildings.

The train slowed; few people stopped to watch who would get on or off. Uncle Mario stood and got everybody ready to get off. Nana noticed a slight smile as he took his wife's hand. Nana understood that smile as a sign of happiness that the journey was at last over and that they all had arrived healthy.

"Simons!" a conductor yelled as he walked to the iron steps of the door to their car. Nana watched him grab an iron handle and swing his body over the gravel. He waved his arm and the train stopped.

The man whom she had seen from faraway now stood in front of a delicate iron bench. He waited at the door. Two years had passed since she had seen her father. Paquita and Nana recognized him immediately. Their two-year-old baby sister Jesus didn't, for he had left El Barral just days after her birth. They all pushed through the door to step on permanent soil and hear some word from the silent man who seemed to hug them with his eyes.

Malaquias de Leon reached out to shake hands with his brother-in-law Mario. He smiled and thanked him for accepting the responsibility of guiding Lorenza and their three daughters through the perilous trip north. Lorenza quietly waited for some kind of acknowledgement from her husband. He finally went to her and gently embraced her. Then he hugged his oldest daughter, then Nana, and took the baby Jesus in his arms.

"I am grateful that you have arrived healthy. Now follow me," he said.

The two sisters walked side by side, observing the new buildings and houses that had recently been constructed. Everything was so new and modern. Simons was a marvelous and beautiful place, a mysterious city full of strange machines and sounds. As they advanced with their father, men passed into the center of the brickyard from where polyphonic sounds originated and from where men emerged with faces and clothes covered with red dust and mud. The people seemed to have a destination and Nana wondered where her father's might be. She hoped it was one of those beautiful white houses with potted flowers at the edges of the little front porches she saw on Vail Avenue. These were wonderful and beautiful places compared to the house in which they had lived in El Barral.

Now Nana walked alone behind her father, turning and exploring the town. She hoped that he would take them to one of those white houses where she promised herself she would take care of the flowers. There were only three more houses on the street they traveled. Nana's face revealed disappointment as her father led the family away from the last one. Ahead a small grocery store appeared in their path. Malaquias opened a wooden gate next to Acacio Newman Delgado's grocery store. He entered a small fresh garden of ferns and exotic flowers. Connected perpendicularly to the back of the store was the Delgado residence. It was much larger than the other houses in Simons. On the porch was a small loveseat swing on which Nana and Paquita immediately sat. Malaquias knocked and moved Jesus to his left shoulder. From the side of the house a happy voice said hello.

"Your family has come, Malaquias! The rooms are ready. Come with me, señora. Here you will stay until they finish the new houses. It will be a matter of two weeks at the most. Those carpenters work very fast. Isn't that right, Malaquias?" Maria Delgado said, almost screaming and speaking rapidly.

Malaquias did not attempt to interrupt and gestured to Lorenza not to try.

"Come on in, please. What beautiful little girls. They will be very happy here. There is a lot to do and they also have school. I brought you extra blankets for the girls. The two beds are big and comfortable. I think you will be fine. Food is served to our guests at seven in the morning, at twelve and at six in the evening, every day, of course."

Maria Delgado opened the door to one of the rooms in the back of the house which she rented to single men. Malaquias had stayed with the Delgados for two years since his arrival in Simons. He had asked them for an extra room for his family until he was given a house. Gonzalo Pedroza had promised him one of the new houses constructed in Simons. Suddenly Malaquias and Lorenza realized that Maria Delgado's rapid talking voice was no longer present. She had left as fast as she had appeared. Malaquias laughed with his wife and daughters.

"I'm going to buy some fruit and milk for the girls," Malaquias said.

"¿Adonde se fue Mario y su familia?" Lorenza asked, surprised that during the time they walked from the depot to the Delgado house she had not noticed that Uncle Mario and family were no longer with them.

"They went to Uncle Epifanio's house," Malaquias answered and felt disappointed for not having a house for her. "Don't be upset, Lorenza. In two weeks we will have our new house." He left and she turned to make a home for her family in two small bachelors' rooms. Lorenza found herself sitting on the edge of a bed covered only with a sheet. Her two oldest daughters played behind her. Her youngest cuddled her blanket and felt cozy and warm. Lorenza was secure and safe now that she was with her husband. Throughout the trip north she never felt safe. Always she dreaded what might happen to her daughters. But now there was a future, hope and a promise of a good life.

She told Paquita and Nana to ask Maria Delgado for a broom. Lorenza wanted to clean immaculately the two rooms. She began to unpack the few bundles of clothing. She folded and looked around for a place for the family's clothes. She folded the only material objects she had saved from Mexico. The worn clothing blurred in her vision as she remembered her neighbors in tattered apparel. Ripped clothes were a metaphor of Mexico's peasants. The tears were so deep and great that they could no longer be repaired. Either they must be destroyed or new ones must be created. Mending and sewing new clothes from old material was a gift and talent she enjoyed. Lorenza separated the salvageable from the wearable. Nothing would be thrown away.

Lorenza sat quietly on the side of the bed. She put her hands on her lap and stared out the open door of the room. The early afternoon sunlight softly caressed her feet and ankles, climbed her legs and swelled in her hips and between her thighs. Her soft brown eyes gleamed with a sure power in the warmth of the sun. Lorenza sensed her life was important. She was not just a woman sitting on the side of a bed. Her brown eyes searched beyond the door to the side of the Delgado house and to the fern garden. Her face was transformed into a cactus leaf and her daughters into cactus plants growing strong and thorny. Her insides were a tightly-knit net of cactus thorns. Her husband had penetrated her body, had painfully broken through the thorns, and surely she would give birth again to another cactus child.

In the garden Maria Delgado flung water from a bucket on the hard red clay. The water spread like cold ice on the ground. Lorenza and her three daughters stopped before the watery plain and saw an image, a feminine face trapped in the shiny ice water. The face contorted, opened its mouth and screamed silently. They heard no sound, yet Lorenza understood that the woman had screamed. Lorenza and her daughters could do nothing as the image twisted into a drowning agony. It had traveled terrorized through the water and wetness of the universe. Lorenza moved forward. The three women stepped on the image and it disappeared.

Lorenza and the children walked toward where the builders constructed the de Leon family house. It was only a matter of a few days until Gonzalo Pedroza would turn over the key and the house would be theirs. Only two days to pack.

Finally the day came. Malaquias rented a horse and wagon from Gonzalo and arrived after work at three in the afternoon to move the family. He loaded the wagon with boxes full of clothes and kitchen utensils which Lorenza had packed that morning. At last Malaquias drove his family to their new home on Jalisco Street in the middle of the Simons mandala. Nana clutched her doll as she proudly observed the world pass by from the back of the wagon. She was proud of her father, her mother, and her sisters. She felt special to live in a beautiful new white house.

That evening Lorenza located the girls in their bedroom. Malaquias had brought back from the general store two new beds, five chairs and a table for the kitchen, blankets, rubber mats for the side of the beds, and a small wooden chest with three drawers to store the food he had bought.

"Tomorrow early they will bring the icebox and the stove," Malaquias announced to his family.

"Papa, I want some pots to plant some flowers in front of our house," Nana said clearly and confidently.

"Yes, of course, m'hija." Malaquias smiled and put his arms around Lorenza.

Nana went outside and sat with her doll on the front porch, calculating where she would place her potted flowers. She sat there listening to the conversations of neighbors strolling by the house. She noticed the children who would soon become her play and schoolmates. Lorenza had prepared Nana and Paquita for these new experiences. Two women stopped five feet away and argued about a church that Mr. Simons had ordered built. The women fussed over the location of the church. The last statement Nana heard made sense to her.

"Our sacred church will be very beautiful," one woman shouted as she moved away from the other woman who looked at Nana and strolled to the house next door.

Nana watched the woman enter as she returned to imagining where she would locate her beautiful flowers. She was happy and promised that she would take special care of her colorful flowers. At that moment the woman next door came out and flung water out into the dirt street. Nana saw in the window of moisture an image of a suffocating, drowning woman. She shivered but held her ground and stayed in the middle of her imagined garden.

The original granite cornerstone for the Catholic church was placed on May 1, 1913. One week later it was removed by orders of a priest who stated that the Church would not support any Bolshevik dates. The priest profusely condemned the stone for fear that it might inspire subversive activities among the Mexicans of Simons. Father Zarrutia warned of the subversive actions of many Bolshevik sympathizers in Mexico and reminded the Simons brothers that the Mexican Revolution was at its most violent stage. Every day thousands of Mexicans died and thousands of refugees entered the United States to escape the atrocities of Bolshevik madmen.

Rosendo and Gonzalo listened to the man dressed in black and interpreted what they heard as some exotic fairytale about devouring monsters called Bolsheviks. For Rosendo and Gonzalo, these political monsters were far from real and represented no threat to them. Walter comprehended the priest's great fear as mere cowardice and considered him the greatest of hypocrites for failing to offer his God as a source of security against the Bolshevik monsters. Joseph listened carefully, constantly nodding, seemingly agreeing with the priest's words.

"We must not give them any indication that they will find sympathetic ears here!" Father Zarrutia said and kicked the cornerstone. "I don't care where, but destroy it. Bury it somewhere. Get it out of our sight! Prepare a new stone with a different date." He went to his wagon and rode away, knowing that his word would be obeyed.

Joseph had ordered William and Gonzalo to have the stone destroyed. Rosendo shook his head and laughed. He did not understand the urgency to do away with a date and a block of granite.

"The priest is right. There is a danger. We don't know who's coming from Mexico," Joseph remarked to Walter and the other men.

"Poor desperate people who want peace and a job are coming from Mexico," Walter responded to his brother.

"You have a problem, Walter. You want to be everyone's father. Not this time. The stone shall be destroyed or else no church," Joseph answered to the point, impatient and angered. "Let's go, Rosendo!" he ordered.

The wind stirred up dust that surrounded Walter, alone, looking toward where his brother Joseph had disappeared. This is the last time you tell me what to do, or for that matter, tell my men what to do. Not here, Joseph. This is my yard and you don't rule here, brother!. . .

The wind whirled around him. The red dust thickened. A wall of violent dust prevented him from seeing the world. . . .Someone will be entombed, Walter thought spontaneously and wondered from where and why that idea had come to him so clearly. He approached the railroad tracks, crossed the Santa Fe rails, moved to Rivera Road and entered the general store, still thinking and now trying to escape the image of someone buried in whirling red dust.

Libra, the seventh sign of the zodiac, is like the cross and the sword and symbolizes equilibrium on both the cosmic and the psychic planes. However, October of 1913 was total disharmony and the month of an unexplainable, insane and tragic event. What occurred late one cold night in the middle of October left Melissa Simons in a psychological stupor. She later functioned and spoke normally, but her gaze was always as if her pupils were fixed on a vision that was not present in this time or space. It seemed as if she were blind yet seeing.

The night was unusually quiet; wild animals prowled closer than normal around the Simons homes on California Street. Joseph observed coyotes near the entrance to Walter's house. Their shiny eyes fixed on him and steam from their hot damp mouths formed a cloud around them as the pack moved into the nearby fields and on to the hills. Up there beyond, against and inside the mountain, light flickered from electricity caused by the hot and cold winds and unstable conditions that floated on the surface of the great moving mounds of earth.

Everyone was safe and comfortable. Laura and James had retired. Walter and Sarah's bedroom light was on and next door their mother had retired at her usual ten o'clock hour, while Orin Elmer probably worked, or read, or did whatever he passed the time away doing until early morning when he usually fell asleep. Often he did not change clothes and slept with what he wore that day. Joseph went to sleep a little after twelve in the

ALEJANDRO MORALES

morning.

Perhaps the strangeness arrived about eleven-thirty and moved into Melissa's home, passed by her room and found comfort near Orin Elmer. No one person of the family, nor friends, children, adults or Mexicans knew the precise moment when the strangeness embraced, penetrated and swallowed Orin Elmer. Quiet dominated the three houses when Orin Elmer turned off the lights and threw himself on his bed. He began to feel in his body a great thirst rising to his brain. The extremities of his body became active as if they had been possessed by an independent energy. They moved, twisted, and pulled against and away from the whole. He lay in bed not knowing what to do, afraid that his hands, arms, penis, legs, feet or head would drag him away. With this great fear, a fever arose that seeped out from the core of his flesh and mind.

Orin Elmer sat up and heard the deep silence of the fever. He craved water to quench the fever that was beginning to devour his subconscious mind and, his most internal flesh. He rose from the bed and found his way to the kitchen. In the dark he groped for a glass and placed it under the faucet, but to his desperation there was no water. He moaned at this unexpected, illogical condition. When he turned both faucets, a hiss emerged from deep within the plumbing. He needed water, if only a cup, to sip and dampen his lips and suffocating body. He uttered nonsensical remarks and turned toward the refrigerator.

On the top was a small bottle of water. He could not recall why the bottle was there. He decided not to drink but to dampen a washcloth and place it on his face. He did this constantly, moaning louder and stumbling several times against the furniture, knocking to the floor pans and plates. He found himself leaning into the sink where unwashed dinner dishes had been left. He reached for one dish and turned it to find hundreds of crawling insects. He looked again and now the insects had completely taken over the sink and were dispersing onto the counter. He turned both faucet handles to wash the crawling bugs away. But from the mouth of the faucet came a louder hiss, followed by silence and a stream of thousands of insects which enveloped the bottle of water he held. He moved to protect the bottle. With each step he crushed hundreds of brown bugs. They now blanketed the floor, the walls, the ceiling.

Orin Elmer's delirious language became a terrifying scream. He staggered to his bedroom. The insects were taking over the house. His bed was covered with creatures. He could not escape them. The beasts were now crawling onto his legs. They fell from the ceiling. Orin Elmer crushed and pulled them from his hair as he screamed and struggled to exit this image.

Melissa rushed to Orin Elmer's room. Three steps into the hall, she felt the insects ankle high. In that instant a wave of bugs flooded her bedroom. Not even the bright lights made them disappear. The light caused the top layers of insects to sink down into the masses that were below. Melissa, covered with brown bugs, screamed to her son to leave the house. She grabbed his arm and forced him to step through the foot-deep layer of oozing life to the porch and out into the yard.

Joseph and Walter arrived. Their faces were panicked by Orin Elmer's screams and by their mother's horrifying expression as she violently brushed the brown insects from her night gown.

"What the hell!" Walter exclaimed, staring at the house from which came a strange papery sound.

"Don't go in the house! It's full of insects!" Melissa screamed.

"There's no water! I'm burning and I need water!" Orin Elmer spat insects at Joseph.

"Oh, God! Orin Elmer is contaminated!" Joseph prayed. "Walter, we must stop them from spreading to the other houses!"

"I don't think the insects will spread. They belong only to this house and they don't want to go anywhere else. If you want to destroy them you must burn the house, and there's no guarantee that will work!" Walter declared.

"Ride to the yard for Rosendo and a crew to dig a trench around the house. Fill it with oil and fire it up. I'll take Mother and Orin Elmer to my house," Joseph said, helping Orin Elmer who cried for water and spat brown insects from his mouth.

As Walter rode off to the Pasadena yard, neighbors walked over to the invaded house . . . I hope they don't panic when they see those bugs, he thought as he spurred the horse to full gallop.

By three in the morning Melissa's house was surrounded by a ring of flames. Walter and Rosendo had returned with twenty-five men who immediately dug a one-foot trench, filled it with oil, and set fire to it. But at the time of their arrival at the house, the strangeness was gone. The insects had disappeared, leaving no trace of their existence. Nonetheless, not once did Rosendo doubt Walter's description of the invading insects. Rosendo suggested that they proceed as planned and had the house surrounded by fire. Walter could not believe that the insects had gone without a trace. The house stood as if nothing had ever crawled through it. He searched and did not find even a dead insect. Walter observed Joseph's house where their brother lay burning with a fever. The strangeness had burrowed itself in Orin Elmer, who throughout the daybreak hours gagged and coughed up pieces and at times whole brown insects that came from deep within his body.

Convinced that his brother had been bitten by some kind of animal, Joseph sent for a prominent Pasadena poison specialist. The horrible putrefaction of Orin Elmer's insides could only be caused by a poisoning of some kind. As the doctor rode up in an elegant carriage, Rosendo and the men tended the last of the flames. Rosendo knew of this ostentatious doctor and was sure that he would not help Orin Elmer.

An hour after the arrival of the doctor, Walter emerged from his house and went to check on the burning. He approached Rosendo who stood watching the front of Joseph's home. Walter noticed Rosendo's disharmony. With his hands Walter motioned to Rosendo to speak.

"That doctor cannot cure your brother," Rosendo said.

"Why not? He's the best!" Walter responded, angered.

"Your brother is not ill with fever, nor is he poisoned. He is hechizado," Rosendo said knowingly.

"Hechizado! Who would want to put a curse on him?" Walter answered, bothered by Rosendo's comment.

"I do not know about that, but he needs to be seen by a curandero." Rosendo spoke with an insistent tone.

"Do you think Joseph would permit that?" Walter asked, giving into Rosendo's idea. Walter believed that his brother was gravely ill and beyond the help of doctors.

"If you want your brother to live, allow him to be seen by a curandero," Rosendo stated firmly.

Walter watched Rosendo strike a shovel into a burnt trench. Rosendo worked as if he were angry about the possibility that Orin Elmer would not have the privilege of being cured by a curandero. He understood that Orin Elmer was poisoned spiritually and that the Anglo logic of one of the Simons brothers would not permit Orin Elmer's salvation. Rosendo identified Joseph as the obstacle. Walter would allow a curandero to see Orin Elmer but Joseph considered curanderos quacks who thrived on the superstitions of the Mexicans.

Rosendo became almost violent with the thought. He slammed his shovel into the trench and flung the dirt as if he were burying one of the patrones. The Mexicans who worked with him felt his annoyance and believed that the powers of the strangeness would be victorious. The brown bugs thriving inside Orin Elmer's body were a result of a telluric-human curse. Rosendo and the men filled the trench and, as each one offered the last shovelful of dirt, he looked toward the house where Orin Elmer lay strangled by the insects pouring from his mouth.

At eight in the morning Joseph came out to find the men watching, waiting for the terminal word. Joseph responded furiously at the men's knowledgeable gaze.

"What are you waiting for? For me to tell you he's dead? You're like vultures waiting for a corpse. Get out of here! Go back to the yard!" Joseph screamed.

"Calm yourself, brother!" Walter urged. "How is he?"

"Orin Elmer is dying," Joseph declared softly as if speaking to himself.

"Joseph, let me go for a curandero," Walter suggested.

"Damn you, Walter, neither Orin Elmer, nor I, nor mother believe in witches, in stupid Mexican superstitions! I will never allow my brother to be treated by ignorant Mexican Indian witch doctors," Joseph said firmly.

"But that's the only chance he has! Maybe they can do something for him!" Walter screamed, trying to break the stubborn crust that covered Joseph's mind.

"No, Walter, I don't believe in your damn Mexican superstitions! Orin Elmer will have the best medical care that money can buy. He will survive!" Joseph's voice was insane with fury and hatred for Walter who dared to offer a witch to cure Orin Elmer.

At ten in the morning the frowning left and a great wail came from the wooden heart of Joseph Simons' house. Melissa cried over the atrocity of her son who lay dying, being strangled by brown insects that flowed from his mouth. Walter had asked Joseph a third time to call for a curandero. Joseph's response was to insist that Walter leave. Walter declared that he would go for the curandero despite Joseph's denial. Upon hearing this, Joseph physically and violently threw his brother out. While the violence between her sons intensified and her cry became a loud gagging shrill, Melissa observed, fascinated, as the brown insects covered the body of her beloved Orin Elmer. The beasts crawled in and out of every orifice in his face and torso.

At eleven in the morning Orin Elmer drowned in a cocoon of brown insects. His engulfed body gave off putrid odors and gushy popping sounds. His family was never able to brush the plague off his body. As his mother undressed him, the insects insistently clung to the skin and left his clothes immaculate. When Orin Elmer was placed in a casket, millions of bugs surrounded his corpse. Only when the box was closed forever did the multiplication of insects seem to subside.

Orin Elmer was buried at Pasadena's Christian's Presbyterian Cemetery. Only the immediate family attended the service. After Orin Elmer's death, a deep silent hatred remained between Joseph and Walter. From that moment on, Melissa was silent and blind, seeing secretly into the future forever.

In the third week of October of 1913 the first official Mass of Our Lady of Mount Carmel Church was celebrated. What should have been a joyous event was converted into a solemn moment to celebrate the entering into paradise of Orin Elmer Simons. It began early in the morning with the arrival of Bishop Connaty, accompanied by Father de Fives, Father Juan Zarrutia and Father Arcan Rose. By eight that morning a red-faced William Melone, the chief usher for the occasion, saw to it that Walter and Sara Simons, Joseph, Laura and James Simons were seated. Mrs. Arcadia Bandini de Blake, a benefactress, joined the Simons family in the front pew. As the Bishop prepared for the High Requiem Mass he was reminded of the grant of land and donation of construction materials and labor given by the Simons family. He was informed of Mrs. Arcadia Bandini de Blake's funding of the altar, its artifacts and the images and paintings that decorated the church's interior.

The Bishop, satisfied that he and his assistants were ready, gave a signal to William to allow the Simons folk to enter. Few of them knew that they were about to hear a Requiem Mass in Latin, but as the word circulated here and there, sobs were heard. The cries and sobs multiplied and half-way through the Latin Mass most of the older women mourned the death of Orin Elmer Simons, a man whom none of them had ever met.

After the Mass, Bishop Connaty paid tribute to Father Rafael de Fives for his excellent missionary work. He thanked Mrs. Arcadia Bandini de Blake for her generous contribution that would never be forgotten by God's servants. He acknowledged the great sacrifices made by the Simons brothers and he urged the Mexican people of Simons to follow these unselfish, self-sacrificing examples of Christian love. The Mexican women, who understood very little of the Bishop's comments in English, thought that he continued to talk about the departed Orin Elmer and they sobbed loudly in between sentences. The Bishop urged them not to cry but to show their gratitude to the Simons family, Mrs. Arcadia Bandini de Blake, Father Rafael de Fives and the other Benedictine fathers who loved by being obedient workers and faithful followers of Jesus Christ.

After Walter and Joseph and their families rode away to their homes in Pasadena and Mrs. Arcadia Bandini de Blake was escorted to the Simons depot to catch the mid-day train to Los Angeles, Bishop Connaty gathered the Simons faithful outside their new church and announced that Father Rafael de Fives would be their pastor. He then blessed them and left for Montebello.

That afternoon Father Rafael de Fives, William Melone, and Gonzalo Pedroza organized an impromptu fiesta to honor their new pastor and church. All of Simons cooperated and they organized the first of many gay and exciting jamaicas. At one in the morning Malaquias and Lorenza de Leon took their family home. They walked under a sky blanketed with stars that lit their path. Nana, happy and content next to her mother, skipped all the way home.

What seemed large and mysterious became smaller and familiar to Nana as she explored the Simons Brickyard and the company town. She roamed the company grounds and the agricultural fields and discovered a baseball diamond in the meadows of wild flowers on the north side of Vail Street. Every day at three in the afternoon twenty men practiced throwing and hitting the ball. The men ran to the points of the diamond and at times were able to make it back to where they started.

Nana often watched the team practice. Each man performed superhuman feats. They ran faster, hit the ball farther and threw the ball harder than Nana could imagine. These men were giants who surprised her every day. On Saturday and Sunday when the Simons team hosted visitors Nana coaxed her father into taking her to the ballgame. She never fully understood the game but enjoyed the spectacle and excitement. Nana liked the Simons baseball players' uniforms: baggy green shirts and short pants tucked with garters below the knee. The shirts had red rounded priests' collars, and lettered in white down the front was the company name "Simons." The men wore long white socks with red tops and green caps with short bills.

There were times when Nana, Paquita and their father were astounded at the rowdiness of the crowd watching the game. At times the fans became drunk and threatened the players and each other. Nana had witnessed several fights break out. Most often the men were silly, so inebriated that they could not harm themselves. However, on one occasion that Nana never forgot, blood flowed heavily.

The Simons team had a black first baseman, Glory, who was called "La Gloria" by the Mexican players and fans. Nana had never seen a black man. The first time she saw Glory she was astonished by his deep blackness, wide, flat nose, thick lips, big bright eyes and shiny, curly hair. She stared at him in amazement. Glory noticed the little girl scrutinizing him. He walked up to Nana, looked her right in the eye and said "Boo!" and laughed loudly, celebrating his joke. Nana, surprised and scared, felt his laugh and began to giggle. She never stared at anyone else again.

Glory would always say hello and Nana would sit with her father or

Paquita next to Glory's family. During a game when his wife, two daughters and son were present, two members of the opposing team called Glory ugly names and made obscene motions toward his wife. Nana saw the Simons players calm Glory and sit him on the bench. His wife took her children in her arms and turned their sight away from the obscene men.

When Glory came to bat, the insults began again and the visitors' fans joined the name calling. The first ball pitched to Glory was at his head, causing him to fall. William Melone protested vehemently. Glory got up again to face the pitcher and once again the horrible words were directed at him and his wife and children. The pitcher threw the ball and hit Glory on the shoulder and neck. Glory fell, grimacing in pain.

"I got me a real black nigger! After the game I'll get that big-titted black bedwarmer over there," the pitcher yelled proudly while the visiting players and fans cheered and applauded.

Glory's wife ran to her husband. The children remained seated next to Nana and regarded what was occurring. From the Simons bench bolted the players who went right at the pitcher and knocked him down. Glory got up and charged his attacker and beat him about the head. Both benches emptied and the visitors' fans started for the field when five Simons men blocked their way. They drew their revolvers and fired above the visitors' heads toward the empty fields. The melee suddenly stopped.

Gonzalo Pedroza, who had come by at that moment, was told what had happened. He ordered the visitors to retreat and walked over to where Glory sat on the pitcher. Gonzalo turned to the visitors' fans and fired his gun into the sky and screamed at them to leave. He turned to Glory and the bleeding pitcher.

"Hit him until you're satisfied," Gonzalo said to Glory, who sent his mighty fist crashing three times into the defeated pitcher's face.

Glory raised the battered man over his head, walked to where some visiting players waited surrounded by Simons fans and flung the pitcher at their feet.

"Thanks for the game, boys," Glory said and went to his terrified family.

Nana waited next to Glory's children. She never forgot the hatred she saw in the faces of the visitors and she always remembered the horrible words in Spanish and in English that were directed at the Mexicans for allowing a black man to play on the Simons Brickyard Baseball Team. The hatred went beyond the surface of what she had seen. It was directed at the color of their skin.

Glory's blackness and Nana's brownness were shades of light that floated in her mind as she and her father walked home by the new Vail School building. The fields were covered with purple, yellow, and white wildflowers which reminded Nana to water her flowers on the doorsteps of the front porch. Walking with her father was a silent affair. He never said much to his daughters. The morning and evening greetings and commands communicated few real feelings stored in his heart. Nana observed that silence was the dominant nature of father-daughter relations.

They were now next to Vail school. Nana's feelings towards school were ambiguous. She enjoyed the academic, intellectual exercises that she understood in spite of the impatient teacher. Nana attended school with the other Simons children. Among them she found many friends and a few treacherous teasers, such as the five Pedrozas: Francisco, Maria Pascuala, Ramon, Jesus, who was as old as the six-year-old Nana, and Elvira.

During the first few weeks of school the children who had recently arrived in Simons were always the center of curious attention. The new kids seemed to move in the middle of a circle of children. Nana was placed in the second grade and as she walked to her class Jesus, Elvira and Francisco watched and giggled close behind. Glad to see each other back in school, the smiling veterans entered the class.

Nana took a seat at the front, not by choice but because she was one of the last to enter. She sat by the window at the head of the first row of desks. The crisp-warm autumn morning, clear and beautiful, invited Nana to enjoy nature through the window. She deliciously contemplated the birds outside flying from trees to swings to monkey bars.

Suddenly Nana sensed that it was her turn to present herself to the class. The teacher realized that Nana was a recent arrival and called her up to the front. Once more Nana glanced to where the birds flew freely. She had no alternative but to obey. Acting automatically, she followed the teacher's hand-motion to the front of the room from where she saw seventy eyes peering at her. From amongst those orbs Jesus and Elvira Pedroza smirked and giggled with delightful malice at observing Nana's nervousness and embarrassment. Wearing a light rose dress, hair parted down the center with pigtails and white bows, she stood alone. Nana, with hands together, gazed at the floor while she heard the teasing comments of the Pedrozas. The teacher placed her hand on Nana's shoulder. From the teacher's red smile came words that Nana understood but did not particularly want to hear.

"And what is your name?" the teacher asked.

Nana fell into her self; shoulders caved into her chest, arms stiffened, hands clasped and pushed against the inside of her thighs. The wry-faced Pedrozas leaned forward to hear. Everyone waited through the silence.

"Look at the class and tell them your name." The teacher nudged Nana forward.

Jesus and Elvira Pedroza regarded the other children, and with mouths half-opened on the verge of hilarious laughter, leaned over their desks again and exaggeratedly turned an ear to Nana. Without moving her head, she saw the Pedrozas for an instant. From deep inside she slowly pronounced her name with a fearful, embarrassed child's tone.

"N-a-n-i-t-a," she said, her eyes searching the floor for an object to concentrate on for safety.

"N-a-n-i-t-a," Jesus Pedroza mimicked.

Elvira laughed and imitated the name with a baby voice. Now the entire class mimicked and laughed at Nana.

"You may sit down now, Nanita." The teacher placed her next to Elvira, who could not sit still nor contain her laughter.

Jesus repeatedly leaned over to see Nana. He opened his mouth wide, bobbed his head and enjoyed a silent guffaw which brought laughter from the class.

Nana and her father now moved down the hill, through part of the Vail School playground, toward the arroyito which always had water. They crossed easily and moved up the hill to their home in the Hoyo. There was no reason to go home by this way. In fact, the route was longer. Her father chuckled to himself. What made him laugh, Nana wondered. They passed by a house with a heavily and colorfully burdened clothesline.

"I brought some coats for the girls," Malaquias told Lorenza as he placed the shopping bags on the kitchen table.

"They need them. It's getting colder," Lorenza said, unwrapping the package and holding up one quilted, multicolored, butterfly-patterned bathrobe. "How pretty, Malaquias! Tomorrow they will wear them."

Lorenza took the three bathrobes to the girls' room.

"Look, Nana, the coats that your father bought for you," she said to Nana, who reached for a red bathrobe with chromatic butterflies. It fit her. Paquita was fitted into yellow and Jesus received a green bathrobe. Nana dreamed of the next day when she would wear her brand-new quilted red coat to school.

Nana's mother, an early riser, had awakened Paquita at five. Today Paquita would stay home from school to help with the house chores. Paquita wore her yellow bathrobe. She lingered awhile, wondering why she had to arise at this hour of the morning while her sisters slept. She knew the answer—being the oldest it would always be this way. Although disappointed about not going to school, Paquita was excited for Nana who would wear her beautiful red coat. Paquita was sure the children would comment and the Pedrozas would be envious. Tomorrow Paquita would wear her yellow coat and walk proudly next to her sister.

By seven-thirty Nana stepped out the back door and waved good-bye to her mother and Paquita, who cried silently. Nana moved down the dirt street through the Hoyo already bustling with workers. Simons Brickyard was growing rapidly. Nana ran to feel the wind through her hair. Soon she reached the downgrade to the arroyo. Below, about to cross the water, Jesus, Elvira and Francisco Pedroza teased three of their followers. Jesus threatened to throw the smallest boy into the water. Elvira and Francisco grabbed the boy's legs but he resisted, yelled, cried and ran off. Nana had reached the Pedrozas during their attempt to teach the boy how to bathe.

"Look who's coming! La Nanita!"

"And wearing a clown's bathrobe!" Elvira pointed out as Nana started to cross the arroyo.

"Why did you bring that bathrobe? Don't you have a jacket?" Francisco asked Nana who stood on the other side of the arroyo.

Puzzled by the remarks, Nana pulled together the lapels of the coat.

"My papa bought me this coat," Nana answered angrily.

The Pedrozas ran across the arroyo. Jesus caught up to Nana and tugged at the red bathrobe.

"This is not a coat. It's a bathrobe for wearing after a bath!" Jesus broke into great laughs.

By now other students had noticed the girl, Nanita, with her red, quilted, butterfly-covered bathrobe. Nana ran to her classroom and joined the line with the rest of the children who stared and giggled. Jesus and Elvira butted to the front of the line, joking all the while about Nana and her sobretodo. Nana now understood that the garment she wore was not supposed to be used as a coat since it was something called a quimona, a garment related to taking baths. Clothes that you would put on to cover the naked body immediately after bathing you would never wear in public. It was like wearing underwear. Nobody must ever see it. Paquita would probably wear the bathrobe to the store. Nana stacked the embarrassing thoughts in a precarious tower in her mind as the children marched into the classroom. The teacher stopped her.

"Why are you wearing your bathrobe, Nanita?" the teacher asked, half-angered and amused. And with a wry expression of disbelief she put a hand on Nana's shoulder and slightly pushed her back to study the multitude of chromatic butterflies. Nana did not look up. Embarrassed and humiliated she only shrugged her shoulders.

"Go in and sit down, Nanita," the teacher ordered.

As Nana went to her seat the Pedrozas struggled to contain their laughter. Other children followed the Pedrozas' lead and chuckled.

"Look what a pretty bathrobe Nanita is wearing," a child commented.

"I like the colors," another added.

"And the butterflies! Be careful they don't fly away with you!" a boy shouted from the back of the room.

At this comment general laughter flooded the room. Nana sat silently crying. She wished that the butterflies would fly her away. The teacher brought the class to order. Before the children stood for the flag salute Nana turned with teary eyes and wet cheeks, stared right into Elvira's pupils, and noticed her face and the great difference in skin color. Elvira's skin was as dark as chocolate. Elvira turned to face the flag. Nana scrutinized the face of Jesus and Elvira Pedroza, faces she would never forget.

During the first recess the teacher offered Nana a sweater from the lost and found box, but Nana embraced her quimona and walked out to the playground to suffer the teasing that would surely come from the Pedroza children and their cohorts. Nana did not pay attention to them and soon the children forgot about the quimona and invited her to play.

After school, still wearing her quimona, Nana ran home and found Paquita waiting in yellow and covered with butterflies. Nana described what had happened and both girls hung their quimona behind the bedroom door. Lorenza had already placed her daughter Jesus' quimona there, for early that morning she had discussed with one of the neighbors the purchases which Malaquias had made the day before. In the conversation Lorenza discovered that what Malaquias and she thought were "sobretodos" were "quimonas."

The end of the school year of 1914 found Paquita, Nana and Jesus in wait of the arrival of a new baby. Their mother had tried to hide her pregnancy as long as possible but size had become an undisguisable factor. Nana and Paquita curiously asked questions concerning their mother's protruding abdomen.

That the summer would be extremely hot was the neighbors' consensus as they gathered and chatted outside the Simons white washed homes early in the morning. The night before, Malaquias gave the girls each a white bonnet decorated with a long red ribbon. He had told them it was to protect their beautiful skin from the fire-like sun.

Nana and Paquita went off to school playing with the ribbons on their new bonnets. On the way other children commented on the beauty of the bonnets. Both girls were quite happy and proud of their lovely hats, but even amidst all the attention their thoughts were with their mother and they hoped that by the time they returned home she would have had the baby. The girls passed the arroyo and moved up the hill to the Vail School playground. Suddenly a hand knocked off Paquita's bonnet, which fell into the arroyo. Paquita turned and watched her white bonnet slowly float away. Nana immediately recognized Elvira Pedroza run up the hill and not look back.

"Come on, let's get the bonnet. The water will take it!" Nana urged her sister.

Nana and Paquita cautiously moved to the edge of the riverlet. Paquita, who was downstream, had picked up a long twig with which to snag the hat as it floated close to her. Attention focused on the moving white object between them. Nana reached with a shorter twig, and suddenly two bonnets appeared in the stream. A scream broke from the surface of the water as Nana sat incensed and watched Jesus Pedroza, who had pushed her in, escape to the classroom.

At the top of her voice Nana expressed her fury in unintelligible utterances. Paquita walked into the water to help her sister and fell. Nana and Paquita sat leaning on their arms and hands stretched out behind them and watched their beautiful white bonnets with the red ribbons float faster out of sight. They rose slowly and stepped toward home. In a few minutes they arrived gasping from the hard run and could barely make sense to their mother. Finally, at the kitchen table, after their clothes had been changed and their hair wrapped in a towel, the girls calmed down enough to explain what had occurred.

"Who is going to stop those Pedrozas?" Nana asked softly . . . They are the children of Mr. Gonzalo Pedroza and he's capable of kicking out any family who touches them. . . These thoughts Lorenza did not share as she prepared hot chocolate for her daughters. Lorenza moved slowly, for her unborn child was always in front of her. She served the chocolate to Nana, Paquita and Jesus, who listened sadly to the story of the loss of the two white bonnets. Lorenza left the children in the kitchen and exited to the back garden to start the laundry.

All that morning and afternoon Nana had repeatedly created the images that crashed into her vision and mind. The feeling of the helplessness of watching the water take her bonnet away persisted. And Jesus and Elvira Pedroza were to blame.

Nana waited amidst her potted flowers, hoping that by chance the Pedrozas had taken the long way home. Her patience proved to be productive. They advanced alone—Jesus, Elvira and Francisco—whistling, laughing, kicking a can and hoping for the opportunity to tease Nana again. The Pedrozas saw Nana on the porch, stopped, conferred and approached her. But this time Nana had determined that she would stand up to the Pedrozas. She did not know exactly how, but whatever the consequences the Pedrozas would never again pick on her and Paquita. The Pedrozas admired the potted plants.

"What pretty flowers, Nanita," Jesus teased.

Elvira reached for one of the pots and Nana grabbed her hand and squeezed. Nana pushed Elvira to the ground. Her light skin contrasted with Elvira's chocolate tone.

"Don't touch it, blacky!" Nana defended her territory.

"Don't call me that!" Elvira yelled.

"Blacky, blacky! I'll call you what I please, blacky!" Nana shouted.

"Please don't call me that!" Elvira pleaded.

"Don't call my sister blacky!" Jesus demanded.

"Blacky, blacky, blacky!" Nana's sisters Paquita and Jesus joined the chorus.

Attracted by the melee two other children neared to find Elvira in tears, her brother Francisco crying and Jesus Pedroza yelling at the de Leon girls who repeated the chorus. Minutes later five more children sang. The chanting became unbearable to the Pedroza children.

"Blacky, Elvira the blacky, blacky, Elvira is a blacky, blacky!"

The children had surrounded the Pedrozas. Jesus pushed his sobbing brother and sister through the circle and they ran home, trailed by a singing tail of thirteen unafraid children. The Pedrozas reached their front gate and the chanting stopped. Jesus, Elvira and Francisco looked back and discovered that they were alone.

Chapter 7

Laura and Sara rejoiced at seeing the family enjoy the dinner they had prepared that afternoon of July 4, 1916. Although it was a special day Joseph and Walter decided to celebrate quietly together at Walter's home. An early dinner was the order of the afternoon, and afterward the family planned to sit on the porch and watch Rosendo direct five men in lighting fireworks purchased in the Chinatown of Los Angeles. Joseph, Laura and James strolled about the rockets, fountains and bombs being set up. The sun glimmered off the shiny silver firework cannisters that would lie in the street for three hours until night when they would streak through the sky to burst into multicolored flowers.

Sara went to Walter, who was seated in a comfortable chair on the porch. No words were exchanged; instead a smile and a touch were shared with confidence. She moved out to the street to where Laura watched the rockets being readied. From where he sat, Walter watched them and felt comfortable. His stomach satisfied, mind rested, passions gratified, body healthy and soothed by the afternoon sun, he would not move. His desire was to hold the feeling forever. The family moved in and out of the house. Outside they bathed in the sun but impatiently hurried its descent.

At dusk Melissa was brought out to experience the fireworks from the seat that Walter had abandoned just minutes ago. Walter could see his mother from the street where he checked the last installations of the fireworks. It grew darker and Melissa stared straight ahead, motionless. When the fireworks began she never changed her posture, nor was she startled by the great booms and fierce beautiful lights of the bombs and rockets. Everyone held their fingers to their ears and stood sideways to the rockets. An excited James was stopped from going out into the street by Joseph who scolded the boy and sat him down on the steps. Laura and Sara joined James while Joseph stood with Walter next to Melissa.

"She doesn't respond to anything anymore," Joseph said to Walter who followed a rocket into the sky. "Orin Elmer loved fireworks!" he declared, angered at Walter for not saying a word about their mother.

"At least I didn't refuse him any chance he might have had to live," Walter said rapidly.

"What do you mean by that?" Joseph asked sharply.

Boom! Millions of bright colors fell from the sky.

"Come on, don't shut up. Nothing could have saved him. Not even your Mexican witch doctors you wanted to bring to him," Joseph said angrily, looking at the curtains of red hanging in the night sky.

"I don't care what you want to call them. They just might have been able to save his life," Walter retorted and started down the steps.

"Now wait a minute! You're not going to blame me, damn you! It was those insects that killed him!" Joseph shouted.

Boom! Patriotic fire brushed across the stars.

"He might have been saved if you had allowed the curandero to see him!" Walter tried to keep calm.

"Don't say that, Walter." Joseph's lips tightened at the use of his brother's name.

"I don't have to because everyone knows it." Walter hurt his brother.

Laura, Sara and James stepped between the brothers and pushed them away from each other.

"Damn you, Walter! Why don't you go live with your Mexicans?" Joseph challenged.

"Why should I? This is my home. This house belongs to me. I earned it!" Walter shouted.

"You're wrong. This house belongs to my son and he shall have it," Joseph responded furiously.

"Go home, Joseph. Go cool off and I'll see you tomorrow," Walter suggested.

"I'll see you in court, beloved brother," Joseph said.

"Good. It's about time we settled matters." Walter gave a signal to Rosendo.

Boom! The fireworks lit the night with magnificent colors and holiday gaiety. Joseph walked with Laura and was in the street before James could react to what had occurred. James, at a loss as to why he could not see the fireworks with his grandmother, uncle and aunt, hurried after his parents. He would enjoy the artificial fires while sitting on the steps of his own porch.

Joseph opened the gate door and glanced up to wonder about what he had threatened to his only brother. Laura and James joined him on the porch.

"Walter is the only brother you have left," Laura said, kissing him and hugging her son.

Perhaps family was more important than economic possessions or brotherly rivalry, Joseph mused. His father was dead and his mother was not with them mentally. Orin Elmer had been eaten by insects and madness. Walter was the only brother alive. His three sisters, back in Iowa, seldom wrote. They declared no claim to what he and Walter had built.

The brick factories were his and Walter's. The Los Angeles, Pasadena, Simons, Santa Monica brickyards and the yard they were considering developing in El Centro belonged to them and their heirs. Nonetheless, they had to come to an agreement as to which one of them would administer what yard.

Joseph didn't want the Simons yard. Walter had usurped that yard and made his town. Joseph disagreed with the paternalistic way in which Walter operated the Simons yard. He was uncomfortable with Walter being the great father to the peasant Mexicans. A written agreement must be reached, he thought as the last volley of rockets shot into the sky.

"I'll go for Mother," Joseph said to Laura.

"But please don't argue with him," Laura worried.

Joseph nodded, walked across the street, went to Melissa and started to guide her back. Walter came to the porch as Joseph closed the gate door. Walter went down to the gate.

"Good-night, Mother," Walter called and wished she would answer.

Joseph stopped and stared into Melissa's eyes and hoped. But not the slightest response came from her eyes, mouth or body.

She stood like a stone, looking outward until someone or something moved it. Walter was at her side now and kissed her.

"Joseph, we must meet at my Simons office tomorrow. It should be done as soon as possible," Walter said.

Joseph, bothered with the direct way Walter made a decision for him without any consideration as to what his plans might be for tomorrow, mentally repeated Laura's warning and agreed to meet Walter.

"At ten tomorrow morning, Joseph." Walter waited for his brother's answer.

Joseph took Melissa by the hand and started to his house. "Tomorrow at ten," he called out. "But not at Simons. It's too far to ride. Tomorrow we can talk here, in your house or in mine, or right here in the middle of the street. Not in Simons!" Joseph shouted.

The next day, like the men who worked at Simons Brickyard producing thousands of bricks per day, Walter did not rest. He woke up at four-thirty and could not find sleep again. The meeting with Joseph immediately came to his mind and refused to leave. By five he was dressed and had coffee brewing. Sipping a cup of coffee he went to his study, opened a large iron box and took out three ledgers in which he recorded the Simons Brickyard sales and personal dealings concerning buyers, contractors, employees, and comments on his methods of administration and decisions.

Walter knew every aspect of the machinery, production and human maintenance needed to make a profit at Simons Brickyard, which was fast becoming the largest of the yards owned by the Simons brothers. Aware of the growing potential of the yard, he had decided that he deserved outright ownership. As he perused the ledgers he concluded that the El Centro property was the basis for another yard like Simons.

He sipped at his coffee and thought of his father and mother, how their house was empty, how Orin Elmer's rooms were quiet. He searched the walls that surrounded him. He experienced an intense feeling of belonging to those walls, that room, that house. He would not surrender the house or the Simons yard. He felt that he had created and belonged to both places and that both places belonged to him.

Joseph did not wait until ten. He too had had a restless night. The images and words of the night before intruded his sleep. He awoke tired and irritable, moved slowly through the house, and made his way to the kitchen where he prepared a cup of coffee.

As Joseph stepped out the front door, he decided that the Los Angeles, Pasadena, Santa Monica and El Centro brickyards would be his. His mother would have to move to where Walter presently lived, to James' future house. Joseph would insist on keeping the house which he had built for his son. Walter and Sara could move to the house where Melissa lived, Joseph thought as he made his way across the street, which he took for granted, like most of the other objects in his life.

Joseph did not bother to knock on Walter's front door. He moved quickly to the study where he found his brother under a warm yellowish light concentrating on a stack of papers. For seconds Joseph watched Walter read, pick up a page and turn it over onto the pile of papers reviewed. Suddenly Walter felt a presence which went beyond his brother who stood at the entrance to the study. A decision had been made by both men which meant much more than the possession of material objects. For the sake of family peace they had to settle the ownership of the brickyard and the properties, separate the authority, and break an old bond of silent trust. Dependence on one another had become a burden which could only be relieved by financial independence.

"Come in. Sit down," Walter motioned with an open hand to the chair in front of his desk, not the seat at his side. He felt that talking behind the desk, from behind a pile of company documents, created a power position from which he was the stronger and his brother the weaker.

"Well, what are we going to settle?" Joseph leaned forward, placed his forearm on the desk and looked straight at his brother under the light.

"It's time that we work at our own pace, work independently. Do what we want to do and not bother the other. But help the other if and when help is needed." Walter decided not to waste time.

"What do you propose?" Joseph responded.

"We should separate. I want the Simons yard, El Centro and this house. You can have the rest. We must operate independently with the understanding that if you or I have difficulty keeping a yard solvent, then the other has the duty of taking over and making the defaultee a full partner of that property only. We must do this to keep our properties within the family, to insure ourselves, to develop at our own pace." Walter stopped and wondered if Joseph understood. Walter placed his forearms on the papers, leaned forward and waited in a silence communicated by a stare which said he had nothing further to say until he heard his brother's response.

"You can't have the house. Build your own," Joseph said and smiled.

"I ask for only three properties. Let's not be unreasonable," Walter responded with subtle anger in his tone.

"Unreasonable! You're the one who wants to break up the business! Besides I built this house for my son! And you knew that!" Joseph raised his voice.

"I have kept it up. You haven't spent a cent on the maintenance or changes which I have made. You never said a word about the changes! The simple fact that I have invested thousands in the house should convince you that it belongs to me," Walter replied tight-lipped.

"You're being stubborn. I told you from the first that the house would be for my son." Joseph pushed himself up from the chair.

"I won't give it up!" Walter yelled, turned off the lamp and walked over to a window. He drew the curtains open and the sun of the morning after the Fourth of July invaded the study.

"I was right then," Joseph said.

"About what?" Walter asked with his back to Joseph who moved to the doorway.

"I'll see you in court," Joseph answered, disheartened.

Walter faced his brother and nodded. "Fine. We'll talk later," he answered, feeling that at last they would resolve what had bothered them for years.

The brothers faced each other for a moment. There was no other way. Decisive footsteps on the wooden floor, the front door opening and closing: the sounds dissolved in the morning heat.

By court order J. R. Allen, accompanied by Joseph and Walter Simons, traveled throughout Southern California photographing every building, machine and animal which the Simons brothers owned. By early 1917 the judge agreed with Joseph Simons' petitions which requested control of all the properties except the Simons yard. However, Walter wanted ownership of the Simons yard, the El Centro properties, and the Pasadena house and filed an appeal against his brother. Realizing that his brother would not abide by the court decision and wanting to avoid a time-consuming and costly legal dispute, Joseph capitulated to Walter's demands.

By spring of 1917 Walter Robey Simons had gained complete economic control of the properties he desired. The deed of the house was sent to him by special courier. From the moment Walter accepted the package, the relationship with Joseph had ended and begun anew. On the surface peace had come, but the hurt and bitterness remained.

Throughout the court proceedings Walter never felt any remorse for what some acquaintances described as a terrible, sinful economic betrayal of a brother. If anything, it was the change in Joseph's relationship with James that deeply hurt Walter.

James, who had turned seventeen years old at the time his father decided not to continue legally to fight Walter's claim to properties that had long ago, even before his birth, been designated to him, became incensed at the loss of his house.

A quiet young man, James suddenly turned aggressive, and the first to suffer the brunt of his verbal anger was Joseph.

Walter never forgot the night when James attacked Joseph. The many verbal insults of "failure," "betrayal," "coward," "worthless" and Laura's cries whirled in Walter's mind.

The insults and humiliation devastated the respect that had existed between father and son. The stress caused a paralysis to slowly overtake Joseph's body. He lost the use of the thumb, index and middle finger of his right hand as well as the forearm. Although he could hold a pen, writing was difficult and he used his left hand to carry his right hand across the paper.

Laura was sure that the paralysis was caused by the tension and worry brought about by the court action, but most destructive was the decrement of James' respect for his father. Joseph walked head down, never directly looking at anyone in the eye, and his facial expression was weighted by the loss of a son whom Joseph never really knew.

Walter sat at the desk reviewing the week's orders. Ballast for ships, he thought. With Wilson beginning a second term, peace would come soon. He liked the amount of brick ordered by Los Angeles-based international ship brokers. Thousands of brick to be used as weight on Russian ships.

He did not question the use but had William investigate the economic soundness of the company. Nonetheless, he ordered that shipment be sent immediately to the Los Angeles dock. He instructed Gonzalo to operate all twelve machines and set up number thirteen. The number did not bother William or Gonzalo who listened to Walter place an order for more mules and wagons.

Looking out the window, Walter saw Roberto Lacan dismount and tie his horse to a post. Walter thought about Pancho Villa who had crossed the border with guerrillas and raided Columbus, New Mexico, killing seventeen Americans. General Pershing had pursued Villa with six thousand troops but could not find him. Roberto Lacan, a cunning maderista, had probably wanted to be with Villa. Roberto walked by his boss and wished him a good morning.

"You're not going to leave that horse there? It will crap and we'll have it inside. It'll smell like a stable," Walter said sternly.

"No, Mr. Simons. I will move the animal immediately." Roberto abandoned his intention to mount a new shoe display before the general store opened at eight o'clock. In a minute Roberto and horse were out of sight.

Walter returned to his work to finish sorting the order invoices. As he automatically pushed the paper, the early morning with Sara rushed to him. She felt him get out of bed, wash, and dress. When he returned from the kitchen to kiss her, she muttered words that she had used three times before. When she told him, Sara cried. They both were afraid of losing this child. Three times before, she had miscarried. He told her to sleep, and left.

Walter reached for another stack of orders and wondered what it was about the Simons men. Joseph had only one child. Walter had none. He wanted more than anything to have this child. Sara deserved the baby. He placed the last order on the local stack and noticed that its job description read residential housing. At that instant he decided that Sara needed a change of environment. The house in Pasadena, the house that he had struggled so much to make his, he would leave. Walter laughed at the silliness of it all as he pushed himself away from his desk.

Walking into the general store, Walter saw William and Gonzalo drinking a cup of coffee which Roberto had brewed. Walter held the residential housing order up high and looked straight at Gonzalo.

"I'm going to build a house," Walter said.

The declaration came out of nowhere and caught the three workers by surprise. They stood with cups in hand, not knowing how to respond to Walter's revelation. William drank his coffee as Walter watched the steam rise from the coffee cups.

. . . And I'll huff and I'll puff and I'll blow your house down! One pig built a house of brick, stronger than his brother's, so strong that nothing would bring the house down. It would be the sturdiest and safest house in the world. There had been three little pigs but now there were only two. Brown insects had eaten the third; worry and the loss of respect in the eyes of his son was short-circuiting parts of the brain of the first pig. The second and first pig had buried the third. The second watched sparks perpetually fly from the head of the first pig. The second pig would survive by building the best brick house in Los Angeles . . . Walter's mind allowed the pig faces to fade away. He blinked and found three human faces staring at him. He motioned to Roberto for more coffee.

"Gonzalo, the brick you use to build a house, it's the common, regular brick?" Walter inquired.

Gonzalo nodded.

"I want you to choose and separate the best shaped, colored, strongest brick we produce. In a few days I will tell you where to deliver it," Walter said pensively.

"Yes, Mr. Simons." Gonzalo put his cup on the counter. He grabbed his hat and the door closed behind him. His horse whinnied and broke into a gallop.

Walter returned to his office and packed two saddlebags with company paperwork. By one o'clock that afternoon he had begun preliminary negotiations for the purchase of residential property in an exclusive section of Los Angeles. The next day he signed contracts to purchase in cash three lots on Plymouth Street. He immediately sent word to William and Gonzalo to begin transporting brick to the site.

The morning that Walter announced he would build a house and gave orders to select the best brick he produced, Gonzalo left the general store in a full gallop. With Walter's orders to select the best brick echoing in his mind, he rode to the bachelors' quarters to see if any new men had arrived. On his way he remembered that he had had a discussion with Malaquias de Leon that needed to be concluded. It had turned out that Malaquias, an excellent worker who came to Simons around 1910, had become somewhat of a rebel. He refused to obey the understood Simons rule which demanded that workers buy groceries, clothes, shoes, and other living necessities at the company general store. For years Malaquias and Gonzalo had nurtured an ongoing feud. Gonzalo insisted that the rules be obeyed. Malaquias believed he was free and that after he put in twelve hours at work the rest of the time was his own. Malaquias demanded the right to spend his salary when, where and on whatever he desired. He did his purchasing outside of Simons in the neighboring towns.

What bothered Gonzalo most were the two horses and carriage that Malaquias bought and kept in the backyard of his Simons house. These animals exemplified Malaquias' freedom. He was completely and independently mobile. He placed no limitation on himself and quietly encouraged other workers to do the same.

Soon Lorenza would give birth to another child, for she was well advanced into her sixth pregnancy. For his family's sake Malaquias would not limit his freedom and basic right to make survival a little easier, more prudent than what Simons offered. Hard work was his ethic; he considered work a privilege. No matter how difficult it might become, he had learned to move forward, and as he did obstacles disappeared, fears were understood and life became more meaningful. Not a talkative man, he was known as a calculator to enemies and as an hombre pensativo to his acquaintances. He was not a man to count on friends, but everyone knew that once he gave his word, they could count on Malaquias. He was a respected man who kept to himself and performed well on the job and as a provider for his family, the measure of a good father in Simons.

With this history in mind and a basic dislike for Malaquias, Gonzalo approached the house. Gonzalo heard that Malaquias had been going to Downey and intended to buy a third horse, which was absolutely unacceptable. He had given the workers permission to have hogs, goats and even milk cows whose milk, cheese and butter were sold at the general store, but Malaquias had never asked for permission to own horses. He had acted without consulting Gonzalo, who categorized this lack of consideration as an affront to his authority.

Gonzalo dismounted while a four-year-old girl came to the door. Moments later Lorenza, holding two-year-old Leonardo, stepped onto the little path on the porch. Nana's potted flowers had grown into beautiful, fruitful plants. She cared for them and the family respected where she had placed them six years ago.

"Malaquias is not here, don Gonzalo," Lorenza answered, moving the baby to her right hip.

"I want to see how many horses he has out back."

"Only two, don Gonzalo." Lorenza placed herself and the child directly in his path.

"Very well, let there be only two and not one more!" Gonzalo spoke with an angered tone.

"That is impossible, don Gonzalo. Malaquias has just bought the third one and he will pick it up this afternoon." Upon finishing her statement Lorenza suddenly realized the possible consequences.

Vexed, Gonzalo mounted his horse and went looking for Malaquias. He had assigned him to machine number five, where he found him placing wet brick on drying racks. Malaquias worked right up to the moment Gonzalo called his name.

"Buenos dias, Mr. Gonzalo Pedroza." Malaquias continued working.

"I told you two horses was enough! You can't have the third one!" Gonzalo insisted.

Two men who worked with Malaquias came closer.

"My horses don't harm anyone. Who has complained?" Malaquias raised his voice over the machine's grinding noise.

"I'm telling you not to bring any more animals. If you insist, get out of here!"

"Look here, Mr. Gonzalo Pedroza. I'm not afraid of you. You don't scare me like you do the other workers. I'm bringing my horse tonight. And don't worry because within a week we will leave Simons." Malaquias and the other workers left Gonzalo standing alone.

An unexplainable sensation, something more than anger, made Gonzalo call out to Malaquias. Gonzalo would have the last word. He would impose his power.

"Hey, Malaquias. Tomorrow morning at five sharp go to kiln number six. You are going to sort brick for the patron's new house."

Gonzalo spurred his horse and went off to inspect the other machines. As he galloped he felt satisfied that Malaquias had been bothered and had shown anger upon the refusal of his horse. Now Malaquias was probably seething about the onerous task of selecting brick. Gonzalo's square face broke into a smile. Abruptly he turned his horse for home. Pascuala, with child, had had a difficult morning. A desire to smell and feel her body and arms about him rose to his head. At full gallop the horse felt strong between his legs.

When Malaquias reported to kiln number six, he saw Octavio Revueltas and his father Damian, who had been living in Simons for four weeks. Octavio had been assigned to build drying racks while Damian worked loading clay onto the wagons that transported it to the machines. The night before, Gonzalo had visited the Revueltas and asked them to report to kiln number six to select choice blue brick.

That morning Gonzalo waited for the three men, who arrived punctually. He instructed them on the color, texture and strength of the brick Walter wanted. When he finished he turned to the three-dimensional brick rectangle that loomed above him.

"This kiln has a lot of blue brick inside. Find it and stack it here." Gonzalo motioned with both hands to the spot where the blue brick would be stacked.

The three men watched Gonzalo tie his horse to a post and walk into the general store, probably to review with William the day's activities. Octavio leaned against a ladder. His vision followed the railroad tracks, the same tracks he and his father had walked to reach Simons. Somewhere just outside his day-trance, he heard Damian and Malaquias solve the breakdown of the brick monolith.

"From the top to the bottom," Malaquias suggested.

"Octavio, bring the ladder over here," Damian called to his son.

Malaquias climbed to the top of the kiln and pointed to a spot half-way down the side. He told Damian to dig out an area wide and deep enough for him to stand. By the time the area was gouged out and reinforced by wooden planks, Malaquias had accumulated several hundred blue bricks at the edge of the kiln just above Damian's head. Malaquias looked down to where Damian had inserted himself into the wall. Below Damian waited Octavio.

"Octavio, place the ladder in front of your father," Malaquias called down. "Damian, stand with one foot on the ladder and the other on the kiln. Now look up to where I am. "

Damian did exactly what Malaquias instructed and saw him standing above, holding what seemed to be an armful of bricks.

"I'll throw them down to you and you pass them on to Octavio," Malaquias called down the side of a stacked arm. "Octavio, be ready. Here they go, Damian!"

The brick throwing and catching chain began. At first Damian and Octavio dropped most of the bricks. But quickly they learned to give with the weight and easily fell into the rhythm. Like their confidence, the stacks grew until the men were catching nine bricks a throw with ease. They worked straight through the morning. Their conversation was sparse, just a word of encouragement to each other. Damian and Malaquias changed places twice. At one in the afternoon they decided to lunch and rest.

"We're doing fine," Malaquias assured.

"Yes, but it's going to be very hot," Octavio commented while he unwrapped the tacos his aunt had prepared.

"A nice cold beer would really be good now," Damian suggested.

"Yes. You know that soon they will stop selling all types of alcohol," Malaquias said.

"Here in Simons?" Damian asked.

"Throughout the country. There is a national movement to prohibit the production and sale of liquor. They even want to stop selling beer." Malaquias shook his head in disgust.

"Why's that?" Octavio asked and bit off another piece of his second taco.

"I don't know. First because of the war, then because they want to stop alcoholism among men." Malaquias drank from his water canteen.

"They won't stop anything. There are too many people who make their liquor at home. My papa knows how to make it," Octavio countered.

"This is true. We won't miss anything," Damian said.

"The law is in the Congress and I believe that it will be approved soon." Malaquias took an orange out of his paper bag.

"It's a stupid law. It will cause more problems than it will solve," Damian said while he removed his hat.

Malaquias sat against the blue brick Octavio had stacked. "When did you arrive? I have not seen you around here," he asked.

"A few weeks ago. And you, Malaquias?" Damian replied.

"It's been years that we have lived here. But Gonzalo has just kicked me out. He gave me one week to find a home," Malaquias said and nodded his head in the direction of the general store.

"That's the way it goes," he continued. "For awhile I have been thinking about renting some land. I'm one of those ranchers who has to be up to his neck in earth to feel free. I don't feel free in Simons."

"Explain that to me, please," Octavio queried.

"Gonzalo controls it all. We must buy in the company store. We have to ask his permission to purchase an animal. Here you work and spend in the same place. And bear it, because if you don't Gonzalo will fire you. He does not scare me with his square brick face. I'm taking my family out of here. Finishing this week, I'll get paid and goodbye." Malaquias angrily wiped his hands.

"We will stay for awhile. Until Mexico stabilizes. And then we will return," Damian said softly.

Octavio heard his father but understood him differently. He sensed a half-truth in what his father had said. The house, land, Mexico: he remembered. Images of the difficult and dangerous trip rushed to his mind. For now Octavio would work and wait for the opportunities that Simons would offer in the future. His mother would soon arrive to make a home for the family here. He had faith in her.

"Now it is my turn to throw from above," Octavio said. He climbed the ladder and went to work on top of the brick monolith.

Octavio refused to wait for his father. He loved to get out into the daybreak sun and run with the wind, feeling the strength of his body. He did not bother to look back for his father; he was sure that Damian would get to the job as he always did. No matter what was said about Damian, whether he drank too much, chased women, or mistreated his wife, he faithfully provided the essentials of life for his family.

Octavio saw Simons awaken into activity. In the houses the women prepared breakfast and got the family ready for the day. The street soon filled with workers who moved past Octavio and headed to their places at the brickyard

On the fourth day of labor Octavio, Damian and Malaquias had lowered the kiln to where two men could break down, select and stack the remaining brick for the patron's new house. Several times Octavio had accompanied the delivery of material to the lots on Plymouth Street. The arriero, a Portuguese man about as old as Damian who controlled the four mules and large wagon, was a player on the Simons base ball team. Jimmy, hired by William for his hitting and second-base talents, talked throughout the trips to and from the building site. His conversation concentrated on baseball, on how to handle horses and mules and on the rumors that Walter planned gradually to replace the costly and slow beasts of burden with efficient and faster trucks.

Like many others, Jimmy was opposed to the change, for he felt that mules and horses were more dependable than trucks. Octavio felt comfortable with the idea of motor machines, but horses seemed more reasonable and easier to handle. Animals understood and obeyed commands while trucks and automobiles, bloodless technological tangibilities controlled by mechanical means, lacked vital organs, brains and decision power.

Octavio stopped at the entrance to the street where Malaquias lived. By today, Malaquias was ordered to leave Simons. Perhaps he will refuse to abandon the house his family occupied for six years, but the consequences for disobeying Gonzalo can be severe and Malaquias was not a foolish man, Octavio thought as he approached the de Leon house. The wide open front door offered Octavio an answer. Boxes, mattresses, tables, chairs, and other articles had been placed around the samll porch. The de Leon family had prepared for the exodus.

Malaquias appeared from the back of the house guiding two horses that were pulling a large wagon, with a third horse tied to the back. In fifteen minutes Malaquias, Lorenza and the children loaded the wagon. Lorenza, heavily pregnant, assisted the children onto the wagon, climbed onto the driver's seat, took the reins and waited for Malaquias' order to move ahead.

Proud of his wife and family, Malaquias spurred the horses forward and never looked back. Perhaps only Nana, holding one of her potted plants, had a parting thought for the house and the porch she had beautifully decorated. With the clip-clop of the horses and as the porch became smaller, she promised innocently that someday she would have a home from which she would never be forced to leave.

"Goodbye, Octavio. Good luck," Malaquias called out.

Nana caught a glimpse of a young man standing on the edge of the street. For an instant their eyes met. She quickly turned away to face the oncoming road.

Octavio waved and silently watched the de Leon family leave Simons. The idea of survival dominated his mind. Octavio would never allow Gonzalo to step on him. Like Malaquias, Octavio would rather face the consequences than live enslaved by fear. Octavio continued toward the job site. The families of Simons were engaged in the day's chores. His mother, brothers and sisters came to mind. He wanted them present, accounted for and happy with his father. He shivered in the morning sun at the thought of his father falling back to the vices he had enjoyed in Mexico. To him, the first-born, fell the responsibility to protect and support the family. If Damian relapsed, Octavio would willingly accept the charge.

Octavio analyzed the relations of power in Simons. Gonzalo's power rested on his relationship with the patron, but there was one other element that Gonzalo respected: money. As his purchasing power grew, Malaquias had become a danger to Gonzalo. Malaquias had expanded his material wealth by the purchase of horses which allowed him the freedom of movement and choice. He could buy and sell in any Mexican barrio he pleased. He did not depend on Simons and never saw himself at the mercy of Gonzalo. Malaquias represented an option opposed to the Walter Robey Simons philosophy of the Mexican worker, and thus he was not tolerated in Simons.

In a few minutes Octavio would arrive at the job site and for the first time in his life Damian's presence did not matter. Survival depended on Octavio and not his father. Octavio Mondragon Sandoval made sure of personal survival, but he honored traditional teachings: obedience, respect, and loyalty to the family patriarch, regardless of his actions. However, for the welfare of the family, Octavio justified an adjustment of values. From today on he would contribute but a portion of his salary to Damian. He wanted to save money for the future. Perhaps he would build or buy a home for his mother, brothers and sisters. Hard work would earn him a steady amount but he was interested in adding to his earnings. Periodically the square face of Gonzalo appeared and jabbed his brain.

Ever since he started playing, Octavio had won in games of chance. He had rejected gambling as a source of income for it often led to confrontation among friends. However, he possessed a special talent, a gift of special intelligence, a genius manifested in the extraordinary ability to calculate and memorize the number of times the faces of cards appeared in a hand. Poker, cunquillan and malilla were his specialities, and dice were a challenge. He considered himself qualified to play and win at any card game that was held in Simons. But before setting out on the path of chance, which could be dangerous, he decided to observe the gamblers who came to Simons to practice their skill. . . . Observe, study, be the best gambler in the world, trust no one and work hard to hold the family together, Octavio thought as he took off his sweater and prepared to stack brick.

The decision to make extra money through gambling and not to give his earnings to his father showed in Octavio's face and his manner in dealing with the man who had engendered him. A split developed between father and son. As Octavio became increasingly independent, Damian could see the grip he once had on his first-born's life weaken rapidly. That morning when he awoke and discovered that his son had left, Damian realized that he would have to work harder to keep up with Octavio.

When Damian arrived at the job site, he found his son setting brick up for loading onto the wagon that would transport it to Plymouth Avenue. He did not communicate a word to Octavio. He placed himself in front of the wagon, a signal he was ready to load. Instead of stacking seven bricks on his hand and forearm, Octavio readied nine. He looked at his father and tossed the nine. Damian's face manifested surprise at the odd number which his son threw. He caught the bricks and hoped that Octavio would not throw that many again. His wish was not answered.

Chapter 8

In comparison to life in Mexico, the years between 1910 and 1920 were peaceful building days for the people of Simons. By 1920 Malaquias and Lorenza de Leon and their children Paquita, Nana, Jesus, Andrea and two boys, Leonardo and Juan, were farming ten acres of rented Japanese land on Telegraph Road in Downey. Although Malaquias had left Simons, he had not burned his bridges and he kept his family close enough to the brickyard in case of a purge on the Mexicans by the gringos. For the moment Malaquias, Lorenza and family existed by caring for each other and producing for the good of all the community.

Damian Revueltas settled into the life he chose to live. He became a superior brickmaker, mastering every step of the brickmaking process. Within a year he had earned the highest paying job in the yard, that of quemador, burner in charge of a kiln, a big responsibility since a slight change in temperature could cause the loss of hundreds of thousands of bricks. Damian accepted the responsibility with great seriousness, and when he was on the job Gonzalo was sure that Damian would not make a mistake. Besides establishing himself as one of the best workers in the yard, Damian was seen by the community as an excellent provider for his family. He had been given one of the nicer houses on Southworth Street where he had taken his wife Milagros the day she arrived.

Damian was proud to offer Milagros a home and a material life much better than what she had in Mexico, but the old vices again swallowed Damian. He drank, chased women, listened to mariachis late into the night and often stayed away from home for days. For years Milagros had not allowed Damian to touch her. He had known other women, had explored and tasted the moisture of their bodies. To Milagros, Damian's hands would always remain dirty. Neither water nor blood could ever cleanse the violation of her person, body and holy marriage vows. Damian had condemned himself forever from his bride's white sheets. He absented himself from the sight of his wife and children, confident that his oldest son would provide for the family. Damian's attitude penetrated Octavio's heart and mind as a burning, heavy rancor, but Octavio always came through.

The United States, Octavio decided, was the place where he would build a house for his own family. Mexico retreated into fading images in his memory, and life in Simons and in Los Angeles became more exciting every day. He worked hard during the day and in the evenings went out to gamble with his uncle Ignacio Sandoval, one year his senior. At first he just observed, but soon he calculated the feel of the luck of the cards. He developed a sense of when to enter and exit a game, when to bluff, when to raise or pass, and he studied the reactions of men when they won and most important, when they lost.

Within months Octavio had men betting on whether he would win or lose, and more often the bets were made on how much he would win. Several financial backings were offered but Octavio refused, preferring to remain independent and not share his winnings or compound his losses. His calculative genius gained him constant money in his pocket, credit from anyone and respect from the men of Simons. He never asked for money but he was always willing to lend to responsible fellow workers. He was considered an intelligent man with a special gift.

Octavio gambled in Los Angeles, East Los Angeles, Belvedere, Whittier. Monday through Thursday he played poker, cunquillan or malilla at his home table at Simons. When his father entered the room where the game simmered, Octavio became uncomfortable and after a hand or two, winning or losing, he would fold and walk away from the game. Damian would then buy in, taking Octavio's place. With a look, Damian would indicate to his son to leave and Octavio always obeyed. To Gonzalo who played often, beating Octavio became an obsession. When Octavio would get up to leave, Gonzalo, noticeably angered, would throw his cards down.

"Stay, man!" Gonzalo would yell as Octavio pushed away from the financial meal.

"There will be another night for revenge," Octavio would reply, acknowledging Damian who, to Gonzalo's irritation, sat next to him.

Gonzalo respected both men but he had paid a high price for the great admiration he had for Octavio . . . Some day your luck will run out and I'll beat you, thought Gonzalo as the door closed behind Octavio.

Although Prohibition had been imposed, Octavio and Ignacio, his constant companion and fellow gambling traveler, found good Mexican whiskey easy to get in La Calle de los Negros, located at the plaza de Los Angeles in the Mexican section of Los Angeles. The closed bars were transformed into restaurants, facades for the infamous speakeasies where whiskey, wine, and beer were as available as before Prohibition.

Liquor was never difficult to purchase for Octavio, the Simons workers and the general population. At first there was a scarcity of alcohol, but soon after the implementation of the law, bootleggers produced enough whiskey, wine and beer to supply most of Los Angeles. Certain parts of the city became known for producing the best wine, whiskey or beer. Spirit production went underground and became a bigger business than before the dry law. For some winemakers, going underground meant the survival of a family tradition, a way of life and meeting an economic need.

In his gambling adventures, Octavio had met several alcohol producers who gladly gave him the liquor he needed. In Simons several families fermented wine or had whiskey or beer distilleries. Simons never lacked in alcoholic beverages. For home bootleggers and gamblers and a number of Los Angeles gamblers and prostitutes, Simons was a safe enclave from law enforcement agencies, including the federal and Montebello police.

"Payday!" Saturdays were dominated by tremendous human activity. Vendors came into town at about six in the morning to set up stands and park their wagons full of the products and services they sold. The bootleggers displayed bottles of spirits to the Simons residents and to outsiders who had been invited by the men to enjoy the excellent card and dice games that developed on Saturday night. At the time the payroll line formed, the prostitutes were brought by a man and woman known only as the Benicasim to whom Gonzalo rented two rooms. One was the cocktail lounge where the men got to know, choose and come to an economic agreement with the woman desired. The other room was partitioned into as many cubicles as there were women working, usually seven to ten daughters of joy, with portable folding screens painted with pornographic scenes. The women started to service the clients when darkness overcame daylight, no later, no sooner, and worked until daybreak.

With the night the area behind the general store appeared like a circus. Men, some women and a few children drank whiskey, wine or beer and chatted or played. The men discussed the week's work, counted their money and evaluated the different levels of gambling that the night offered. Octavio Revueltas was always mentioned among the top competition and highest stakes, but never did he allow himself to get enticed into the prostitutes' rooms.

Small groups of men gathered around the Benicasim doors waiting to buy their turn at a moment of intense feeling in the vagina, anus or mouth of one of the loving ladies. These activities became known to the people of Montebello who already had negative opinions about Mexicans in general and the workers of Simons in particular. Sodom and Gomorrah were children's playgrounds compared to the Montebelloans' images of what went on in Simons. The little that most Montebelloans saw of Simons was from the bluff off Date and Maple streets. From there they looked downward into the brickyard. This descending point of view, coupled with what was heard about the occurrences in the brickyard, resulted in "the hole," a name given by Montebelloans and translated to El Hoyo by Simons residents.

Payday gathered momentum at ten minutes to three in the afternoon. The men who finished the day's work early started to form a line. Exactly at three, William and Gonzalo, armed with handguns and Winchester rifles, escorted James Simons, who carried a small metal payroll box. James drew a pistol from inside his coat and calmly introduced it behind his belt buckle. Afraid of being robbed, he insisted on armed security during payroll call. He would never be able to live down a loss of control over the workers and he believed such an incident would be symptomatic of psychological weaknesses passed on to him by his father, Joseph.

On one particular Saturday, Walter Simons arrived at the brickyard early in the morning to deliver the bimonthly payroll box. His nephew James entered and immediately started to prepare the wages. James's face revealed tension and his tired eyes communicated the heavy hatred he felt for his father. Through most of the morning uncle and nephew did not speak.

With the work finished, Walter thought of his brother whom he had not seen for some time. He decided to see him during the weekend. He spoke to Gonzalo and William and started for the door.

"James, say hello to your father," Walter said sternly, expressing the disappointment he felt because of their constant quarreling. James attempted to smile.

Outside, Walter saw the church and prayed that he would always get along with his children. He was needed at home, for Sara could give birth at any moment. At least that was what she had told him that morning. She felt the baby would come today, tomorrow or yesterday. Walter chuckled at Sara's yesterday. He moved past machine number seven and headed toward the library which Sara had insisted on building. It was filled mainly with magazines from Mexico and children's books written in English. The clinic was next to the library. From Monday to Friday, from eight in the morning to two in the afternoon the doctor tended to the ill, injured, and pregnant.

Two pregnant women entered the clinic. Walter understood in those two full wombs a metaphor of Sara. . . . Women get and are pregnant the same way, no matter who or where they are, he reasoned. His mind shifted from making babies to constructing houses. He worried whether the prefabricated house packages that he had designed would sell. He had invested thousands on this idea of selling a one-family preconstructed dwelling which was planned to the last block. The workmen had only to put it together. The predesigned packages were all the same: a ten-room house, 74' x 54' overall. The total cost of the hollow tile house delivered on the job was $407.

The horse ride home was peaceful. For a greater part of it Walter thought of the five trucks that William had ordered. They were scheduled for delivery by the end of the year. He would have to learn how to drive. The trucks certainly moved faster than the horse that Walter whipped. Sara waited for him at home, possibly giving birth this instant, he thought, and whipped the beast again.

An hour passed and the animal tired suddenly. He was close to his home but space became larger as time seemed to crawl. Bothersome frames of the past appeared, making the way difficult. Large anguished chunks of Orin Elmer's death superimposed themselves on the sights of the road. He needed to get home as fast as possible, but the more he hurried the exhausted horse, the slower time moved. Walter pushed his wet hair back and wiped his perspiring face. He felt near his home. At the end of the road, a series of brick walls appeared moving toward him, and as they passed he understood that he had reached his brick house. Before the front gate, a fear invaded his mind and he refused for a moment to look at the front. When he did, he saw Joseph and Laura.

"Damn it!" Walter whispered. Of course they had come to help with the baby, but Sara had a nurse and the doctor said he would come by that morning.

In the living room, Melissa described inner walls, fluids and blood. As she spoke Walter saw in the depth of his pupils a ripped picture come together. One Simons vacuum double-wall system, a hollow wall of solid brick which he could simultaneously see from every possible angle, was streaked with blood, flesh, fingers, a tiny hand, an adult foot, a baby's leg, a woman's breast dripping milk, an infant's head, a woman's arm struggling to escape, a baby boy's testicles and penis, and Sara's beautiful face peering from within the hollow minute space. Suddenly a scream surged from Walter so loud that no one heard. Exhausted and drenched, he saw through his red eyes the door to the bedroom where his Sara and their son lay in state.

Late that evening, Joseph, Laura, James, Melissa, the doctor, a nurse, a few neighbors, two police and two ambulance attendants heard deep sobs coming from the bedroom. Joseph, relieved that his brother finally cried, went to accompany him. At one in the morning the doctor signed the death certificate. Walter allowed the bodies of his wife and son to be taken to the Christian Presbyterian Mortuary. He asked to be left alone. After everyone left, he sat in his and Sara's bedroom and saw millions of brownish square insects overrun the house.

Not long after Sara's death, Walter discovered he could not continue without the companionship of a woman. He let it be known that he searched for a wife. He did this knowing that some people would scowl at the short mourning period he offered Sara. Walter was convinced that the love which Sara had given him needed to be expressed and not suppressed in tears and black clothing for the length of time society deemed proper for mourning. What he had experienced with Sara he would feel again, and because of Sara he would love more intensely. Walter cultivated a circle of friends, members of the clubs and organizations his mother belonged to. Laura, who was excited about the idea of a new wife for her brother-in-law, encouraged him to attend her social club functions. She held membership in an organization that particularly interested Walter, the Pasadena Dames of the Red Earth, which was made up of women whose husbands were related to the construction industry. Speakers invited by the club presented topics dealing with building in Southern California. Joseph had spoken on several occasions. He had embarked on a writing and lecturing campaign about the contributions and benefits of brick to the Southern California economy.

On a blustery summer afternoon Laura had invited two talented and important people to perform for her assembled guests. Joseph Simons was the keynote speaker whose lecture "A Few Things About Brick, Mortar, Masonry, Terra Cotta and the Bixby Hotel Disaster as Viewed by a Brick Man" addressed a recent tragedy in Long Beach. The other guest participant was Edit Marian Chalk, a classical pianist who would open the evening activities with music by Mozart, Beethoven and Chopin.

After an hour of aperitifs and conversation, the group of seventy-five were seated. Laura sat Walter in the front row corner seat from where he could see perfectly the lovely face and body of Edit. Not one word of the introduction did he hear. Upon pronouncing the last word, Laura observed her enthralled brother-in-law staring at Edit. When Edit completed her performance, she stepped to the front of the appreciative public and bowed. Walter's applause seemed louder than the others and he smiled, letting her know that he thought she was the greatest pianist in the world.

She moved toward him and acknowledged his enthusiasm. He kept applauding and smiling. Edit walked to the back of the crowd and disappeared into the house.

Laura came to the front and introduced Joseph, who graciously thanked the audience and took the podium.

"Let me assure you that this will be short, for I too want Miss Chalk to enchant us again with her beautiful music," Joseph said as he smiled at his audience.

Walter loosened his tie, crossed his arms and thought about Edit. With the words "In conclusion. . ." pronounced by his brother, Walter realized he had missed Joseph's entire speech. He walked to the white French doors leading into the living room, searching for Edit. By the time he found her, he had already decided that she would be his wife. As he came face to face with her, Laura made the introductions and helped break the awkwardness. Walter did not know exactly what he would have said to Edit if it were not for his sister-in-law who began to tell Edit about the beautiful home Walter was building in Los Angeles.

"Ask him to tell you about it. Better yet, you should take Edit to see your new home," Laura said and walked away.

"I bet it's made of Simons brick" Edit smiled.

"The world's best," Walter said comfortably.

"Good brick and good mortar, like your brother said." Edit built Walter's confidence.

"Would you like to see the house?" Walter asked and prayed.

"Wonderful idea," Edit answered.

Walter followed her to the garden where she played two original compositions to the delight of the guests. By the end of the evening Walter was enchanted beyond hope. He did not admit to being in love but he knew he wanted to share the future and his fortune with Edit, the most beautiful, talented and intelligent woman he had ever met.

By the spring of 1922 Walter had found a wife, Edit Marian Chalk, who immediately began to administer the home Walter had taken her to see on their first outing. She had decorated the house to reflect her musical tastes derived from her years of study in the best schools of music in Canada and the United States, an achievement which made Walter more proud of her. Edit became involved with the Los Angeles Symphony and other musical organizations to which she contributed money and devoted time. She was sincerely excited about the many possibilities that her husband's cute little town had to offer. She was a woman who, along with her husband, enjoyed experimenting with the social structures of the time and felt strongly that Walter, like his brother Joseph, should be a spokesman for brick.

Edit continued her involvement with music in Los Angeles and through her affiliations introduced Walter to associations that would advance him in the area of construction. They entertained many Eastern and Midwestern brick manufacturers until finally the association members voted to have their national convention in Los Angeles. It was the first time the large national industrial body, the Common Brick Manufacturers Association, had crossed the continent to hold its annual convention in California, the place where paradise trembles.

Walter and Edit dedicated hours to the success of the conference. They arranged two special trains which brought the delegates from the Midwest and East to Los Angeles, where the sessions were held at the Biltmore Hotel. Regardless of the long distance which most of the participants had to travel, attendance at the meetings surpassed that of any previous convention. The visitors were profuse in their praise of Western hospitality and especially the arrangements made by Walter and Edit.

One afternoon the delegates visited the brick plants and enjoyed a special entertainment at Simons provided by Walter and Edit's Mexicans, as the visitors referred to the men, women and children who played instruments, sang and danced to traditional Mexican music. The Simons Mexicans prepared an exceptional variety of regional dishes, the culmination of which was the barbacoa. At the plant the workers had been ordered to build a stage covered on three sides and roofed with palms. A theatrical performance celebrating the Mexican holiday, the Day of the Dead, was presented for the guests, who were fascinated by the costumes and music. The candy skulls and skeletons were especially a big hit.

After the food and entertainment ended, Walter extended greetings to the brick men. He said that it was an honor to welcome the association to Los Angeles and he hoped it would come back every year. But most important to the brick manufacturers were Walter's comments on the future of brick in California.

"Los Angeles has an impressive record of more than $200,000,000 worth of building done during 1922. While Los Angeles is a fine city, more fireproof buildings should be erected. Here lies the great opportunity and challenge for brick manufacturers: whether or not we can keep up with the growing demand for our product. Brick is the material with which great fire calamities, such as the one which befell San Francisco, can be avoided." Walter looked at the audience, pleased that they seemed to agree with him.

"We must educate the people about the safety advantages that brick offers," he continued. "We must have publicity to enlighten the public and to secure legislative enactments that will be fair to brick. We must fight against interests who attempt to deceive or mislead the public. No lie can live. Give the public the truth about brick and we can ultimately win the market. We must do this together. This is the day of cooperation. The man who lives within himself is not a success and will never succeed."

The enthusiastic guests stood to acknowledge his vision of the successful future. Just beyond the circle of light in which the elite brick manufacturers sat, two hundred and seventy-five Mexican workers waited eagerly to produce the brick to build California and make Walter's dream become reality. Among the Mexicans, Octavio neither clapped nor cheered. He watched impassively, rubbing together two twenty-dollar gold coins in each of his jacket pockets.

Chapter 9

By March of 1922 most of the horses and mules were gone from the brickyard. Half a dozen horses and three mules were pastured in the fields between Vail Field Airport and Simons. The horses were more a reminder of past and changing times than practical animals, except that Gonzalo had chosen the six best horses of the herd for his pleasure. He considered them a reward for his many years of dedicated service to Walter. William did not object to Gonzalo's ownership of the animals. Nor did James Simons, who kept exact figures of equipment and animal inventory, ever question Gonzalo's possessions. James considered it a good idea to keep a few horses available in case the delivery trucks broke down, or if his uncle wanted a careful inspection of the property.

The transporting of material was now accomplished by trucks owned by William Melone and Sons. The fleet was housed and maintained in Simons. Although the maintenance was the responsibility of William's company, he took advantage of the Simons brickyard equipment and mechanic. As the fleet of trucks grew, so did the number of mechanics. By the middle of 1922, four Mexicans with mechanical experience had been found and hired by Gonzalo.

At the zenith of his power, Gonzalo put four of his best horses up for sale. Gonzalo, in charge of the Simons general store, decided that it would be an innovative idea to convert one of the small rooms near the general store into a restaurant. In three small bachelor rooms he set up a kitchen and tables. The menu was simple, and after dark someone served homemade beer and wine from a window in the back. Success struck the restaurant and Gonzalo hired another cook.

Early one morning, while Gonzalo and William were being served breakfast at the restaurant, both cooks announced that they would have to leave the job in one week because their husbands had returned from working in the north and required attention. And besides, they had both discovered that they were en estado and did not want to work for fear of losing the embryo.

"We would work up to the last moment, but our husbands have returned. You understand, don Gonzalo," one woman said.

"We will not abandon you. My sister Amalia will come on Friday. I will show her what she has to do. She is a good cook. You will see," the taller of the two added. They both moved to the kitchen area.

ALEJANDRO MORALES

The day Amalia started work at the restaurant, Gonzalo sat down and faced the back of the tall slender woman who worked at the counter top chopping onions. When she turned to see the customer, Amalia noticed the large square face and recognized the man so many times described by her sister and friends. Struck by her natural beauty, Gonzalo was not able to say a word.

From that moment on rumors began to circulate throughout the town. Men, women, and children talked about Amalia and Gonzalo, who began to spend most of his time at the restaurant talking with Amalia when business was slow. When alone, Gonzalo would sit at his table and discuss what Amalia needed to run a more efficient restaurant. Well-organized and fast working, she easily accomplished the work that was formerly done by two women. Gonzalo's admiration changed to a desire to possess her, and her curiosity changed to feelings of caring for the man with the ugly square face.

One night Amalia stayed after closing hours to clean the floors and get ready for the next morning. This was not out of the ordinary for she often stayed after hours to work, but in her zeal to finish as much as she could, she did not notice that she had worked until nine-thirty. Her job was hard but she treated the restaurant as if it were her own home, and she would often spend time dreaming about how she would like her life to become.

At ten in the evening when Amalia went to the door to leave, Gonzalo entered. At the moment she saw his block face, she understood that the restaurant would be her home. They kissed and embraced. He could not and would not resist the passion.

That evening Gonzalo and Amalia shared their caring and need for each other. He took her to an empty bachelor cabin and brought her water and towels. Amalia asked Gonzalo to stay the night. She slept comfortably with a newly discovered sense of liberty. He lay at her side, eyes open, thinking of Pascuala.

His desire to be with Amalia developed into a basic need and soon he gave orders to extend a room from the restaurant, which had already been enlarged. This was to be Amalia's room, which she accepted without question. Here she worked and waited late in the evening for Gonzalo to walk from his first house to his second. All of Simons knew what Gonzalo and Amalia did at the restaurant but no one dared mention it to him or Pascuala, who was filled with child again.

Amalia lived in that room for six months, until one day she demanded a house somewhere outside of Simons where she was to give birth to their first-born. Gonzalo said nothing when he heard his love announce the results of their playfulness. She had been worried about his reaction, but she heard no roar from the large, square-faced man who tenderly embraced her. It was then that Gonzalo decided to sell four of his horses. He sent out several men, including Roberto Lacan, who was marked to be fired, to announce the animals for sale.

Roberto was given the special task of visiting Malaquias de Leon who had expressed interest in two of the beasts. Malaquias had remained in contact with the people of Simons, and Gonzalo often sent him men to be cured of homesickness, bad colds or stomach problems caused by what most people believed were psychological forces gone awry. Malaquias was not a curandero, but he was always willing to help a person in need of rest, which was what he offered.

"If an ill individual rests in the house of Malaquias de Leon, that person will be cured," the people would say after a few days' stay at the de Leon ranch. Malaquias, although stern and outwardly unloving with his family, had a reputation of being a generous, kind and helpful man with neighbors.

Malaquias thanked Roberto for the message and rode back to Simons with him. When Roberto and Malaquias entered the store, they found Gonzalo and William with what seemed to be a new employee. Roberto noticed the three men trade glances in the sudden solitude of bad tidings. Roberto, aware that Gonzalo wanted to replace him, understood that this was the last time he would see the inside of the general store. No introductions were needed. Roberto knew the tall man was his replacement.

Gonzalo reached into his inside coat pocket and pulled out a cloth bag of gold coins.

"You are fired, Lacan," Gonzalo said with a slight smile.

"It makes you laugh? Don't feel so sure of yourself, you cockled prick, because at times things are not the way one perceives them," Roberto laughed.

"Watch your mouth because someone can break it!" Gonzalo moved toward the young man.

"That might be, but you won't be the one; you can't even break through the pussy hair of your concubine," Roberto yelled.

"Get out of here because you are in danger!" Gonzalo placed his right hand on his gun.

"Leave, Roberto! I can't assure you your life!" William shouted and cocked a rifle.

"Now you have a reason to fire me!" Roberto shouted outside. "Mr. Gonzalo Pedroza is no one's father! I swear it with what hangs between my legs," Roberto repeated as he walked on Vail Street out of Simons.

That afternoon William prevented Gonzalo from committing a murder.

Nonetheless, the damage had been initiated in Gonzalo's mind. From that moment on he began to doubt Amalia's faithfulness. He did not intend to abandon her but each time he thought of Amalia's growing womb he heard the cursing insinuations of Roberto Lacan.

Malaquias looked at Jacobo Ramos, the tall stranger in the store with Gonzalo and William. Jacobo was from New Mexico and could read, write and do mathematics exceptionally well. He was hired as a regular worker in the brickyard but asked to be placed in a higher position of responsibility. He was capable of managing the general store better than or at least as well as Roberto. That was all that Gonzalo needed. He had often observed Roberto talking intimately with Amalia and several times had interrupted their conversation at the restaurant, conversations that Amalia seemed to enjoy. It did not matter to Gonzalo that Roberto was from the same town as Amalia. He disliked the relaxed manner of her conversation with this man, and the confidence that evolved between them threatened Amalia's dependence on Gonzalo.

"Good afternoon, Gonzalo," Malaquias said, emerging from the corner where he had witnessed Roberto being fired.

Gonzalo instructed Jacobo to restock the shelves, looked at Malaquias, and motioned to the exit. As they rode to where the horses were pastured, Malaquias asked about the condition of the animals and Gonzalo inquired about the farm. He assumed Malaquias' efforts had been profitable since he was interested in purchasing two horses. Suddenly Malaquias stopped abruptly.

"I intend to buy some properties on Maple. I hope you don't oppose my living near Simons," Malaquias said, surprising his fellow horse lover.

"There is no need. You don't represent any danger. You can do what the hell you want. Look, there are the animals. Which ones do you like?" Gonzalo replied.

This gesture of choice was understood by both as an opportunity for friendship beneath the surface of the warring facades. That afternoon Malaquias arrived home guiding two horses. Gonzalo counted the money from the sale. He would sell the other animals and soon accumulate enough to rent a home outside of Simons for his Amalia.

It was not surprising that in January of 1923 the Walter Robey Simons dream factory was recognized by the Common Brick Manufacturers Association of America as the largest brickyard in the world. The Association took it upon itself to take a series of photographs for publicity and distributed them to the membership, workers and public. Two photographs became popular with the Simons workers. The first one showed all the buildings of the brickyard. The workers liked the photograph because they could see the powerful producing brick factory they helped to build.

The second photograph held with special regard by the workers was a photo of the entire Simons work crew. The men received free copies of the photograph and some bought extra copies to send back to Mexico. In the opinion of the men, the photograph captured the sense of living in Simons and the sense that they were part of a great working family. Two women, however, interpreted the photo differently.

Milagros Revueltas, dressed in black, expressed her opinion to her family and husband during dinner at a time they were together and outwardly happy. When Damian handed the photograph to Milagros, she first studied it. The family waited anxiously to hear Milagros' reaction to the image. She handed the black-and-white back to Damian.

"Do you like it, Damian?" Milagros asked calmly.

"Don't you?" Damian retorted, somewhat surprised.

"Well, no," Milagros began. "It is a photograph filled with repression. The men are stiff, tense, as if they were dead, all with hats on. The serious faces are faces of fear or hate. Very few of the men are smiling. It is a photograph of sad prisoners, of tired slaves. Of men angered for being where they are at. As if they are forced to do what they do, not want to do."

She moved the photograph closer to Damian before continuing. "Look at yourself. How do you look? Don't tell me that is the face of a happy man. I don't like the photograph because it is the result of a machine that reduces men. It makes them tiny; it squashes them and smears them on a piece of paper. And that way we cannot embrace them." Milagros stood up slowly and walked to the stove.

Octavio noticed his mother's body tremble, struggling to control the hurt rushing from deep in her heart and mind. Her body shook. She fought back the sobs and continued to work. Octavio sat back and turned to his father who continued to eat, oblivious to Milagros' emotional state. Damian finished and looked up to see his children's eyes fixed on him. He pushed himself away from the table and rose.

"Well, what do you want me to do?" Damian yelled directly at Octavio. Everyone around the table had an answer, but at that moment none dared to speak up.

Pascuala Pedroza talked about the photograph to her sons and daughters while she sat in the living room prior to retiring. The children discussed how the men looked. They joked and laughed about this person's father and that person's uncle. Gonzalo talked about the photographer and how he had told the men that the photos taken that day were to be given to many other brick manufacturers and customers. He told Gonzalo and his men they were the working force of the biggest brickyard in the world. Pride beamed from Jesus, Elvira, Francisco and the other children's faces as they listened to their father explain the importance of the photographs. Finally the photograph came to Pascuala. The children urged her to respond to what she held in her hands.

"Gonzalo, you look tired, completely drained. It's because you work day and night. That is not right, Gonzalo. The children miss you at home. All these men are tired of working. There are many men, Gonzalo, few smiles. They seem to be covered with dust. You can have your photography; it is an exercise of another world. I'm afraid that someone, if they want to, could burn it and you too would burn." Pascuala let the photograph fall from her hands.

"Pascuala, don't speak that way. Can't you see that you scare the children?" Gonzalo spoke sternly. "It's time to be happy. The brickyard is producing at maximum capacity. We have so many requests that we can't keep up with them. Now we have more trucks, and a train that Mr. Simons bought will multiply production. I wanted to surprise you. I think that what I tell you next will make you happy. They gave me a raise in salary. And do you know what we are going to buy? I bet you can't guess."

Gonzalo looked at his children who were sitting at the edge of their seats shouting what they thought their father would buy.

"Wait." Gonzalo held his hands up, bringing silence to the children who waited eagerly. "We are going to buy an automobile so that we can take you on vacation, Pascuala."

Gonzalo smiled at his wife before getting up. As was his habit three to five times during the week after dinner, Gonzalo left the house. He would return at dawn, have breakfast and go to work.

Pascuala tolerated this life, never admitting that her husband had another woman. Despite what was common knowledge in Simons, she never acknowledged the fact that Gonzalo fathered children other than hers. When she contemplated the pride and excitement her children had for their father, she dared not complain. Now, at nine in the evening the children slept. Gonzalo was with the other woman and Pascuala sat alone sipping warm milk, hoping that sleep would come to her. Lying on the kitchen table were hundreds of men looking at her from within the encasement of the photograph.

Octavio found his three brothers Federico, Maximiliano and Jose discussing the merits of different makes of automobiles pictured in a car magazine Federico had bought during an excursion with friends to the various Mexican dance halls and nightclubs in Los Angeles.

On Friday Octavio had finished work, cleaned up and left for Maravilla to a poker game which went on until early Sunday morning. He had just returned tired but filled with the feeling of success that only five hundred dollars in bills and gold coins could give a winner. He said hello to his brothers and stepped into the outhouse. When he came out, Federico and Maximiliano, dressed in dark pinstripe suits, stopped arguing about which was the better car for the money. Federico tilted his white cap and put his hand to his hips.

"Brother, how did it go?" he asked.

In the moments before the answer, Octavio experienced a weight of responsibility. He felt as if he had brought them to Simons and that he was duty-bound to them. Federico was twenty years old and seemed restless. Often he talked about leaving the house, perhaps going to work in another yard. Maximiliano, who at eighteen had shown hard-working brickman's skills and a great passion for women, lately revealed a sickly paleness on his face. Jose, sixteen, talked a lot about impossible goals, played an excellent second-base and worked hard when he desired. Rogaciana, their fourteen-year-old sister, had recently blossomed into womanhood. She was a little uneasy with her brothers but Octavio understood that to be natural. Felicitas, ten years old, was the youngest, a child who demanded everything and usually got her way.

Octavio heard his mother scolding Rogaciana who again could not find her shoes. Felicitas screamed that they would be late for church if they did not hurry. Octavio heard them all—all except his father.

"It went very well, Federico. So well that I can tell you that soon we will buy our own car," Octavio said.

The three brothers immediately brought the car magazine up and showed Octavio the different makes.

"Octavio," Milagros called and slowly stepped down the three steps from the kitchen entrance. Rogaciana and Felicitas joined the others, excited about the possibility of purchasing a car. Milagros walked her son toward the street.

"Octavio, your father has not given me any money for the house. The girls need shoes and dresses for school. And you and your brother need work clothes."

Milagros knew her son's reply; this was not the first time she had turned to him. She felt sad for him. Although she believed that the oldest son was obligated to contribute to the household to a higher degree than the others, she silently cursed Damian for making Octavio's burden so heavy.

"Here Mama, take this."

"Why does he make us carry this heavy cross?" Milagros thanked Octavio and went off to church with her daughters.

Octavio watched them for a while. Rogaciana and Felicitas turned to wave to their big brother. He took a deep breath. He was unshaven, clammy and hungry.

"Come with us. We are going to Montebello Park to the Ceballos' picnic birthday party," Federico implored.

"No thanks. I'm taking a bath and then I'm going to Gonzalo's restaurant. Maybe I will find our father there." Octavio started for the house when Jose approached him.

"Hey, Octavio. Have you heard about the orchestra?" Jose asked.

"What orchestra?" Octavio asked, unsure.

"Simons will have a big band. They already have been practicing for a few days. All the musicians are from Simons." Jose raised his voice.

"Well, those boys have played together for a long time. They always play at Simons fiestas," Octavio said, unimpressed.

"But this is going to be an official band. Mrs. Simons wants an orchestra with a conductor whom she will send to us. The orchestra will be hers. They will practice this afternoon at the big hall," Jose called back from the gate leading out to the street. He looked back again and waved to his oldest brother.

Octavio entered the house, took off his clothes except for his boxer shorts, and shaved as he filled the tub. He sat in the warm water, relaxed and dozed off to sleep in short spurts of time. He enjoyed this state of drowsiness. He could savor that precious condition of sleep for intense short moments. The soap smelled clean and fresh. He rinsed with a hose attached to the bath faucet. He did not like to rinse off with the same can that everybody in the family used. One of these days soon he would build a shower outside and shorten a hose and connect it up high on the bath wall. The family would have a shower inside and out. He considered the thought amusing as he dried his body.

He adjusted his tie, put on his cap and walked out of the house. Since the Simons amusement hall was on the way to the restaurant, Octavio decided to walk by. Perhaps the band, or as Jose had said, the official Simons orchestra, would be there getting ready to practice.

As he drew nearer to the hall he heard silence. The Simons musicians were there unloading garment bags and boxes from a truck. Octavio knew most of the men. He greeted them and walked into the hall where other men unpacked red and black trousers, green jackets, white frilly shirts and long black velvet scarves. From the boxes black bolero hats were drawn.

"Octavio, do you like our uniforms?" Don Vicente Limon asked.

"Yes, beautiful, don Vicente," Octavio answered.

A short man with baton in hand and dressed in a Simons Brick Company Orchestra uniform entered the hall.

"Gentlemen," the conductor said, demanding complete attention. "Put your uniforms on and we will begin to work immediately. Thank you."

He tapped the baton against a chair and went before a podium. As the men undressed and dressed, they passed by the conductor who handed them each a book of music.

"Excuse me, Octavio, but we are going to practice. Stay and listen." Don Vicente Limon, decked out in his uniform, put his flute together, received his music, placed it on the stand and took his place in the front row.

Within ten minutes the Simons Brick Company Orchestra was in full uniform, assembled and ready to practice. Octavio, taken in by the excitement and rush of the musicians, moved back and found a seat. His mind was hooked by a musical note from a flute, then one from a trumpet, a tuba, a clarinet, a french horn, a trombone, a violin, a viola, drums, and a baritone saxophone. Finally the instruments were tuned. The conductor tapped the baton, raised his hands and the band began to play "Rhapsody in Blue," "April Showers," the Mexican national anthem, and the United States national anthem.

The conductor then worked with each musician on individual passages. He smiled all the while as the men perspired, trying their best to impress this man sent by Edit Simons. He spoke often, at times encouraging, at times scolding, often repeating her name, for she was his superior. The conductor demanded excellence from the band and insisted that each member strive for achievement beyond himself. After the musicians had gone through the individual parts, the conductor again began "Rhapsody in Blue."

The music followed Octavio in the direction of Gonzalo's restaurant. For half an hour he walked to his destination, but somehow he advanced slowly, meandering aimlessly through pieces of space and moments of time, allowing his vision to be filled with the changes that were occurring around him . . . Everything is changing so rapidly, Octavio thought, standing before a row of about ten trucks . . . Before they were mules and horses. And they changed as if by magic. And now by magic we have an official band. I bet they will take them to play for the gringos. He saw a plane landing at Vail Airport, then another and soon after another landed . . . Machines will dominate the world . . . He remembered what he had told his brothers about driving a car. He forgot one thing: he did not know how to drive . . . I will learn.

Octavio stepped onto the general store porch and entered the restaurant. He took a table across from Gonzalo, who sat with Amalia. Jacobo Ramos drank a cup of coffee. Octavio said hello and searched the room for his father. Damian was nowhere to be found. The general conversation in the restaurant centered around the new conductor and band. The baseball team and the band would bring fame to Simons, but for the moment Octavio could give a damn about that for Simons. His main concern was where the next meal for the family would come from. He admired the band but felt that Edit could have used her money in a better way for the residents of Simons.

Several young men entered the restaurant and ordered two glasses of homemade beer.

"Hey, is that the Simons band?" one man asked all present.

Most nodded their heads affirmatively, and a few yesses rang out.

"They're taking a lot of photographs of the band. Mrs. Simons is with the photographer. I heard her say that the musicians would get a photograph and also that they want more musicians. It's true, this place is modernizing," the young man said and took a long swig of beer.

About half-way home Octavio followed the tracks for the new rail system that was being installed. The conversation of the young man in the restaurant came to him. One word—modernizing—danced in his mind. He understood the word to mean a force of reading, writing, mathematics, machines and everlasting change. He would allow that force to take him just so far.

The tall woman rang the doorbell and the piano music inside stopped. Two minutes went by and the woman grew impatient. She rang the doorbell again and finally the door opened. A noticeably pregnant Edit Simons shook Kaila Morisson's hand and slowly led her to the library where they went through the formalities of offering and accepting afternoon tea and then setting the ground rules for the interview.

Kaila, a freelance writer and sociologist, was preparing an article that was to be published in one of the leading California sociological journals.

She had long wanted to interview Edit Simons, for she had heard of the wonders which the Simonses had accomplished with housing for their Mexicans, the subject of Kaila's study. Earlier that week Kaila had interviewed Joseph Simons at his home in Pasadena. The interview was short and not informative. Joseph seemed unwilling to speak freely and was uncomfortable when it came to discussing his brother's factory in Simons.

As the interview with Edit started, Kaila realized that questions were not needed to help Edit speak about the Mexicans housed at her husband's brick factory.

"My husband's workers are all Mexican except for the supervisor and a few of the truck drivers. They are excellent, faithful workers. Our Mexicans are not those heavy-lipped, sleepy-eyed Latins reclining in the sun, too lazy to seek the shade. No, Miss Morisson, these men, women and children are lovely, hard workers.

"Yes, I am aware of the thousands of Mexicans who come to Los Angeles yearly seeking a job. You must consider that behind those dull eyes lies the tragedy of a nation. I agree, the Mexican is basically lazy. Their idleness is caused by a lack of mental development resulting from decades of violence and oppression. As people they are content with very little, but I believe that is but the heritage of generations forced to adapt themselves to bitter poverty and horrible tyranny." Edit poured tea and paused to rest.

"Mrs. Simons, what do you think of the housing you provide?" Kaila asked, moving to the edge of the chair and reaching for her tea. She sipped, put the cup down and prepared to take notes.

"Excellent. Mr. Simons and I are aware of the horrible housing conditions poor people are forced to live under. We have seen the Mexican courts, the one and two-room shacks where they cook on a very poor makeshift stove, where there are no electrical lights, no plumbing, no furniture, only a trunk where the family guards their most valuable possessions.

"We do not approve of unscrupulous landlords who provide only one toilet for an entire court which may house five families or more. This is inhumane treatment, not decent. Simons housing, on the other hand, is excellent. You will not find any of these deplorable conditions at our factory," Edit said, watching Kaila transcribe her words.

"Why don't the Mexicans complain to the authorities?" Kaila asked as she put a fresh sheet of paper on top.

"Because they are accustomed to very little in Mexico," Edit answered, "and therefore they accept the very worst living conditions that Los Angeles offers. They are usually content with very little. They have been forced into the worst sections of the city. And I am sure, Miss Morisson, that you know the results. The city has been forced to increase its public health staff. The damp, unsanitary, dark homes of the Mexicans are constant sources of tuberculosis. And because of the crowded conditions, social diseases are rapidly spreading among these people. Alcoholism, prostitution and gambling are rampant in the Mexican areas.

"These evils can only be erradicated by providing better homes and offering basic services as we have done in Simons. We provide excellent housing, a school and library, a health clinic, a baseball team, and we have even organized an orchestra that will perform in the Rose Parade this year. My husband and I take great pride in the way we treat our Mexicans. And in return they are totally dedicated to the factory and to Mr. Simons," Edit said, handing Kaila a photograph of the orchestra.

Kaila placed the photograph in her briefcase and reached for her tea. The women traded glances and a smile, both satisfied with the manner in which the interview progressed.

"Back to what I was saying earlier," Edit continued. "The Mexicans are childlike in their desires and accept what they are given. Seldom do they question their situation. If they are housed in ill-drained buildings, with insufficient light and air, with poor sanitary plumbing and small rooms, they will remain lazy and shiftless. Mr. Simons and I believe that the Mexicans must be made self-reliant, independent and proud of their efficiency. We have created a town in which the Mexicans can achieve these goals." Edit looked out to the garden at the side of the house. The sound of gurgling fountains entertained the minds of both women.

"Your home is very beautiful," Kaila commented. "Is there anything else you'd like to add?"

"I must confess a strange thought that just came to me," Edit replied. "Mexicans, like cockroaches, are extremely adaptable. They will survive anything. Many might perish but there will always be survivors to propagate the race. They're just like cockroaches."

Edit moved next to the window and brought out Leaves of Grass which she had been reading prior to playing the piano before Kaila's arrival.

Chapter 10

Prior to the de Leon family move in 1925 to Maple Avenue in south Montebello, bordering Simons, Malaquias de Leon had moved his family to Downey where he had rented thirty acres owned by Eliola Garcia Pardo, a Spanish widow who lived secluded in a large home near the governor's mansion. The thirty acres rented to Malaquias were surrounded by parcels rented to Japanese farmers. Malaquias preferred living with the Japanese rather than at Cantaranas, a part of the Santa Fe Railroad Mexican camp nearby.

Soon after moving to the Telegraph Road ranch in Downey, Malaquias bought three cows and a bull which soon multiplied his stock to six milking cows. The milk was sold to Japanese families and to families living outside the community. The Japanese made Malaquias a successful farmer. Matola, Ajimba, Matusaki, and Yokohira taught Malaquias many farming techniques which made his thirty acres produce bumper crops yearly. In return, he shared his tools and his time in helping them transport their crops to the market.

The Japanese were considered rich by people on the outside. They did not require much to keep them going and most of their money was sent to the mother country. Nana, who helped Malaquías, often worked with the Japanese and would talk to the women. She would ask them if they saved their money in the bank and the women would reply: "No bank, send money Nipon, Nipon."

Late in 1921 some of the most successful Japanese families suddenly abandoned their homes, leaving tools and fields that needed to be tended. These sudden evacuations continued to occur. Malaquias asked Matola, Ajimba, Matusaki and Hokohira why their neighbors were leaving. The men either could not or would not give any explanation. Then in July of 1922, Matusaki and Hokohira both left without notice. Two weeks later at mid-morning Matola went to the de Leon home and asked to speak with Malaquias. From the kitchen window Lorenza and her children watched Malaquias motion in the negative to the request of Matola. Lorenza and the children sensed that the Matolas had to abandon the ranch. After Matola left, Lorenza and the children joined Malaquias outside and watched their friend disappear forever.

"He is going, right?" Lorenza asked.

"Yes. He gave me tools and what they left in the house. He said that tonight a group of men will come and take what is left and burn the house."

Late that night strange men entered the ranch and burned every house that the Japanese had occupied. Screams were heard by the people watching the fiery glow in the sky, and throughout the night and early morning Malaquias, surrounded by sharp farm implements and machetes, guarded his family.

The sun played hide and seek with the rising grey pallor that streaked the early morning sky. In a matter of hours, from one day to another, life had radically changed. Malaquias, Lorenza, Paquita, Nana, Jesus and Andrea smelled the smoldering remains of the Matola home. As he walked through the ashes, Malaquias pondered why the forces that ejected the Japanese had not struck him. Obviously he would be next. The Japanese had been there for years doing good work, and unbelievably all that remained of their existence was black ash that the wind would spread into the fields.

"You practically kill yourself to get ahead and look what happens!" Anguished, Malaquias spoke to Lorenza and Nana who listened while riding in the cab of the family panel truck heading home.

"It's because they are Japanese and we are Mexicans. If we were black it would be worse." Lorenza's words sounded like a prayer. Nana's eyes were hypnotized to the road that rushed at her.

When Nana recognized a black automobile parked, waiting at the front of the house, her heart dropped to the pit of her stomach. Lorenza dreaded the thought of moving. She leaned on her husband and placed her head on his shoulder.

"La señora Garcia Pardo," Malaquias whispered to Lorenza as he reached for the handbrake.

The chauffeur opened the back door and out from the 1924 Ford four-door sedan emerged la señora Eliola Garcia Pardo dressed in deep black.

"Good afternoon, Malaquias," señora Garcia Pardo said, offering her hand and smiling. "Malaquias, the Japanese have left. We can't count on them. The majority of my land is empty and there is no one to attend it. Some day this land will be worth much money. Well, then, for being an excellent worker and for knowing how to treat the land, you can stay. I have also come to offer you ten acres of virgin land. Stay, Malaquias, work the land and you will become rich."

By the time señora Garcia Pardo had finished delivering her offer, she had circled Malaquias' truck and perused the ranch.

"I can't buy that land. I barely have enough to feed my family," Malaquias answered candidly as she went to the door of her automobile.

"Five thousand dollars is nothing, Malaquias. Think about it. Try to get the money. Let me know in a week." Señora Garcia Pardo closed the door and sped off into the edge of the afternoon.

Malaquias spent the next four days planning how to get the five thousand dollars, but no one could guarantee the money without enormous cost. He wanted the land but had to admit that it was impossible to purchase it honorably. While searching for the funds, Malaquias kept hearing and seeing unfortunate situations which stood out like omens telling him that perhaps it was safer not to buy the land.

One of the strangest occurrences was the mysterious death of Rosendo Guerrero. His death took place in the Pasadena hills in a secluded chapel-like structure constructed with adobe by Rosendo and other acquaintances who, people said, gathered there to pray.

The horrible state of Rosendo's body was such that the man and child who discovered it went mad. The body had been dismembered and arranged in a large round kettle with a narrow neck which flared at the opening just enough to hold Rosendo's head, while the rest of him cooked. The room had frescoes painted on three walls. A man with Indian features sitting on a sea shell, perhaps a nautilus shell, was painted on the west wall. The man, depicted naked except for a rope knotted around the waist, sat with forearms resting on his knees and large tears streaming down the cheeks. The eastern wall was adorned with a large, perfect, yellow-orange circle. According to several accounts, the northern wall depicted a man severing his own left arm that was placed on a round stone. On the southern wall there was a painting of a kettle with a fire under it and a man's head protruding through the opening in the top.

The rumors were that Rosendo committed suicide or sacrificed himself or united himself with God by following an ancient Indian path known precisely to only a few people and enigmatically to all as El Sendero Luminoso del Sol. Malaquias returned home in the late afternoon with images of the sacred sacrifice of Rosendo Guerrero.

At dusk a car slowly moved on the road leading to the de Leon house. Nana, Paquita, and Andrea watched the black mechanical insect turn off the illumination of its eyes. Doors opened and closed and the mysterious black bug crawled closer to the house. It moved off the road and parked on a rise under a walnut tree. Two men spread a blanket and stretched out. A third stayed in the car and pushed a cap over his face. Men had parked on Telegraph Road before, but now they began to venture on Malaquias' property.

Malaquias had prepared for these intrusions by purchasing a rifle which he never wanted to use. But tonight, before the night stole all the sight from the day, he would have to ask these men to leave, threaten them if necessary, and kill them if forced to protect his family. The images of bizarre deaths, disappearances and murders of Mexican children had haunted his mind for days. Nothing would deter him now from saving his family. He walked the short distance from the house to the car, rifle strapped to his back. At speaking distance he rested the rifle across his belt buckle.

"What do you want here?" Malaquias asked as he positioned himself to see the man in the front seat and the two men now sitting on the blanket.

"We're tired and it's gettin' late so we gonna sleep right here," the one on the blanket said.

"No. This is private property. Leave or I'll shoot you!" Malaquias lifted his rifle to the man's head.

The car started. The man who had spoken was in the back seat. The other grabbed the blanket and went to the front seat. The car drove around Malaquias, who pointed the rifle at their heads. The car sped to Telegraph Road, turned right toward Whittier and was lost to Malaquias' view. Lorenza was at his side now.

"Those men can come back. We can't stay here any longer. It's too dangerous," Lorenza said, going back to the safety of the house."

In the two weeks that followed, Malaquias sold most of his own tools and those acquired from the Japanese. The animals, except the horses he bought from Gonzalo, were sold. He found a house and property on Maple Street near Simons Brickyard. On a Friday morning he loaded the family belongings on the Ford truck, seated his children in the back and tied three horses to the truck bed hooks. As he drove away from the ten acres of prime land he could have had, he felt a knot of sadness grow in his throat and a great desire to cry. But he did not. What he felt then turned to bitterness and an image of failure. What could have been his biggest prize he had lost. He stopped the truck, looked both ways and turned left on Telegraph Road toward Simons, in the opposite direction which the three men had taken two weeks ago. Perhaps they would never return, he thought as he moved slower, carefully leading the horses.

Nana had finished washing and hanging up her brothers' and sisters' clothes, while at her feet the baby, almost a year old, played on a blanket. A few yards away Leonardo and Juan played with wooden blocks and cars.

Towering above them silently, heard only when the winds shook their branches, eucalyptus trees marked the wide limits of Maple Street. Inside Nana's yard a willow's branches brushed the smooth hard earth. The melodies of a Mexican ballad entered her mind.

Nana picked up Rafael and walked to the kitchen where her mother and Paquita prepared dinner. She listened to the sounds of the house. It was alive, she thought. Everyone, even the baby, busied themselves with living. But Nana considered what she did at that moment, simply listening, different from what everyone else felt important. She felt lonely. Often Nana watched young women walk by the house with their fiances. She wondered about what they said, how they touched, what they felt when they embraced, how many times they kissed. Damn them, she would say to herself. How did they meet? How did they achieve the relationship they had? The love, the caring, the tenderness expressed in such intimate, soft, graceful actions. People in love are like flamingos in flight, she thought. She tried to remember where she had heard that strange statement about humans and birds.

"Mama, why don't you buy a phonograph?" Nana asked at the moment Malaquias hung his coat and hat behind the kitchen door that led to the backyard.

"No, no phonograph, no phonograph! Instead, she should buy you boots and work clothes so you can help me load the manure. I need you to help me until your brothers grow up." Malaquias spoke to both his wife and daughter. He reached for a towel and went out to bathe in the large tub next to the garage he had built.

Lorenza's face was streaked with embarrassment when Nana's eyes screamed rebellion. Everyone knew the unspoken truth: Lorenza was unable to defend her own children from their father. Usually Nana was the target of his anger, his accusations, his failures. Nana had sacrificed school, domestic jobs, and training in a doctor's office. Perhaps that was the origin of Malaquias' anger and constant bitterness. His face was forever tense as if he had a sour lime in his mouth.

Nana placed the baby in the crib and walked to the porch where she had again begun a garden of potted plants. She watered the plants and studied the people who strolled through the late afternoon to the onrushing bright stars. Celia, the young woman who lived two houses away, waved and said hello. She walked with her friend Federico Revueltas.

It had been a quiet ride from the doctor's office. Nana held Juan wrapped in blankets, silently looking at whatever came upon his eyes. Malaquias drove the truck to the front door and watched his wife and daughter take Juan into the house. The doctor had told Malaquias, Lorenza and Nana that the lower intestine protruding from Juan's anus would have to be removed if it did not regress with the treatments.

Lorenza heated the water to just below uncomfortable. Four-year-old Juan, with his intestine hanging out, had to sit in the warm water. Everyone hoped he would survive that black thing dangling out of his body. Although somebody prayed for his death it was never revealed who, but the fact was felt emotionally by Juan.

Days passed and the treatments did not work. Juan would have to suffer a dangerous operation. Nana prepared for the trip to Whittier with her mother and Juan. His condition had deteriorated to where he could no longer walk normally. Juan advanced with his legs spread apart wide. People stared and said things that he was too young to understand, but the discomfort he endured clearly made him realize that this condition was terribly wrong.

The doctor at the clinic in Whittier had gestured the action of a cutting scissors to Lorenza. Nana's translation was not needed. Lorenza and Juan knew what the gesture meant. It was definite, sure as the date set that Juan's condition required a trimming of the bowel. On the return home riding La Paloma, the black and white trolley, Lorenza and Nana spoke little. Both women sat close together. Juan, snuggled up against his mother, his feet warm on his sister's lap, slept all the way to Simons. When they alighted off La Paloma, Juan refused to walk. The thing felt thicker and longer. Lorenza checked her son.

"The intestine is blacker and more swollen," Lorenza said, kissing Juan and carrying him.

"I'll help you, mama," Nana offered.

"No, let me be. I want to feel this child in my arms." Lorenza moved ahead.

They rested at the water tank. Nana splashed cold water on her face and washed off the red brick dust. The day, neither hot nor cold, was comfortable weather in which other people strolled peacefully. Nana drank and sat next to the cement tub to watch the silver gush forth from the open spigot. Through the running silver cylinder she saw a deformed figure coming towards her. The man rode a black Arabian horse with a fancy saddle. Dressed in a black suit and tie, he removed his hat, dismounted, cupped his hands and swished water over his long hair. Nana noticed the strange long earlobes that dangled in the wet grey hair which touched his shoulders.

"Buenas tardes, doña Lorenza."

Lorenza had immediately recognized him.

"How are you, señor Lugo?" Lorenza smiled as if this man relieved a little of the worry and pain she felt for her child.

"Why are you carrying that child? Let him walk. The day is for walking." Señor Lugo detected the suffering in Lorenza's sudden weak smile. "The child is sick?"

Lorenza nodded yes.

Fascinated by his mannerisms, Nana moved closer to listen to and watch this man whom Lorenza addressed as if she had known him for years.

"Tell me about him." Lugo knelt in front of Lorenza and Juan.

"Juan has an intestine that is hanging out and the doctors want to operate. It is a horrible black swollen thing that came out from him," Lorenza declared and slightly rocked Juan. She stopped and allowed señor Lugo to see the protruding colon.

"Do not believe those scientists. They do not know what they say. I have had several fine horses that have suffered your child's ailment. But only the fine ones suffer that illness. Listen to me, doña Lorenza de Leon, because I will give you the medicine to save your son." Señor Lugo spoke still on one knee, his voice changed as if he were composing a special poem.

"Get a brick and heat it in the fire of your stove. Open a roll of cotton. Then ask for fig leaves, olive oil, alcohol and urine from one of your other children. Put these liquids in a pan and boil them. Take the brick out of the stove. Wrap it with the cotton and pour on the potion. Wrap all this with a black cloth. Lay the child down and place the medicine brick next to the intestine. Cover the child with heavy blankets to trap the vapor. Be very careful not to burn him. Repeat this treatment for seven days and nights and you will see that your son will be cured on the ninth day. Forget about the operation. Return to your home in peace. Goodbye, doña Lorenza, goodbye."

Señor Lugo walked away to the west. Nana remembered all he said. She watched him mount the horse and climb the hill on Vail toward the Simons general store. She imagined him crossing the railroad tracks and passing by Mount Carmel church. She now knew the identity of the man. He was a Lugo, a rich Mexican family who had lost their land. They lived in a large two-story square house off Garfield. It was rumored that one of the brothers was insane.

Nine days later, Nana thought that if this Lugo was the insane one, his insanity was strangely wonderful, for as she entered her yard on Maple Street, she noticed that Juan was cured and running after a stray hen.

Nana looked into the bedroom where her mother spoke with thirteen-year-old Andrea who was terrified at the sight of blood running down her leg. Lorenza never explained menstruation to her daughters. They would hear of it from friends who had started. Nana remembered her first experience, at fifteen. She had been at school listening to the fifth grade teacher. Suddenly she felt her pants were wet and asked permission to go to the bathroom. She screamed at the discovery of blood and carefully cleaned herself. The nurse explained what had occurred and sent Nana home where Lorenza quietly gave her the necessary hygienic items.

If this was natural, why must women be terrified of the first blood, Nana thought as she watched Andrea come out of the bedroom with Lorenza. Nana smiled and her sister did likewise.

"Take her outside and sit her in the shade," Lorenza said.

Nana and Andrea sat and talked about womanly subjects. Andrea stopped shaking and crying after Nana explained that it was all right to be afraid the first couple of times. Soon Andrea would become accustomed. Nana left and went to tend to her porch garden of potted plants. While she watered, Celia strolled by with her friend Federico Revueltas.

"Nana, are you going to the dance? At the Rodelos' house. We'll look for you. All of Federico's brothers will be there." Celia giggled suspiciously about something that Nana was not privy to.

Nana had tried to go once before but Malaquias had refused to allow his three older daughters to attend. However, since that denial Nana had spoken with don Angel who explained to Malaquias that he could not keep his girls penned up like prisoners. They were women and if they were to grow up normal, Malaquias had to allow them to dance and express themselves as women to other women and to men. Nana decided to ask her father and went to Andrea to solicit her help in taking care of their brothers.

Nana and her sisters Paquita and Jesus lay in wait for Malaquías to arrive. When he entered the house he sensed that his three older daughters were waiting for the perfect time to spring the question. He had been indirectly warned by don Angel's conversations concerning the children, but he had not decided what his response would be. His daughters had prepared a delicious meal and Lorenza had fussed through dinner about how hard they had worked for him. He ate and listened. For dessert they had even made his favorite empanadas de manzana and wonderful hot chocolate with a tinge of cinnamon. When Malaquias finished he pushed away from the table, sat back and crossed his legs.

"Gracias a Dios," he declared, contented.

Paquita, Jesus and their mother passed around a glance which stopped on Nana. Leonardo, Miguel, Juan and Rafael played with their food. In a few minutes Malaquias' patience would end. Nana thought about her father's comment . . . Thank us who prepared dinner, father, she steamed mentally.

"I'll take care of them," Andrea blurted out, responding to the mess the boys had made on the table.

Her sisters' and mother's eyes urged Nana to ask. Malaquias unbuckled his belt and rubbed his stomach. He was about to react to the boys when Nana moved to the edge of her chair.

"Papa, please, Paquita, Jesus and I want to go to the dance at the Rodelos' home tonight. Please give us permission to go." Nana felt relief in her chest when her father gave his assent.

The women were about to leave. Nana noticed that her mother had a curious look. She proudly primped her daughters' hair and adjusted the collars on their dresses. Malaquias came up to his daughters and reminded them to sit and return home with don Angel who would be leaving the dance around one in the morning. Nana noticed that her father and mother were in a splendid mood.

Nana was happy as she and her sisters walked down Maple to the Rodelos' home from where the music came. The three young women were met by Celia who was talking with two female friends in the front garden. Celia accompanied the de Leons to the back where the dance was happening and sat them at a long table next to don Angel and his wife. Celia sat next to Nana and from there flirted with the men sitting, standing, leaning around the dance floor.

"Look, here comes Federico Revueltas. Do you know the family? He has brothers," Celia said excitedly.

"Oh, you," Nana replied, hiding her interest in wanting to hear more about Federico's brothers.

"The oldest is Octavio. He has a reputation for gambling but they say he is responsible. There comes Maximiliano. He is serious but fun also. Then my Federico, and Jose is the youngest. He is immature. They should be here any moment." Celia fished and reached for Federico's arm as he arrived at the table.

"Sit down, Federico." Celia pulled Federico down to the chair between her and Nana. Federico took off his cap and adjusted his tie.

"Federico, this is Nana, Paquita and Jesus de Leon. They are the sisters who live down the street in one of don Angel's houses." Celia spoke, smiling at the women.

The band struck up a romantic bolero. Celia, with dance in her eyes, turned to Federico when two men stepped into her view. Maximiliano Revueltas and Cuco Lopez spotted Federico and began to circle to avoid the dancers. Directly through the dance floor advanced a third man. Octavio Revueltas presented himself before the table; his brothers stood behind him. He slowly removed his cap, all the while exploring Nana's face. A strange, exciting sensation took hold of his heart, forcing him to search for a deep breath.

Nana, although uncomfortable, did not retreat her eyes from his, nor did her lips break a tiny smile, yet inside she felt a desire to laugh hysterically about the possibilities that ran amuck in her mind. She was relentlessly staring into Octavio's almond, yellowish brown-green eyes dancing among long curly lashes. Nana finally smiled and thought about the spiritual togetherness she sensed in her parents earlier that evening.

That night Octavio asked Nana to dance three times. Neither he nor she knew how to flutter or flicker to the waltzes, boleros, corridos, tangos and the latest dance crazes coming out of the Hollywood Paladium and the Bolero Club. Octavio sat with Nana while Cuco Lopez, Maximiliano and other gentlemen asked Paquita and Jesus to the dance floor.

Octavio and Nana were shy so they did not speak much of the happenings outside of Simons. Most of the night Octavio fussed over Nana's soft drink, making sure that she always had a full glass. He asked the appropriate questions about her family, if she worked, how she helped her father and mother. She asked about Octavio's work, his brothers and sisters. Whenever Octavio's question was answered, Nana would follow with her own question. Nonetheless, their conversation was interspersed with moments of silence.

Several men who did not know Octavio asked Nana to dance. She did not refuse anyone. All the while she danced, Cuco Lopez repeated that he thought Nana was the most beautiful woman at the dance and he would never get over his love for her. Octavio considered Cuco's comments and evaluations manifestations of too much alcohol. In fact, before he became unbearably obnoxious, Cuco went out to the sugarcane patch where at the top of his voice he began to compare Nana to the infinite beauty of the Milky Way . . . Madmen and drunkards tell the truth, Octavio thought as he waved goodbye to Nana.

Chapter 11

Walter and Edit Simons' first child was born without complication at home. The parents named her Helen Reubena. Walter had wanted to name her Sarah in memory of his first wife, an idea which Edit rejected from the first mention. She did not want the memory of Walter's first love to parade in the name of their first-born. Walter opted to give the child the name of his father. Helen was Edit's mother's name. The compromise was acceptable enough to reestablish peace between the two debating spouses. Helen Reubena was born on a stormy March 25, 1925.

Eight months later on November 1, Melissa Elledge Simons passed away from a massive stroke which she suffered at dinner at Joseph's home. Death was acceptable, but not the manner of death nor the condition of the body after death. Melissa Simons began to choke on a kernel of brown rice. Her family, realizing her condition, began to slap her on the back. Suddenly she reached for her own neck and squeezed with unbelievable strength, puncturing with the thumbs through to the esophagus. When this occurred, Joseph, with Laura at his left and James at his right, stepped back directly behind his mother who, perhaps trying to get a last glimpse of at least part of the family she dearly loved, turned her head one-hundred and eighty degrees without moving her body and died staring at the space between Laura and Joseph and James. When the ambulance came the attendants, unable to turn her head, laid her with her face up and body backwards. After exhaustive efforts the last consideration was to sever Melissa's head. This alternative was rejected by the family who, for the first time in twenty-five years, had gathered together. Lola Ellen, Mary Francis, Emma Lisa, Joseph and Walter agreed to bury their mother face up, body down.

"We simply have to accept these occurrences. The more technologically advanced we become, the stranger the happenings," Walter said softly at the funeral reception at his brother's home.

None of his sisters nor his brother wanted to discuss the condition of their mother. They preferred to forget.

After Melissa's death, Walter felt liberated from the dread of hurting her. When she was alive he lived with the fear of embarrasssing her. She was always on his mind when he made decisions that might affect the family image. But not any longer. Now he would do whatever he decided and the hell with what people thought. Walter considered himself the

Henry Ford of brick production. He knew he could produce the best product for the best price faster than any of his competitors. He was convinced that some day his product would be transported in trucks and trains throughout the United States. He had already sent material abroad to Mexico, Panama, Japan and even Russia for ship ballast. But boats were extremely slow. He envisioned great airplanes flying in a day or two across the ocean delivering Simons brick to any country that wanted the best building material in the world.

In the same room on exactly the same day at the same hour one year after the birth of her first daughter, Edit gave birth to Drusilla Melissa. On the morning of March 14, 1926, to pass those last hours, Walter cleaned out his desk drawers. In a magazine that had been misplaced, he admired an announcement of the seven new locomotives he had bought for his brickyard. When he heard the cry, Walter dropped the magazine and rushed to the door of the bedroom. A nurse came out and Laura followed. She smiled and stepped out to the middle of the hall.

"Congratulations, you have a beautiful girl!" Laura said and rushed off, following the nurse.

Walter received the news with half a smile that fell as soon as he was alone. He had been so sure that this child was going to be a boy, a male heir for the Simons Brickyard, a son that he wanted to prepare and educate as he had done with James these past years. Walter wanted his own son. They would simply have to try again and again.

"How is she?" Walter moved with Laura toward the room.

"Tired, but fine. You may see her and the baby as soon as we do a little tidying up. Wait in the library. Joseph will be here soon," Laura said.

He remembered that at Helen's birth there were more people waiting, and all the family had waited for James. Now Walter waited alone in his beautiful library looking out to the garden of the brick house on Plymouth Avenue in Los Angeles. He sat quietly, listening and waiting for whoever would rescue him from the loneliness with which he had wrapped himself. He thought of what it would take to impregnate his wife with a man-child. He envisioned her in the normal positions which so far had produced exclusively females. He would have to try acrobatic, exotic positions, and above all, he thought, he must educate her to accept his penis in her mouth. Until now, Edit had always refused, but no longer, for he was convinced that if she swallowed his sperm a male child would result. Spurred on with disappointment and anger, Walter prepared to penetrate his adored wife through every love tunnel he could imagine. He had never taken images like these seiously. Feeling uncomfortable, he went to the window.

"What is it, Walter? A boy or a girl?" Joseph had saved his brother.

"A girl," Walter, caught off guard, responded, mimicking joy and excitement.

"Congratulations, Brother." Joseph offered his hand. "By the way, in a few days you will receive a check. Open an account for your new daughter."

Joseph pushed his coat open and placed his hands in his trouser pockets and rocked.

"Walter, I sold Mother's house," he continued. "You'll receive your share. It's not much, but give it to your children."

Joseph moved over to the window. "That garden is truly beautiful. Another matter you will have to deal with soon is your house. Much is happening today, ah? What I mean is that James wants to buy your house in Pasadena." Joseph contemplated the intense greenery in the garden. It seemed like another world. A stillness fell, a rest between thoughts and words.

"Fine. I'll sell it to him. I'm planning to build a house at the beach," Walter responded and noticed Joseph tilt his head to the side and back, questioning. "I bought a lot on the Newport Peninsula."

Walter leaned against the wall and allowed the garden to take him back. "How we fought over that Pasadena house," he spoke softly.

"And you spent so much money keeping it," Joseph chuckled.

"And who's going to end up with it?" Walter silently said good-bye to his garden although its image remained in his mind.

"James wants to move in by December." Joseph smiled at Laura who had just entered.

"Fine."

Walter walked out first. Joseph and Laura followed to visit the newborn child and her mother.

The instant the photographer's shutter clicked on December 29, 1926, the gleam in the newlyweds' eyes reached out through time and space. Octavio and Nana stared beyond the best man and maid of honor, the photographer, his wife and his assistant. The gleam was hope for the children and grandchildren and great-grandchildren they hoped for and were seeing at that moment. The photographer applauded and his wife and assistant threw rice as the couple ascended to the back seat of the 1925 Plymouth four-door sedan chauffered by Ignacio Sandoval, best man, and

Tati Sandoval, maid of honor. They drove directly to Ignacio's house where a small celebration had been organized by Federico, Maximiliano, and Jose Revueltas and Paquita de Leon.

Octavio, on a cane armchair, sipped cognac. Nana, also on a cane chair, held his hand and watched the few friends celebrate the marriage. At times her happiness was interrupted by memories of her father's face. Malaquias had twice refused to give Nana's hand to Octavio. There had been some friction—a misunderstanding about his gambling and his associates. Octavio had even sent a priest from Saint Benedict Catholic Church to explain his honorable intentions to Malaquias. But still Malaquias refused.

On Christmas Eve, Octavio drank a toast to the season with Ignacio Sandoval and offered Nana a sip. She kissed the cognac and took Octavio's arm and led him to where Tati had arranged a white and gold nativity set by the window. A four-foot Christmas pine tree decorated with handmade straw decorations waited for the new year. Tati had bought the nativity set in Tijuana, and the tree was given to her by Gonzalo Pedroza and Jacobo Ramos who distributed the trees to the families one week before Christmas. From far away, music from the Simons band rehearsing for their second appearance in the Rose Parade came to Octavio and Nana.

Walter and Edit Simons also heard the music on Christmas Eve as they led a group of fifty business colleagues and wives to observe the distribution of the Christmas gifts. That night Simons was a showcase town, an example of the success of Walter's benevolent exploitation and control of Mexican labor. Many in the group considered the social unit of Simons a utopian achievement. Everyone affiliated with Simons seemed happy and content. The newspaper reporters and observers from the East were amazed at how well the workers were served for their toil. The guests experienced a beautiful Christmas filled with Walter and Edit's generosity.

That night the eight hundred little Mexicans and their mothers were introduced to the American custom of decorating a Christmas tree in honor of the Christ Child and the distribution of gifts commemorative of the Three Wise Men of the East. Ironically, most of the donated toys and clothes for the children came from the Eastern businessmen. Walter, Edit, and the invited guests saw the happy children receive their toys, mufflers, frocks, shoes, hats, caps and other sensible presents while the mothers rejoiced in the receiving of shawls, shoes, household items and colorful material for new dresses.

Corpulent Walter Simons watched with great satisfaction and beamed with genuine pleasure. His guests witnessed a man who seemed to be an exceedingly happy individual because he had given joy to so many children and their mothers each recurring year for the last decade. His actions proved the sincerity of his purpose and the sense of accomplishment that he gained from the custom. Truly, the guests felt, to see the merry-faced, brown-skinned youngsters carrying off their treasures after a two-hour romp around the gorgeously decorated tree was to recognize a new light on the melting pot of America.

Most of the children had been born in the town of Simons and educated in a grade school of substantial red brick. Built by Walter, the school was a high point in the tour of the little model community where the teachers imparted English and American ways to the four hundred brown pupils ranging from five to sixteen years of age. Another inspiring sight was the hospital maintained by the patron. A visiting nurse made a continual round of the cottages and sanitation facilities as well as provided first aid instruction to the mothers and workers. Of course she also cared for the sick and the injured. There was even a special oxygen room for those workers who, after years of laboring in the red brick dust, developed nagging coughs and breathing problems. The company doctor, Emil Strayhorn, dispensed medical care four days per week.

Most certainly the vision of Santa's little elves sprang into the minds of the visitors when they entered the model Simons woodshop cottage in which the furniture was made by the older children of the grade school. The little Mexican elves displayed their ingenious collection of useful articles made out of wooden dry goods boxes, shoe boxes and roughly-finished lumber saved by the Simons store manager, Gonzalo Pedroza. More than several of the guests purchased the Mexican-made articles as mementos of the inspiring tour. They bought little bureaus covered with chintz, neat benches, kitchen tables, bedstands, a cradle, chests of drawers and a score of miscellaneous articles for the home created to lighten the housework and afford general comfort to the family. This display of products created from material that normally would have been thrown away manifested the Simons virtues of thrift and economy.

The Simons community of four thousand Mexicans seemed happy and contented. The rent paid for the three and four-room cottages was $1.25 a room per month, which included water for house and garden. Many families nurtured a little green patch which yielded vegetables according to the taste of the humble, shiny-faced cultivator. A company store at which the women did most of the buying operated during the week.

That evening of national religious glory Octavio and Nana confessed their love for one another. They kissed and embraced, and for the first time Nana allowed Octavio's hands to roam over her shapely figure. When they emerged from the dark where they had been caressing on a bench under a large walnut tree near the amusement hall, they heard the speeches and the children applauding Walter, the patron. Octavio smiled to the world for the wonderful gift he had discovered in Nana. The promised couple went to watch the children receive their gifts.

Near them a group of distinguished visitors talked with Walter about the founding of Simons. Walter indicated that early in the establishment of the company town, remembering what he had seen in Mexico, he realized that poor living conditions were as obnoxious to Mexicans as to any other people. With this in mind he attempted to build, step by step, dollar by dollar, in such a manner as to allow free rein to the employees in all matters outside of actual business affairs. The preference of the Mexicans was considered when houses were constructed and the company store was opened. Walter had it stocked and operated by people who understood and respected the national tastes of the Mexicans.

"Ladies and gentlemen," Walter said to the visitors, "in this way I have tried to solve the problem of satisfying labor and thereby avoiding any talk of unions. I felt that if I could succeed with this project, production and quality would rise, costs would be down, and profit would be more than satisfactory. You have seen the results and proof of the wisdom of the course."

Walter had always been interested in the individual concerns of his brown workmen. Mexicans were like the earth; Mexicans were the earth, he often would say to himself when alone. By keeping in close touch with his employees and taking care of these men and their families, although it had been an onerous task, the patron had been well repaid. When it was revealed that the annual labor payroll at the plant was less than its primary competitors, that the company had enjoyed the uninterrupted production of a high quality article of brick and had successfully out-earned the keenest competition, there was great applause from the special guests and magnificent praise for the humanitarian policies pursued by Walter.

Throughout the company's growth, Walter had endeavored to establish an equitable, mutually agreeable wage scale. In addition he had been able to inculcate a spirit of loyalty among his Mexican employees that was the envy of all the Eastern businessmen who toured the plant. They agreed that the Simons Brick Company had attained one of the most remarkable industrial records in the country.

Octavio felt proud when he heard the man say ". . . in the country . . ." During World War I the Mexican employees had the proud record of subscribing in greater volume for Liberty Bonds and war stamps, in proportion to numbers, than at any similar plant in the United States. The Mexicans, although few were United States citizens, matched their loyalty and patriotism with their hard-earned money and their lives. Moreover, at the suggestion of Walter and Edit the men wrote letters to relatives in Mexico telling of the wonderful living conditions in the company town of Simons, as well as the goodwill of Americans towards Mexico. These letters did much to counteract German propaganda damaging to United States interests as the letters were passed around freely and widely read in Mexico.

In Simons, whistles never blew nor bells rang to mark the beginning or end of work time. Walter was opposed to any methods of labor handling which savored of slave-driving. This attitude paid large dividends in both morale and increased production. When on double shifts, the plant with a daily single shift capacity of seven hundred thousand bricks easily produced one million bricks per day.

Octavio and Walter crossed glances. The group of visitors shifted position and moved slowly toward the center. Walter continued to explain his success. The masterminds of Simons were Walter himself and Rosendo Guerrero, whose directional mandala plan had evolved beyond what they both could have imagined.

After Walter's model Christmas Eve program, Octavio and Nana planned for their elopement. Malaquias had not been receptive to Octavio, and Nana was sure that her father would deny Octavio her hand. And so they waited for the right hour when Nana would walk out of her house and start a new life with Octavio.

For days before Nana's departure Octavio made himself somewhat of a nuisance and alerted Malaquias that Nana had a serious suitor. Octavio would walk past the house and talk to one of Nana's brothers and give him an envelope. About ten love letters had been exchanged. The decisive final letter from Nana was deliverd to Octavio by Ignacio Sandoval on the morning of December 27. She had instructed Octavio to come for her at six o'clock in the evening.

At about five o'clock on that not too cold afternoon Ignacio and Guadalupe Sandoval drove by the de Leon house. Nana and Paquita waved to them through the screen door and heard Guadalupe call out "six o'clock." Nana and Paquita returned to help their mother in the kitchen. Lorenza knew that her older daughters were planning something. She had a hunch that Nana might not be home the next morning. Sadness, happiness, excitement, worry and love pounded her heart as she observed Nana nervously checking the clock and searching out the front door to the street. Malaquias gathered his family round the table and Lorenza served.

"Where is Nana?" Malaquias asked, turning to his wife who continued to serve around the table.

"She's not feeling well, Papa. She is resting in bed," Nana's older sister responded.

The clock marked three minutes to six. Dinner had started early. The front door was left open and from where Malaquias sat at the head of the table he could see through the kitchen and living room to the street. Lorenza warmed the tortillas. The boys, not aware of what was about to happen, talked and ate happily. Paquita looked to Nana and her bedroom. When Octavio arrived, Nana would have to walk through the living room in front of her father. Paquita drank a glass of milk without breathing.

"Well, look how hungry you are," Malaquias remarked to his oldest daughter.

"Yes, papa, I'm very hungry," Paquita said and noticed a blue car drive past the door.

Ignacio's car was black and Paquita relaxed for a moment. Then a black car drove to the front of the door and stopped right before Malaquias' view. Paquita's heart palpitated. Nana would have to leave now. Malaquias saw the car but continued to eat. Nana, carrying her shoes and a small valise, went to the front door. She turned and before pushing the door open looked back at her family. Her mother smiled. Nana was out the door and ran to the car where Octavio waited. They embraced, got into the back seat and drove away down Maple Street. They heard one cry from Malaquias.

"Nana!" Malaquias, in the middle of the street, saw his daughter looking back and getting smaller.

That night Nana stayed with Ignacio and Tati. Octavio went to his home and finished the extra room that he had added to the Mondragón family house. This would be the room that he would give to his bride. Early the next morning, on December 28, Friday, Octavio and Nana were married in a Los Angeles civil court. On the next day they were married by the church and celebrated at Ignacio and Tati's home.

Octavio and Nana kissed. This time they would be alone together for the first time in their relationship. She was unsure as to what he might expect and he worried about how he should treat her that night. The evening was clear; the December stars were bright. The month of December had become so special in their lives. Octavio was born on the twenty-fourth of the month and they were married in December, and perhaps by next December they would have their first child. Nana gently pushed Octavio away.

"Octavio, we should return to your home." Nana urged Octavio to stop.

Octavio and Nana approached the Revueltas kitchen and were surprised to find Octavio's father, mother, brothers and sisters bearing gifts for the newlyweds.

"Octavio, you are the oldest son. For Milagros and me your marriage is very special. We have come to congratulate and welcome you and your wife Nana," Damian said slowly and carefully.

Milagros nodded in agreement. Octavio waited for a few seconds and embraced his father and mother. Milagros immediately went to Nana, welcomed her with a mother's hug, and sat with her for the rest of the evening. From that moment on, Nana was accepted by the family and known to society as a Revueltas.

The wedding celebration continued until the early morning but Octavio and Nana left at eleven and walked under the cool night sky. Octavio took Nana to the room he had built on the side of his parents' house. Nana accepted the room and the house but wanted her own home. Octavio lit a candle and watched the shadows on the wall. Nana undressed all the while her husband admiringly studied her body. That evening they made love once and fell asleep, satisfied with each other.

After the new year Nana settled in the Revueltas home and tried to feel comfortable living with her in-laws. Although she made an honest effort, it was not what she had hoped married life would give her. She became close to Milagros and willingly helped her wash, cook, and clean. As the year progressed, however, it became more and more difficult to avoid petty clashes with her sisters-in-law, and at times her brothers-in-law asked her to wash and iron for them as if she were more like a servant than a wife of their older brother. Often Nana would run to her private room to escape being ordered or yelled at by Damian who proved to be a selfish and demanding father-in-law. There were moments when she felt like a kept whore when Octavio would arrive from work, bathe, eat, make love and leave to gamble. As she waited through the night worrying about Octavio, she vowed that some way or other she would get a home for herself. It was in late February that she announced to her husband that she was pregnant and demanded her own house for her children.

"Don't you like it here?" Octavio asked, disappointed.

"Think of your child, Octavio. We need a house for our family," Nana answered with an angered tone.

"Don't be mad. I am very happy we are going to have a son." Octavio picked up his coat.

"Where are you going?" Nana asked angrily.

"To win money for our family." Octavio's last word was pronounced half-way to the door.

Nana heard the screen door close, Octavio speak with Ignacio, and the car drive off. She fell on the bed and cried. After a while she realized that crying no longer helped. She stopped and would not ever again cry for his leaving to go off to gamble.

Months passed, and to the world Nana always showed a happy face. She was visited several times by her sister Jesús who was well on her way to having her first-born. Jesús, Paquita and Andrea were Nana's only contact with her family. Paquita described how Malaquias became depressed after Nana's elopement. Life around the house was not the same. Nana's sister and brothers feared their father and kept out of his way. Malaquias worked from sun up to sun down, blaming his plight on Nana. He was furious at her abandoning the house when they needed her the most. Nana could not go home to visit and her mother, sisters and brothers were forbidden to see her.

"Tell Mama to wait for a grandchild about the first of November," Nana proudly told Paquita. "I know she will be very happy. And give her a big hug from me. Please, Paquita."

Nana felt miserable at not being able to see her mother.

Late in June, on a warm Sunday on a weekend that Octavio chose to spend at home, he asked Nana to put on her finest dress. He told her that they were going to see one of the greatest men in the world and his miracle machine. Nana immediately thought of the circus but Octavio explained that they were going to see an airplane. The day was beautiful; the morning fog had been burned away by the warm sun and the sky was as clear as crystal blue water. Octavio hurried her along, for the plane was to land at eleven, stay until one and depart for Los Angeles. It would probably never return again. Octavio did not want to miss the great plane and its pilot.

They started on their way down Vail Street to the dirt path that led to the baseball field and the arroyo separating Simons property and the Vail Airport. They climbed up and over the embankment of the arroyo. When they reached the top, they were amazed upon discovering scores of cars lined before them. Hundreds of people had congregated. Most of the men like Octavio wore suits and ties, and Nana was in her party best.

Nana noticed that she and Octavio were the only two brown faces among the huge crowd who hurried to flock around the plane hoping to get a glimpse of the miracle bird that had flown across the great Atlantic Ocean. The brave man who accomplished the feat stood under the propeller answering whatever questions were asked. Nana realized that as they got closer to the plane and the man, the crowd got whiter, almost porcelain and sickly to the eyes of people who had never seen a large concentration of the Aryan race. She and Octavio kept walking right through the crowd, passing lines of modern automobiles until finally they saw the aircraft hangar beyond a fence.

"An airplane, Octavio?" Nana questioned with irony.

"It's Lindbergh's Spirit of St. Louis. It crossed the Atlantic." Octavio pulled her toward the fence.

"How small and fragile to fly to the other side of the world."

Nana's eyes followed the fence and the faces peering in at the plane. No one knew she was there. She raised her hands, reaching up to the upper horizontal pole of the fence. She felt as strong as anyone there and her baby felt comfortable, as if he were stretching his body with joy. She brought her hands down and walked away from the fence. Octavio followed behind. Adjusting his cap he stopped her.

"We'll lose our place!"

"But I don't want to be squeezed against the fence," Nana said moving toward the Vail Airport runway.

"Don't you want to hear what Charles Lindbergh has to say?" Octavio walked alongside, moving away from the excited crowd.

"No," Nana replied.

They advanced along the runway. The voices faded, the sun got hotter and they were alone in silence.

"Let's go for a soda at Acacio Delgado's store," Octavio suggested.

"Good idea. Let's go."

Nana took her husband by the hand and headed in the opposite direction to Maple Street, close to where her family lived. They again passed by the crowd around the Spirit of St. Louis.

"Look, Octavio. It's Mr. Simons!" She pointed and Octavio immediately pulled her hand down.

They watched Simons shake hands with Charles Lindbergh and embrace him twice. Walter and Charles Lindbergh were joined by a group of men and women who escorted them into the hangar. As Octavio and Nana neared they saw the celebration in honor of Charles Lindbergh's feat and Walter's accomplishment in getting the famous pilot to land at Vail Field.

The Revueltas crossed over to the side of the arroyo and over the next barranca down to where the Simons locomotive tracks lay connecting the clay pit above Washington to the machines in the main yard. They enjoyed the warmth and each other's company. By Vail Elementary School Nana sat down on one of the benches against the administration office. She felt her abdomen, caressed her child. Octavio placed his hand there and felt life. A smile, intimacy and peace reigned.

"Help! Help us!" a woman screamed.

Octavio and Nana focused in the direction of Washington from which a woman ran towards them.

"Please, someone help us!"

The woman was almost to them. Behind her rose black smoke. The woman reached for Nana and fell to the dirt. Octavio ran beyond her, toward the screams of children trapped inside a burning makeshift wooden cab attached to an old Ford pick-up truck. From the back of the bed, sticking out over the tailgate, a man's large legs kicked, struggling to move out backwards. Octavio grabbed the man's feet and pulled. Suddenly a man emerged clutching a child in his arms. The man fell on his back, the child rolled off his chest, and the truck was overcome by flames. Octavio dragged the man and child to safety. The woman noticed the man on the ground and the crying child.

"Where are my other two babies?" the woman asked and reached for the truck.

Nana stopped her advance. The woman realized that they had been consumed. A shrill inhuman scream shattered the air around Simons.

Now other Simons workers had come. Gonzalo Pedroza ordered someone to drive into Montebello and summon the police and firemen. In an hour the police and firemen investigated the truck carcass. The firemen treated the man, woman and child while others cooled the metal steel and smoldering wood. As the firemen began to rip apart the metal and wooden house shell, the people who had gathered waited for the extraction of two corpses. When the moment came to pull the babies out, the police pushed the spectators back, which gave Nana a direct view into the open bed. The two and three-year-old children were not burned but had died of asphyxiation from toxic smoke. They seemed to have wanted to protect one another, for they died embracing each other. The man and woman sat and watched the firemen load the two corpses onto a large red truck. A fireman called to the parents who picked up their living, crying child and joined the rest of their family in the truck.

The police did not care to ask questions about ther accident. After the family was driven away the police and firemen left. The crowd dispersed and Octavio and Nana were left alone as they had begun the day. Nana protectively touched the child in her womb. The people who had suffered the tragedy which she and Octavio witnessed were some of the many that kept appearing around Simons. Most looked for a job but were turned away by Gonzalo or William. They were people who carried their belongings looking for a place to sleep, eat, rest—a place to make the search end. That family lived in that truck. Even if Octavio did not like it, she would have a home for her children, her family, Nana thought.

Nana looked at Octavio and did not like him at that moment. He felt that she should live with her mother-in-law. In that way she would always be protected when he was gone. Nana did not want to be protected, much less mothered by Milagros who had major problems with Damian and still had most of her children at home. Nana could not understand how Octavio enjoyed living cramped in that room attached to the house. She walked faster and Octavio was left behind. Finally he caught up.

"Octavio, I want my own home!" Nana demanded with fear and confidence.

Octavio kept walking.

In a sunburst of color, Octavio moved in tall brown work boots, blue pants, long-sleeved white shirt, sleeveless brown thick sweater and brown hat. His right arm swung freely, his left crossed his stomach, and his legs took long strides. His brown face and clear dark eyes glistened under the shadow cast by the rim of his hat. He marched happily. Alone, abuzz with excitement, he played and advanced over a bed of lapis lazuli, grey, yellow greenish, brown, rust, black foliage; the husks of the sugarcane his father planted rotted over the earth. He threw bread crumbs of leftover Mexican sweet bread. Three crows swooped down to beak them and exploited him awhile.

He marched away from the large sugarcane field bathed in the golden radiance from the core of the sun. The painted yellow sky brushed a haze, a vibration which he had felt many times when he walked on the earth alone. He breathed deeply. He lacked the words for what he felt: exaltation and ecstasy were not in his vocabulary. Behind his right shoulder, far off in the horizon, a blue house, a red roof and two meager trees grabbed onto the field against the sun's brilliance. Trees, towers, stacks, buildings stood far off to his left, silently repelled by the powerful advancing sunlight. From the direction in which he was headed, diagonally to his right hip, came a golden path that trailed off to the left of the sun.

Octavio moved in a sea of colors which he enjoyed. He took a deep breath and looked around at the beautiful world, a beauty that brought images of his beautiful wife. He had no doubt that he was a fortunate man. Nana would soon deliver their first child. Their constant love had proven pleasurable and fruitful.

In those days Octavio and Ignacio had been assigned to the work crew which was constructing the Simonses' retreat cottage on the Balboa Peninsula in Newport Beach, California. The house was a four-bedroom, large kitchen, dining and living room entertainment getaway for Walter and Edit. Walter had planned this second home for some time, and upon closing the deal with his nephew James, he had decided to build it. He searched for a lot near the beach where there would be future development. Newport Beach offered quiet seclusion and promise of a profit in years to come.

Octavio had worked on the construction since the house began to rise. He learned all that he could about building a home for he realized that, although he would be perfectly happy living the rest of his life with his parents, someday he would build his own house. As Octavio neared his parents' house he could almost see himself and his sons working on the Revueltas family casa. He opened the gate and wondered about Nana . . . Would it be tonight or had she already given birth . . . With his last thought he was overcome with excitement, for at the front door waited Tati with a smile that almost hid half of her lovely face. The smile transferred a genuine joy to his mouth and face. Tati hugged him and whispered the child's gender. Octavio moved to the bedroom and heard an infant's wail . . . What a screamer! he thought. He laughed with joy when he saw Nana, pale and tired but proudly holding the infant.

"She is beautiful!" Octavio said, not remembering that he had wanted a male for his first-born.

"Oh, Octavio!" Nana cried softly and disappointment vibrated in her voice.

Octavio shook his head no. He could not speak. Tears welled in his eyes. He sat beside Nana and held her and his daughter. He did not speak while Nana cried in happiness but also frustration at not presenting him a man-child. He knew why she cried and felt she was funny for that, but if he dared laugh he would let out a wail for the wonder of it all. Tati had observed quietly for some time. How she envied Nana.

"I'll bring you some hot tea with honey," Tati said, waiting for a response.

Octavio and Nana nodded yes. As she left the room Tati glanced once more at the beautiful couple and their daughter Micaela. She entered the kitchen where her husband Ignacio had arrived. Milagros had started some tea, Damian ate dinner, and Maximiliano, Jose, Rogaciana and Felicitas had gathered in the exciting warm heart of that hogar.

Chapter 12

December of 1927 promised to be a cold and dry Christmas season. The temperature dropped to below freezing several times during the first week of the month. The dry cold weather created hope that perhaps it would snow in Los Angeles. The possibility of snow, the excitement of it all, was sufficient to tolerate the real state of economic affairs that dominated not only Southern California but the entire country. Misery and want were beginning to walk throughout the country. The poor were becoming poorer; the rich, richer. Nonetheless, the United States population was enjoying the highest standard of living ever attained anywhere.

Walter's Mexicans lived well compared to other poor in the country, and compared to their own kind in Mexico they lived like the affluent. The Mexicans of Simons worked to their utmost capacity for Walter. However, they were never trained to slow down. Their diligent and effective work was so productive that their capacity to make brick had outrun the capacity to consume it. The brickyard slowed but did not lay off any workers. Everyone still had work and lived in relative comfort, although some workers were better off financially than others who did not share in the general prosperity of the company. These economic levels were brought about by the maldistribution of profits. Walter's profits and dividends had risen much faster than the wages he paid his workers. The time of great gains was becoming the age of disillusion and despair for the general population living outside of Simons. People became desperate with the fear of losing whatever they had saved. They feared the possibility that there might be no tomorrow.

With the advent of the Christmas season, strange and horrible deeds began to occur. Young people who looked expectantly toward the future were the most affected by this spirit of doubt. The weather, by changing radically to an uncommon warm, enhanced this feeling of uncertainty. And in that mid-December heat there appeared in Simons a woman who looked about fifty-five-years old but was in fact only thirty-five.

As if coming out of a slit in the canvas of reality, the woman walked down Vail Street. She wore a black hat with white inverted triangles, a black velvet dress, black stockings and shoes and a long black fur coat. With her right hand she clutched a small black handbag against her breast. With her left hand she held the black leather handle of a bright silver leash attached to a golden collar around the neck of her seventeen-year-old son,

William Edward Hickman. The young man was impeccably dressed in a black suit, white silk shirt and black tie, hardly the attire of a distraught poor boy. As the boy walked along, he placed his hand in front of his face when people stared. He hid his face as if he were hiding the thousands of freckles that gave his countenance an angelic sigh. Innocence had been carved on his face. But he walked afraid of the look of other people.

Mother and son moved in the direction of the house of doña Marcelina Trujillo Benidorm who waited at the entrance. Hickman's mother had earlier asked doña Marcelina if she would cure her son of the horrible visions he observed at night. Insanity was a unifying blood vessel that ran in William Edward Hickman's family. His grandmother was known to be insane, and two uncles manifested an irrational religious calling to heal the well and destroy the sick. A male and female cousin were imbeciles who toured with a foreign circus. His mother, in her opinion, was seriously but gloriously disturbed throughout her life. She, like a black widow spider, had been accused of literally devouring Hickman's father by killing, mincing and eating him as meat patties throughout the year that she nursed Hickman. Charged with murder, and while never convicted of the crime, she was institutionalized in an asylum for one year of observation until declared perfectly sane by the psychiatrist. She then returned home to raise Hickman.

Mrs. Hickman brought the boy to doña Marcelina to erase an image that the teenage boy had described repeatedly to school officials. He had visions that his mother, thinking he was asleep, regularly stood over him at night with a butcher knife in her hand contemplating and praying for God's instruction for either her death or his. In the morning she would lick the boy's face to place spots of Christ which, according to her, had been pricked on her tongue throughout the night by God. It was not uncommon for the boy to suffer epileptic attacks on his way to school. Children and adults would gather round him and watch until the seizure subsided. If he suffered the attack at home, his mother would remove his clothes and lick the boy's body until he fell asleep exhausted from struggle.

Doña Marcelina spent the morning analyzing the boy. She rested to regain her energy, for the child's condition proved to be multiple and severe. She dedicated the afternoon to experimenting with various resolutions but none was successful. When the sun began to set, she turned to Hickman's mother and declared that the boy had won, that she, doña Marcelina Trujillo Benidorm, could do no more, that her energies had seen the boy's destiny and it was irreversible.

"He is one of the chosen. I can only pray for you," doña Marcelina said to the mother and son as they prepared to leave.

"He has been chosen to do God's work," Hickman's mother laughed as she proudly helped her son with his coat and locked the gold collar round his neck. Both mother and son knew that it was impossible to cure their destiny. She was the mother of a Judas and he would carry out his betrayal terrifyingly well.

Doña Marcelina walked the Hickmans to the edge of her property and pointed to Telegraph Road in the direction of Los Angeles and hoped that there Hickman and his mother would find in the vale of reality a rip to step through. Doña Marcelina watched them disappear. That evening the great curandera wept for the sure victims of these miserable people, victims whom, although she could see, she could not warn.

On a warm Thursday, the fifteenth of December, Octavio returned from work early and told Nana to get the baby ready for an excursion to Los Angeles. Nana prepared a lunch, diapered Micaela and wrapped her in light blankets. She placed the lunch and extra diapers and blankets in the back seat of the 1923 brilliant blue, four-door Rekenbaker sedan that Maximiliano and Octavio had recently purchased. Maximiliano arrived with Ignacio and Tati, who carried a lunch basket. Tati immediately went to the baby.

"How is my precious baby, comadre?" Tati held Micaela.

Nana noticed how Tati had addressed her—comadre—Tati's way of indicating that she wanted to baptize the baby. Nana had not considered anyone but Tati who had accompanied her throughout the ordeal of labor for the honor of being a godparent. Nana went to Tati and put her arm around her.

"Secure in your arms, comadre," Nana smiled.

"Well, what are we waiting for?" Tati asked satisfied. She took Micaela out to the car where the men waited. Nana went for her purse and joined them.

"And Octavio?" Ignacio asked.

"Here he comes. He was in the bathroom," Maximiliano answered jokingly but factually, for from where they waited he could see the outhouse.

"Well, how much did you confess to the spiders, Octavio?" Ignacio drew laughter from the family. Octavio opened the door and handed the keys to Maximiliano.

Maximiliano pulled away from the fence and drove slowly toward the general store. As the car passed Guadalupe Sandoval's house they saw Milagros sitting in the garden under the giant alcanfor at the side of the house chatting with her brother and his wife. Maximiliano stopped the car.

"Mama, we're going to Los Angeles to see the Christmas lights," he called out and waved goodbye.

Milagros nodded her approval and made the sign of the cross in her goodbye wave.

By the time they broke through the Los Angeles city limits, Nana and Tati had indirectly received the evening's agenda. At first, all Nana knew was that they were going to Los Angeles. Then she heard that they were to see the city Christmas lights and finally eat at the plaza where there was to be a performance of Christmas carolers. It would have been nice if Octavio had told her a day before of the plans. She remembered Tati's calling her comadre. Had the godparents of her child been decided without her opinion? Tati still held Micaela in her arms. Nana sensed how much Tati desired a child of her own. With that thought Nana's anger subsided. Nonetheless, she felt strongly that Octavio should consult with her about whatever plans he wanted to make concerning their family. Octavio and Ignacio conversed all the while; seldom did they address Nana or Tati. Maximiliano drove carefully, fascinated by the rapid growth of the city of Los Angeles.

"Los Angeles has more than a million people now," Maximiliano thought out loud.

"Yes, a million gringos and perhaps a million Mexicans that the gringos don't want to see," Ignacio rejoindered.

"They think they all work in Simons," Octavio chuckled.

"Did you know they fired five men today?" Maximiliano stated.

"The most recent arrivals and with family. It's because there is less demand. They are reducing production everywhere," Octavio said.

"That's why Federico is leaving. He thinks work is more secure at the other Simons brother's plant," Maximiliano said.

"It's the same as here. Federico is going because Celia says there are better schools, a house to buy, also because Celia has relatives over there. There is no job security at any brickyard," Ignacio responded, somewhat bothered by what Maximiliano said.

Nana thought of having her own house.

"That's why we need a workers' union to protect the workers and their jobs," Octavio said in a strong tone.

"If you start on about a union they will fire you," Maximiliano replied.

"Old man Simons is against any kind of union. He has said that unions are only good for creating dissatisfaction among the workers."

Maximiliano started to lower the sun visor. Suddenly he stopped. He looked out the window toward the Montebello hills, past them through the time and space housed in his mind, and from a corner of his left eye from infinite miles away he saw traveling across the vast whiteness a brown insect reaching out to him. Perfectly calm and pale Maximiliano contemplated the ever-laboring insect. Unafraid of the enormous beast that approached, he waited without breathing.

"The old man thinks that by treating us like pet children he blinds us from what is happening outside of Simons," Octavio said, interrupting his brother's vision. "No, Maximiliano, times are bad. Lots of people are out of work. What or who is going to stop Simons if he decides to throw us all out to the street and then gives our jobs to the gringos?" Octavio stated with anger.

"Look at the little angels, the candles, Santa Claus, such pretty decorations." Maximiliano braked for a red light and then drove through the main downtown streets. Finally he stopped before the railroad station and turned into the parking lot.

"From here the plaza is not far," he said and stepped out of the car.

As the group neared the plaza, individuals, couples, families—all Mexican, only a few Anglos—paraded before Nana's eyes. These people were moving in every direction around Octavio and her. They seemed confident, far from what she felt about her married life at the moment. Married life was a necklace of discoveries which Nana experienced every day, both alone and at times with Octavio. Often Octavio returned home only to change clothes, eat and go off to work. Survival was the rule of every day and night.

Nana could feel Octavio as he walked next to her. She looked for the best place to sit down for their picnic dinner. An open space was on the right of the stage that had been built by the city Recreation Department for the entertainment that would step forth shortly to sing about Christmas cheer. Maximiliano spread a blanket on the dirt. They all sat down and Nana and Tati passed out food. Octavio and Ignacio drank wine. Nana and Tati refused to drink and sat with Micaela, who had fallen asleep at the moment that the Department of Parks and Recreation's three hundred volunteer carolers began to march in and vibrate the Los Angeles basin with the lyrics of "Hark the Herald Angels Sing." Nana, amazed at the size of the choir, took in the beauty of the voices which seemed to be singing to her. She held her baby next to her heart, rocked gently, and hummed the Christmas songs which she heard for the first time in her life.

The melodies danced in Nana's mind throughout the intermission when a woman whom Octavio, Nana, Ignacio, Tati and Maximiliano should have known came up on the stage. A priest spoke of her as a friend of the community.

"And why not say it? A friend to the Mexican community of Los Angeles. I give you Edit Marin Chalk Simons, the organizer of this year's Christmas Carol concert," the priest said.

"That's old man Simons' wife?" Ignacio asked.

"Yes, she is, and here comes Mr. Simons." Octavio pointed to a large man walking up to the stage to stand next to Edit. They did not speak to the public, only bowed, shook hands with some of the carolers and exited into the warm December night.

Earlier in the afternoon, about two o'clock, a young man appeared at the Mount Vernon Junior High School and spoke with the registrar. He gave a false name and identified himself as an employee of Mr. Perry Parker, the manager of a local bank. The innocent freckle-faced young man with black curly hair communicated that Parker had suffered a serious automobile accident and that the family had authorized him to pick up the Parkers' twelve-year-old daughter, Marion. The young man sat up properly and waited. His calmness caused the school personnel to act immediately, for the boy's words and tone announced that Parker was in imminent danger, that death lurked close by his hospital bed. Without question, the believing school officials released the child.

Parker came out of a staff meeting and was confronted by a Western Union messenger who handed over a telegram. He thought of his parents or in-laws who were well advanced in age. The first death of his young family and during Christmas, he thought as he entered his office to open the envelope privately. When the messenger had left, the office staff was alerted to the possibility of an untimely death in the manager's life. The staff became worried when after half an hour Parker did not come out of his office. His secretary entered and found him crying like a child. A few minutes later, the office was taken over by Los Angeles police. The bank closed when the police arrived, and shortly after, the news of the kidnapping began to leak out to the public.

Parker still held the telegram when his wife Jasper burst into the office. The telegram informed the Parkers that their daughter was unharmed and that they should do nothing until they received a special delivery letter.

Jasper let the telegram fall to the floor. She sat and cried openly for a few moments and then resolved to get her daughter back. She stood up and took her stunned husband by the hand.

"Perry, we must go home," she declared positively, for up until that minute everyone in the room had been gloomy and negative. Jasper told the investigating officer that they would wait for the letter and the return of their child at their home where Marion would want to be returned.

At ten o'clock that night, as police began to question neighbors and family acquaintances, the Parkers stood just outside their front door. They felt that their house had been raped and that the heart of their family had been ripped out by some unknown power that probably observed their agony.

On the morning of the following day, the Parkers heard a knock at the open door. There stood a postman who wanted to dispense with the formalities of having one of the Parkers sign for the letter, but who was instructed to proceed with business as usual. Mr. Parker scribbled his initials while Jasper took the larger than usual envelope and went to the living room where the police investigators waited. She gave the envelope to her husband. He opened it and extracted three different-sized papers. The largest of the three was a set of instructions from the kidnapper.

Use good judgment, don't panic and keep this a private matter. Get $1,500 in twenty-dollar bills. Instructions for the exchange of your daughter for the money will follow.

If you want aid against me ask God, not man. Jasper took the other papers. One was a note from Marion.

Daddy, Mommy, I'm o.k., please help me. Marion.

The third paper contained another statement from William Edward Hickman, the kidnapper.

Remember, don't get excited but do get the money. I'm watching you. The Fox is very sly, you know.

Immediately Parker left alone for the bank. He discussed the situation with the bank owner who was briefed of the kidnapping by police and was requested to cooperate. The bank owner did not hesitate to give Parker one thousand five hundred dollars. The banker and a police detective who had been with him all morning put the money in a leather bag and sadly watched Parker walk out to the street and drive off through the modern streets of Los Angeles. At seven forty-five that evening Hickman called Parker and in contorted monstrous tones told him to wait closely by the telephone for more information. He repeated that the rich man should try no tricks. Mr. Parker put the phone down and waited.

Outside, within a one-mile radius from the Parker home, the police were watching all the telephone booths. The police traced the call to find that Hickman had placed the call from a booth outside the area. At eight forty-five the chimes on the grandfather clock marked the third quarter hour and blended with the ring of the telephone. Again, in terrible sounds, the kidnapper told Parker to drive to the corner of Tenth Street and Gramercy Place, park and wait. He did not mention the money but Parker took it with him.

Hickman wanted to make sure that his demand for secrecy was being kept by his victims. He realized that the police had been notified but he wanted to deal with Parker alone and not be interfered by meddling police officers. Hickman had made his last call from outside the Wilshire Police Station, and after he hung up the phone he observed the police run to their automobiles to get to the appointed rendezvous. He laughed aloud and restrained himself as he started his car. With a smile like a porcelain doll he steered his car into the long line of police cars. He giggled and patted Marion on her left knee.

As he drove to his apartment on Bellevue Avenue, Hickman became increasingly angry at Parker for not keeping the abduction of Marion a private family affair. He sat and contemplated what to do about Parker's unfaithfulness. Finally he feverishly composed a furious note which had to arrive in the morning, he thought, as he sealed the envelope. For Parker to receive the note by the next day it had to be mailed by two o'clock in the morning.

Marion was now beginning to get tired of the game. At first she had considered her kidnapping a funny trick but now she wanted to go home to her mother and father. She had even told Hickman that she had dreamed she had been separated from her parents by a strange power. Marion's dream buttressed Hickman's belief that he had been chosen to be a Judas, that all the sins of the world would fall on him. He was convinced that he must not give Marion up, that she must accompany him until Parker turned over the one-thousand-five-hundred-piece golden fleece.

Hickman saw Marion becoming more restless and uncontrollable. He could no longer risk traveling through the streets of Los Angeles with her in the car. He decided that he would decorate her and leave her in the apartment. He cut up a white sheet into strips which he used as ribbon to bind the terrified girl. He told her not to yell because if she did the ribbons would get tighter. He then dragged the child under the bed and tied her bound legs, feet, arms and hands to the four legs of the bed. He warned her not to cry out for it would disturb the neighbors and above all would cause the ribbons to shrink. Marion could only nod yes. She could not speak from the pain and fear of what might happen next. Hickman smiled, looked down and imagined what was under his bed, giggled strangely, quietly shut the door behind him and ran out to mail the letter.

Muffled cries and thuds crawled and climbed through the area bordering Hickman's door. He listened and was angered at her lack of understanding and cooperation. He opened the door slowly, hearing the sounds from Marion's efforts to kick the floor in a desperate attempt to attract someone's attention. He lowered himself to the floor and said hello.

Marion, panic-stricken, now struggled violently to free herself. Her body, energized by fear, contorted itself in impossible positions. She banged her feet, her buttocks, and back against the floor. Near exhaustion but never giving up, she began to slam her forehead against the iron crossbars of the bed frame. She stared with eyes ablaze with fear at him, the unimaginable beast that tortured her and those she loved. Now Marion's thoughts were riveted on her mother and father. Why didn't they come to help her?

Hickman shook a behave-yourself finger at Marion. He sat up and studied the room. A strange smell began to invade it. His nose sniffed and explored the air. From the doors, windows, and cracks in the walls seeped a blue fog which seemed to fill the air. Out of this vapor appeared a personage of biblical bearing, a person with eyes that compelled obedience. A being who was dressed in a white suit, shirt and shoes, immaculately clean, stood before Hickman and spoke for his ears only.

"Strangle her," the figure said calmly and smiled.

Hickman felt blessed, chosen and privileged to be commanded by this beautiful power that he thought existed for him alone. A blue fog had filtered into where his brain once was nourished by blood. Now a blue fluid circulated rapidly through the arteries, veins and capillaries. A chemical unknown to his physical makeup thickened in the body of the sweet-faced American boy who once wore a gold collar with a silver chain held by his mother. He held a long red towel, threw it over his neck and went down to untie the horrified Marion. Her body was limp from struggling, her forehead battered blue and bloody. He dragged her out from under the bed. As the blue fog swirled around them both, a white human shadow still glided in Hickman's pupils, urging him to fulfill the Judas deed that he knew for a fact would take him to paradise.

The child rested for a while, preparing herself to fight again for her freedom and by now aware that the battle would be for her life. She felt her tormentor's hand glide over her forehead, wiping blood onto her hair. She saw him reach for the red towel hung around his neck. He lifted her head onto his knee and slipped the towel around her fragile neck. She felt the damp cloth being crossed over her throat. She screamed through the gag and fought with all the energy and force that she could possibly surge through her twisting body. The towel pulled taut as the all-American boy separated his hands slowly. He sat on his calves with Marion's head slightly lodged against his knees. As he looked down at her mask of ebbing life, he saw her eyes search his and he deviated his face. His hands kept pulling apart the ends of the towel until the convolutions and throbs ceased in Marion's body. His arms and hands fell to his side like massive weights. He fixed his vision on the white presence that seemed to be moving away. As it faded, Hickman closed his eyes and slumped over Marion's corpse and slept peacefully.

Hours later he stretched with the feeling of life rested by deep sleep. He cleared his head, rubbed his eyes and saw Marion dead by his side. The extreme pallor of her murder wailed hatred at him. Outside, the modern world began to wake up. Hickman pushed back her beautiful dark curly hair. She died and now I'll never collect the money, he thought as he rushed about reasoning an alternative plot. Finally he pulled himself together and settled on a resolution to his dilemma. He placed Marion's body on the bed and contemplated her nacre beauty, then rushed out to a drugstore and purchased cosmetics.

Returning to his apartment he waved to his neighbors and went happily to his room. When he entered, his hands went for the body of Marion Parker. He stripped her and carried her to the bathroom, laid her down on the floor, and began to dissect the corpse. In her quietness and stillness Marion was beautiful, angel-like, he thought. He tenderly lowered her remains into the bathtub. His hands caressed and lovingly slit her throat and let the blood drain. The experience of working in a chicken slaughterhouse gave what he considered to be adequate knowledge of human anatomy to dismember a human. Marion's rigid arms resisted being cut at the elbows to remove the forearms. She twisted and turned when he meticulously severed the torso at the waist and carefully disemboweled it. He let the water run and cleaned the parts, torso and face of the silent, obedient Marion.

Hickman neared the makeup that he had bought and held the head with his right hand while he painted over the mask of death a ghoulish approximation of a happy Marion. Suddenly he was stunned by the realization that his created beauty was asleep. Her closed eyes must open again to gaze on the living. He searched the rooms of his apartment until finally the answer came from a picture frame on the wall. He took the thin, shiny wire and used it as a silver thread to sew open the painted eyes.

He then spread thick layers of newspaper beside the bathtub. With his bare hands he placed the entrails of the butchered Marion in the middle of the newspaper and wrapped the first bundle. The offal was enough to create three thick, carefully formed newspaper parcels. He drove to Elysian Park and threw the packages into an arroyo. He drove around Los Angeles with Marion's remains at his side. He had dressed her torso and placed it in the front seat, propped on economics books. Her legs, forearms, and hands lay at his right.

At about seven-thirty on Saturday, December 17, when night already had overtaken the day in Los Angeles, Hickman went to a telephone booth and called the terrified Mr. Parker.

"I am the Fox. Come immediately to 493 South Manhattan Place. Make sure you come alone with the money," he demanded.

Parker, against the advice of the police, insisted on going alone to meet with the beast who possessed his daughter. He slowly searched for the correct numbers and upon reading them over the house entrance felt a cutting of hope go through his heart. He parked the car, turned off the headlights and strained to explore the space in which he waited with heart pounding and mind agonizing, wishing, pleading and promising to give up everything he had accummulated for the return of his daughter. All the while Hickman, with the painted, smiling Marion at his right, watched the desperate father.

As soon as Hickman was satisfied that Parker had come alone, he drove up alongside Parker's car and surprised him. Parker had been thinking of the wonderful trips he and Jasper would take with Marion when he realized what was happening. In the diminished illumination thrown down by the street lamps, Parker squinted at the figure that sat in the front seat of the devil's car. Marion was there; that was her dress, but her face was shadowed by an invisible atmosphere, a nimbus of blue vapor.

Hickman accelerated the motor. Parker held up his hands imploringly. He threw the package of one-thousand-five-hundred dollar bills through the lowered window of the beast's car. Abruptly, Hickman sped off heading into the darkness. At that instant a clown's grotesque mask appeared on Marion's face. Parker got out of his car and ran after the hateful kidnapper. Ten strides and he stopped. He understood that he must return to his car and save Marion. He fumbled hurriedly to start the engine when he saw that down the street Hickman stopped and opened the door and repulsed out into the world Marion's members, torso and decorated face. Marion was scattered horribly on the grass between the street and the sidewalk. Over the curb her grinning head hung from her torso. Parker ran hysterically forward and found his daughter. He began to cry, and in Los Angeles an eternal and terrible fear began.

Don Vicente Limon read the newspaper as he moved ever so slowly away from Mount Carmel Catholic Church where he had attended the eight o'clock morning Mass. Father Rafael de Fives had prayed for the soul of a child who had suffered a terrible fate unimaginable, until this morning, to the people of Southern California. In Simons the priest's words of fire and damnation for the murderer of Marion Parker were repeated by the workers as they greeted Father de Fives after Mass. Parents held their small children and told the others not to wander off. Their daughters were held by the hand and were not allowed to leave their sight.

"That monster deserves to be hanged immediately," a mother said to her husband.

Anger and fear were communicated in looks, gestures and words. At the general store a crowd gathered around don Vicente. Many bought *La Opinión* and several had asked don Vicente to read aloud the story of William Edward Hickman and Marion Parker. As he read the details of the kidnapping and the condition of the child's body, prayers were said and groans of disgust and soft cries of horror and fear emerged from the crowd.

"What should we do?" a woman cried out.

"We will have to take our children out of school," a mother rejoined.

"Well, I'm going to Los Angeles to get that animal. How many are going with me?" a young man shouted and was answered by several others.

"We must watch our children always and close the doors and windows day and night," an old man suggested and all agreed.

Don Vicente folded the newspaper and listened.

"Is there anything else, don Vicente?" a man shouted from the back of the crowd.

"Nothing," don Vicente said softly.

Silence fell on the people gathered there. Perhaps for an instant their minds brought Marion back to life. There she stood with their young daughters. The people of Simons, concerned with the possibility that such a friend like William Edward Hickman could enter their town, called to Jacobo Ramos who was tending the general store and requested to speak with Gonzalo Pedroza.

"Calm down. Don Gonzalo is aware of what has happened. I assure you that there is no lack of security here. Only out there in that world." Jacobo turned and entered his commercial domain.

Not convinced, the workers went home watching their children. Most of the Simons Mexicans felt directly tainted, affected, touched by the patron's world. Hickman came from the mass society outside of Simons, a society which rejected them, and now a beast created among the gringos was infiltrating and interacting psychologically with them. In the back of their minds lurked the possibility that the gringo beast could enter their world, or that Walter Simons would allow the police to go into Simons Town and invade their homes in search of the beast. The rumors multiplied.

Now, in front of Octavio Revueltas's home, don Vicente stopped to say hello to Octavio and Federico who chatted with Ignacio. Federico read from the *Los Angeles Times* whose headline roared "This Fiend Must Not Escape!" The entire force of two thousand Los Angeles police were mobilized to search for Hickman. The department requested the cooperation of Los Angeles' leading citizens and the surrounding police agencies. An unpredictable, volatile hysteria settled over the city. People gathered and circulated aimlessly through the streets, waiting for more news about the progress of the search. Fearful citizens donated funds for a reward for information leading to the arrest of the killer. By Sunday morning authorities had amassed twenty-five thousand dollars to capture the Devil.

"Like I've said, don Vicente, it will become dangerous for Mexicans. The newspapers are saying that the Fox has black curly hair. They will stop all of us who have hair like that. You'll see how the police will harass the Mexicans," Federico said assuredly.

"And now that they have a reward they will stop us even more," Ignacio added.

"But do you think they will come into Simons? The gringos don't enter here nor will criminals like the Fox," Octavio said and put his arm on his brother Federico. "You will have to be more careful because you are moving closer to them."

"When do you move, Federico?" don Vicente Limon inquired.

"After the New Year," Federico answered and opened the gate for his mother Milagros who had returned from Mass with Nana and the baby Micaela.

Morning greetings were exchanged. The two women moved toward the house. Nana turned to Federico.

"Celia told me that you will leave the house after the New Year. Has anyone asked for it?" Nana asked, adjusted Micaela's blanket and looked to Octavio while Federico responded.

"No one that I know about, Nana." Federico waved and left for home.

Ignacio and don Vicente went off toward the bachelors' quarters where they would drop in to see how the card games were progressing. Octavio had only an hour ago returned from there. He reached into his right pocket and felt the thick roll of twenty, fifty and hundred dollar bills.

"Octavio, come and have breakfast," Nana called.

Octavio reached to adjust his cap and went to open the door for his wife. While he ate breakfast, comfortable and safe within the walls of his father and mother's home, there roamed beyond the parameters of Simons a murderer, William Edward Hickman, who, with his obscene acts, had wrenched the lid off Pandora's box and released a modern image of fear that hungered, fed and grew.

The last posada culminated at Mount Carmel where the townspeople gathered to sing the traditional hymn of asking for shelter. A boy costumed as Joseph and a girl dressed as Mary, on a donkey, went to several houses before they were invited to stay in a stable which waited for them at Mount Carmel Church. For nine nights they had sought a place to stay and found none, but on the twenty-fourth of December the couple found shelter at an inn. On the last evening of the ceremonies most of Simons participated, carrying candles which lit the way. When the priest declared that the holy couple had found refuge, the celebration began in earnest. To the disappointment of the priests on that particular Christmas Eve, Simons workers and their families returned home early. The visions of William Edward Hickman waiting in the night behind a bush encouraged parents to rejoice the birth of Christ in the safety of their homes.

The Revueltas family, talking, arguing, eating, and laughing gathered closely together around Damian and Milagros to celebrate Christmas and the birth of their first-born child, special even though Octavio and Nana had borne a daughter. Enjoying his family in the small company house, Octavio felt the future when he saw Nana and Micaela. For next Christmas Nana envisioned her own house. The desire for her own dwelling stirred to greater emotion when Federico and Celia discussed their imminent move to Gardena.

On New Year's an identical scene could have been photographed. Mila-gros made dozens of tamales, and a large pot of menudo simmered late in the night waiting for the bachelors of the family, Maximiliano and Jose, to return from the fiestas they had attended. Federico and Celia announced that they soon would be blessed with a child. For an instant Milagros sat motionless, resting among their movement, energy and growth which she felt tugging at her heart. She smiled and went to stir the menudo.

Almost two years, a matter of hours, since she had been brought to live with Milagros, Nana thought as she changed the baby. She would have no more living as if she were everybody's maid. She would have a home for her children and freedom from restraint, from always having to consider first the other members of the family, never hurting Milagros. Octavio had not responded to Federico's plans to leave. The likelihood of renting his brother's house, located next door to his parents, seemed never to cross his mind. Why did Octavio ignore her desires, Nana silently asked.

During the week from Christmas to New Year's the friction between Nana and Octavio had mounted. He had not mentioned that Federico would leave on the third of January. He kept this information to himself. Octavio wanted to tell Nana but he kept forgetting. Gambling had kept him away at night for most of the week. Although he won large sums and always placed plenty of money on top of Nana's bureau, she was not happy with his chronic absence from the house at night. If he could give himself the privilege of gambling to all hours of the morning, she would give herself the right to an individual house.

Gunshots rang outside in celebration of the new year as the men of Simons fired their pistols and rifles to the stars as if they attempted to puncture tiny holes in the firmament in search of where last year had gone.

In Pendleton, California, William Edward Hickman, startled by shots, erratically drove a stolen green Hudson past two local cops. The next morning Los Angeles newspapers heralded the apprehension of the Fox. The district attorney and half of the Los Angles Police Department big-shots took the first train north. There they found Hickman housed in a cage in the middle of the local jail, the townspeople circulating around him freely. Under heavy guard Hickman was immediately returned to Los Angeles by train. The mob-minded people that the police expected did not materialize, and strangely, as the trial opened the public's fervor dwindled to mere curiosity, especially because of Hickman's plea of innocent by reason of insanity, which was quite new to the courts. The prevailing attitude was to insure him a fair trial and then hang him. The trial was over in a few days. The jury took less than an hour to reach its verdict. William Edward Hickman was adjudged to have known right from wrong at the time he kidnapped Marion Parker and in the moment he killed her. Hickman was sane. Judge James Trubucco quickly sentenced Hickman to be taken to the death house at San Quentin prison and there hanged by the neck until he was dead.

By the fall Hickman's name had virtually been forgotten. Consequently on the day of his execution the Los Angeles newspapers published articles reviewing the horrible crime committed by the Fox. On that day Hickman sat in his small cell, consoled by a phonograph recording of "In a Monastery Garden." For his last meal he ate ham and eggs, grapefruit, potatoes and a waffle. It was as ordinary as anything in his life had been with the exception of the crime he had committed and his death.

Three men stood with sharp knives poised against separate strands of rope. Only one was connected to the trap door at Hickman's feet. The knives were drawn, and the ropes cut.

As the trap door opened, Hickman appeared to slump forward rather than fall. His body hit one of the uprights and had to be guided by guards. For ten long minutes, as the body twisted in midair, the sounds of agonizing death filled the room. When silence finally came, a doctor stepped forward and after listening with a stethoscope, pronounced William Edward Hickman dead. But his neck was not broken. He, like Marion Parker, strangled to death.

Chapter 13

Federico and Celia had been gone for almost two weeks and still their house remained empty. Celia had kept the rooms clean, and the roof and floor were in excellent condition. Nana had checked. She watered three small hydrangea cuttings potted and placed on the tiny front porch as she always had wherever she lived. One step down she talked and served water to each one of the five pruned roses. Nana wanted her plants to bloom on the porch of the house that she stared at in the early January morning chill. She had visited Federico and Celia's house on many occasions and now empty, she found it unbearable. Nana missed its kitchen, its bedrooms, living room and small porch which, ever since Federico had announced their departure, she had decorated and redecorated. The pail stood empty now. She started to the back of the house to the water pump when someone called her name.

"Good morning, Mrs. Revueltas," Jacobo Ramos greeted her as she approached the fence gate. He carried a lunch bag and a folder stuffed with papers. Nana smiled and nodded a good morning.

"The house has been empty for weeks now." Jacobo pointed to Federico's home. "Octavio has not told me if he wants it. The thing is, a new worker and his family have arrived and he is interested. . ."

"I want it," Nana interrupted. "Yes, sir. We will move in on Saturday," she said confidently.

"Well, fine. How do you want to pay the rent?" Jacobo inquired. His face revealed a puzzled thought.

"Take the money out of Octavio's pay," Nana ordered.

"Mrs. Revueltas, have you spoken to your husband about this arrangement?" Jacobo expressed his confusion.

"Don't worry. Octavio and I have talked. But I ask one consideration." Nana paused, placed her left hand over her right hand which held the empty bucket and stood straighter than ever before in her married life. "Please don't tell Octavio about our conversation," she implored. "I want to surprise him by moving in by myself."

"Done, Mrs. Revueltas, done." Jacobo moved on to the general store.

Nana filled her bucket with clean, clear water and returned to moisten the earth of the plants that she would soon place on her own front porch. The sooner the better, she thought when she heard Milagros call from the kitchen. Nana did not want to hurt Milagros in any way, for above anyone else she was the kindest and most understanding mother-in-law. She admired Milagros, the great mother umbrella that invisibly and constantly hovered over the house, for her simplicity, strength and love.

There, pouring water over the rose bushes that ran along the front fence, she thought of her father. He would not acknowledge or speak to her. It was as if she had been cloistered from Malaquias who still, after all these years, would not see her or his first grandchild. Stubborn he was, stubborn he and I will be, she thought and noticed the rings of her tears in the little puddles of water around the knotty trunks of the naked rose bushes. Angrily she wiped the tears with part of her dress and went inside to Milagros, who called again. Before she went in, Nana stopped and glanced at the space she had claimed for herself and her family.

The Saturday that Nana took over the house, Octavio left for work later than usual. This slight delay in Nana's plan made her uneasy and irritable. A few minutes after his departure, she went outside to make sure her husband had not stopped to talk with one of the neighbors and unknowingly run into her plan. No, Octavio was well into the roads and mechanical internals of the brickyard, which had grown to be a giant among its kind. Nana returned to the house, went to Rogaciano and Felicitas' room and reminded them that they had promised to help her move. The girls turned and tucked themselves comfortably under the covers, mumbled a yes and went back to sleep. Nana went to her room where she found Milagros gathering boxes that she had collected from the general store. Both women paused to contemplate the baby who slept in her crib.

"Nana, here are the keys Mr. Ramos just gave us. If you need more boxes, just ask. I have a lot more." Milagros smiled and started out of Nana's room.

"Thank you, Mama Milagros," Nana called after her.

"I'm going to get the girls up to help you."

In a few hours she would be living in her own home and would not have to concern herself about trying to satisfy everyone in the household. She and Octavio had not accummulated much. Octavio did not want to move. He was happy living with his parents, so he did not buy much for a future home. Nonetheless, Nana had begun to collect blankets, tablecloths, dishes, pots and pans, kitchen utensils, two chairs, a small lamp table, a bed, bedspreads, linens, three pillows and four lamps. Now she packed carefully and placed the boxes near the door to make Rogaciana and Felicitas' job easier. Nana pulled the linen off the bed and threw it in a corner. She struggled with the mattress to stand it on edge on top of the box spring. Suddenly she felt it going over. She clung on only to topple over to the other side and land on the floor against the wall. She sat there with the mattress partly on her legs. Still sitting down, she checked Micaela, who slept comfortably.

"Mama sent us to help you," Felicitas said, entering the room.

"How long are we going to take?" Rogaciana whined.

"I don't have very much, those boxes, the bed, all that you see here, that is all," Nana explained to the girls who were upset at having to get up so early on Saturday.

"We'll start with the boxes," Felicitas suggested.

"I'll open the door. Put everything in the living room. I want to clean the rooms first." Nana started for the door.

"That is not necessary. Since very early my mother has been there cleaning. Thank God you're only moving next door." Rogaciana was annoyed at all the attention Milagros gave to Nana's move.

Milagros wanted her daughter-in-law to move into a clean house, for she considered this to be Nana's nuptial home and it should be as clean as the pure white linen of her honeymoon bed. Milagros had been cleaning the rooms since early that morning. She asked Damian to stack firewood just outside the back door which he did with clandestine joy about his oldest son obtaining his own place to hang his cap and coat. Damian continued to stack wood and to clean the garden in the back and front. Neighbors came by and asked about the house, or if Damian was moving. While Damian took time to explain that Octavio was taking the house, other folks joined the conversation. As Milagros directed her daughters as to where Nana wanted the boxes, she engaged in the chit-chat with the group. After a short time Rogaciana and Felicitas simply stopped working and sat next to the gossipers who talked about everything and especially those delicate matters that must be kept among married adult couples.

Nana, who was busy putting paper in the kitchen cabinets, realized that she was by herself. She went to the front door and observed nine people enjoying an impromptu gathering. They had forgotten whatever business they had to attend and enjoyed a break, sharing news that concerned family, work, Simons, Montebello, the world. Rogaciana and Felicitas each sat on the ground next to a box of Micaela's clothes. The two were sorting through the clothes and laughing. Nana put her hand on the door jamb and leaned against it, almost hiding. In the middle of the group that had gathered to chat were two people who seemed to have forgotten the past that had separated them spiritually and physically. Damian, with his arm around Milagros, talked with her and the others. She in turn rocked in his arms, enjoying his conversation. For that instant they seemed to stand together as a happy couple, not dominated or directed by personal events of the past.

As fast as it had gathered, the group broke up and returned to the normal morning activities. The smiles of Milagros and Damian slowly changed, and on their faces their normal expressionless mouths settled again. Milagros turned sharply away from her husband and walked to her house. Damian looked around and realized that his daughters were playing with baby clothes at his feet. Rogaciana and Felicitas immediately threw the clothes into the box, rose with the box in their hands and ran to Nana. Damian stared at the three women standing by the door. He felt a rhythm in his heart which he could not share. He waved to the three women and moved away toward the interior of the brickyard.

As Damian retreated, Nana saw that under his hat there was no head, no neck. At the end of his shirt sleeve there were no hands. While she traced the enchanting figure of cloth, Rogaciana and Felicitas returned home to bring the few pieces of furniture which Nana had collected. Micaela's cry interrupted Nana's mind which struggled to understand the phantom of cloth that masqueraded as her father-in-law. Nana took her baby in her arms and fed her . . . Damian, neither your wife nor your sons nor your daughters know you, she thought.

Nana kept looking out toward the direction in which Damian had left her sight. Milagros appeared carrying a large chair. She put it down and sat in it to rest. Milagros rose holding the chair behind her asked Nana to open the door of the house so that she might find her a permanent place. Milagros the chair found a comfortable niche next to the wood-burning stove in the kitchen. The location was perfect. She found four small indentations in the wooden floor, as if a chair had stood there before. Milagros the chair communicated to Nana that from that chair in that place she would always be with her, and that if Nana ever needed her advice she would only have to sit in the chair, a simple oak straight-back chair which now meant so much to Nana and Milagros. Nana placed her hand on the back of the oak rest and Milagros, transfigured to herself, embraced her daughter-in-law and her woman child. Nana had now become the true center of her family. She embodied synthesis, stability and unity in her words and actions. Through Milagros the chair, she had learned these values, and in the embrace they shared they had silently vowed to act out on each other the concepts of support, exaltation, equilibrium and security. Again the two women embraced.

The results of Nana's labor were in evidence by three that afternoon. However, she was not satisfied and began to make plans as to the pieces of furniture she would buy to make her house into a practical and comfortable home. The baby fed, changed and napping, Nana took a moment to rest and enjoy a cup of tea in silence, alone in her own house. She waited for Octavio to return.

He proudly pronounced his name loud and clear. He had done nothing wrong, never harmed anyone. His conscience was clean. And he was the best card player in Simons.

"Octavio Revueltas," Jacobo Ramos repeated to James Simons who counted out the payroll cash to the workers. Gonzalo Pedroza and William Melone stood guard as they had done for years.

"Octavio Revueltas, thirty-seven, fifty," James declared and placed the money on the table in front of Octavio who did not move.

"Thank you, Octavio. Next, please." James motioned to Octavio to move out. Octavio still did not move.

"This is not complete," Octavio said as he looked at Jacobo and turned to his fellow workers with an expression on his face that asked for patience.

Jacobo now remembered that Octavio's salary was incomplete because of the house Nana had rented. He put his hands up to calm Octavio and the men growing impatient. He explained the situation to James, and with his permission turned with a tinge of a smile, placed his hands on the table, leaned forward and spoke softly to Octavio.

"The two-fifty they took out are for the house your wife has rented," Jacobo said calmly.

"What house?" Octavio, shocked and surprised, raised his voice. "And who authorized it?" he shouted, leaning on the table, nose to nose with Jacobo. Gonzalo pulled at Octavio's left arm.

"Go and discuss it with your wife," Jacobo responded sternly. James reached to feel the snubnosed shotgun waiting under the table. He would not hesitate to blow off Octavio's head.

"Pick up your money and move it, Revueltas." With a rifle, William pushed Octavio out of line.

The tension subsided as Octavio walked away from the payroll table. The men who were closest had observed the altercation. Some saw only the violent manner in which William had used his rifle to shove Octavio out of line. The men had tensed up and no one knew where the battering of a fellow worker would lead. Their eyes followed Octavio, watching to see what he would do. Jacobo Ramos, James Simons, Gonzalo Pedroza and William Melone were sensitive to the unified energy of the workers. They could feel their power and their anger. A dangerous moment had passed and only the men in power had recognized it. The workers had simply lived it.

Octavio walked as fast as he could, almost at a run. No one, nothing could have slowed him down. He pulled the fence gate open and reached for the front door of his father and mother's home. As the door slammed behind him, his mother looked up to acknowledge her oldest son. Octavio went to the room in back of the house where he and Nana had spent wonderful months together, where they had conceived their first-born. The room was empty. It had been devastated, violated without his permission. She had left nothing but three hairpins that lay on the floor where the chest of drawers stood . . . She didn't even talk to me about it. Why didn't she tell me?. . . Octavio entered the kitchen where his father ate. Milagros turned a tortilla over on the stove and waited.

"Where is Nana?" Octavio asked with a slight sense of fear. Only for an instant did the thought of her walking out on him pass through his mind.

"At her house, Octavio." Milagros pronounced the sentence with a secret feeling of triumph and pride for Nana. She pointed next door.

"Where Federico lived!" Damian shouted, bothered by Octavio standing stupefied at what Nana had done. "Go!" he waved and continued eating.

Milagros placed a tortilla at the side of Damian's plate. She looked up to see her oldest son disappear.

Nana had heard Damian's angered voice and knew that he had spoken to Octavio, who walked aggressively to the door. She saw him approach. She noticed how the tiny squares of the screen door blanketed his entire body. The baby was playing quietly in one of the bedrooms while Nana waited, sitting in the kitchen in the chair which Milagros had given her that morning. It did not matter how angry he would become; she was ready and confident. From where she sat she saw the little squares swing away and her husband appear. Octavio rushed into the living room, but as he entered, the lack of furniture and the cleanliness that reigned in that house established by Nana, the woman he loved, diminished his irritation.

"Why did you do this?" Octavio insisted.

"Because you did nothing and I did not want to be forgotten in that little room. You wanted to have me there like a bird in a cage. Whether you like it or not, now we have our house," Nana said calmly.

"Sure, and I almost got into a fight with Jacobo Ramos because he took the rent out of my salary. 'Who authorized this?' I asked him. And he told me to talk to my wife. If it hadn't been for Gonzalo, I would have broken Jacobo's mouth. You must tell me what you are going to do. If you don't, you make me look like a fool and put me in danger." Octavio moved to the stove, closer to Nana.

"If I had asked you for the money to rent this house you would have said no. Jacobo was going to rent it to someone else. I had no other choice, Octavio. I was not about to lose this house," Nana said, sensing that she had won. "Besides, we are going to need more rooms for the new baby." She reached out to touch his hand.

"Nana, we don't have any food here. I'll go right away," Octavio said, conceding to Nana's logic.

"I'll get coffee ready. When you return we will have dinner, thanks to your mother." Nana walked Octavio to the door.

"Make the coffee strong. I'll need it for tonight," he said as he left for the general store.

When Octavio returned with two large bags of groceries, Milagros had dinner warm on the stove and was about to finish a cup of tea with Nana. He placed the bags by the cupboards and sat on one of the two chairs Milagros had brought with a small table.

"Thanks, Mama. I spoke with Jacobo and he explained everything. Tomorrow he will send some furniture," Octavio said and began to eat, feeling comfortable with his mother and Nana and the new house she had acquired.

At six o'clock Milagros took her leave. Octavio had a second cup of strong coffee at six-fifteen. He washed, dressed and sat on the side of the bed. Nana, in a nightgown, played with Micaela and studied Octavio's nervousness. She knew that he would leave shortly to gamble in the rooms provided by Gonzalo. She hated Octavio's leaving her alone, sometimes for days and nights. How she worried about him. But she could never stop him from joyfully fondling those cards that he carried in his coat pocket. Under his left lapel, next to his heart, he did not carry a photograph of his beautiful wife, but a pearl handle thirty-eight. The thought that her husband would ever have to use that weapon frightened Nana more than anything else.

Voices rushed to her as she lay in bed watching him push away after kissing her and his daughter. The blurred image of a notorious gringo gambler dragging his shattered knees through gravel ran in her mind. Above, his pearl handle gun smoked. Nana could not identify the man who held the gun. From out of the dark night someone called "Octavio!" and the fearful image vanished. Octavio faced away from the chest of drawers where he had left money. Nana put on a robe and took the baby from him.

"Be careful." Her voice became a whisper.

Octavio smiled and in moments was out of the house, sitting in the front seat of Guadalupe Sandoval's car. What lingered for a few seconds after Octavio left Nana was the sound of the machine that transported him through the Los Angeles night.

From far above, the gamblers were seen sailing through the waves of life moving upward to Los Angeles' most msterious place. People entered there only to improve on their talents, gifts and powers. The enclave was situated high above Los Angeles in Chavez Ravine. From the Los Angeles basin, Barrio Margarito always glowed with enchantment. Polylustrous, it existed ready to offer its pleasures. Sentinels watched the approaching people, the advancing automobiles. Some would be allowed to pass; others were sent back to their point of origin.

As Guadalupe and Ignacio Sandoval, Maximiliano and Octavio Revueltas slowly drove in, several men forced them to stop. Dressed in Arabic robes, the men pointed down the road. They had not asked questions. They merely peered into the car and seemed to recognize the visitors and allowed them through. The three guards moved away laughing. Now Octavio observed that under the robes they held rifles and other weapons. These men whose language was exotic and unrecognizable were the preamble to the marvelous world of Barrio Margarito.

Although known as a Mexican barrio, an international, interracial and intercultural flavor permeated life in Barrio Margarito. The barrio was a boiling pot of races, each respecting others and living in dignity. There were Mexicans, Blacks, Arabs, Jews, Indians, Asians, native Americans, and gypsies who lived in this magic place above Los Angeles. The people's native dress added to the cosmopolitan atmosphere. And it was correct to assume that people from around the world came to this town— people with special talents, gifts or powers. Barrio Margarito was the Andorra of Southern California, receiving every kind of natural and synthetic product: alcohol, exotic narcotics, gold, silver, jewels, books, male and female prostitutes of all ages as well as the many gods of the cosmos. The architecture was a mixture of Mexican, Oriental and Arabic buildings and numerous different-colored tents. Even at night when Octavio entered, the brilliant, many-hued colors of the town struck his eyes.

Octavio alighted from the car and found himself before a crowd standing in a walkway below a mosque-like building. Women dressed in black or brilliant green, beautifully patterned, multicolored silks passed by him.

Some women, scantily dressed, moved about as naturally as the others. Men, women and children walked by quickly, carrying objects valuable to them. Barrio Margarito was a circus which never failed to amaze, never stopped to rest.

The four men were now out of the car, each fascinated by what he saw in different directions. Music expressing the multicultural ambiance came to them and left. Delicious aromas floated by the four as they waited for Pierre Menard, the man who had invited Octavio to participate in the richest and most enchanting poker game in Los Angeles. Octavio had met Pierre at the Italian Bank of Los Angeles where Octavio had a savings account. It was not until the third invitation, however, that Octavio elected to gamble at Barrio Margarito.

"Hello, Octavio, boys. I'm pleased that all of you could come," Pierre Menard called from the ingress of the mosque.

Octavio acknowledged him and headed into the house; behind him came Guadalupe, Ignacio and Maximiliano. Pierre shook hands and escorted Octavio to a large upstairs room. In the center of the room, a lamp hung over a round table with five chairs, three of which were occupied. Pierre introduced the gentlemen to Octavio's right as Humberto Peñaloza, Federico Robles and Stewart Josia Teaze. The chairs to Octavio's left belonged to Pierre, who sat down, and to Octavio himself.

When the five were seated, a betting audience began to enter the players' chamber. Among the bystanders were Guadalupe and Ignacio who stood, and Maximiliano who sat as close to his brother as the guards permitted. Once commenced, the game could last for days, but Octavio had only until early Monday morning when he would have to stop—win or lose—to go to work. This was understood by the four gentlemen.

Three Japanese men came forth with a new deck of cards. Pierre dealt the first hand. As the hands fell, were played out and dealt again, Octavio learned that his fellow players were the best cardsmen he had ever confronted. He felt that these men were concerned more with the art of gambling than with the winnings. They, like Octavio, shared in the gift. In Barrio Margarito gambling games were considered an art, and those people who had superior rapport and could communicate with the materials of the game were considered to possess a sixth sense. Octavio enjoyed the challenge, and by two o'clock Monday morning when he announced his departure he had won a large amount of money. Federico Robles and Pierre Menard had lost the most to Octavio. Both men encouraged him to return whenever he could.

Maximiliano had waited for his brother while their uncles Guadalupe and Ignacio had gone home and returned for them. The four were again driving through the night. Octavio relaxed and pushed his shoulders against the back seat. Soon he pushed open the gate that led to his wife and family. Nana silently let him in and returned to bed. Octavio placed a roll of twenty, fifty and hundred dollar bills on the chest top, changed clothes and closed his eyes until six. In silence he ate breakfast and left for work.

Chapter 14

In early March of 1929 Nana's potted garden on the front porch suffered from over-population. There was no more room for the pots that she insisted on placing there. The potted flower crisis forced Octavio to expand the area. He extended the porch by running it along the front of the house. When Nana saw the porch being built she experienced an unexplainable physical feeling of happiness. She moved slowly about the new porch, sobbing from the ecstasy her pregnant body generated in seeing a large, clean place for her potted plants. Nine months pregnant, about to give birth at any time to their second child, Nana became hysterical upon viewing the new porch. Octavio hugged her.

"Don't cry. Calm down and rest," he said lovingly and escorted her inside.

Guiding her step by step he suddenly realized her bravery. Nana sat on the new couch she had picked up at Montebello Furniture. He cushioned her back and lifted her legs onto the couch. He sat at her feet on the braided rug. Her sobbing and laughter subsided. Octavio smiled.

"What happened?" Octavio held her hand.

"I can't explain it. I felt that I drowned in a strange happiness and the only way to save myself was to laugh and cry at the same time," Nana said softly and stared out the window.

"You scared me," Octavio said after they both heard birds chirping somewhere in their garden.

"Octavio, I'm fine. Don't worry about me. Your mother is just next door. She is watching me. Now go to work. I'll be fine." Nana kissed his hand.

Octavio changed into his work clothes. He went to the kitchen and poured a cup of coffee.

"Octavio, why do you go in so late?" Nana asked from the couch.

"Gonzalo and William are cutting hours. And it looks like they're going to lay off some men." Octavio sat on the small sofa facing Nana and stirred his coffee.

"What is going on? I see the workers very restless." Nana struggled to sit up.

"That is because we don't know who they will fire. It can be anyone. It doesn't matter how many years you've been a slave. Things are bad everywhere. They ask us to produce less every day," Octavio said soberly.

"And Mr. Simons always on his trips," Nana said. "Why doesn't he do something?" she added angrily.

"What concerns him is profit and if he concludes that it is necessary to fire workers he tells Gonzalo and William and they decide who to fire." Octavio pushed the door and from outside he waved good-bye.

Nana placed her hands on her full womb and breathed deeply, relaxed and looked at her feet . . . What will this all come to? She breathed deeply again.

Octavio stopped and pushed his cap back, wiped his eyes and peered out at the drying racks. Beyond them giant machines murmured. He adjusted his cap forward and walked right at them.

Layers of grey black clouds sliced across the sky heading southeast. The wind raced and molded them in to strange, beautiful formations. Below the clouds, struggling to break away, several kites danced. Three boys maneuvered back and forth and around each other trying to avoid a tangle-up. When they saw Damian and Octavio hurrying by, the boys started to roll up the string, for the sun was now setting and hunger began to tug at their stomachs. The wind came a little sharper and colder now. Octavio stopped to pull up his coat collar. Damian lit a cigarette and offered one.

"No thanks, Papa," Octavio said. "Are you sure it's time?" he asked, worried.

"Yes, Dr. Cushner saw Nana and asked Milagros to send for you." Damian puffed on the fast-burning, sweet-smelling tobacco.

"Thanks, there is nothing we can do then. Just now they fired fifty more men." Octavio showed five fingers.

"I hope we don't get the ax," Damian said.

"Many leave and men arrive daily wanting jobs. Most would work for the food only. Even if they don't get work they make camp near the train tracks. Lots of hobos live there. We are living in bad times. Some of the workers are talking about returning to Mexico, that they will put up a business of some kind. They say that it is a good time now to return because the United States government will pay for the trip," Octavio said and chuckled.

"What they want to do is kick all the Mexicans out of the country and never let them come back again. They have said publicly that the Mexicans are a main cause of the economic problems of the country," Damian replied and stopped.

With the sun below the green of the giant cypress which had grown unmolested for decades, surrounded by cactus and maguey plants at the foot of the barranca on Español Street, Octavio and Damian passed by the dump. The people from Simons found it easy to throw their trash at the foot of the barranca. Often residents of north Montebello would deposit truckloads of garbage, rubble, debris of all kinds. The dump became a dangerous attraction for curious children. Rumor had it that a child had been swallowed up and never seen again. Recently more people, not children, but adults with families scavenged through the bags and boxes hoping to find edible food or something of value to sell.

As Octavio and Damian came closer to the dump they regarded a man moving away rapidly. He carried a brown bag, and when he saw Octavio and Damian he looked towards the dump and started to run in the opposite direction. The man's trajectory was like a breakaway kite twisting, turning, falling. A pleasant smell rose from the heaps of waste. The frames of several wrecked trucks and cars lay silently abandoned in the wasteland.

Damian grabbed Octavio's arm and made him stop. He pointed to one of the trucks. From beneath the wreckage of a truck propped on top of two others a powerful black arm, another arm, a grotesque head, and a torso slowly emerged. Two legs pushed the ape-like phenomenon out of the cavity it had occupied. Moments later there appeared another, and another came soon after. While Octavio and Damian watched astounded and tried to see if these unknowns were human in any way, six more black figures egressed from under the truck's skeletal remains. The unknowns gathered in a circle and seemed to communicate a plan of some sort because they immediately went off in pairs. Two headed in Octavio and Damian's direction. As they neared, the blackness of their bodies shone in the reddish light of the setting sun. From different parts of the bodies hung black fibers of varied lengths and widths which danced in the cool wind. Octavio and Damian braced themselves for what was about to happen, for now father and son stared directly into the eyes of the two beasts who went to a pile of wood scraps and gathered a bundle each.

"Good afternoon," one beast said.

Octavio and Damian, shocked at what they heard, did not respond.

"We are going to build a bonfire. With this wind it will be very cold tonight," the beast added.

Finally Octavio recognized that the material that made up what seemed to be the beast's skin was rubber—black automobile and truck tires cut up into pieces and somehow joined to make shoes, pants, vests, sleeves, gloves, masks and round caps. The two rubber men were half-way to joining their companions, who had already started a fire, when one stopped and turned to Octavio and Damian.

"Come with us, boys!" the rubber man yelled.

Octavio raised his hand and waved good-bye. The light from the fire was stronger now; only a red hue remained in the western sky. Octavio and Damian glanced back at the rubber men who danced like apes around the fire in the center of a garden of waste. Octavio smiled as he walked away from those ingenious people who survived in the dumps of the cities.

Damian entered Octavio's house and found Ignacio Sandoval pouring a straight shot of Scotch. Tati and Milagros cooked at the stove. Maximiliano, Jose, Rogaciana and Felicitas with Micaela on her lap sat at the kitchen table eating and talking excitedly about the new baby. Ignacio lifted his glass and smiled at his brother-in-law. Tati's and Milagros' hands formed tortillas while they acknowledged Damian standing at the threshold of the kitchen. Maximiliano got up and went to the stove and poured a cup of coffee. Jose continued to eat. Outside by the back door in the garden Octavio washed off the red dust from his face, neck and hands and dusted his clothes. The water stopped running and the family could see him standing just on the other side of the screen door.

"Octavio!" Tati exclaimed joyfully and opened the door to urge him inside.

Octavio waited for some indication as to whether Nana had delivered the child.

"You have a son! He has arrived!" Milagros joyfully cried.

"Gracias, Mama. How is Nana?" Octavio asked softly.

"Resting. Go in. I will wait," Tati encouraged.

"Well done, brother!" Maximiliano shouted.

Ignacio walked up to Octavio, hugged and kissed him. "You are a blessed man. Happy Octavio Revueltas," he whispered.

Octavio tenderly pushed Ignacio away and while still holding his arms, nodded agreement that he understood what he felt. Octavio moved to the door behind which Nana and their son waited. Octavio closed the door and looked up to contemplate a powerful woman. Nana, on the edge of the bed, her feet heel-to-heel on the rail of the bed frame, her naked knees and legs gleaming in the dim light of the bedroom, held a newborn child against her breast. She sat up straighter when Octavio came closer and sat next to her.

"How do you feel?" Octavio asked, helpless to find the words to describe his emotion for her and the child.

Nana nodded, sniffled and smiled. She leaned on his chest and he embraced her and then took the baby from her.

"You are tired. Sleep a while. Your son and I will be here at your side. We'll watch over you."

Nana closed her eyes and in a few minutes was asleep. In half an hour Tati came in carrying the sleeping Micaela.

"Put the baby in the crib and give your daughter a kiss because she is going to bed," Tati ordered.

Octavio watched Nana and his first-born son Arturo sleep for a long time into the night.

The rubber men multiplied, the bonfires grew larger and more men and women seeking work or simply escaping from boredom and hopelessness began to set up campsites around Simons. As these desperate people came to the doors of the Simons residents begging for food to feed themselves or their families, the people of Simons realized that suddenly, almost overnight, the world's richest country, the world outside of Simons, had been thrown into a downward spiral of economic destitution and human destruction. As months went by the economic condition of the country plunged. The great confidence in the growth of the economy that Americans felt in the previous decade was replaced by disillusion, despair, unemployment, hunger, idleness, futility and complete worthlessness.

The Mexicans living in the Los Angeles area also suffered from the great Depression. They became the targets of racial violence from the Anglo population who saw the Mexicans as a major cause of the Depression. The Mexicans became the scapegoats. The Mexicans were the problem: they took jobs from American workers, they were parasites on welfare rolls draining the relief funds, they were illegal aliens and should not receive any public service designated for American citizens, and they did not want to learn English.

By October of 1929, businesses began to fold daily and the stock market declined until late in October when the buildings on Wall Street shook and economic security crashed, ruining hundreds of investors, large and small. In the evening the bodies were counted; many died of self-inflicted wounds, others of burst hearts. Thousands wandered through the streets of the cities, psychologically devastated, their minds scrambled, never to recover again. The collapse had occurred and millions of jobs were lost. Banks failed, and familes lost their life savings, their homes and were rendered penniless and homeless.

By the early part of 1930 jobless men, women, children and street families congregated on the outskirts of cities setting up Hoovervilles, colonies of cardboard shacks. These people begged and scavenged for food, clothing and other useful items in the garbage bins and dumps of the cities and recognized their plight as a result of the many Mexicans in the country. The government agreed and started to discuss a policy of repatriation for all Mexicans. Government officials declared that Mexicans would be deported, and city officials distributed leaflets in the barrios of Los Angeles declaring that there would be an all-out campaign to return the Mexicans to where they came from. The *Los Angeles Times* ran articles which created an omnipresent fear in the Mexican community of being arrested at any place and time, day or night, by immigration authorities who would invade the house and drag whole families out, throw them in trucks, transport them to the stockyards, load them on trains and rush them to Mexico.

The Mexicans of Simons struggled through these bad times. Their ingenuity and tenacity to avoid hunger and malnutrition, which were common conditions during these harsh years, became an inspiration for the people who associated with them and for their patron, Walter Robey Simons.

Eventually Walter appeared alone walking on Vail Street toward the general store. He had arrived at five o'clock that morning and surveyed the condition of the brickyard: the machinery, the racks, the housing, the school, the clinic, the library, the mechanics, the garages and trucks, the trains, the bachelors' quarters, the rooms where the prostitutes entertained on payday, the gambling rooms, the church, the water tanks and the men. It had been years since he had overtly toured the brickyard. He would send his orders and decisions through James Simons or William Melone and Gonzalo Pedroza. They would meet with Walter in his home in Los Angeles or in Newport on the Balboa Peninsula. In those years Walter and Edit and their two daughters Helen Reubena and Drusilla Melissa spent the warm summers and damp winters in their Balboa Peninsula brick cottage.

Although Walter had been absent physically from the brickyard, he still controlled every aspect of the business. It was he who decided how much brick to produce, how much to cut back and how many men would get fired. He also decided to let most of the men with families who had lost their jobs stay in Simons housing and continue to buy at the company store. He realized the difficulty that most families would have if he expelled them from Simons. However, his primary objective was to have available a corps of indebted labor to begin full production once the crisis ended.

As he walked through the brickyard he recalled when seventeen machines were operating at full tilt. Now only three were producing at a slow pace, and probably, he concluded, he would have to cut back to one. Inspired by the dedication of his Mexicans and their willingness to work, he was sure that there would be an upswing in the economy. Unlike his brother Joseph, Walter still had hope, and the measures he would have to take now were to save the business from the total disaster that Joseph predicted.

Walter entered the general store and perused the shelves. Jacobo Ramos had cut back on the orders of non-essential items. He stocked only the basic clothing and foods to sell. Walter went to his office where Jacobo, Gonzalo and William waited.

The sound of chirping birds broke the silence that overpowered the space where the men sat. William was at the desk, Gonzalo sat in a chair in front and Jacobo stood by the door holding the general store ledgers. All three men stared out the window, meditating on a better day. Walter observed exhaustion and fear in their faces. Jacobo was nervous and tentative in his movements. He held the list of men that the three would suggest to be fired. William looked out the window at one of his family trucks. Only three were transporting material, and within the yard, not to a construction project. The remainder of the fleet was idle. Gonzalo thought of Pascuala and Amalia.

By the spring of 1931, Gonzalo and Pascuala had engendered seven children, the youngest being Walter, named after Walter Robey Simons. Like most men with families his first concern was feeding his wife and children, but Gonzalo had a double worry in that Amalia also demanded financial attention for herself and her three children whom, in nights of blind passion, Gonzalo had fathered. Supposedly neither Pascuala nor her children ever found out about Gonzalo's other family but as gossip would have it she probably knew of his second house. Gonzalo never acknowledged Amalia publicly as his lover, although she worked in his restaurant right up to the early part of 1931 when it closed.

Amalia lived outside of Simons in a small work camp known as Montebello Gardens. There her children went to school and there Gonzalo had visited her for the past years. He often heard his Amalia's voice crying, asking how they were going to live, how they would buy their food and how she could help him support their family. Pascuala never criticized him but on the contrary offered help. Amalia's requests were screams of anger and threats of exposure. She demanded money to feed and clothe her family. If she did not get her share of attention she threatened to go to Pascuala and reveal the hypocritical secret that everyone in Simons knew about except her lover's legitimate family. Gonzalo's face had grown tired, thinner and uglier. His square face became cubed and his neck thinned and wrinkled. Everywhere he went people would turn and look at this strange phenomenon. He carried in his mind the responsibility of two families and the guilt of one and the shame of the other. Walter knew of Gonzalo's circumstances and he considered him a man about to be broken by the results of his own decisions, consequences that were gnawing away at his physical and psychological being.

Walter felt tired. He took deep breaths and at times could not get the air to the deepest part of his lungs. He exhaled slowly toward the center of the room. As he studied Gonzalo's cubed face, images of his brother Joseph stumbled through his mind. The daylight shone through the window, filling the room with warmth. Outside dogs barked and played. Birds sang and flew from trees to the ground to the fields and back to the trees.

"We'll stop payroll on about one hundred men out there. We'll keep about seventy-five on payroll and we'll run only one machine. The men who are living here can stay." Walter looked at each of the men. "Do you understand?" he asked softly as if he were telling them that he had no other choice if he were to saved the company.

"What do we do about this union talk that has been going around?" William put his elbows on the desk and leaned forward.

"We don't want unions here. We can handle our own problems. Warn them once. For those who insist, tell them to leave. I will not tolerate union talk here." Walter raised his voice.

"I want one machine in operation daily," he continued. "I've wanted to build a house on my piece of property on Poplar Street. Now is the time to build. This Depression will end and I want to be ready to build." He turned to Jacobo. "Is that the list?"

Jacobo handed the folder to the patron.

"No, you three men can handle that. I approve the list." Walter pointed to the names. "Gonzalo, I want you to keep this place under control. I don't want any trouble in this yard." He went to the door and exited.

William, Jacobo and Gonzalo left quietly to execute their charge. They slowly disappeared into the images of Simons Brickyard, into the juggling finances and properties, in between the scenes of the powerful past, the dangerous present and the hopeful future.

Walter knew he could save the company. He was sure that the Depression would not destroy his creation. He would not fold, go bankrupt like so many. He would not give up, commit suicide, give in to despair, nor go mad. Each brick building he drove by renewed his spirits and confidence in the future. Brick would again be the main construction material, and when the economy mended and upsurged he would be ready with the product. He had invented a process to improve building construction by combining reinforced cement material with stone and brick. He had applied for a patent and was sure the United States Patent Office would grant his request. Surrounded by the despair of the Depression, Walter nonetheless felt elated by the possibilities for the future.

Now, before Joseph Simons' house, he remembered the good times there and the battles—some won, some lost—with his brother. The grass was dry in the front yard. The shrubs struggled to push buds from stems, branches, trunk and roots. The garden seemed unattended. It was as if time itself had been abandoned to do what it would do and people so drastically depressed cared nothing for the future. Walter entered the house and recalled how neat it used to be when he lived across the street. Now the house was cluttered and dusty, reflective of a man who had stopped functioning in this world. At fifty-seven years of age, Walter stood waiting in the living room wondering about the condition of his demented brother.

"Are you here, Walter?" Laura asked as she went to the sofa and sat down to look out the window in silence.

Her face had grown old, her hair silver and her body frail. She had dedicated her love and time to caring for her husband. Ever since 1929, when Joseph claimed to have seen millions of brown insects rise from a pit in a field near his home and devour a family of street people, his mind had slipped slowly into itself until his words and actions became inside out, absurd. Simultaneously he lost competence in administering his business, and when the crash came he panicked and liquidated most of his investments, except for the Los Angeles and Santa Monica brickyards which were now on the verge of being shut down and taken over by Mexican workers.

Joseph had lost everything that he had created. His madness was self-destructive. He would not eat human food; he preferred insects. He would not bathe or properly attend to his bowel movements; he lived in his own filth. Doctors from throughout Southern California came to treat him but all failed, and Joseph grew happily weaker in his illness. One day when Walter went to visit his brother, he knew that Joseph had not slept for five nights. When he encouraged his brother to sleep, Joseph answered that he did not understand what sleep meant and if he did before, he had now forgotten the concept. He would die from being wide awake forever.

"Where is he?" Walter now asked.

Laura stared out to the garden. Walter moved to the window which framed an oak tree. A brick planter encircled the trunk, and alongside in a pool of blood lay Joseph with his skull split. Walter ran to his side. Joseph had fallen backwards, breaking his head against the planter. He lay with eyes opened. Wide awake forever. When Walter pushed his brother out of the blood, hundreds of brown insects scattered from underneath Joseph's back. Thousands more scurried away. Walter, infuriated with the beasts, crushed as many as he could under his shoes but the insects kept coming from someplace under his brother's body. Walter screamed at Laura who continued to sit with her silver hair and her ancient face peering at the millions of crawling brown insects that covered her husband's corpse.

Joseph Simons' many friends were surprised to hear that the funeral ceremonies were private. They would have liked to have said good-bye to the pillar of the brick industry, to the man who had brought the brick manufacturers to tremendous power and importance. Hundreds and hundreds of potted chrysanthemums, wrapped bouquets and wreaths began to arrive the day Joseph's death was announced. So many flowers were sent that Laura was forced to pile them until mounds of flowers almost reached the ceiling of the library in which Joseph lay in his simple casket. The pungent perfume floated throughout the Joseph Simons home. Flowers kept coming until finally Laura asked the delivery men to leave the flowers in the front garden. Mountains of multicolors sang Joseph's passing as cars drove by the house to stare at the strange happening.

On the day that Walter and Edit, Helen and Drusilla, and Laura and James Simons transported Joseph's body to the Pasadena gravesite next to his parents, Walter had ordered three Simons Brickyard trucks to move the tons of flowers to the cemetery. As the hearse, two limousines and three trucks loaded with flowers drove from the Simons family home to Joseph's final resting place, people stopped to watch the procession of color and perfume. The overloaded trucks dropped a blanket of flowers on the streets they traveled. The fragrance stopped people everywhere and invited them to come and hold a flower. The peaceful scent entered the buildings and houses bordering Joseph's route to his bed in the earth. People came out of their workplaces, businesses, homes to pick up a flower. They went on for another and another and followed the carpet of colors that led them to Joseph's private ceremony.

Walter realized that there was no way of preventing the people from coming closer. The crowd grew constantly. He ordered the casket to be lowered into the ground and at the same time he asked the drivers to dump the loads of flowers. The casket situated, the trucks deposited the tonnage of bereavement on the side of the gravesite, but the loads overwhelmed the area and buried Joseph Simons. The children in the crowd jumped on the mountains of flowers and the people threw bouquets onto the mounds of aroma and color. Walter observed the multitude and then indicated to James that the family should abandon the site. The funeral director agreed and escorted the Simonses to the limousines. Walter looked back at where his brother lay and saw children and adults jumping into the mound of flowers that covered the casket. As the limousine drove to the gate, the crowd closed the road behind. Even if Walter had wanted to go back to dig up his brother and see his face once more, the crowd had made it impossible.

That evening in the library of his home in Los Angeles, after writing letters to his sisters Lola Ellen, Mary Frances and Emma Lisa who had sent enormous wreaths but for reasons of health and distance did not attend Joseph's funeral, Walter reviewed his brother's documents and ledgers. James had given him all the records pertaining to his father's business. He had studied the material and expressed his willingness to cooperate with his Uncle Walter. After an hour Walter put down the ledger. His eyes focused on the three letters to his sisters who were far away physically and estranged emotionally from him and his family. Time and space were the enemies of brotherhood and sisterhood, he thought. He had seen them slowly die in his mind and heart. Now at this time Walter could not say he loved any of his sisters, nor would he miss them if they died. And he knew he would not go to their funerals, though he would not send an obnoxious huge wreath but a small and simple bouquet. He couldn't even imagine their faces. They had been blurred by absence.

He picked up another ledger and studied it. By three o'clock that morning he finished and decided that he would suggest to James to liquidate all remaining properties and work with him in administering the two largest brickyards: the Santa Monica and the Simons yard. With the patent of his invention, Walter was sure that the Santa Monica yard and especially the Simons yard would again become the most productive in the country and the world.

His no-name invention was a faster method of building stronger and cheaper brick walls. He believed that his invention would solve the problem of expansion and contraction of steel-reinforcing bars used in brick walls. His method provided for a structure erected at a low cost and assembled rapidly and efficiently. The unique way the metal reinforcing bars were connected was the key to the invention. He had invested thousands of dollars in architects, engineers and lawyers to prepare his statement to the patent office. Walter, convinced of the efficiency of his invention, claimed that a structure, no matter how large, made by his method would resist the greatest shock without a complete collapse. The invention included not only the general wall construction method but also specific individual bricks designed especially for the Simons method. Walter declared that his invention was not limited to the specific construction described, and illustrated in the patent petition some of the variations that could be made for the adaptability of any structure desired.

Walter had decided that his Mexicans at the Simons Brickyard were not only going to produce the material for the invention but would also serve as the builders of the projects contracted. In late January of 1933, William, Gonzalo and Jacobo explained to the fifty-five workers present the new deal that Walter had outlined and declared it to be the direction that the brickyard would take. The men listened and glanced at one another as William detailed the brick walls they would produce. Jacobo stepped forward and explained the wages that the workers were to receive. There were no raises, no improvements in anything. During the past three years most of the workers had borrowed from the company store and had a substantial debt. The patron had helped them through depressed times and now he expected his Mexicans to cooperate with him in launching the new direction of the Simons Brickyard.

Octavio, who stood among them, received the news with disdain. Why should they have to work without a raise or improved family benefits. Octavio did not owe the company one cent. He paid his bills without fail. He and his family were financially free of debt. Only fifteen other men found themselves in the same envious position, most of them Revueltas and Sandovals. Not even the square-faced Gonzalo could claim financial independence from Walter Robey Simons. Gonzalo, Jacobo and William owed everything they possessed, accomplished and desired to Walter, and consequently they carried out his bidding.

Octavio, dissatisfied with Walter's offer of work in order to rebuild the economy and the country, recalled what he had heard at a meeting of the Congress of Spanish-speaking People, that the patrons would attempt to pay lower wages because of the Depression or maintain the salary scale implemented before the bad times came. Octavio became annoyed at the suggestion that the Mexican workers, who had been working hard all along, should work harder for no additional compensation to maintain a flame of hope for a better society in the future. He disliked the word hope.

Hope, he believed, was a concept of oppression used by the dominant society to rule the mass of people. Hope represented non-movement, never advancing forward, never bettering the workers' economic state. Hope was a void, a holding zone used to control. Octavio would not be controlled. He rejected hope and searched for a plan of action against Walter.

Octavio disengaged from the group and signaled to his brothers that he was leaving the union meeting. Organizers from the Cannery and Agricultural Workers' Union as well as three men from the newly-formed Confederacion de Sindicatos de Campesinos y Obreros had previously visited the Simons Brickyard. Octavio had attended all the meetings. . . . Who will survive will be Octavio Revueltas, he reassured himself as he walked away.

Jose now walked next to him. After a few minutes Octavio stopped. He knew that Maximiliano followed behind, but he would never catch up to his brothers. Octavio sensed that a negative energy seethed in Maximiliano's body. For six years this burning had fed on Maximiliano's will to live. Most of the time his condition was normal, but at times a heavy weakness took hold of his body and nearly incapacitated him. Recently, after the coming of the new year, the seizures of fatigue multipled in occurrence and intensity. Maximiliano had sought medical help but the doctors concurred, after examining him for tuberculosis, that he was simply overworked or perhaps malnourished. He cut back on his hours at the brickyard, which angered Gonzalo who accused Maximiliano of being un huevon, lazy. Milagros took the doctors' comments about malnutrition as a personal insult as well as an order and a challenge to feed and save her son. She began to make enormous meals and practically force-fed him. However, these efforts did not change Maximiliano's condition. He deteriorated relentlessly and no one knew why or how to stop the process.

"Hurry up, man!" Jose yelled, insensitive to Maximiliano's effort to walk faster, to catch up to his brothers, not to slow them or their lives down.

Octavio needed only to give Jose one stern look to tell him that he was dangerously out of line. Octavio reached for Maximiliano, who took his arm and leaned on his older brother the rest of the way home. Maximiliano became rubber-legged and Octavio struggled with him, encouraging him that home was not far. Jose ran home to tell his mother that Maximiliano had suffered another attack. That afternoon as Maximiliano slept, Octavio discussed his brother's state with Milagros and Damian. Obviously something dreadfully powerful attempted to take over his body. That energy had to be destroyed, equalized and balanced. Milagros decided to take Maximiliano to doña Marcelina Trujillo Benidorm for her analysis.

Early the next morning Octavio awoke with concern for Maximiliano uppermost in his mind. He did not disagree with his mother about taking Maximiliano to see doña Marcelina but he felt that Maximiliano needed a complete physical analysis which would require a stay in the hospital. Maximiliano was in a battle to live. This unexpected turn of events in his brother's life convinced Octavio that better salaries and benefits as well as improvements in working conditions were long in coming. Simons workers had inhaled red dust for decades and no one had ever complained when a worker coughed and spit up his lungs in puddles of blood and globs of red pebbles.

Octavio and Nana walked along Southworth Street toward the giant oak that rose on top of the hill overlooking the arroyo on the back side of Vail School. They stopped and looked toward the dairy. The cows mooed; their huge udders swayed as they headed toward the milking barns. Octavio and Nana laughed at the lumbering cows constantly mooing. She was grateful, happy to have gotten out of the house. Being with children, talking to them all day and cleaning house made for a long day. Their second male child, Javier, seemed to demand too much of her. Javier, born on April 23, 1932, seemed insatiably hungry to Nana. On their stroll they talked about Javier's birth and how perhaps they should have only one more child. Throughout the conversation Nana relived the day of the birth. She recalled how the event had been exactly the same twice before. The same people were present to help, she lay on the same bed, the water boiled in the same white porcelain pot, and the same white towels and linens were used by Tati, who had not yet conceived her first child. But there was something different.

"Maximiliano was very worried. Do you remember, Octavio?" Nana remembered.

Octavio looked out over the Vail School.

"He constantly asked Tati about my condition. 'Has Nana given birth yet?' he would ask. I remember his strong voice just outside the room. But now his voice is very weak. Maximiliano should live, Octavio." Nana clenched her hands and shook them, imploring the firmament.

"He'll recover, he'll recover." Octavio embraced Nana and kissed her neck. "What did doña Marcelina have to say?"

"That day Mother returned very scared. She did not mention the fear she carried within but it was so heavy that it showed in her expression, in her movements, in her voice. I asked her to tell me about Maximiliano's examination. Your mother was tranquil but with an iron stare told me that doña Marcelina discovered millions of black spiders circulating in the oceans of blood in Maximiliano, and that the black spiders are burning him internally. And that Maximiliano will be devoured by the fire of his own life. That's what your mother told me." Nana smiled as she saw her daughter.

From the Vail School kindergarten classroom, children excitedly ran across the playground. Among them ran Micaela. Nana walked down the hill to the arroyo to help her daughter cross the brook. Octavio waited under the giant oak at the top of the hill. As Nana and Micaela carefully crossed the brook and walked up the hill, he thought of how easily people and events are forgotten. Nana had only moments ago described the death of Maximiliano whom they both loved but whose existence was now blanked out by the sudden overwhelming presence of their beautiful first-born. In watching them come nearer to him, Octavio thought about how much he loved his children and how they would get the best that his work could afford.

And Maximiliano would get the best medical treatment possible. There was still a life before his children, but for his brother there was only one choice: to go to Whittier Presbyterian Hospital for a complete physical and series of tests to find out if doña Marcelina's painful road of death was true.

Nana picked up Micaela and handed her to Octavio.

"How did it go today?" Octavio kissed Micaela and put his arm around Nana's neck.

He looked toward Simons Brickyard. Screw old man Simons. We need a union here. Screw this place. We have to change it. He silently cursed the place which he could never leave nor be far away from. He saw himself like the old oak tree under which minutes ago he had stood. The oak struggled to grow, breaking the ground around it with enormous roots. The old oak would never move. It would die there where it grew.

Chapter 15

The stars began to wink in the dark grey blue of the sky. From atop the hills overlooking Los Angeles, from Barrio Margarito, Octavio noticed that the red hue from the setting sun hung on for a long time. He walked down the outside staircase leading from a second-story room where he had just won one thousand dollars from a man who did not know when to quit. Octavio had left the man with empty pockets, pitifully crying. The man cried out that his children would not eat because of Octavio.

Ignacio and Guadalupe Sandoval and Vicente Limon met Octavio at the bottom of the stairs. The three men moved across a large plaza which sloped down to a fountain in the center of Barrio Margarito. They went to a small second-hand shop which sold books, statues, lamps, furniture and paintings. In a room at the back of the shop were hundreds, perhaps thousands of Oriental paintings. Octavio heard someone say Japanese woodblock prints. Ignacio, Guadalupe and Vicente followed Octavio to a large terraced room. A long table took up the center of the upper part of the room, and beyond that windows displayed the evolving night sky and its dancing stars. As Octavio and his group walked up to the table, a man whom he had seen before across poker tables in Barrio Margarito passed him carrying one of the Japanese paintings. They acknowledged each other and moved on. The evening's host, Armando Takahashi Subia, pronounced the man's name Stewart Josia Teaza, a patient gambler and a great admirer of Japanese woodblock art. He was returning to Tokyo where he resided. Armando spoke of the man with great respect as he guided his Simons Brickyard guests to the dinner table.

That evening the four men from Simons listened to Armando explain the need for workers to be organized. He presented the history of the Cannery and Agricultural Workers' Industrial Union as well as the historical process of worker organization. When dinner was being served, a young woman entered the room. The woman looked up to where the men dined. The night sky and the stars showing through the windows created the feeling that she would be dining among the stars and that the stars were not so big and far away as humanity thought. Armando waved her up.

"Caroline Decker. She has been with us ever since we started organizing." Armando introduced the woman without male and female formalities, which he believed were obstacles to social progress. He treated

Caroline Decker with respect and confidence. He explained that her task for the evening was to talk about the organizers that offered to help the men, women and children of Simons.

"Actually, most of the young people in the CAWIU . . ." Caroline paused and observed her listeners' eyes. "I'm sorry. Do you understand English?" she asked and looked to Octavio for an answer for the men who accompanied him.

Ignacio smiled. Guadalupe and Vicente leaned back in their chairs and indicated yes with long vertical movements of the face. They did not want to give the impression of boredom and ordered another beer from the waiter who waited close by for orders.

"Well, good. I'm glad," Caroline continued. "We are a group of people dedicated to our mission to save the exploited workers of this country. We are poorly paid and overworked. If someone were to ask me if we had Communist affiliations, I would have to say yes we do. We are ideological communists, progressive Americans with a social conscience who believe that with the organization of workers we can achieve equality. People will not suffer hunger, will not lack medical help, will not lack decent housing, nor an education, nor a job, nor clothing. Equality means freedom from the lack of basic human necessities which capitalism inherently denies to eighty percent of the people who live under its economic exploitive system." Caroline considered her beautiful, powerful words. She scratched her nose.

"We can help you. We can organize you into a strong successful union that will guarantee equality and freedom from not being able to meet your basic needs." She searched Armando's eyes, perhaps for approval, perhaps for an indication that he was going to speak.

"It won't be easy and it might be dangerous, depending on how the boss reacts to your efforts," Armando added.

"What do you say? Can we help?" Caroline directed her questions to all of them.

Octavio and the rest of the Simons brigade consulted through looks.

"Yes, we need your help," Octavio finally said.

"Good. Begin to talk to the workers at the yard. Tell them to expect us in three weeks. By then the owner will have made his first move to stop you," Caroline finished.

As Armando walked the Simons proles to the door, Caroline waved from the top tier of the room. Octavio wondered about what he had done and what the consequences would be.

By the fountain at the center of Barrio Margarito Plaza, Octavio saw the man from whom he had won one thousand dollars. The man seemed to be in a drunken stupor. Octavio studied him for a while. His light complexion, his suit, tie, and shoes were those of a smart gringo. The man opened his eyes and reached up to Octavio.

"Ignacio, give him the flask," Octavio suggested, smiling. Ignacio pulled out a flask of bourbon from the inside pocket of his coat. The man grabbed the bottle and gulped down the whiskey.

"Drown, you imbecile," Octavio whispered.

The man put down the almost empty pint. Ignacio looked at Octavio in disgust for having to waste a full bottle of good whiskey on a drunkard. Guadalupe and Vicente walked away, laughing at Ignacio's ironic anger. Octavio stared into the wino's eyes.

"Thank you mister, you're my friend! You're my friend!" the man did not stop yelling.

From Barrio Margarito, down toward the ocean, Octavio saw a strange red glow and sparks rising and jumping from the earth. Now he could barely hear the man's words.

Micaela, Arturo and Javier, comfortable in warm, clean clothes, waited for dinner. Nana had decided to have a light meal since, to her anger, Octavio had gone to Los Angeles to gamble or to do something with the union that the workers wanted to start. She felt vulnerable because Octavio persisted in his involvement with these strange people. The Japanese-Mexican and the woman Caroline Decker had visited the brickyard on several occasions. They had talked to the men and had influenced them by the manner in which they spoke about the workers of the world. These gatherings had been kept secret, but now that the workers planned to meet in the company amusement hall, Nana feared that trouble would find her husband and that the Simons foreman would retaliate. Somehow Gonzalo Pedroza had found out about the secret meetings and had reported them to William Melone and Jacobo Ramos. They, in turn, had communicated the union activity to Walter Simons who was vacationing in Europe. William had received a reply indicating that Walter would return in two weeks and that they should find out who the leaders were of the union activities.

Nana stirred the simmering albondiga soup and worried about Octavio. She went to the small front porch and tended to her potted plants. Next door, in the room that Octavio had built for them, lay Maximiliano, weak, resting to accumulate energy to be active in the morning. He usually tired easily but at times he felt strong. Nana felt guilty worrying about her husband and the relationship with her father in comparison to what Maximiliano must be feeling about his health, but she could not control her thoughts.

She loved her parents and on several occasions had seen her mother at Paquita's house. She had forgiven her mother for not being strong enough to defend the rights of her daughters. Nana admitted, however, that she could not find the place where forgiveness for her father was hidden. She needed to forgive Malaquias for his attitude toward her marriage, her elopement, which he had condemned as a disgraceful abandonment of Nana's sisters, brothers, mother and father when they needed her the most to help support the family. It was as if Malaquias would have never allowed Nana to pursue a life of her own.

Bitterly, Nana realized that she could never forget how Malaquias had acted when she went to him at her uncle's house to ask for forgiveness. She compromised the fact that she had done nothing wrong in order to bring peace and unify the de Leon family for her mother's sake. On her knees Nana asked for forgivenenss only to have Malaquias totally ignore his daughter's presence. Never looking the child in the eye, he held his granddaughter Micaela for a moment and quickly handed her back to his sister-in-law. He had humiliated Nana and left her sobbing on the floor. At that instant Nana's respect and love for Malaquias gave birth to a powerful parallel hatred that she sadly carried in her mind as a horrible memory.

Nana cleared her eyes and again looked toward where Maximiliano lay sleeping. She would send him some soup later. She breathed deeply and wondered when Malaquias would move to Norwalk. Octavio had told her that he had talked to one of Nana's younger brothers and that he mentioned July.

In the direction of where her parents lived there suddenly appeared uncommon lights. Staring at the strangely-moving illumination she experienced a chill and felt her hair electrify. A fear overtook her, and at five-thirty she quickly went inside to her children and the safety of her home.

Javier cried, Micaela called, Arturo yelled.

"Ahi voy!" Nana shouted, running to Javier's crib. She picked up the baby, and when she left the bedroom she stood still and saw strange colors dancing on the falling night. As she locked the front door she glanced at the street. No one was out there where stone silence vibrated in space. Birds, cars, people seemed to have ceased functioning.

Nana walked rapidly to the kitchen. She placed Javier in a large basket on the kitchen table where Micaela and Arturo waited. She listened to the deep silence and with a smile reassured the children, reached for the plates and made noise as she set the table. Nana dipped a spoon and tasted the soup. She picked the pot up with her right hand and turned carefully toward the table. Her eyes looked at her children's faces as they were raised above her. She felt herself pushed and stretched onto the floor. A string of blood ran down her chin. Her knees collided with her mouth and separated. Nana, elongated on the floor, searched for the hot pot of soup. At a distance of five feet with not a drop spilled, the pot of hot soup rested on the floor. Unsure of up or down, Nana attempted to stand. Micaela and Arturo remained seated. Javier still lay in his basket on top of the table, but now he was in a different part of the kitchen. The house moved as if being rowed on the sea. Nana gathered the children and went to the back door. A deep constant hum filled the silence that had bothered her only moments ago. As she looked out over the brickyard she saw waves move through the surface of the earth.

"An earthquake!" Nana was overwhelmed at the energy that moved through everything she saw.

"Mama?" Micaela questioned Nana's fearful tone.

Nana did not want to panic the children. The rumble from deep within the earth became stronger. She watched the walls to see if they would crack, to stop the debris from falling on her beautiful babies. She could not go outside; the earth undulated and opened. Nana would take her chances inside, in the center of the kitchen, around the sturdy table that served her well.

She placed Javier underneath the table and sat down to watch the walls and ceiling. In the living room lamps fell, furniture moved; in the bedrooms photos fell to the floor, windows broke. The hot stove danced but held together. Nana found herself with her children underneath the table staring at the hot pot of albondiga soup that miraculously did not move while objects around it were made to dance by powerful telluric forces. She snuggled Javier in her arms while Micaela and Arturo embraced her.

"I think that in a little while we will eat those albondigas," Nana laughed. A loud sound and terrible jolt hit the house but the pot of soup still did not move.

The massive blow of the Long Beach earthquake caused men, women and children in the Southern California area to experience strange physical and mental occurrences. Some people fifty miles away from Long Beach instantaneously blacked out. Others reported that they had experienced the quake approach like a wave of earth which grew over their heads. Suddenly they rode the top of the crest, and as fast as it came it shot out from under and left them behind to flatten out miles away. One man reported that he had stood in the living room when the quake hit but found himself relocated in the kitchen at the opposite end of the house when the quake was over. His neighbors had gathered and walked around his curious house. He went out to discover to his amazement and pocketbook grief that his house had moved one-hundred-and-eighty degrees. The house had been ripped from and made to straddle the foundation. In other places, all sorts of strange lights and illuminations were reported. People saw lightning bolts, fiery showers, blurred explosions and falling stars dance and die like a Fourth of July sparkler.

The earth moved around dinner time, and the reaction of many people was to rush outside where the kinetic energies were just as terrorizing as inside. Brick buildings buckled and collapsed; brick chimneys snapped at the top; high posts swayed and fell; telephone and electrical cables swung, sparkled and snapped. The rumble of the uncomfortable earth was constant, like the unbearable shrill of howling dogs.

Nana moved from under the table and placed the soup pot back on the hot stove. She sat the children at the table and caressed Javier sleeping in the basket. Milagros and Maximiliano came to mind. She hoped that Octavio would come home immediately. She wanted him now to help pick up the fallen objects, to check the doors, windows, walls and roof. Nana needed a guarantee that the house was safe for her children. She searched for soup bowls, found one and dropped it. The bowl shattered. The uncomfortable stillness and the silence had been invaded and made to retreat by the shaking earth and a broken kitchen, too. She served the albondigas in two large cups. Micaela and Arturo were satisfied. They ate slowly, tentatively. With every noise they stopped and waited. Outside the wind returned to play with the trees. A muggy and silent evening covered Simons.

For hours parts of Southern California were cut off from outside areas. To some people Southern California had suddenly vanished, prompting the explanation blurred in small town newspapers across the country: "California Falls Into Pacific." The Long Beach earthquake measured 6.3 on the logarithmic scale. The possibility of a higher magnitude quake lessened because the epicenter was offshore. Notwithstanding, terrible damage occurred throughout the Los Angeles basin. Property destruction was great and millions of Depression dollars were lost. One hundred and fifty-three people perished in the earthquake.

The 1906 San Francisco earthquake had revealed the importance of the availability of excellent fire-fighting equipment. The Long Beach tremor provided a lesson in how not to construct in earthquake country. Nana remembered hearing about the San Francisco earthquake and how the workers of Simons had produced the material to rebuild practically the entire city. She also recalled the great Tokyo jolt in 1923 and how the men worked double shifts to produce the bricks needed by the Japanese to reconstruct Tokyo. Simons Brickyard and the workers were important to the world, she thought.

Nana moved Javier over to her right hip and took Arturo by the hand. Micaela sat down on the porch. Residents began to come out of their houses. Milagros opened the door and waved.

"Are you alright? The children? Oh, what a scare!" Milagros motioned that she would return in a minute to talk more.

Nana imagined that soon all the machines in the brickyard would start to operate. The demand for brick to repair the damage caused by the quake would be great. Considering the power of the quake, Nana concluded that the damage had been extensive. She moved about in silence and thought about the importance that Octavio had given the establishment of a union for the workers.

Milagros fanned herself with a white handkerchief which contrasted with her black dress. She had gone to check on Maximiliano. "I don't know how he slept through the earthquake," she said and made the sign of the cross.

The quake made the priests of Mount Carmel Catholic Church come to the forefront to help. Mount Carmel was a strong edifice. Most of the other brick churches in the devasted areas of Los Angeles had disintegrated. Their brick exterior walls had crumbled, leaving the roofs to fill the void below. In many cities, two and three story buildings stood naked. Their interior walls were exposed because the outer walls had tumbled down into a pile of rubble. The brick veneer in thousands of buildings had failed miserably. Simons had suffered no major destruction. A few cracks here and there and broken objects that might have caused a tear, but Simons stood solid like a fortress.

The earth had attempted to violently tear itself apart. The aftershocks of this internal vehemence continued to jolt the surface and terrify dwellers well into the night and dawn. By eight o'clock in the morning children played in the streets. Some families, fearing the collapse of their homes, slept outside; others had taken a stoic attitude to the shaking earth and like Nana and her children had slept in their beds. When Octavio arrived at three o'clock in the morning, Nana did not speak to him.

"We could not arrive sooner. The roads are blocked," Octavio explained and checked the four members of his family huddled together in Nana's bed. He slept on the couch.

The morning paper had been delivered late to the general store. Simons workers had been coming and going, buying extra canned food, warm clothing, blankets, tools for survival in case the earth shook again. Octavio read through *La Opinión* slowly while he drank coffee. Nana focused on an article which described the heavy damage suffered by the school buildings.

"Imagine, Octavio. What would have happened if the school had been in session?" she asked and continued to read next to him.

The newspaper reported that the earthquake had struck at five fifty-four in the afternoon. If it had hit during school hours, thousands of children would have been killed. Elementary, junior and high schools were badly damaged; many were complete losses. Geologists and architects reported that school buildings were particularly vulnerable because of the manner and material of construction. School boards had ordered educational structures to be built with brick because it was considered the cheapest and most durable material. Only until March 10, 1933 did school boards throughout Southern California consider brick construction to be safe. Now, as people of Southern California observed the thousands of mounds of brick rubble, it struck them that perhaps brick was not the material to construct the buildings that held important documentation, that provided essential physical and spiritual services, and most important, that housed their children.

After the earth had almost shaken itself apart, the fear of a natural disaster of this magnitude occurring again faded and became unimportant to the people. The earthquake did not eliminate the long bread lines, nor the thirteen million jobless men and women. The earthquake, in fact, closed down businesses and put more people out of work. Ruin, hunger, and illness still lurked in the shacks of homeless city workers and farmers; they remained in the eyes of children playing on the back streets of the big cities or the dusty rural areas; they rubbed elbows with professional classes as well as the rich living on the grand avenues in the nation's great cities.

In Simons there was always food; no one starved. If Walter Simons did not provide credit, which he almost always did, a neighbor would offer food, or the church would donate a basket. Octavio made sure that there was never a lack of food, clothing, medicine, blankets or shelter in his family's life. But good health he could not guarantee.

Months had passed since the quake. The big rush for brick that Walter had predicted had not yet hit the brickyard. And it seemed as if the patron worried little about the lack of work. He and his wife had traveled to

Europe on a musical tour organized by Edit for the members of the Los Angeles Music Guild.

In the middle of June, Octavio and Nana visited Milagros and Damian who were sitting in the back garden of their home thinking of Maximiliano's suffering. As the warm caressing wind played across their faces, the four talked about Maximiliano and reached the same terrifying conclusion.

"We have to take him to the hospital. They will give him blood. His body needs oxygen," Octavio said.

"The general hospital is far," Damian commented.

"Jose will take us," Octavio spoke directly to his mother.

Milagros nodded slowly. Her eyes glittered in the afternoon sun. She knew that another transfusion would prolong Maximiliano's life but would not save him. Maximiliano had become so precious a person to her, the family and the people of Simons. Milagros rose from the straight-back chair and headed into the room where Maximiliano lay. She sponge-bathed and dressed him. Maximiliano's head bobbed from side to side as if his neck could not support the beautiful head. Milagros sobbed quietly. Her son could not hear her; her son could not see her. His eyes were always shut, his breathing labored. Milagros could not understand how Maximiliano had fallen victim to a disease that she never knew existed until now. Six, seven, eight months ago he was a healthy strong man. She held him in her arms and put her mouth next to his.

"Give me the animals that eat my son's blood. Allow me, oh God, to eat them. Let them eat me. Oh blessed God!"

"Mama, we must leave. They are expecting him at five," Octavio's voice called just outside the door.

"Maximiliano is ready. Come for your brother," Milagros replied.

Maximiliano spent the last two weeks of June in the hospital. The family, with his consent, allowed experimental transfusions to which he responded positively, but the effects lasted for only a day or so. During the last week Maximiliano consented to experiments that had never been tested on humans. The first was extremely painful; the second put him in a coma for three days. When he awoke, his strength had miraculously returned. He felt cured and immediately requested that he be allowed to return home. The doctors told him that the euphoric state of strength was temporary and that the relapse would be severe or perhaps fatal if he were not in the hospital. Having been told the consequences, Maximiliano made his decision. On July 1, early in the morning, he signed the release papers and walked out of Los Angeles County General Hospital. In his mind, he was cured and was going home to his brothers, sisters, father and mother.

By the end of the day Maximiliano felt cold. His fingers, toes, the tip of his nose, ears, and penis felt as if he lived in an ice cold climate, but he remembered it was July in Southern California and hot. I will leave this life. I don't know for whom I lived it. I don't know what it is all about now . . . Maximiliano sat at the dinner table set in the backyard garden. He ate as if he had a hundred years to live. He found in his mother's garden a beautiful red rose . . . It will also disappear. While his brothers, sisters, uncles, aunts, and other relatives and friends discussed Maximiliano's miraculous recovery and drank to his health and future, Maximiliano went to his room, got into bed, and fell into a warm deep sleep.

In the morning, light came to Simons. Poles and wires had been brought into the yard only six months ago. Today electricity was hooked up to the houses. With only one connection, residents wired an entire wood structure. Electrical cords ran over the walls and ceiling. It was not uncommon to see dozens of black electrical and white medical-tape balls covering the wire splices. Octavio tacked the white cord with the bulb socket and brass chain swinging freely from the center of the kitchen above the table. He had dedicated the morning to the arteries of power which now ran through every room of his parents' house as well as his own. Octavio stood on a chair and held out the clear glass bulb for everyone to see.

"From this little thing enough light will emerge to illuminate the kitchen?" Rogaciana asked skeptically.

"How pretty!" Felicitas exclaimed.

"Put it on, Octavio," Damian ordered impatiently.

Octavio smiled in agreement. He moved the bulb to the mouth of the socket. The fingers of his right hand slipped their position on the bulb. Everyone followed the bulb to the floor. The loud pop and flying thin glass caused the family to protect their eyes. Laughter filled the kitchen . . . Damn scientists, why don't they make things right? Octavio thought as he pointed out to Jose the package of bulbs on the sink counter. Jose handed another bulb to Octavio who connected it without further mishaps. Octavio made sure all eyes were on the bulb before pulling the golden chain. He pulled and light filled the room.

"They are so expensive," Milagros exclaimed as she swept the floor.

"It's about time Simons supplied electricity for the houses," Octavio said, satisfied with his electrical work.

By seven-thirty Octavio returned to his home. Nana had breakfast ready. The children were up and playing in the living room.

"How did he awake?" Nana asked about Maximiliano.

"He was still asleep. Mama said he slept through the night without awakening."

"Octavio, do you believe they cured him? People are beginning to talk about a miracle," Nana said.

"I don't believe anything. Time will tell." Octavio sat at the table to breakfast.

Maximiliano, Federico, Jose, and Octavio walked into Acacio Newman Delgado's grocery store on Date Street at one in the afternoon. Maximiliano had gotten up at nine and was delighted that his mother had electricity in the house. He ate well and at ten-thirty visited with neighbors who came to say hello and wish him well. Some of the folks seemed to be saying good-by rather than welcoming him back. Maximiliano expected this reaction and understood, for after all he had almost died from leukemia. He talked for an hour until his brothers picked him up to listen to Acacio's radio, the first in Simons that was near enough so the people could listen to national news reports from the Spanish radio station. On the hour without fail, Acacio's grocery store was filled to capacity. Few people bought groceries; most were there to say hello and listen to the radio.

When Acacio saw Maximiliano come into the store, he whisked him over to the chair right next to the radio and brought him a cup of coffee.

"How are you feeling, Maximiliano?" Acacio poured more coffee.

"Just fine. I returned to remain at home forever." Maximiliano paused and drank. Several people moved toward the radio.

"What a beautiful radio." One man leaned an ear closer.

"It's very expensive," another man commented from the back.

Maximiliano nodded at Octavio, Federico and Jose who stood nearby guarding him, constantly watching him as if something were about to happen.

"That's what electricity is for Simons. More business and more money for the rich," a third man shouted from the back.

"You'll see, our women will want to buy all the electrical apparatuses they offer them. Now we have a swarm of vendors selling electrical junk to make it easier for the women. No sir, electricity is a gringo plague that will infect us and make us sick. They will make us like thousands of stupefied moths attracted to and trapped by this pretty light until we burn. Just look at how you are swarmed around that electrical idiot box," the third man continued near the door.

"Hey friend, stop your bitching and leave. We want to hear the news reports," Linacero Guerra, one of the three toughest men in Simons, threatened.

The third man waved Linacero off and walked out into the afternoon of the third of July. Linacero reached up and turned the volume louder. He patted Maximiliano on the shoulder, assuring everyone in the store that no one would interrupt Maximiliano from listening to Acacio Newman Delgado's new radio.

The Spanish voice that shouted from the electric box began to report a litany of terrible events around the world and in the United States. The electric voice yelled about Adolf Hitler and the Nazis in Germany, Mussolini's Fascist party, Emperor Hirohito, Mexican deportation, the repeal of prohibiton which brought on cheers and applause from the listeners, Franklin Delano Roosevelt's New Deal, and the end of the Depression; but what most affected Maximiliano was the voice's description of the burning of mountains of books written by non-Nazi and Jewish authors in Germany. Maximiliano felt tired after the battering of information. On the way home a burning sensation snaked through his veins and burst into his mind at the image of millions of books consumed by fire. He was blinded momentarily. He closed his eyes once but suddenly thought that if he closed them again he would lose his brothers forever. He decided that no matter what the cost he would keep his eyes open for eternity.

Milagros and Damian waited together on the porch for Maximiliano, who embraced them both. For a long time the three held on to each other, not wanting to let go, afraid of separating. Octavio and Federico pulled them apart. Milagros sobbed. She could not contain her fear any longer, A dark bruise had encircled each of Maximiliano's eyes. Federico and Jose, not knowing what to do, turned to Octavio who calmly smiled and took Maximiliano toward the room in the back.

"I want you to rest. In a few hours all the family and your friends will come by to say hello. You want to be strong to receive them and to drink a few shots with your buddies." Octavio opened the door and watched Maximiliano enter.

"Octavio, you know I can't sleep. I have to keep my eyes open forever. I will never shut them, brother." Maximiliano leaned against the door. "Wait until after I'm gone before you call the ambulance. Please, brother. I ask this of you because I love you very much."

Octavio's face contorted with sorrow and anger.

Abundant food and drink kept the relatives and friends in pleasant conversation. Aunts, uncles, cousins, and the heads of families had brought food, and the comadres and compadres had made sure that Damian had plenty to drink for the adults and the children. Summertime in Simons brought freedom for the children more than any other season of the year. The hot weather invited them to run barefoot through the agricultural fields that surrounded the brickyard. Exploration was the children's favorite game. Fields of corn and sugarcane made hide-and-seek a challenging activity. Children's screams and laughter filled the summer afternoon at the Revueltas home. To celebrate life was the order of the day.

Maximiliano was strengthened by the overflowing honest love that fell on his head, neck, shoulders, arms and hands. The love given him was his responsibility and he would respond by not feeling ill. A forever smile and a handshake thanked all who had come to celebrate his return. He maneuvered to the couch in the living room. Maximiliano constantly wiped his eyes. Now the rings had become wider and blacker. Reddish-blue blotches appeared on his neck and hands. His lips grew purple and his smile fainter. The men would bring him a drink and he would lift up a glass showing that he had one, two , three and the hundreds of other drinks his relatives and friends wanted to have with him.

The food diminished and by six-thirty it was gone. Although Damian and Milagros had prepared plenty, the people had eaten all of it and now began to leave quietly. Some went to thank Maximiliano for the wonderful party and encouraged him not to give up. Others, seeing Maximiliano's condition deteriorating by the minute, thanked Damian and Milagros. They looked over to Maximiliano as they said good-bye to the Revueltas. In their eyes and tone of voice they communicated pity and irony. They did not believe in what they said, and to cleanse their hands of creating false expectations they left Damian and Milagros with "Esta en las manos de Dios." At seven in the evening the house had been abandoned to the family.

The warm silence of the comfortable summer afternoon, periodically interrupted by the explosion of cherry bombs and firecrackers, provided Maximiliano with the belief and the desire that the moment would never cease. He sat snuggled in the couch, safe for eternity. He would never move; here forever he wanted to remain in this space and in this time, never moving forward nor backward, never changing. His eyes were set deep and the rings had become bruises. The explosions of the night multiplied. With each detonation of the outside world, Maximiliano perished cell by cell. He would never give up. Maximiliano rested, his head back, his mouth open, every fourth breath gasping for air.

At eight o'clock his breathing was consistently heavy. He was cool but drenched in perspiration. Octavio and Federico carried their brother into their parents' room. Maximiliano vehemently pointed to the kitchen door to the outside. He wanted air, wind, the open space of the garden to help him breathe, help him find oxygen. Octavio and Federico held him up and walked him around the garden. Nana came up to dry his brow. His legs weakened. He could stand only with the help of his brothers. Octavio moved him toward the outside bedroom. Maximiliano grew weaker. He could no longer hold his head up. Milagros cried at the foot of the bed. Damian held fast against a corner. Octavio watched Nana wipe Maximiliano's face, neck and arms. Outside, Federico, Jose, Rogaciana and Felicitas listened to the thousands of explosions that invaded the warm night.

Octavio remembered Maximiliano's request not to call the ambulance until he was well on his way to death. Rest and peace lay on Maximiliano's countenance while outside the innocent laughter of excited children ran away down the street. His breathing was shallow and erratic. Milagros had administered medicine that was to have strenghtened Maximiliano enough to be returned to the hospital. But the chemicals did not take effect. Maximiliano seemed not to suffer pain. Octavio ordered Jose to call the ambulance. By the time the ambulance arrived Maximiliano's breathing had practically ceased and became difficult to ascertain. Several times the ambulance attendants, while preparing Maximiliano for the trip to Los Angeles General Hospital, asked if Maximiliano were dead. Milagros considered these questions cruel and insensitive to the mourning family. iano will never die . . . Milagros went to her son's side. Nana stepped back to allow Milagros to hold her son and see what only she could see in his eyes. She smiled an ancient smile and he responded likewise.

"Mama!" Maximiliano called out with a strong fresh voice.

"What do you want, son?" Milagros fought back from the deepest part of her soul not to cry out with him in her arms. With his head against her bosom, he reached the distance from which no living being has ever communicated.

Damian pushed himself against the wall. Tears overran his strength and his face became wet, his nose filled with salty anger. He would not wail with anger at losing his beautiful son. Damian climbed into the ambulance. He would accompany his son to the hospital. Octavio observed the attendant close the door slowly. Damian sat straight, hand on lap and eyes fixed on Maximiliano's blue face. Octavio, Federico, Jose and Ignacio Sandoval followed.

That afternoon Octavio had accepted the inevitable death of his brother. He was grateful to Maximiliano for telling how he wanted to die, where he wanted to spend his last moments. Octavio glanced at Jose driving and crying silently. The image of his father sitting helplessly next to his dying son kept reappearing, jumping at him, symbolizing an unknown explanation. The siren and the red and yellow spinning and flashing lights broke the world up and lessened the sorrow, the pain and the anger. Octavio walked into the hospital with a roll of hundred dollar bills. At ten in the evening he paid a fifty-dollar deposit required by the hospital. Octavio, Federico, Jose and Ignacio joined Damian in the emergency room and waited. At eleven-thirty a doctor approached the family and explained that Maximiliano's condition was terminal. He would die at any time.

"There's nothing we can do now. I'm sorry. You can go in now." The doctor rapidly moved away.

Maximiliano's brothers, father and uncle talked to him and held his hand. They were not sure if he could hear them, but if he could they wanted to show him that he was not alone. As Octavio spoke there walked into the brick-walled room a boy whose face he had almost forgotten, a boy who had died in 1918. Julio smiled at his brothers, walked around the bed and whispered into Maximiliano's blue ear. Octavio squinted, rubbed and closed his eyes to rest them for an instant. Julio was gone. Maximiliano's body lay empty of energy. Jose sobbed openly. The other four stood silently, feeling the weight of Maximiliano's death in their minds, hearts and throats. Julio had entered the room at 1:02 and left with Maximiliano at 1:03 in the morning of July 5, 1933.

At six in the morning Federico followed the Moritz Funeral hearse. Octavio and Ignacio waited for Maximiliano's body to be readied, while Damian, Federico and Jose drove home to prepare the family and to organize the wake. Milagros, dressed in a new black dress, greeted her family and did not ask for explanations as to why Octavio and Ignacio had not returned. She had alreay made a special place in the living room and with the help of Tati, Nana, Rogaciana, Felicitas and neighbors had begun to prepare food for the mourners who would visit her son, Maximiliano Revueltas.

At midday Maximiliano lay in state in his home. Maximiliano had returned home and again would receive family, friends and neighbors. Most of Simons town came to pay their respects. Among the early arrivals were William Melone, Jacobo Ramos and Gonzalo Pedroza who weakly embraced the bereaved parents. They left immediately after they visited the family. At this time there was no need to test the tensions between Octavio and the foremen.

A priest from Saint Benedict Catholic Church in Montebello recited the rosary once and immediately left. Two women alternated leading the mourners in praying the rosary. While the town women accompanied and prayed for Maximiliano's soul, the men drank and reminisced about Maximiliano's good times. By eleven the people began to leave the house. By twelve Damian and Milagros had retired.

"Octavio, I'm going to rest," Nana said.

"I want to be with him a little longer," Octavio replied and kissed Nana good night.

Octavio found himself alone with his brother's cold body. On one of the small end tables he contemplated a photograph of the four Revueltas brothers taken eight years past. He picked up the photo and felt proud of his brothers Federico, Maximiliano and Jose. The four were dressed in their best clothes. The photo was Milagros' favorite of her boys. Octavio's eyes found the couch, the same place where Maximiliano had sat the night before thinking of forever. Octavio brought the photo closer to his eyes. Maximiliano, with his hands on Federico's shoulders, seemed powerful standing behind him. Jose smiled like a child. Octavio, straight and serious, brought Jose closer with his left arm. Federico leaned to his left and showed a devilish smile. Octavio's and Maximiliano's lips were like the Mona Lisa—emotionless. What had been the occasion that had brought them together so happily? In that photo and forever, the Revueltas brothers touched, connected by flesh, blood, mind and a special vision. Octavio fell asleep on the couch. In front of Maximiliano's coffin his hands covered the photograph which lay on his chest.

The early sunlight warmed his eyelids. Through them the darkness of the night had gone. Octavio opened his eyes and lay perfectly still. His sight searched to the left and to the right. A strange house, he thought, and the light brightened the space of his living . . . This is the day in which I bury my brother . . . . He felt the photograph on his chest. It was he who had the financial responsibility of burying Maximiliano; he who had to pay the medical cost; he who had to pay for the funeral; he who had to pay for the drink and food for the wake and funeral; he who had taken Maximiliano to several doctors and he who could not guarantee Maximiliano's health; he who saw Julio walk into Maximiliano's hospital room; he whom father and mother had confidence in to make the correct decisions. It was always. ". . . Whatever Octavio says . . . Maybe Octavio will give you some. See if Octavio gives you permission. . . . Octavio has money . . ." At that moment Octavio sensed the family's weight on his chest. It was difficult to arise but Octavio knew that he had to. He loved them and that was enough. Milagros, Damian, Ignacio, and Tati waited for him to awaken.

"Octavio, come with me. Nana has made a delicious breakfast." Tati led her compadre to his house. The rest of the family listened for the Moritz hearse that would transport Maximiliano's remains to Mount Carmel for a High Mass.

The church was filled. Friends stood against the walls in the aisle and outside in the gardens. Cars were packed into the dusty church lot, all along Church Street and on both sides of Rivera Road. People liked Maximiliano. He became a kind of hero, an intelligent, dignified man who made just decisions and lived his life with intensity. He was a beautifully brave man, they said repeatedly.

The long serpent of cars cruised down Whittier Boulevard and turned into El Calvario Cemetery where, after a prayer and a blessing, the casket was lowered into the ground. One by one Maximiliano's family and friends gently tossed a flower on his casket. Doña Marcelina Trujillo Benidorm, from amongst the mourners, began to sing:

De colores, de colores se visten
los campos en la primavera,
de colores, de colores son los
pajaritos que vienen de afuera,
de colores, de colores es el arco
iris que vemos lucir,
y por eso los grandes amores de
muchos colores me gustan a mí
y por eso los grandes amores de
mucho colores me gustan a mí.

Octavio was surprised that most of the people began to accompany the woman. He noticed that Milagros, Damian, Nana and the priest were singing along. The song was beautiful, happy, and Maximiliano would have approved. Octavio picked up Arturo and went to Nana who held Javier in her arms. Micaela hugged her mother. The five of them moved away from the crowd.

Chapter 16

With the death of Maximiliano the world began to fall apart. Acacio Newman Delgado's stationary radio—he never moved it because he did not want to upset the radio's entrañas—screamed assassination after assassination, atrocity after atrocity, blood bath after blood bath: the Ku Klux Klan marched on Washington, Asians slaughtered Asians, the Spanish Civil War errupted, Franklin Delano Roosevelt was reelected President of the United States by a landslide, Chiang Kai-Shek declared war on Japan, Trotsky was exiled to Mexico. With more houses acquiring electricity the voices multiplied. More radios appeared in living rooms, kitchens, or bedrooms. As hearing space grew smaller, the voices were often pitted against one another. Gonzalo Pedroza had to threaten the people that if the sound of the radio was not lowered he would have to take the apparatus away. Nonetheless, the voices continued to scream throughout Simons.

The world never heard of the little local tragedies that occurred. Radio reporters never screamed about Jesus Romo racing his pick-up truck down Vail, speeding over the bridge, flipping over and killing his six-year-old twin daughters. Neighbors crowded into Jesus Romo's small wooden company house during the wake to see the two beautiful innocents and to observe how the young reckless father responded to the tragedy. The night progressed, cramming people into the living room where Jesus Romo twisted, tore, beat his body. At times he would scream and struggle to run away or he would smash into the crowd begging to be beaten, hanged, killed to end his sorrow and remorse. Just beyond the kitchen, enshrined in a large casket, lay the twin girls. The rosary, a humming, never ceased. Suddenly a loud roar surged from the center of the living room and the world caved into itself. The weight of the people in the center of the room facing the casket caused the wooden floor to break in half. The praying bereaved fell through to a deep hole in the ground which apparently had been dug up during the construction of the house but of whose existence no one was aware. The floor split in two, the center caving into the unknown and the outside areas rising, causing those people who were standing near the walls to slide into and on top of their fellow neighbors. A panic danced before two angelic twins dressed in beautiful white gowns.

"Jesus, Maria y Jose!" a woman screamed as she went down.

"God punishes us!" several mourners announced.

"Because we are sinners!" a high shrill yelled repeatedly, hanging on to the edge of the floor.

"Jesus Christ, forgive us!" A fat man fell into the dark hole.

"Don't touch me, you scoundrel!" a middle-aged woman cried out.

"Bury me, punish me with the bodies of sinners, Jesus!" Jesus Romo begged at the bottom of the wet pit.

The screaming continued while people crawled out of the hole and from under the house. Most were wet and covered with mud as they emerged cursing Walter Simons and his plant stooges. Brown insects crawled on the victims and on the ground. A woman had broken an arm and agonized in pain. An old man with a hunched back came out walking on his feet and hands looking for a cavalry to bury the twins. Other men emerged coughing up red dust collected in their lungs through decades of working in Simons Brickyard. Men and women, as they slid rapidly into the pit, cursed Walter for permitting the world to sink into the abyss of Golgotha. Octavio and Nana were about to enter the house when the ground swallowed the mourners.

With the new use of electricity, wiring and overloaded female connector terminals became a common cause of fire. Panfilita Cora lived with many hens and roosters in her house. She was blind and at ninety-five simply did not bother to distinguish outside and inside. To her it was all the same; nothing stopped her from being where she wanted to be at whatever time she desired. The women of Simons cared for ancient Panfilita. They chased the chickens and roosters out, cleaned her house and made sure she had plenty to eat. The women asked the men to install electricity in the house. This would enable them to visit Panfilita in the evening, make sure she had eaten, iron her clothes with the new communal electric iron the women had bought, and ensure a relatively comfortable life for the senior woman. The women who visited at night always left the kitchen light on.

One evening after Panfilita's friends left the house, she opened the back door for her animals to enter freely. Early the next morning she went into the kitchen to prepare her breakfast. Five chickens roosted on the table and Panfilita sent them scurrying. Three of the five flew up onto the worn wire connecting the bulb over the table. The chickens landed on the wire and a moment later Panfilita smelled burnt fowl. The light went out and the hot wire came to rest on a pile of tissue papers that Panfilita saved to start the stove. Before the residents could organize a bucket line the house had burned to the ground. Miraculously, Panfilita stood by her stove, stoking the fire to heat tortillas. She had worked through the conflagration, and when the people found her still next to her stove slapping out some thick tortillas in her hands, not a burn marked her body.

These strange, alarming events were the results of powerful energies maneuvering for advantageous positions at the starting line of a violent primitive race towards complete power over their own lives. The world of labor was not exempted from the violence. In El Monte, Mexican and Filipino farm workers joined together and struck for higher wages, improved housing and better working conditions. The violent strike involved approximately seven thousand men and their families. The news of the strike and the wage gains it won spread throughout Southern California. The victory augmented the confidence that was growing in the Mexican worker in the area.

Octavio, Armando Takahashi Subia and Caroline Decker discussed the positive and aggressive attitude of the Simons workers who had attended the third meeting of CAWIU at Barrio Margarito. Carlo Lanzetti, a fellow organizer from the Long Beach office of the CAWIU, had spoken about the possibilities of organizing a strike against Walter Simons, and in particular the Simons yard on Rivera Road and Vail Street. Lanzetti described what the workers could expect during a strike. He spoke about how difficult it might become and urged the men to prepare themselves and their families. Lanzetti set a meeting at Simons Brickyard to officially invite the workers who could not show up for the present session. Discussion at the Simons meeting would detail the state of negotiations with the patron.

Loud cheering, yelling of "¡Viva!" and clapping broke from the forty-five men when they heard the possibility of a huelga and consequently a victory for higher wages, better medical care and job security. The men's spirit, confident that they would win a strike, prepared them psychologically for the oncoming confrontation. Octavio was aware that the men would fight. They were more afraid of the results of another Depression-like situation than the silent threats made by William Melone, Jacobo Ramos and Gonzalo Pedroza who had the power to fire but would not execute the threat for fear of a strike.

If the superintendent and foremen lost control of the workers, they in turn lost their jobs, Walter had declared upon his return from Europe. He had been frustrated in his efforts to spur brick production. The earthquake had stopped the large orders he once enjoyed. Now it seemed that contractors turned away from brick as the main building material and used it mainly as a decorative facade. Walter now faced his militant Mexicanos to whom he had given everything they needed to survive, and who now threatened to stop production completely by declaring a strike.

Octavio thought that Simons owed the workers compensation for faithful service and insisted on higher wages for more complex, technical work. He remembered the phrase "trabajo complicado y tecnico" as he paid the house to enter into a high stake poker game in Barrio Margarito. Jose Revueltas, Guadalupe Sandoval, Juan Juarez and Isidro Olague accompaned him.

Octavio played until six in the morning. At the table was a man who had lost every cent, had borrowed several hundred dollars from the house and was down to his most precious possession—a pearl-handle pistol—which he put in the pot to call what he calculated to be Octavio's bluff. When all the cards faced up for the men around the table to see, the man cried in disbelief that he had lost. He sat stunned. Armando, who had joined the group, warned Octavio to leave immediately because the man he had humiliated was a member of a notorious gang of thieves who usually arrived about this time to help their friend make up any losses incurred. The men from Simons heeded Armando's suggestion and by seven-thirty had turned off Washington Boulevard onto Vail Street.

Octavio gambled and won obsessively. It was one way he took revenge on the decadent, obscene, diseased world which had infected and murdered his brother Maximiliano. It was the world created by the gringo which tainted everybody with their pleasure-oriented values which he felt caused "un daño en el cerebro," a wound in the brain.

"Erfath, erfath, ate, ate. Ama, Ama." Eight-year-old Arturo spoke in his backward way to his father as he entered the house through the kitchen. He turned and searched for Nana who had gone for Javier.

Nana returned holding Javier and found Octavio drinking coffee and staring at Arturo happily eating his breakfast. Seeing Octavio sitting there, Nana felt mixed emotions. She was relieved that he was back safe, but she was angered at his carousing, gambling, drinking and union organizing. She would make him breakfast and then send him out to Maravilla for groceries. Nana noticed her husband's weariness. It's his own fault!. . . She placed breakfast before Octavio who ate with Arturo and Micaela, who joined them. Nana left to fold clothes in the bedroom.

"I don't want you to go out to the street," Nana yelled out to Micaela and Arturo who ran outside to play. Seldom, only when she was present, did she allow them to leave their yard to play with neighborhood children.

Octavio reached for a clean shirt on the bed. He reached in his pocket and showed Nana a roll of bills which he had won that morning.

"You know that I don't want that money," Nana said and placed his clothes in a standing closet.

"Seven hundred dollars," Octavio rejoindered.

"I don't want it," Nana said sternly, looking directly at Octavio.

"But save it for me, please," Octavio asked.

"Leave it where you always do." Nana motioned to the top drawer of her clothes dresser where she had her intimate clothing.

Octavio felt around and pulled out a cloth bag where he stuffed the money. He pushed the bag to the back and covered it with his wife's soft, smooth undergarments. As he pushed the drawer shut he smelled the fragrance of cedarwood and Nana's own orange blossom perfume. He stroked the brass drawer handles.

Their love-making had not been the same for some time now. Even before Maximiliano's illness, a distance had begun to grow between them. Octavio's absence in the evenings to meet his gambling obligations and organization activities caused Nana to become cold toward him. It became obvious to Nana that it was more important for Octavio to spend his leisure time with his union organizer acquaintances and gambling than to be with his family.

"Dejame en paz" and "No me toques" became a common phrase expressed by both Nana and Octavio. Their dreams for the future, love-making, their marriage, their communication were minimized to the absolute essential level. Octavio seldom stayed at home more than the five hours he needed for sleep. Nana dedicated her energies to the house and her family and to Milagros who had also long before begun to suffer the same plight. In these years Nana became a solitary woman, a woman finding energy, inspiration and the will to endure from within herself.

At about nine in the morning on a foggy June day in 1937, the eighty-five man crew had converged on what used to be Gonzalo Pedroza's restaurant. Armando Takahashi Subia, Caroline Decker and Carlo Lanzetti received the Simons workers with coffee and Mexican sweet bread provided by the workers' wives. The men, in high militant spirits, joked and kidded as they drank coffee. Three bottles of whiskey circulated, serving "un piquete" to most cups of coffee.

That morning Walter's faithful Mexicans had started working at the normal hour. They cranked up the seven machines, fired a newly-stacked kiln of bricks, revved up five Plymouth locomotives, started up a dozen trucks and commenced to produce brick. At nine o'clock the workers suddenly stopped and gathered at Gonzalo's old restaurant. Peregrinacion Juarez, Domitila Olague, Mirasol Leco and their daughters carried in nine dozen apple empanadas. The men did not wait for Lanzetti to speak; they went for the empanadas.

"They're hot. We must not wait," a worker commented.

"Don't be hogs. Leave some for the men in the back," a man shouted making his way to the trays.

Drinking coffee and munching on empanadas, the workers settled down to listen to Lanzetti who had raised his arms and hands signaling for silence. He began by talking about the history of the ongoing working class struggle and he described Walter as a paternalistic exploiter who lived in an extravagant, luxurious world, known to the workers as the world of "los ricos." It was a world they had never seen much of, less imagined. Lanzetti told the Simons workers that they had basic human rights.

"You deserve, you earned, you have the right to demand higher wages for technical work, better medical care for yourselves, your wives, and your children, a pension, Social Security for yourself and family. All of you have worked hard for these benefits and Simons must cooperate, must meet your just demands!" Lanzetti yelled to every person in the large room. He sipped coffee.

"All of you know that Walter Simons is here today. He came to see if you had the guts to close down the plant. Well, you showed him that you mean business, didn't you!" Lanzetti exclaimed and raised his right fist.

Armando and Caroline, standing at diagonal corners, applauded and cheered. The workers, many of whom understood most of Lanzetti's statements, applauded their agreement. The men who did not understand followed suit. As a group they understood what they had done and what needed to be done to achieve their demands.

The meeting place, located next to the general store, made it convenient to walk over to Walter's office and picket the building. Gonzalo and Jacobo waited with shotguns in hand. None of the men dared approach the entrance. They had completely encircled the building and marched clockwise around it. Lanzetti, Armando and Caroline took a position in front of the entrance. With them stood Jose Ceballo, Juan Juarez, Leon Martinez, Isidro Olague, and Octavio. After approximately twenty minutes of slow, silent marching by the group, William Melone appeared carrying a clipboard, his right hand resting on the handle of a thirty-eight caliber Smith and Wesson.

"Why don't you men go back to work? You're wasting time and losing money," William called out and stepped down to the ground where the five workers waited.

"Jose, Leon, Isidro, Juan, why did you stop working? Mr. Simons has treated you and your families very well. He has provided everything that you need. Did you, did any of you, suffer during the Depression? No, because Mr. Simons gave you credit to get what your families needed.

Now you owe him a favor. So go back to work!" William took five steps to where Octavio listened next to Guadalupe and Ignacio Sandoval in front of the three union organizers.

"Octavio, why did you bring these people here? They are trouble-makers. Mr. Simons says that they are Communists and that he wants them off his property."

The workers stopped marching and crowded around Walter's three stooges who slowly stepped back onto the entrance porch.

"We want to talk with Mr. Simons," Juan Juarez shouted.

"Hey, Gonzalo, call him. Tell him that we will wait for him here," Leon Martinez said.

"We want to discuss our demands," Isidro Ceballos insisted.

"The patron will not speak to you today. You don't appreciate what he has done for you. You are acting rudely. Return to your jobs. I repeat, the patron will not speak to any of you today," Jacobo spoke angrily with the shotgun pointed directly into the crowd. He gestured to Gonzalo and William to enter the office.

The workers resumed their silent march. By now the wives and children had joined. The women and children had made the strike a collective family struggle and brought about the feeling of complete unity. The Mexican families marched on into mid-afternoon when William stepped out communicating a different attitude.

"Mr. Simons has agreed to discuss your demands," he began and was interrupted by cheering. "But not today and not with all of you and especially not with those Communists." William hurried the sentence and braced for the response which came before he had even finished.

The workers insisted on seeing Walter immediately. William asked for quiet.

"He is willing to talk about your demands but he wants to study them. Do you have a detailed list of grievances and demands?" William waited.

The workers looked around and wondered if anyone had prepared a list. Lanzetti passed some papers to Jose Ceballos who lifted the documents above his head and approached William.

"Good. Now Mr. Simons needs to review these documents. In a few days he will call your representative. But he also wants you to go back to work while he studies these papers. What do you say?" William watched while the workers caucussed.

"Fine. We'll give him five days to tell us where he wants to meet," Jose Ceballos answered for the workers.

"Who will represent you?" William asked, surprised at how well organized they seemed to be. Jose Ceballos stepped forward again.

ALEJANDRO MORALES

"Leon Martinez, Isidro Olague, Octavio Revueltas, Juan Juarez, and me." Jose Ceballos at that instant hated William Melone.

It took Octavio to break the dangerous staring trance which both men had created. Octavio placed a hand on Jose's shoulder, allowing him to pull away his vision and not lose face with William.

"We'll work till sunset. That way Mr. Simons can't say that we stole hours from him," Octavio said.

Octavio led Jose, trembling with rage, away into the afternoon. He threw his jacket over Jose's shoulders and calmed him. He noticed that the sun had burned away the fog and cleared the day.

The table that was placed at three o'clock in the afternoon on Saturday, payday, in front of the entrance to the general store was the same one used for years by James Simons. Before he sat down he removed his coat, hung it on the back of the chair and adjusted his shoulder holster and made sure that the thirty-eight caliber pistol slipped out rapidly. Behind him stood William with a shotgun and Gonzalo in his usual place on the right-hand side of the first worker in line. Jacobo, at the right of James Simons, called the men forward.

Before they approached the table, many of the men adjusted their pistols tucked under their belts. Some had hip or shoulder holsters and a few had a shotgun or a rifle of different caliber. Each man walked forward confidently to receive his pay. Octavio was not armed when he took the brown envelope and moved to where his father counted his money. Octavio repeated Damian's action without taking the bills out of the envelope. Jose Ceballos came up counting his cash and stood next to Octavio.

"All here," Jose said.

"They're already stealing from us. They would not dare lower the measly wages they pay!" Damian said for everyone to hear. Octavio smiled and enjoyed his father's sarcasm.

"Octavio, Mr. Simons has asked for a meeting," Jose Ceballos called out.

"When?" Octavio asked.

"The representatives received an invitation for Monday, at twelve, his house in Los Angeles. He invited us for lunch," Jose Ceballos said excitedly and with subtle pride that they had been invited to Walter's mansion on exclusive Plymouth Avenue in Los Angeles.

"You have to dress formal," Jose Ceballos added.

Damian took the invitation from his son. Octavio grabbed it back and read it. He crumpled it and threw it to the ground.

"We don't have to impress him. We must convince him. Monday is a day of work. We'll be there in work clothes!" he said convincingly.

"Good idea, Octavio. Meet here at nine. We'll take my truck. Tell the others." Jose Ceballos threw his jacket over his shoulder and walked home.

Octavio's eyes chased the blue-silver glitter that danced around the thousands of diamond-shaped crystals of the chandelier which seemed to have been stopped from falling from the beautiful white ceiling by smaller diamonds that spiralled to form a marvellous inverted pyramid. The sparkling apex pointed to the silver bowl filled with steaming vegetables being served by a dark-skinned woman. Octavio glanced at Jose Ceballos, Leon Martinez and Isidro Olague who sat across the elegant table touching the silverware, waiting for Edit Simons to begin to eat. Next to Octavio sat Juan Juarez. At the head of the table, Walter smiled and lifted his glass of red wine. Edit peered at Juan Juarez who, as he chewed his food loudly, banged his knife and fork on the china. Annoyed, she frowned at her husband who cleared his throat and lifted his glass higher.

"At this time I think a toast is appropriate," Walter spoke directly to Juan, who continued to enjoy his lunch. "A toast, Juan."

Jose smiled slowly and was glad that Juan felt comfortable. Juan daintily patted his lips with the silk napkin. He raised his glass and glanced politely over to Edit, turned and looked at the patron.

"Mrs. Simons and I are . . . glad that you were able to lunch with us today to go over the statement prepared for you by those union organizers." Walter drank from his glass.

Octavio and the other men looked at one another and touched their lips to the crystal glass and set the ornament down.

"You men have worked for me for many years. Some of you, I think, might have even come from the Pasadena yard. Now I have considered this statement carefully."

"Walter, I would like to talk with the men before you announce your suggestions," Edit said tactfully. "I am very happy that you voiced your needs in such a diplomatic way. You can be sure that Mr. Simons and I are concerned about your welfare and will do whatever possible to help you and your families. After all, Mr. Simons has been very kind to your people all these years. He has given you a job, a home, a school, a clinic, a band. Many other things Mr. Simons has provided willingly. . ."

Edit's words became distant sounds in Octavio's mind as he glanced through the dining room window at the two luxury automobiles parked in the driveway of the mansion. Jose Ceballos' old Model A truck proudly represented the workers of Simons in this unsafe world. Three glamorous cars slowly passed. The drivers scrutinized the workers' relic. "Que miran, cabrones," Octavio thought. Edit's lips still moved as Octavio communicated with eyes and slight gestures to his fellow workers: Don't believe it. I told you they were going to sweeten us up.

"Mr. Simons' suggestions are made especially for you and your families," Edit finished and was satisfied with her words.

Walter drank some wine and cleared his throat. He shuffled several papers before him and reviewed one.

"Now with that said," Walter stated, "I would like to respond to your observations and concerns by making, as Mrs. Simons has said, the following suggestions. The best way to help the crew and their families is to have excellent leadership. That is not to say that I have not been satisfied with the present supervision at the plant. No, instead I would like to add more men to that faithful staff. I believe that you five men are capable of doing the job. Therefore, I am promoting you to foremen with all the benefits. In this way you will be able to provide encouragement to the men to cooperate and produce more, and in so doing I will be able to meet their request at a future time." Walter noticed that Octavio refused with his right hand.

"We did not come to accept personal promotions, but for all the workers. Make them all foremen and recognize our demands and we'll have an agreement," Octavio spoke without hesitation.

"Don't try to buy us, Mr. Simons. Respond to our requests. They won't cost that much. You'll come out ahead. You'll see," Jose said, looking for the opinion of his fellow workers.

The five men presented a unified stand and refused Walter's offer. Octavio pushed away from the table and waited.

"Don't be unreasonable. A union will ruin the company and we are just now beginning to pull ahead. In about three more years I'll be able to meet your demands, without union pressure, and you will be better off. Stick with me. Help me help you. What do you say?" Walter searched and hoped for his answer.

"Thanks for the food, Mr. Simons." Juan reached for his hat on the floor next to Edit.

"Excuse me, I have duties to attend to." Edit left abruptly.

"Let's go. What are we waiting for?" Leon started for the front door. The other men followed.

"Wait. The best I can do is give you a two-cent raise and extend your credit at the company store. No more, that's it." Walter walked behind his

Mexicans.

"Thank you for the invitation," Octavio said from the brick walkway leading to Jose's truck.

"You are extremely unreasonable, Octavio," Walter shouted from behind the heavy screen door of his mansion.

Jose Ceballos started his truck. Juan Juarez sat in the middle. Leon Martinez and Isidro Olague rode in the back. From somewhere in the house someone played on the piano a beautiful tranquil melody which was interrupted for an instant when Walter slammed the front door.

Chapter 17

The shade of the large Simons water tank on Vail Street provided temporary relief at this time of day for a few of the thirty men who picketed the main entrance of the Simons Brickyard. July had turned into a heat wave, and temperatures rose into the high nineties at the end of the fourth week of the Simons Mexican workers' strike. At the general store, patience grew thin as it became apparent that no progress was being made.

July had become a summer month of hardship. The men had no salary, no credit at the general store, and all services provided by Simons were cut off. The strike was more difficult to survive than the Depression. There had been polemics about whether the strike was worth risking the loss of their jobs. Some of the workers wanted to accept Walter's offer of a two-cent raise and extended credit. Others urged the men to take the raise and set up their own store. Finally the workers decided to take the chance and strike, hoping that they could break the patron, make him capitulate to their demands.

Carlo Lanzetti, Armando Takahashi Subia and Caroline Decker organized the picket and work crews. Some men picketed while others worked at odd jobs to bring in money which was deposited in a general fund to support the strikers. Any food brought in was distributed equally among the strikers. Octavio, who worked in the fields and at the docks, donated that money to the strike fund. He kept his winnings from gambling for himself. Nana lived on a strict budget, making sure that the children's needs were met and that there was always enough food to share with Damian, Milagros and their children.

The strikers had barricaded the two main entrances into Simons and blocked the railroad tracks with company trucks. William Melone had protested vehemently the commandeering of his property but his screaming threats did not diminish the workers' determination. Rumors circulated from Walter's foremen that the boss planned to break the strike by hiring scab labor. Two days had passed since Gonzalo confirmed the rumors that today truckloads of men from Watts would arrive and take their jobs. The discussion had been heated among the strikers to achieve the final consensus: "Let's not get into a fight with the Negroes. I don't think they can do the job. Let's stand firm against them. If they go in, let's see if they know how to work."

Wives, sons and daughters brought lunch and drinks. Some families sat under the water tank, others moved under the shade of the trucks, and still others discovered a cool space in the center of the directional mandala. Ironically, a peaceful, quiet mood settled as the workers ate. A slight breeze played with Nana's black hair as she poured another glass of lemonade for Octavio. They had sat at the coolest place—under the water tank where water ran constantly down the tank and moistened the earth, resulting in flowers that permanently grew and bloomed. A blue hummingbird with violet wings flew and drank from each flower. Nana and Octavio, enthralled by the beauty of the ancient holy bird, were sharing a private moment when the repeated panicked sound of a truck horn alerted them to the arrival of the scabs. The lookout stationed at Washington and Vail skidded the truck to a stop, jumped into a cloud of red dust, and was met by his fellow workers.

"They're here! Three trucks of Negros! They're on Washington!" As the lookout spoke, a second man from the general store drove into the clearing dust.

"Three trucks of Negros arrived with Jacobo Ramos!" the worker called out to the group of men, women and children.

There were no more cool spaces. In the early afternoon the heat peaked to one hundred and three when Armando Takahashi Subia arrived from the general store where Caroline Decker prepared for the confrontation.

"Three trucks with Melone and Ramos. The ones on Washington will come soon. Gonzalo Pedroza is leading them." Armando pronounced Pedroza's name with a slight mocking tone. "We know what we have to do. And for the love of your families, don't shoot!"

Octavio turned to Nana who observed the scene by the fertile place under the water tank. Jose Ceballos led the men to positions before the barricade to wait.

Far off a dog barked and a bird cried out in the immense silence where the only human sounds were the occasional deep breaths of men oxygenating their lungs with hot red dust. Soon Octavio heard the powerful motors of approaching trucks. To the hum of marching pistons, whirling fans, turning wheels advancing like a lethargic metal, wooden, rubber, liquid beast, the first truck appeared on the top of the hill on Vail Street and descended, followed by the second and third trucks which transported unarmed men with black sullen faces who leaned against the wooden braces of the trucks and searched for one of their kind among the armed brown Mexicans. As the trucks turned left toward the center of the barricade, the black men realized that they were unwelcome. Words passed among them and from the truck beds they dialogued and called out to the drivers to stop. Abruptly, they faced the armed picket line. Red dust whirled and clung paste-like on their wet faces, necks and arms.

"Calm down! Nothin' gonna happen!" the black contractor who drove the lead truck shouted, leaning out of the truck cab.

Gonzalo Pedroza found himself in front of Armando, Jose Ceballos and Octavio who stood directly at the center of the human curtain which kept Gonzalo from entering the yard. Gonzalo went up on his toes and performed a grotesque ballet, looking toward the blockade over Octavio's right shoulder.

"Move your trucks," Gonzalo demanded.

"You move them, Gonzalo." Octavio stepped to the side and with a gesture of his arm and hand politely invited Gonzalo to take charge of the trucks blocking his way.

Gonzalo took several steps forward and felt his heart pounding and enormous dangling eyes swallowing him up, eating and struggling to devour him. The longer he vacillated the more grotesque his block face became. Under the intense heat of the sun and the ubiquitous red dust, Gonzalo's flesh shook and disfigured itself. His face seemed to be melting. His shirt was soaked with perspiration; his pants were wet at the crotch. Gonzalo's ugliness matched the extremes of hatred held toward him by the minds which destructured and restructured him at that moment. He wiped the sweat from his burning eyes, blinked and focused on the three trucks directly in his way.

"Three men, move the trucks!" Gonzalo yelled without turning his head away from the Mexican strikers.

Three blacks moved ever carefully sideways through the spaces in the picket line. They climbed over the wooden racks and into the cabs of the trucks. The engines started almost simultaneously and the three trucks were aggressively driven afar and slid to stop, creating a muffled dust hurricane.

"Get out of the way. We're going through!" Gonzalo committed himself and the black scabs to make his move.

He slammed the door and the driver raced the engine, dropped the truck into first gear and with a loud shattering crash rammed through the wooden barricade. The second and third trucks passed through without incident. The Mexican strikers had gambled that the hard-working conditions, the difficult learning process, and the heat would take its toll on the black workers. They had gambled that the scabs would not be able to do the work. The strikers lost the bet.

Exactly two weeks to the hour when the scabs had entered Simons, the Mexican workers gathered at a large Four Square church in Long Beach. Octavio arrived with Ignacio Sandoval. The meeting had been called by the workers to discuss what the strike had accomplished. The bright afternoon sunlight brilliantly illuminated the white glossy walls. No darkness was here; everyone could be seen clearly. At the head table sat Lanzetti, Armando and Caroline Decker, the three who had guided them from the start of the strike. Armando and Caroline had accompanied them through the toughest of times and Lanzetti had been present on a few occasions at the front lines, but mostly he had been absent, doing administrative work, he explained.

A few babies cried from different locations in the church hall. The workers were present both individually and with their families. Several men waved and Octavio smiled. He made his way up to the front by shaking the hands that reached out toward him. Octavio stopped at the fifth row where four chairs waited, reserved by Jose Ceballos. He sat silently, listening to the great noise that moved through the church hall. His feelings were dominated by a sense of constant anger, frustration and helplessness at the fact that nothing had been settled. William Melone had told the men that the strike would not end unless they went back to work and that Walter Simons had declared a strike on them and had threatened to shut down the brickyard permanently. To prove that he was serious and not dependent on the brickyard profits, Walter announced that he and Edit would take a month's vacation to Europe. The dialogue would soon be completely severed. The workers would have no one to negotiate with except Walter's superintendent and foremen.

The union organizers stood up and called the meeting to order. Caroline reported on the status of the Simons strike and other job actions in the Southern California area.

"We don't want to hear about how good others are doing," a man from the back shouted angrily. "What are we going to do? I have to feed my family. I have nine children and they're hungry! And we don't have an agreement yet."

"I am tired of waiting and being hungry. We should accept his miserable offer of a few cents and more credit at the company store!" a man on Octavio's right shouted to the organizers.

"Old man Simons is going on vacation. The strike has failed. They have screwed us again. Now look. I think we should return to work," a man on Octavio's left spoke.

"Well, what do you say?" Jose Ceballos shouted to the organizers.

"We know it's difficult. We must be patient and with time we will achieve our objectives," Armando answered the dissatisfaction.

"Look here, we have taken plenty. My children, my wife, they can't suffer any longer. They have the right to eat. And that old son-of-a-bitch Simons doesn't want to deal with us anymore," a man standing behind Octavio addressed the organizers.

"Mr. Lanzetti has another proposal to present to Mr. Simons when he returns," Armando began to explain.

"No, we don't want more plans!" a woman shouted from the back of the hall.

"The waiting is over! Now we want a contract or we will return to work without one!" another woman holding a child said to the organizers.

"If the union could pay more help to continue the strike, at least until Simons returns, we could wait a little more. I can't continue holding out with no food money," an old man directed to Lanzetti.

"We cannot do that. Your benefits, what you contributed, are all used," Lanzetti answered and the response was chaotic and loud.

The Mexican workers had heard enough and let their anger boil over in words. Lanzetti looked to his colleagues next to him. Armando called for order.

"What do you mean we don't have more benefits? Where are our dues?" Octavio asked, disguising frustration with great effort.

"We had to use some of your funds to help other strikers. Your monies went into a general fund for all the strikers throughout the area," Lanzetti replied.

"And now we need it and there's no help. We want our money now. I don't believe that it's all gone!" Octavio shouted.

"You told us to strike with assurances of help when necessary." Jose Ceballos shook his fist at Lanzetti.

"You misunderstood the strike benefits," Lanzetti shouted.

"We understand perfectly. We want our money, our share, right now!" Octavio screamed at Lanzetti. Armando, Caroline, and Lanzetti folded their papers and prepared to exit.

"Shut up, Revueltas. We cannot give you anything back. Now shut up and listen!" Lanzetti screamed.

"No! You listen! You are a bunch of sons-of-bitches. You're the same as old man Simons. Your only interest is in what you're going to gain. You're thieves and exploiters!" Octavio allowed his hatred to speak.

"Revueltas, I could have you banished from every brickyard and field in the state. You would never get a job. You would never work anywhere!" Lanzetti threatened in full rage.

"Anywhere in the world, you son-of-a-bitch!" Octavio went for Lanzetti and was restrained by Ignacio Sandoval, Jose Ceballos and fellow workers who in a human ball held back Octavio.

"Anywhere in the world!" Octavio shouted at the three bodies that walked out the back of the Four Square church in Long Beach.

The warmth of the evening breeze seemed to encourage Octavio to push to the back of his mind the cries from across the sea, the desperation in the country in which he chose to live, from the world attempting to devour itself. He would never let go of his wife and children. He would hold them in his heart constantly, in his mind forever. If he were to let go, the energy invested in caring would surely turn to hate and would explode into a fatal rampage against the oppressive forces, against the enemy which owned everything he possessed. The material objects that surrounded and touched him were temporary, for they could easily be passed on to someone else. . . . Our situation is hopeless . . . Octavio slumped into the living room sofa and silently observed his children. . . . They are not the problem but the world they live in is hopeless. If I were rich, they wouldn't suffer and their future would be guaranteed. I could be rich but I would have to be like them, a lick-their-ass boy like Gonzalo Pedroza, Jacobo Ramos and William Melone. They sold themselves out. I'll never be like them, never . . . .

From the periphery of his right eye a spot of blue entered, advanced, enlarged and became life. Nana, in a blue dress, brought a cup of tea and set it on the coffee table. She reached around Octavio's neck and snuggled up. She too enjoyed the children playing in the living room. Nana contemplated the house that she worked daily to maintain. She smiled at the clean clothes and faces of her offspring. Everything smelled as bright as spring.

"Drink the tea. It's that you're tired. Sleep and you'll see that tomorrow everything will be different," Nana spoke, somehow assured and not afraid of the future.

Octavio drank the tea and relaxed. His heavy eyelids closed. Nana put the children to bed, went for her husband and took him to bed. That evening she told Octavio that she had been pregnant for two months. Octavio laughed, Nana joined in, and gradually their bodies struggled passionately to unite and separate.

The voices in the house moved in and out of Octavio's mind as he thought about the founding of the cooperative store. The voices were the same voices that had surrounded Octavio for years, voices that at times bothered him but that he loved more than his life. The children—Micaela, Arturo and Javier—waited excitedly to meet and see what a newborn baby looked like. Octavio had quieted them and saw them playing in their room. Tati had brought tea to warm him and prevent a chill from the dampness in the air. It had rained for two days, flooded Simons and converted the streets into mud rivers that led into other streets where the Simons Mexicans lived. Ignacio Sandoval lit a cigarette. The flame at the end of the match seemed to Octavio to be pasted against the whitewashed wall of the living room. Octavio had witnessed his compadre's cigarette ritual hundreds, perhaps thousands of times. He realized that Ignacio had been with him during his most critical moments in life.

Ignacio was present the day, one week after Octavio had told the union organizers to go to hell, in which Octavio, Jose Ceballos, Vicente Limon and Ignacio discussed plans for the cooperative store. Octavio recalled the day after the strike. Early that morning the barricades were cleaned, by eight o'clock the men were at their jobs and by late afternoon the brick-yard was well on its way to producing seventy-five thousand bricks. The men had returned to work in silence; not a word had been spoken as they walked to their posts. There was a shared sentiment of defeat that domi-nated the workers that day. Depressed, Octavio still worked hard. It was during a lunch break that he entered into the conversation about the coop-erative workers' store. He, Jose Ceballos, and Vicente Limon were the three men designated as decision makers and possibly the store's adminis-trators. The plan was to have each family contribute five dollars to the cooperative store treasury and with these monies purchase items of neces-sity at discount prices. The workers developed a plan of purchase, credit and payment to be implemented as soon as they established a store. It was decided in a town meeting that the three designated organizers should approach Gonzalo Pedroza, Jacobo Ramos and William Melone.

The workers' representatives met with Gonzalo, Jacobo and William in the half-stocked general store which had ceased selling during the strike. Jacobo had taken advantage of the work stoppage to take a precise inven-tory. He had several books and ledgers which he had prepared for Walter that showed the exact financial condition of the general store and post office. Jacobo was proud of his accounting efforts and hoped that with such an excellent report Walter would allow him to expand the store once the brickyard got back to normal. Jacobo discussed these matters with Gonzalo and William early on the morning that the cooperative store organizers approached the general store.

"Look who's coming," Gonzalo said sarcastically. William went to the window. Jacobo strained to see from where he sat.

"What do they want now? Another strike?" William and Gonzalo laughed.

Jacobo continued to review his ledgers. The transition from strike to production occurred smoothly and without incident. The three Simons administrators had heard rumors of continuing demands from the workers but did not expect any response other than diligent work from the defeated Mexicans. Nonetheless, three men walked up to the general store, entered and closed the door. A tension built which made Octavio scratch the back of his neck. A pause was filled with the sound of birds. Gonzalo broke a jagged smile over his grotesque block face. William stared out the window, across the street to a large camphor tree. Jacobo roamed over his books, oblivious to who had entered. No one in the room threatened him.

"What can I do for you men?" William searched the trees.

"Well, speak up! What do you want?" Gonzalo said aggressively.

Jose Ceballos, Vicente Limon, and Octavio waited, enjoying the uneasiness which their presence caused the foreman and the superintendent. Octavio moved to Jacobo's desk and Jose and Vicente situated themselves along opposite walls of the room. The physical positioning confused Gonzalo. He made a complete circle following the intruders' movement. William kept looking out the window and refused to speak to them directly.

"The workers have decided to have a cooperative store. We need a place," Jose said to Gonzalo.

"I don't think that Mr. Simons will like that idea," Gonzalo said and pointed to William at the window.

"Mr. Melone, the men want to ask the patron for a place," Jose said and watched Jacobo annoyingly turn the pages of one of his ledgers.

"Talk to Jacobo. He's in charge of the general store and you have to arrange it with him. Tell him to ask Mr. Simons for you." William left the general store and never faced the three workers directly.

Five men felt the nervousness of the others as Jacobo came to the end of his ledger. "Why do you want a store? You should use this one," he said.

"We want our own cooperative store. We want a store that will help us, not keep us in constant debt for the rest of our lives, " Octavio challenged the man who pressured the workers by collecting numbers in red, white and blue leather-bound ledgers.

"Like Gonzalo said, Mr. Simons won't like your idea. But if you insist, I'll ask him tomorrow," Jacobo said.

"Oh, so he didn't go on vacation. We want his answer within a week. If not, we'll look for him at his home," Jose replied as he moved to the door with Vicente and Octavio.

The memory of that confrontation caused Octavio to grimace as he placed the bucket on the grill over the fire. When Nana gave birth, Tati asked for buckets of hot water. This time it seemed that more water than usual was required. He watched the flame and listened to Nana inside pushing their child into the world. The wind fanned the fire and chilled his hands. His body felt intensely the process of birth which occurred just a few feet away.

Happiness and sadness lingered in his mind as he thought about Jacobo reporting Walter's decision concerning the cooperative store. The patron had agreed that the workers should have their own store and he demonstrated his support by giving them the place where the Simons general store was located. Jacobo confessed that he had tried to convince Walter to negate the workers' request. Despite his arguments, Walter wanted to give the general store to the Mexicans as a sign of solidarity, a reward for returning to work. Jacobo's work and plans for the general store had been sabotaged by the defeated workers.

Jacobo's job changed in that his only duty became that of rayador, company timekeeper. He kept the same salary and privileges but the responsibilities lessened to the point that he questioned whether or not he merited his salary. The possibility of leaving the company entered his thinking. Jacobo refused to help in the transition of administration of the general store and he never again entered the store.

Guadalupe Sandoval was elected to be store manager, Vicente Limon treasurer and clerk, and Leon and Edit Sandoval store buyers. The store's cooperative constitution was simple: five dollar entrance fee, and member must pay at least half of credit purchase debt each month. If these rules were abused, the member was subject to garnishment of wages or expulsion from the cooperative store.

The abuse of credit was what it came down to. The workers had long been in the business of production and had been exploited and now they, by choice, had launched themselves in the business of selling and buying made easy by the credit installment plan, abonar. This would abolish the Mexican fear of debt. However, it was the installment plan that was the problem with the cooperative store. The saddest thing about all this effort, all the disorganization that it created, was that it had ended in a fight about how much was stolen and who kept what was stolen.

One week after the birth of Flor Revueltas, Octavio and Nana's fourth child, the signal to begin the meeting of the members of the Simons Workers Cooperative Store was given by Guadalupe Sandoval, cooperative store manager, but nobody paid any attention. Guadalupe raised the beer bottle from which he drank and banged it on the table. On the fifth contact, beer ran over the table and onto Guadalupe who stood up and flung the bottomless glass receptacle to the floor. The bottle shattered at the feet of the men sitting in the front row.

"What the hell's happening?" a man yelled.

With the breaking of the bottle, the tone of the meeting was set. Comments and laughter from the members continued as they finally settled down to question the store administrators. Octavio observed from the back of the store. The broken bottles and spilled beer symbolized to him the attitude about credit that had developed among the participating workers. Beer had become the largest commodity sold on credit. Flushed with their new power, the men would come in and take six cases and walk out the store saying "Charge it."

Octavio had always saved money, and he seldom bought anything on credit. To the people who filled the store, however, credit was "una maravilla," but the bad use of it gradually destroyed an excellent idea. As the meeting moved into evening, thousands of accusative words were thrown toward the administrators who flung them back at the members.

"The administrators threw away a page of the book!" a man pointed to Antonio Revueltas, Octavio's uncle who had abused the credit plan.

"Where supposedly your account was recorded, Antonio!" another member shouted.

"I don't believe you paid not even half of what you charged. You owe a lot more than what is in that book," a man standing next to Octavio said.

"It's that none of the administrators carefully recorded what was taken from the store. Many times I have entered the store and seen one of us leave with a six-pack or a bag of groceries and Vicente or Guadalupe or Leon would say 'Oh, we'll record it later.' But no one would record anything," another worker spoke out.

"We went to tell Octavio so that he would tell Gonzalo or William." A man in the middle of the assembly indicated Octavio.

"Everything is registered in the book!" Guadalupe insisted.

"We don't agree. And we have to deal with Antonio's case. He hasn't paid anything on his account and the rules say we have to kick him out," the first man to speak said.

"I don't pay any more than what is marked in the book. I'll pay half of that amount. If that's not enough then I'll leave." Antonio stood up and moved to the door.

"Antonio, please don't leave." Guadalupe saw a huge debt about to abandon responsibility of payment.

"Kick him out if he doesn't pay what's in the book!" a woman shouted to Antonio.

"Tell him to pay, Octavio!" Leon Martinez demanded.

Octavio moved without hesitation to the front of the store, went directly at Guadalupe, grabbed the store credit ledger and headed toward the exit.

"Where are you going, Octavio?" Vicente Limon called out.

Octavio stopped about halfway to the door and raised the ledger above his head. "I'm going to burn this damn book!"

Octavio's last word was answered by his fellow workers and cooperative store members who lunged at him to save the book. The members returned the ledger to the front of the store, to the administrators who placed the credit record in front of the cooperative body. Octavio sat on a bench at the back and listened to the words dance violently in his brain. He felt tired when his name was nominated for treasurer.

"No thanks. I don't accept. Treasurer, well, what am I going to treasure? The debts? You say there's a thousand dollars in the bank. Where is it? I want nothing to do with this. You can have your store."

Octavio walked out into the evening and for the first time in his life in the United States he felt alone. He felt that he had been cut off from the groups and organizations that he should support or that should support him. He headed home, realizing that in the future no one would help him—only Nana, Micaela, Arturo, Javier, Flor and himself.

Chapter 18

Arturo Revueltas' side of the room he shared with his brother was always organized, neat and clean, and mirrored a perfection that passed through his eyes and brain but emerged scrambled around as distorted verbal utterances. He understood what he heard. He could distinguish clearly every word in Spanish. English was more of a challenge; at times the words sounded extremely long and seemingly endless but at other moments he could identify each word. He knew two words well, for they had been used repeatedly to describe his behavior at school and at church. They had become his words. His sign. His social emblem. When Father Charles, the local priest, used the two words to describe him before the neighborhood boys and two nuns who taught catechism at Mount Carmel, Arturo equated the two words to his name.

"Bad boy! Arturo, you are a bad boy!" Father Charles shouted as he picked up Mikey Rodelo whom Arturo had knocked to the ground after Mikey goosed him with a stick.

"Bad boy!" Father Charles repeated while Mikey faked crying.

Now the priest whom everybody respected and even Arturo liked had identified him as a bad boy. He was bad for defending himself, and worse because he did not learn from his teachers. He tried, but when he repeated or wrote or solved math problems the teachers always said he was wrong. Arturo never said or wrote the answers correctly. Although to Arturo his letters and numbers seemed written well, to the teachers, parents, sisters, brother and friends, they appeared distorted.

Twelve-year-old Arturo walked hand in hand with his mother toward the house after a parent conference where Nana had been told that her oldest son was a bad boy. Nana and Arturo were on Vail when Father Charles drove by in a truck. Arturo immediately waved. Nana stopped and watched the priest tip his hat and drive by.

Father Charles, with his eyes fixed straight ahead on the cooperative store, thought about the problems of the Mexican boys he was sent to minister. He agreed with Walter Simons' concept of providing the Mexicans with the basic necessities and enclosing them in a small compound such as Simons town. They were true innocent children of God who required men like Walter and himself to take care of them and guide them through the temptations of life. The Mexicans lived in terrible conditions throughout the city. In the East Los Angeles area, many of the large homes of the millionaire Anglo population had been taken over by charitable institutions, and the smaller homes were becoming the homes of second and third-generation Mexicans.

Many times Father Charles had helped to repair the toilets, baths and showers in these homes; nontheless, the facilities available in the houses were not adequately proportionate to the number of users. Even though these living arrangements seemed to be an improvement over the conditions the Mexicans had left, ten families to a house was unconducive to progressive living. But no matter what he did to help, Father Charles believed that the Mexicans, in time, would allow the houses to deteriorate to the level of the inhumane living quarters of the industrial districts.

Father Charles parked by the cooperative store and walked to the back of the car. The Simons homes on Vail brought on more ruminations about Mexican housing. There were certain spots in the East Los Angeles area that were already as bad as the industrial district ever was. He thought of the Flats district in the neighborhood of the Pecan Playground. Another terrible place was located east of Soto Street and south of Whittier Boulevard. This latter barrio grew because of several appearances the Virgin of Guadalupe had made and the miracles the people had witnessed there. The housing and living conditions were worse than deplorable. Yet the people flocked to live near the holy trees, shacks and gutters where the Virgin had appeared. Most of the Mexican families did not own their homes; therefore, they made little effort to improve the dwellings. The owners, for the most part large corporations in constant need of bottom cheap labor, saw no profit in improving the residences because they might soon want to clear the land for industrial development. Also, it was far easier to find tenants for a shack in this area at ten to fifteen dollars per month than to get a few dollars more after greatly improving the place at considerable expense. Compared to the way other Mexicans lived in Los Angeles, Walter Simons' Mexicans were living in paradise. Father Charles learned that in the industrial areas the Mexican bad boys were more difficult, if not impossible, to control. In Simons it was a lot easier to control the youth. But to control the youth of Simons he had to watch bad boys like Arturo Revueltas carefully.

The Revueltas children sat outside in Nana's backyard garden. Micaela, Javier and Flor played together. Arturo stared up at something beyond the frame in which Octavio and Nana saw him from the kitchen door. Nana poured more tea into Octavio's cup, sat down and stirred the sugar into the piping hot tea in her cup. They had been discussing Arturo's school report. His teacher had identified Arturo as a bad boy who did not care to learn. She suggested that if he did not improve his school performance, Arturo should be taken out of school for he was wasting the teacher's time as well as his own. He would do better working or as an apprentice learning a trade. Nana did not accept the teacher's evaluation or her recommendation. She and Octavio simply did not know what to do next, or whom to see for help. They wanted Arturo to succeed in school but for some unknown reason he did not learn. His speech and sentence construction seemed to fluctuate. At times he spoke well enough to be understood but there were other times when he semed to lapse into unintelligible structures. Nonetheless, Nana refused to give up on her oldest son.

"No, Octavio, those teachers have to do something for him," Nana spoke defiantly.

"What?" Octavio spoke softly.

"I'll never permit them to take him out of school. He's still a baby and he should stay in school even if he doesn't learn anything. Arturo should spend his days in school and not at the brickyard working." Nana drank and Octavio watched the steam from the hot tea rise.

The children continued to play in the garden. Now Arturo had joined them. He played and laughed. He did what all children his age did. Octavio took Nana's hand and held on. He was glad that Arturo was not old enough to be sent away to any foreign war. Across the Atlantic the Nazis continued to over-run Europe. In the Pacific the Japanese war machine stepped up aggression against China and looked on to the South Pacific. Octavio looked at his children and felt compelled to protect them if the enemy dared to attack the United States. But if his son had to fight, he would want him to fight. Los Niños Heroes came to his mind. But he, like many others, believed that no country had the capacity to attack the United States. The distance and vastness of the country rendered an attack impossible. He and Nana agreed with President Roosevelt's plan to send arms, munitions, food and other war supplies to countries that were friends and important to the protection of the United States. But only as a last recourse did he and Nana want American boys to die in Europe. Octavio drank another cup of tea.

The possibility to fight and save Europe from the Nazis and the fascists created a great desire and readiness in the hearts of American youth to go overseas. The Mexican youth of Simons were no exception. The Mexicans were ready to throw chingadazos with the bad guys in Europe.

When it came, it hit with a terrible force and no quarter was given. On Sunday, December 7, 1941, every United States citizen, non-citizen, documented and undocumented resident was stunned by the news flashes of the calculated attack on the United States Pacific fleet at Pearl Harbor.

ALEJANDRO MORALES

The news of the Japanese sneak attack was screamed in English and in Spanish by every radio station in the country. The reports came emotionally charged and were communicated in an intense, exciting manner by Spanish-speaking reporters in Los Angeles. No doubt existed in the opinion of people that the United States would now declare war on Japan. Days later Japan's Axis partners, Germany and Italy, pronounced war on the United States. The whole world followed the latest movements and developments in the European and now the Pacific theater.

In the United States the people now began to worry about the contribution each individual would make to win the war, and in the Mexican neighborhoods throughout the country it was no different. Since the draft began, many Mexicans had volunteered. Latinos from North, Central and South America came to enlist in the armed forces. They were encouraged by the fact that the first draftee from Los Angeles to be picked by President Roosevelt was a Latino. Mexican young men did not even ask. They shouted what their role would be. They wanted to fight the enemy. And so they came and gathered from all the barrios: North Platte, Cheyenne, Maravilla, La Loma, Austin, Limonera, Hollywood, Lorain, Los Dos Laredos, Del Rio, Saint Louis, Rose Hill, Sespe, West Side San Anto, San Marcos, El Hoyo, Barrio Margarito, Quinto de Houston, San Benito, Mathis, Varelas, Ogden, Los Batos, Jackson, Cantaranas, Barelas Verde, Westside Denver, Calle Ancha, Karrimer, La Smelter, El Piquete, Fernando, Corpos, Fresno, Reclas, Las Cruces, La Daisy, La Chicago, El Dorado, La Palomilla, El Jardin, Trinidad, Conejos, El Globo, La Milwaukee, Verdugo, El Ranchito, El Pachuco, Juariles, Garidy, Flats, Magnolia, Jimtown, Chiques, The Camp, Chavez Ravine, Los Marcos, Calle Guadalupe, Buena Vista, La Seis, El Sur, Simons.

From all Mexican neighborhoods the homeboys came ready to defend and die for their home turf, the United States.

Octavio and Nana entered the almost defunct cooperative store. Only the most basic food items were sold by the last people given the charge of running the store. As the cooperative members ceased their participation, it gradually became a private enterprise and holding for Francisco and Ernestina Pedroza, son and daughter of Gonzalo Pedroza who had been caught stealing food and clothing from the cooperative store and selling the goods at discounted prices to willing buyers. When Walter was told of the misconduct of his faithful servant warrior he cried. He ordered the immediate release of Gonzalo from his police and foreman duties and demoted him to apprentice worker.

Gonzalo's hideous cubed head and face now had such an uncountable quantity of sharp corners and points protruding from it that only the men and women who knew him could recognize him. His family and two women loved him still, and to Octavio's and Nana's surprise both women were in the cooperative store purchasing coffee, sugar and canned food. Amalia picked up two full bags from the counter. She greeted Octavio and Nana as she hurriedly went out the door. Nana stepped to the door and saw Amalia get into the back seat of a car driven by two young men in army uniforms. . . . ¡Qué bonitos muchachos! Nana felt in her heart. Octavio moved from the coffee and tea section and placed two cans of each on the counter. Pascuala Pedroza looked at her son behind the counter and pointed to the shelf directly behind him.

"Francisco, give me two boxes of sugar. When will food be rationed?" Pascuala smiled at Octavio and Nana.

"It is, Mama." Francisco placed Pascuala's purchase into a large box.

"Good morning, Mrs. Pedroza," Nana said and raised her hand to Francisco.

"Morning, Nanita, Octavio." Pascuala opened her bag, pulled out a small blue book and gave it to her son.

"How is Mr. Pedroza?" Octavio asked cautiously. Francisco stopped writing.

"Mr. Simons gave him an administrative job. Thank God he didn't put him out in the yard with the workers. He can't do heavy labor. He can't anymore." Pascuala took the book from Francisco and placed it in her purse.

"How are things going for you with this war?" Pascuala asked. The sound of her voice saddened and diminished at the end of the question. She did not wait for an answer. "They took my Wally. Wally is the youngest."

Francisco added the cost of Octavio's and Nana's goods.

The Simons youth were in the thick of battle in the Pacific and European theaters. Sad news came to Simons many times: "He lost his leg, but he's alive. . . . He was shot in the stomach but he's coming home . . . He lost his hearing . . . He's in the hospital . . . He's blind, but he's in Hawaii . . ."

Terrible news came to Simons when Amalia was told by an Army captain that both her boys were lost at sea. Pascuala and Gonzalo Pedroza never said a word when they were told that their Wally was missing in action in Sicily.

On June 2, 1943, Wally Pedroza, after witnessing his company commander and nine enlisted men die and realizing that his company was helplessly pinned by German machine gun fire, picked up a BAR and became a one-man destruction squad. Firing from his hip he moved on the enemy and put out two machine gun emplacements. Wally took two shots to the stomach but still kept advancing forward. . . . ¡Ya estuvo cabrones! ¡Ya me ahuitaron! . . . Wally headed towards a third machine gun. Grenades exploded around him as he moved forward. Wally threw a grenade and wiped out the machine gun nest. He advanced and killed seven more of the enemy. After one hundred yards he confronted a fourth and a fifth machine gun. Wally was instantly hit by what seemed to him a ton of fiery pins penetrating his body. He squeezed the trigger of the BAR for one long eternal burst. Silence and blackness fell on him forever in a small innocent Italian town.

Wally Pedroza was proud of the Aztec blood that flowed through his veins. And once pushed against a corner, pinned down and used to the life of the underdog, used to fighting unimaginable odds and uphill struggles, and having a lot of huevos, Wally could only reason one way and that was to throw chingadazos. He was not going to wait to get his butt kicked. . . . El Wally Pedroza ne se va a rajar . . . He would kick ass. He would do it for the United States of America, for his raza, for his barrio Simons, for his homeboys and homegirls, for his sisters and brothers, for his father and mother. Wally was not going to wait around for someone else to do the job because before he went he saw that every man around him was frozen with fear.

"¡Yo no me rajo!" Wally Pedroza ran forward into millions of butterflies.

Neighbors and family members stared at each other through the silence that followed after Gonzalo knocked on the door of the bathroom where Pascuala had sobbed for the past half-hour. The military man who had brought the brown envelope which held the words of Wally's heroism, death and burial spoke with Wally's brothers and sisters. Octavio and Nana waited behind Gonzalo for Pascuala to exit. The door opened. Nana took Pascuala by the arm and led her to the kitchen. Octavio followed and served hot apple cider. Neighbors talked softly while over their respectable conversation Pascuala's voice and words slowly demanded attention.

"I begged him not to go. I offered to pay his way to Mexico. But he refused. He decided to go so that the gringos would understand that the Mexicans feel just as much American as they do. I didn't want him to go. The Japanese are all over the world. The Japanese killed him." Pascuala raised her hands as she implored the sky.

Octavio and Father Charles moved closer to the sobbing Pascuala. Gonzalo's uncommon face and protruding eyes glared into the noise of people who had come to give their condolences to the family and to cry out the great pride they had been given by the sacrifice of one of their sons. The Mexicans of Simons felt as American as any other American in the United States. The war reports had been interpreted as bad during those days and it was logical to expect bad news again. However, the workers of Simons had discovered a confidence in the death of Wally Pedroza.

"The Japanese killed my Wally!" Pascuala screamed.

Father Charles placed his hand on Pascuala's shoulder to calm her down.

"It was not the Japanese," Octavio, disgusted, said to Nana who agreed and went to comfort Pascuala.

Octavio watched Nana cool Pascuala's face with a wet towel. He remembered watching, over a year ago, a Japanese woman cool the face of her hysterical mother who refused to be forced from her home of more than forty years. In broken English the Japanese screamed that they owned the land and had deeds to confirm their claim. Pearl Harbor intensified long-standing animosity toward the Japanese in California. In Southern California, like an unexpected wave, the army forced the Japanese from their lands and homes and imprisoned them in concentration camps. Octavio, Nana and the children had witnessed these events. On a Saturday in March, Montebello police, federal agents and army troops moved down Vail, Date, Washington, Greenwood and Maple streets, sur rounding the entire area where in the center was located the Japanese school. They found several Japanese families hiding in the basement. Rumors circulated that long distance radio equipment and large amounts of money were found with the Japanese spies. One of the older Japanese men refused to leave and demanded his rights as an American citizen. The police grabbed the old man and clubbed him to the ground. The Japanese were loaded onto trucks.

"My husband is fighting for America!" a Japanese woman with two children at her legs screamed at the agent who pushed her toward the truck.

In the afternoon Nana and Arturo, who had gone to buy vegetables at the Japanese farms on Telegraph Road, discovered the abandoned Japanese houses. They had not taken anything. Food had even been left cooking on the stove. The Japanese had disappeared and those who remained for the time being were soldiers watching over their properties until the government decided what to do with their belongings. Stories ran rampant that the Japanese had been organizing an internal fifth column to sabotage the American war effort. For the Japanese, civil liberties and rights had been suspended. They were considered dangerous, the enemy within.

"Get out of here, lady. Them Japs are all gone and they won't be back. Get lost and don't come back here anymore," the soldier yelled at Nana and Arturo who heard several soldiers rummaging through the house.

Arturo looked away from the house to the fields where he had worked in the summer and in the spring. He felt the world had become eerie, strange, unrecognizable without the presence of the Japanese families. The fields belonged to nobody. The crops would go unpicked, and there would be no job for Arturo. Octavio was watering Nana's plants when Arturo returned home and spoke of the injustice he and Nana had witnessed at the Japanese farm.

At the Pedroza home, Arturo brought another wet towel to his mother to cool Pascua la Pedroza who had screamed that the Japanese were planning to murder all of the people of Simons.

"The Mexicans are in danger!" Pascuala cried in anguish when she saw Arturo and the other young men of Simons.

Not long after the Japanese had been herded into concentration camps in California and Arizona, the Anglo-American population discovered that this action had not solved any pre-existing economic and political problems. And the fear of espionage did not go away. Outside Simons, in a world where fantasy was a way of life, the dominant ruling mentality had decided that the scapegoat replacement for the Japanese would be the Mexicans. The Hearst newspapers launched the first rumors against the Mexicans and set out to effectively and deliberately create fear: "Mexican Crime, Mexican Juvenile Delinquency Rising." Within six months the newspapers had fired up a strong anti-Mexican sentiment on the verge of violent retaliation against the Mexicans. The police of Los Angeles and the surrounding cities used any excuse to arrest and beat Mexicans. The Anglo-American citizenry followed the official example and freely attacked Mexican males old enough to be dangerous. While men were dying in Europe, Africa and the Pacific, the press removed the war news from the front page, paving the way for Mexican blood on the pavement.

Eleven sailors on leave from their station in Los Angeles walked through one of the worst slum areas of the city. The section was predominantly Mexican. The sailors were in an area where few Anglo-Americans, let alone sailors, found their way. Waiting to go overseas to get into some of the action, and bored by military discipline and life, the sailors were driven to an explosive edge. As they later reported, the attack came by surprise. Forty to fifty Mexicans, a gang of zoot suiters, pounced on them and beat them up. By late that evening a vengeance squad made up of off-duty police went to get the Mexicans. The squad entered the barrio where the attack had supposedly occurred and found no one to arrest. Frustrated, they went from house to house searching for any Mexican wearing a zoot suit.

The night after the police raid, two hundred sailors decided to take matters into their own hands and set out to hunt for zoot suit greasers. Near Chinatown the sailors hired forty taxicabs and began to cruise the downtown streets. Minutes later they came across the first victim in a long list of bloodied names. The boy was left naked, badly beaten and bleeding profusely, lying on the pavement. The military task force resumed the search for more gangster Mexicans. The Mexican boys did not have much chance against two hundred drunken sailors hell-bent on raiding the city for Mexican zooters. The police watched the confrontations and picked up the broken bodies of the Mexican youths, arresting them for disturbing the peace, assault and drunkenness. The newspapers reported the sailors' actions in heroic terms, praising the military men's effort to do what the police seemingly had failed to. The papers did not report the resistance on the part of the Mexicans but described them as being rough, cowardly youth fleeing for cover. The Anglo-American populaton was convinced that their Anglo military youth had the enemy on the run.

The Los Angeles press published dire warnings that the Mexicans were preparing to launch massive attacks on Anglo-American servicemen and the community at large. To insure that a million-dollar newspaper riot would occur, the papers published the exact time and place where the Mexicans were expected to attack. In the Mexican communities parents were not allowing their sons and daughters to leave the house for fear of them being brutalized or killed.

Time and history would later write about the days after June 7, 1943, when the movie theaters were invaded and every zoot suiter the military boys could find was dragged out to the street and beaten senseless; when cripples were attacked; when children were viciously taken from their parents and stripped of their clothing and battered with sadistic frenzy and joy; when the Mexican barrios were in constant turmoil; when thousands of Mexican mothers searched frantically to locate their missing sons and daughters; when Anglo-American military terrorists hoodlumized thou-sands of innocent people; when the Anglo-American population, the government representatives and the press applauded the neo-Nazi actions.

"It's too bad the servicemen were called off before they could finish the job," a journalist said.

"That's exactly what we need to end lawlessness: more of the same action being conducted by the servicemen. All loyal citizens should follow their excellent example," a Los Angeles County Supervisor declared.

"Zoot suits are an indication of subversive character. The greasers will do anything to get the Southwest back!" the Ventura Assistant District Attorney stated.

". . . the wearing of a zoot suit is declared to be a misdemeanor," a resolution stated that was drafted, adopted, and enforced by the Los Angeles City Council.

"Speaking Mexican is un-American, subversive and should be declared a felony and unconstitutional. Don't these greasers know that the official language of the United States is English?" the Anglo-American citizenry demanded.

". . . The time has come to serve notice that the City of Los Angeles will no longer be terrorized by a relatively small handful of morons parading as zoot suit hoodlums. To delay action now means to court disaster later on," McAnhester Boddy editorialized and signed in the *Daily News*.

Mexican youth reacted by proudly and defiantly wearing the zoot suit. The boys sported pegged pants with tight cuffs around the ankles, pleats and high waists up under the armpits, wide-shouldered long, loose coats, heavy thick-soled shoes with a glass shine, long gold chains which added glitter to the elegant attire, and duck-tailed haircuts protected by a super fine hat, or tondito. They were not going to be repressed as to what they should wear or the language they should speak.

"A mi nadie me va a decir lo que puedo vestir. Tengo el derecho de llevar lo que me da la gana," a Simons youth declared.

"My three carnales are fighting in Europe, ese, and nobody is going to tell me what to wear," a fourteen-year-old girl said.

"A mi no me importa si me echan en la carcel pero no me quito el zoot suit y no les hablo inglés," a thirteen-year-old boy said.

Arturo carried the neatly folded zoot suit tucked carefully in a brown shopping bag. At home he placed it under his bed. He would don it on Saturday when he went to the show with his cousins Albert and Luis Pino who had sold him the entire ensemble. Arturo had bought the suit two weeks after he left Montebello Junior High, having been in a fight with an Anglo student who had called him derogatory names.

"Mexican greasers do not deserve to walk on the same cement with loyal patriotic white boys," the boy said as he pushed Arturo to the street.

Arturo was forced to defend himself with his fists and in so doing opened a long and deep laceration over the boy's eye. In the scuffle, the boy also suffered deep cuts across his left cheek, the bridge of his nose, and his right cheek when he hit the sharp edge of the sidewalk.

The five witnesses to the fight supported Arturo's testimony. The board of education reinstated Arturo and asked him to return to school, at which time the fourteen-year-old Arturo stated that he had no interest in returning to a school that did not want him.

Octavio and Nana wanted Arturo to continue but their son had made his final decision to drop out. A few weeks later Octavio offered his oldest son an ultimatum: "Return to school or get a job!" and gave him money to buy clothes.

"Oh God, Arturo! Take those clothes off!" Nana exclaimed when her son strutted into the living room dressed in the latest zoot suit attire.

"Mama, sharp this is!" Arturo showed off the newly learned language of zoot suitism. He was proud to wear the zoot suit that Saturday night.

"God forbid your father to see you! Take that clown suit off immediately," Nana said with a look which meant no more argument. "Your father does not like those pachuco suits. And you know how dangerous it is to wear them."

Arturo walked to the mirror in the portable closet in his parents' bedroom. Nana followed.

"Return the suit. If your father sees you wearing it he'll hit you. He gave you money to buy clothes for work." Nana waited for Arturo who admired his pleated pants.

"I spent almost all my money on this suit, Mama," Arturo pleaded for her to understand. Nana turned from her chest of drawers.

"Here, take this money. Buy work clothes and shoes. And show the clothes to your father. Arturo, son, please do this. And take that ridiculous suit off. Your father will be home soon." Nana handed Arturo the money.

That evening after dinner, carrying a brown shopping bag, Arturo went to Luis Pino's home and returned the zoot suit. Luis refused to return the money. Night gradually caught Arturo on his walk back to his house. A silent Simons Brickyard lay before him in the red sunset, and the bluish-black of the silver-studded sky pushed the horizon down far away. The brick-making machines were silent. There were no big orders like the ones long ago that he had heard the men talk about. There would be no work for him at the yard. His father could not help. Arturo knew that Octavio was one of the men marked to be released as soon as the war ended. He wondered how it was in those far-off countries. A truck drove by slowly. The night watchman flashed a light and waved.

"Go home, Arturo!" The night watchman's shout drifted in the December evening.

The truck slowly moved away. Arturo found himself walking alone in silence and darkness. He passed the drying racks. Their constant murmur did not frighten him. The light at the main entrance on Vail revealed the red barren clay, earth that required men like his father to transform it into building brick. His father had worked there a lifetime, Arturo's lifetime, and he had stained his lungs red, like his grandfather. Simons: crown of red brick companies, creator of material to rebuild the crumbling world. Arturo saw the thousands of men and their families with crowns of bricks on their heads, burdens of unrecognized labor carried forever by the Mexicans who worked, lived and called Simons home. His father's face guided him through the night. His mother came to help. His brother Javier and his sisters Micaela and Flor now ran along with him. They all moved effortlessly through the night. He ran with two bricks, one in each hand, when he found himself before his father amidst Nana's garden.

"What's wrong, son?" Octavio asked as Nana neared.

Arturo stood silently and lifted up to his father and mother two red bricks with the name of Simons deeply stamped on each. Octavio took them and, like Nana, puzzled, followed Arturo into the house.

Chapter 19

The March winds cleared the Southern California skies. The sun broke through the persistent clouds and enveloped Nana in a cozy warmth as she fought the wind for the laundry she struggled to fold and place in a basket. A strong gust made her hold the clean sheet to her breasts which felt larger. Soon they would prepare for milk. As they enlarged, Octavio would kiss and lick them and make her nipples rise and he would run his hands over the firmness of her body and she would make him smile. Nana watched the clouds traverse the firmament and thought of her time, woman time, Mexican time, and how none had been fulfilled yet because life was a constant search for Eden. And always, when Eden was thought to be found, Eden became subverted. Life was transformed into a chain of subverted Edens which she wished simultaneously to re-visit and to forget.

She dropped the sheet and felt her breasts. Pride overcame her and gave her strength. She figured that she would have the baby during the first part of October. Nana was thirty-eight and when her fifth child arrived she would be thirty-nine. She was embarrassed by the thought of what other women would say about her having a child at thirty-nine. Having babies was for young girls, certainly not older women of thirty-nine, forty. Nana folded the sheet and reached for the pillowcases flapping in the wind. The economics of the family worried her, especially now when the government had announced that rationing would be expanded to include shoes, meat, cheese, fats and canned foods. How would they be able to feed five of their children? Nana had never before concerned herself with food. Octavio always provided. She and the children had never gone hungry, nor anyone else in the Revueltas family because Octavio never failed to provide whatever was needed. But within a matter of weeks Octavio would be out of a job. He would not work for the Simons Brick Company.

The rumors that had been circulated about Walter Simons wanting to cut back on the number of employees had become a self-fulfilling prophecy. Walter had indicated that the war effort provided enough jobs so that his workers could find other employment. Convinced that the time offered a good opportunity to shorten his payroll, the patron prepared a short list of five names to be fired within a month of the time Nana collected her laundry and a long list of twenty-five names to be announced within a year. The third name on the short list was Octavio Revueltas.

Nana, aware of the social, economical and political problems of Simons, Montebello, California, the United States and the world, would still have this child. During these past months there seemed to have begun a waiting, a period of expecting something to happen. Time moved slowly in the places where she existed. It seemed that the hatred towards Mexicans would never end, that the war was eternal. The child would be born into a terrible world of violence. Nana picked up the basket of laundry and headed to the entrance of her home. She had made the same turn, approached the same door uncountable times before. She stopped to check her plants. She would miss the house if she had to move.

As the war grew more violent, Walter's Mexicans went out to work in factories producing arms and other war materials. The Mexicans did not wait for Simons to announce who was on the list. Many families left. As it was, Walter, it was rumored, suffered from a gradual incapacitating illness that would soon force him to sell the business. The workers knew that Helen and Drusilla Simons had absolutely no interest in taking over the administration of the brickyard, nor did Edit express a strong resolve to continue her husband's business.

Time advanced through the lives of millions of people and the months passed. By June, Nana was five months pregnant and as strong as she had ever felt. She felt as if she were prepared to give birth to a new world when the news circulated that Allied forces had accomplished a cross-channel invasion of German-occupied Normandy. Simons youth pushed onto the beaches with no complaints and never looked back. Like the soldiers, Nana pushed forward.

For the first two weeks of August the heat had been unbearable and made life difficult for Milagros, who had gained an abnormal amount of weight. The doctors had diagnosed cancer of the stomach complicated by high blood pressure and a heart condition. She would have to be operated on and hospitalized for two weeks and spend a month or more recuperating at home.

Octavio brought the family together and polled them about who was able to donate funds to Milagros' doctor and hospital expenses. Federico stepped forward and offered what he could. No one else volunteered money. Octavio, Damian and Federico would cover the costs. Rogaciana, Felicitas and their husbands volunteered time and space but because of their growing families they could not afford to contribute funds. The family gathering took place in Milagros' house but the meeting of the brothers and sisters was called at Octavio and Nana's home. Throughout the evening it became clear that Octavio and Nana would be the people responsible for the major financial obligations. . . . Como siempre, Nana thought as she sat with her two hands resting on a full womb. By seven that evening both houses were filled with family. Nana and Milagros had prepared the usual excellent meal, delicious, with more than enough for everyone. Ignacio and Guadalupe Sandoval promised that they would help pay for their sister's medical bills and reassured Octavio not to worry. They had faith in Octavio's ability to come up with the necessary money.

Milagros entered the hospital in mid-August and one week later returned home to recuperate from the surgery. Regaining strength was a slow process. Milagros, the doctors discovered, had cancer of the uterus and a hysterectomy had to be performed. By September Milagros and Nana sat to enjoy a cup of tea. As Milagros poured, Nana grimaced with pain. The baby had kicked.

"That one is going to cause you problems." Milagros stirred a teaspoon of sugar.

"I'm so tired of carrying him. Look at how big I am," Nana said softly, embarrassed.

"Don't worry. You'll have the child soon. I'll be here to help you." Milagros smiled and wiped a tear from Nana's cheek. "Haven't seen Octavio."

"He's out looking for a job. This morning he went with Jacobo Ramos. Octavio was very happy because where Mr. Ramos works they are going to offer Octavio a job." Nana looked toward the brickyard.

"He's not burning a kiln." Milagros crossed her hands on her stomach.

"Yes, he starts at three in the afternoon. He hasn't quit his job here." Nana pushed her black hair away from her forehead. Both women sat comfortably in a common space and enjoyed one another in silence.

As Octavio reached into his coat pocket to reassure himself that he still had three hundred dollars in cash to pay for the delivery of their fifth child in the antiseptic white delivery room of Beverly Hospital in Montebello. The money was not gambling money but savings accumulated from salary drawn from Phelps Dodge Cooper Corporation where he had been employed since September. Nana would be upset if she knew that he paid for their baby with gambling booty. Whatever way she wanted him to pay was agreeable, although he carried more gambling earnings than salary. Since he had started to work at Phelps Dodge he had saved all of his salary. It seemed that upon acquiring the new job his good luck at the card games he enjoyed had been boosted to such a degree that in the past month he had won more money than in the previous five years of his gambling career. This productive streak of luck had been costly in his relationship with Nana. To make this money required time away from home.

As Octavio waited for the nurse to return with identification papers for the baby, he tried to recall the nights he had spent with Nana during her last month of pregnancy. He worked the swi ng shift from three in the afternoon to twelve at night. He usually left at two to arrive on time. By a quarter to one in the morning, after a shower and a bite to eat, Octavio found that he was wide awake and not tired. It began in that way. After work he would go into Los Angeles, Barrio Margarito, or East Los Angeles to dangerous and mysterious places where he found highly profitable card games. Octavio won and won. It was as if he had been cursed with winning. He would return home at about eight in the morning, sleep four hours until twelve, get ready for work and leave at two. He gambled almost up to the day of the birth. He felt that this child was born an orphan.

To Nana's surprise, Octavio came home the night of the fourteenth of October. The next morning, from one-thirty on he observed Nana prepare herself psychologically and physically for the imminent birth. At twelve in the afternoon Ignacio and Tati Sandoval drove Nana to the hospital. Octavio stayed with Nana until two when he left for work. At about the time he started the powerful machine he operated, Nana gave birth to a son.

Octavio was anxious when the friendly nurse walked into the waiting room and called out his name. Immediately after, Micaela and Arturo entered the room and sat next to their father. The nurse approached Octavio.

"Mr. Revueltas, your wife is sleeping comfortably. I need to know the name of your beautiful son." The nurse smiled.

"Quiere saber el nombre del bebe." Micaela translated, although Octavio understood.

"Gregorio," Octavio answered. Nana and he had chosen the name the morning she entered the hospital.

"Gregory," the nurse translated and wrote. "And the middle name?"

Micaela shrugged her shoulders and looked at Arturo who turned to his father.

"Well, how about Alexander? Alexander is a fine middle name," Octavio finally said. The nurse wrote it down.

"Good, your son's birth certificate is complete. Your son's name is Gregory Alexander Revueltas. Please sign here." The nurse handed Octavio a pen. He signed and the woman in white quickly left the room.

Two days later Octavio and Nana bundled up Gregorio, all paid for, left Beverly Hospital and took their fifth-born home to Simons, his cultural cradle.

Nana prepared Octavio's lunch while he shaved and washed in the brick basin outside the kitchen door. Four hours' sleep, a mild hangover and fatigue quickened Octavio's irritability. Nana, mad at his nine A. M. arrival, was in a bad mood and slammed cupboards, pots and dishes. They both understood the other's mental state. Octavio and Nana made a superior effort to avoid a confrontation. Octavio dried his hands with a towel by the kitchen table.

"There's your lunch." Nana threw the bag onto the table.

"Why did you throw it at me?" Octavio shouted.

"I can hear you, Octavio. You don't have to yell!" Nana moved to the stove and flipped several tortillas.

Within another minute Nana would have screamed about what she considered to be Octavio's lack of consideration and understanding of twenty-four-hour toil as housewife, mother, counselor and companion to Milagros and as instant hot lover to Octavio to satisfy his sexual desire. In turn Octavio waited for Nana's next aggressive outburst so that he could respond to her total insensitivity to and lack of appreciation for his hard and dangerous work to provide a good life for her and the children. They both felt in the right and at any moment would explode to defend their position. Suddenly a knock at the front door interrupted the tense atmosphere. They expected no one. Nana went to the entrance and reached for the door. Beyond the screen door stood two familiar men. Nana's heart fluttered while William Melone and Gonzalo Pedroza politely removed their hats.

"We want to speak to Octavio," Gonzalo said in a firm, raspy voice.

"Is he in?" William moved next to his colleague and peered through the screen to observe Octavio emerge from the kitchen.

"Here I am, Mr. Melone. How can I help you?" Octavio asked as if he knew nothing about why they wanted to speak to him. He opened the door, stepped between Gonzalo and William and went to the fence where he invited them to join him.

Nana, surrounded by flowers to her left and right from the small porch, nervously observed her husband. She too knew why they had come.

"Octavio, you know why we're here. You don't work here but you're still living here," Gonzalo said.

"We have orders to ask you to leave. You must leave the house, Octavio," William said tersely.

Octavio looked at Nana and decided to play a polite hand for more time. "I understand. I'll leave, but I would like to ask a favor. I need some time to find a house. About four or five months."

"Four, five months!" William laughed. "We'll give you three more months and no more. You're to be out of here by the end of February. If not, you know what must be done."

Gonzalo moved slowly through the open gate. He struggled with his body, which now had become a terrible monstrosity of a disfigured, deformed, perverted man, and sat in William's truck. Octavio went to Nana's side in the center of her garden.

"Don't worry. In three months we can find a house or we'll build a new one." Octavio went inside, returned with his lunch, kissed Nana and left for work. From the fence he waved.

"And don't come home at nine in the morning!" Nana yelled.

Now more than before Octavio's gambling winnings were a crucial economic factor for the future. Nana saw Octavio slowly disappear from her sight.

By six o'clock on a spring morning five months later, Arturo had left to work at the slaughterhouse. By seven-thirty Micaela and Javier had walked to meet the bus that would take them to school. Micaela was in her senior year and would graduate in June. Javier was in the eighth grade and was doing excellent work. By seven forty-five Flor had walked to Vail Elementary with her neighborhood friends. Flor was in the first grade and enjoyed school. Gregorio and Octavio slept. Nana sat quietly drinking coffee. She stole a few minutes from the busy day to rest peacefully, in silence. But rest did not come. The month was April, the year 1945 and still Octavio had not found a home for the family. Everywhere he went in the north of Montebello he had been refused. They did not want Mexicans in those areas. The threats which had been made by William and Gonzalo were not executed. During the previous Christmas holidays Walter Simons had fallen seriously ill from some kind of lung congestion. Throughout Walter's convalescent period, William's and Gonzalo's concerns were concentrated faithfully on the patron and the operation of the Simons brickyard. By April, Walter's health had stabilized and he recuperated at the Simons retreat on the Balboa Peninsula.

The war in Europe was ending; Hitler and the German armies suffered defeats on all fronts. On May 8 the war ended in Europe. By late July the

Japanese were brought to the brink of surrender but the Japanese Emperor would not capitulate to the United States, a country, he had declared, whose intelligence was dragged down by Mexicans, Negroes, Puerto Ricans and other mongrel races. The first ray of peace came when the Japanese military was assured that Japan would not be enslaved as a race nor destroyed as a nation. The emperor did not change his mind and the next light his people saw was dealt by President Harry S. Truman. On August 6 and 9 atomic bombs took their toll of life in Hiroshima and Nagasaki. The Pacific war came to an end on August 14, 1945. On the next day the United States began to celebrate. The news traveled slowly throughout the Pacific until finally, weeks later, on September 2 it was hoped that nowhere in the world were American boys dying. And along with all the rest, the Mexican boys from Simons were coming home.

Three months after the end of the war, William Melone and Gonzalo Pedroza repeated the threatening promises they had made to certain workers. The world was now at peace, and the United States celebrated victory. The December holidays were exhuberantly religious, faithful and kind. The new year, 1946, opened the doors to the United States, the most powerful national force in the world. The American soldier symbolized the national collective consciousness of the time. Walter insisted again that past union organizers be ousted from Simons to reward jobs and housing to the brave Mexican boys who had fought for their country.

Octavio was approached and ordered to leave Simons housing no later than March 1, 1946. When Octavio faced William and Gonzalo he simply nodded to acknowledge that he understood. When the middle of January came around, Octavio still had not found a home for his family. He was ignored, refused, and insulted everywhere he inquired about the rental or purchase of a home in Montebello. Racism, segregation and discrimination were the banners of victory in Montebello.

"We don't want Mexicans on our street."

"There are very few Mexican children attending our schools and we don't want to encourage more."

"I don't care if you can pay or not. I don't care if you or any of your tribe was born in the United States. I won't sell to a Mexican."

"Hell, you can't even speak English well enough to keep up with people around here. Your kids probably only speak Mexican. They can't get along with the English-speaking children in the neighborhood. Selling to

Mexicans only means trouble."

"I don't give a damn if your children can speak English well. You're nothing but a bunch of Indians and Mongolians. We don't want Indians and Mongolians in our neighborhood or in our schools. Get out!"

"We don't sell to people that are not of the American race."

"Hey, amigo, this part of Montebello is not zoned for you."

"Mr. Revueltas, you don't want to buy here. It will be impractical since your children will be automatically transferred to the Simons school."

"Get out of here, greaseball! We don't want your kind around here!"

"True, the Hidalgo family does live in the area but Mr. Hidalgo is one Mexican with outstanding economic influence and quality upbringing that requires an exception. The Hidalgo family has credentials that allow them the privilege to live among us."

"Sorry, but we don't want any spics near our women. We believe in one God, country, language and race."

"For generation after generation we haven't allowed Mexicans here. We don't give jobs to them or to niggers. Our churches are not open to their worship. The Montebello plunge is off limits to them and we don't like them to visit the city park."

"You can't buy in Montebello. Go to Simons. There's where you belong. Old man Simons has provided everything there for you. He's created a real Mexican paradise. Now get out of my office, you pachuco breeder."

After he had been verbally assaulted in his last attempt to buy housing, Octavio passed several houses recently built by Simons workers who had left the brickyard for factory jobs. These men had been fellow workers who advised him to purchase land on Date or Espanol Street and not to be so proud as to want to live among the gringos who rejected him. . . . Pride, shit! Don't I have any right? Why did our kids die in the war? When our boys return, don't they have the right to live wherever they want? . . . Octavio walked home from work at one o'clock through the cold and drizzly morning of February 1, 1946.

The driving rain against the bedroom window awakened him. He opened his eyes and made his way out of bed. He stood over Nana who slept a little longer, not yet quite sensing his movements. The baby in the small crib at her side slept cozily. With white jockey undershorts, his right hand on his genitals, Octavio went to the window. Since he had arrived early that morning the rain had fallen constantly. Now the wind whipped the water against the wooden Simons house. Octavio felt a chill and returned to bed to cuddle.

He woke up to the smell of bacon, eggs, tortillas and chili. As he washed, shaved and dressed he realized that he had slept well into the late morning. He would have to hurry for he had promised one of the workers that he would work half of the young man's shift so the young man could go to a party with his friends. Octavio did not mind. The extra money would come in handy for gambling purposes, especially now that he would have to buy property to build a home. When he saw Nana's face that late damp morning he had already decided that he would build on the lot that don Sebastian Pantoja had offered for three hundred dollars.

Nana served breakfast and smiled. She left to check the baby and returned to turn three torillas heating on the yellow wood-burning stove.

"We're going to buy a lot on Español, the lot that don Sebastian offered us," Octavio said and waited.

"And . . ." Nana waited for him to finish the sentence.

"And there we will build a home," Octavio rejoined.

"Whatever you say, Octavio. But where are we going to live while you build the house?" Nana asked, somewhat annoyed.

"Don't worry about that. I'll take care of it." Octavio paused. "Make my lunch because I have to go in early."

"What time do you go in?" Nana asked, already wrapping the tacos.

"When you finish making those tacos." Octavio thought about walking by the bachelors' quarters for a few hands of poker.

Nana finished with the lunch and placed the bag on the table and picked up the dishes to wash.

"Where did Arturo go?" Octavio asked.

"He went with Alberto. I'm not sure where. He said he was going to buy something to go to a dance tonight," Nana answered and noticed Octavio's face tightening with anger.

"Javier went to work," Octavio stated.

"Yes, Octavio." Nana affirmed her husband's thinking out loud and for a moment saw him as a psychologically exhausted man.

"Micaela?" Octavio murmured.

"She has to study catechism. Soon she makes her confirmation. You know that, Octavio. What is wrong with you?" Nana stepped toward him.

"Nothing." Octavio reached for the lunch and bundled up with a sweater, jacket, overcoat, heavy scarf and grey English sports cap.

"Flor is playing with Gregorio." Nana smiled and shook her head.

"Take care of them for me, like always. See you tonight." Octavio closed the door behind him and entered the damp and drizzly afternoon.

Chapter 20

Everything was normal. Micaela saw her mother finish stacking the diapers on the sofa and sit in the rocker. Nana stretched back her neck and breathed deeply, an instant rest. After a few moments she pulled out the pins that held her molote in place. The right side of her hair tumbled down over her back and right breast. With two pins in her mouth she reached for the left side and released the rest of the obsidian waterfall.

"Micaela, we'll check the bread and then go outside." Nana pushed off the rocker and led her daughter to the stove.

"This damn stove gets too hot!" Micaela exclaimed.

Nana placed the bread on the table. Micaela sprinkled a little more cinnamon on the golden brown bread.

"It stopped raining." From somewhere deep in her mind Micaela heard her mother. Faint voices muffled by the thick moist air came to the women.

"What's that?"

Nana shrugged her shoulders. Micaela rubbed her hands and put her coat and galoshes on. She and Nana moved away from the warmth and exited through the back door. The wooden outhouse sat in a corner toward the South Montebello Dairy property almost against the back wooden fence that marked the limits of each lot. Nana thanked the heavens for the brick walk leading to the privy and around the house. Momentarily both women focused their flashlights on the brick basin around the water fountain. Octavio had made these improvements and many others in his spare time to make life a little easier for his family. Nana felt a chill as the flashlight cut through the dark and projected a beam on the handle of the outhouse door. She was instantaneously confounded by the blinking, flashing and flaming of a light that should not have been there. In an instant she froze as her mind translated the silhouetted, undulating code: fire!

Nana turned toward the panicked voices of neighbors. Over and beyond the apex of the adjoining house, flames danced and cracked from the wooden walls and tar-papered roof of the third residence away from where she stood. Micaela held her hands to her heart as she observed the black cloud pierced by fire rise in the moist air. She stared at the leaping, advancing flames. At her side, her mother gazed at the raging heat-full, bright-flame energy.

"Micaela, our house is going to burn!" Nana shouted.

Nana began to perspire heavily as she grabbed Micaela and looked directly into her eyes. Nana's heartbeat, rapid and intense, traveled through her arms to her strong hands and shook Micaela by the shoulder once.

"I'll go for your sister and brother. You go to your Uncle Elias and tell him to get your father at work and move Arturo's car out because it's full of gasoline. Run!"

Micaela repeated the instructions in her mind and on her lips as the last powerful word from her mother's mouth made her run along the side of the house to the street where she yelled for her uncle. Nana watched her oldest child run to the gate where neighbors met her. Smoke and sparks caused the electrical wires carried by high posts planted along the front fences to jump and squirm. The fire would soon be upon all she possessed in the world and all she loved in her life. Flor and Gregorio lay in their beds asleep. Not the hottest flames imaginable could stop her from getting to her children. Her five-foot-two body, drenched in perspiration, threw the doors open. Her face was firm with anger and determination. She wept without crying as she passed the objects she and Octavio had worked so hard and long to accumulate. Her peripheral vision seemed to capture everything as she moved quickly to where the baby slept. She wrapped the sleeping Gregorio in a blanket. As she entered the girls' room, her vision caught family photographs, dressers, her wedding ensemble, and the children's toys. Nana held the baby with her left arm, went to Flor and maneuvered her to a sitting position.

"Flor! Get up, Flor. It's time to go. Put your jacket on," Nana spoke calmly.

She took her youngest daughter by the hand and guided her to the front door from where she could hear voices screaming for her to get out. The baby slept in her arms. Flor held back an instant and then clung to her mother's hip. Nana reached for the door; it opened. Relieved, she stood on the small front porch and waited. On the right, Uncle Elias' house began to burn. His sons and daughters ran in and out, saving what they could from the intensifying flames. Micaela came to her, embraced her, took Flor and guided Nana from the house to the middle of the street where people watched the conflagration.

Of the ten houses on the street, eight were burning. Three were rented by the Revueltas family. Octavio and Nana's was the middle home, Uncle Elias lived on one side and on the other side, in the last house on the street before Vail Street, lived Damian and Milagros. Nana felt someone tug at the baby. She recognized a young woman, a niece, who took Gregorio to where Micaela and Flor sat on chairs that had been saved. Nana thought of Arturo's car and saw it parked far down on the opposite side of the street, safe. Damian's sons and daughters carried furniture out; theirs would be the last house to burn, which gave them plenty of time to save most of their belongings. Uncle Elias' house was aflame and forced the family to stop entering. It was difficult for anyone to believe that even in this cold, extremely wet weather the houses were burning like tinderboxes. Although the fire leapt and advanced rapidly, Nana's house had not yet started to burn.

. . . The children's clothes . . . Nana bolted through the front door. She grabbed what she could and ran out. Neighbors attempted to stop her but she broke away again, still holding on to the children's clothes that she had taken out. The second time she ran to the boys' clothes chest and took the shirts she could carry. Outside she threw them on a table, started toward the house again, but was held back by Damian.

"Nana, don't go in! Look, the house is burning. Sit here with Milagros and your children."

Damian helped Nana sit next to her mother-in-law, who sat on a kitchen chair, tapped her fingers on the kitchen table and shook her head at the incredulity of the whole scene that evolved about her. Their bedrooms, living rooms, kitchens, and intimate objects had been spilled onto that muddy street in Simons, California. Now neighbors and strangers walked through, sitting and touching the furniture as if they were customers strolling through a furniture store showroom. But the primary attraction was the spectacular fire whose illumination could be seen for miles. Nana's house burned slowly and intensely hot. She could feel the heat from where she sat. Damian moved his family back away from the fire. For a moment Nana's sight strayed from the burning house and searched up and down the street for the firemen. Had not Walter Robey Simons assured the residents that they would have the protection and services to meet any emergency? Nana could not find one fireman. If they had come, her house and Milagros' surely would have been spared. Her house was not that far gone.

The people did what they could. Earlier, to fight the flames, a bucket brigade was formed and garden hoses were used until the pressure subsided to a trickle of water. . . . If only the fire department would come! Nana thought. She noticed Milagros staring into the night toward the top of the Español Street canyon at two Montebello fire engines parked with headlights on, red and yellow lights flashing. Nana's house was in full flames and Milagros' would soon follow, but the fire trucks stood poised, not a move to help. Some of the older children ran to call them down to the fire, but the fire chief refused to help.

"I was ordered to stay put here," the chief laughed at the end of his response. "I'm making sure the fire doesn't jump to the Montebello side."

He pushed his hat back and pointed to Nana's house. "That house is gonna go any minute," he laughed as the children ran back to communicate his message.

The workers of Simons would never forget the negative and devastating decision that condemned them to watch their homes burn to the ground. Nana placed her hand over Milagros' hand, stopping her nervous, angry tapping on the kitchen table. The fire chief's message in children's voices echoed in Nana's mind. . . . Why did they come to the edge of the barranca? Someone stopped them at the last moment, someone from Montebello and someone from Simons. . .

For the past few months Walter Simons and the City of Montebello had waged a feud over the location of the Simons Brickyard at Mines and Maple streets in Montebello. Walter wanted to build on-site housing for the workers at the Montebello yard. The City refused to grant the building permits on the grounds that that kind of housing would bring undesirable elements into Montebello. Confronted with an impasse, Walter asked the City to incorporate the main Simons Brickyard located on Sycamore and Vail which had housing for three hundred families and bachelors' quarters. The City again responded in the negative, repeating that it did not want to introduce that kind of element, Mexicans, as permanent residents. Walter countered with refusing to finance part of the bridge and drainage rebuilding expenses on Maple and adjoining streets. He also refused to water down the dust at the brickyard, a decision which resulted in major consequences. The dust rose, formed clouds and penetrated through the windows and door screens, settled and covered walls and furniture north of Olympic Boulevard.

Rumors and facts spread concerning the effects of the uncontrolled red dust. The death of three elderly ladies found dead in their beds covered with red dust made headline news. Autopsies performed by Los Angeles County pathologists found large amounts of red dust in the victims' lungs. The Red Lung Disease, coined by the workers, caused the women's death. To offer proof of the danger of the brickyard, the survivors of the victims came to a city council meeting with three jars filled with the red, dust-infected, stained lungs of the loved dead ones. Following the directions of a doctor, the sons and daughters of the deceased unfolded the congested human bellows in front of the city council. The council members gasped at the doctor's explanation of the women's suffering and at the fact, according to the doctor, that the Mexicans were able to breathe the red dust and survive. The presentation provided the necessary convincing evidence to allow everyone in the council chambers to conclude that the Mexicans were subhuman creatures, cockroaches equipped by nature to be unconsumed in such horrible living conditions. The city and the people were in danger of being polluted by Walter Robey Simons, the brickyard, the Mexicans and the red dust. Better to let them burn.

On the still-smoldering street, a man stood by Nana as she contemplated Milagros' face, a profile of pure simple endurance. Damian brought Micaela, Flor and Gregorio to their mother. Nana, devastated by what she witnessed, wept as she saw the people no longer running, rushing. The panic subsided, and people stood and watched the light of the flames reflected off their faces. No need to hurry any longer. The fire had won.

Nana sat on a kitchen chair with Gregorio on her lap and watched the house burn and shadows interrupt the flames. Flor embraced her mother and the baby and understood that everything was gone. Micaela touched her mother's shoulder and somehow worried about her upcoming confirmation in church. Although in a state of shock, from the deepest and strongest part of Nana's heart came words for those around her at that moment—a simple statement pronounced unwaveringly.

"We'll start anew."

Uncommon for this time of year, two giant kilns burned behind them. Their fire and illumination climbed like a creature into the night sky.

At the time of the fire Javier walked past the checkstands and waved goodbye to the manager and the women checking out the last customers of the evening. The door closed slowly. The bus driver read a magazine while he waited at the southwest corner of Montebello and Whittier Boulevard. Crawford's Market was on the northwest corner. From this point Javier, dark-faced, smiling, bright-eyed, sprinted to the front of the bus. He was proud of his speed, both in running and in working. The manager told him that he was the fastest and most careful boxboy they had. The junior high school coaches considered him the fastest sprinter on the ninth grade track team. A hard worker, outstanding athlete and excellent student, Javier represented the exemplary good Mexican boy. He possessed such extraordinary mathematical abilities that the algebra and science teachers allowed him to advance at his own pace. Once Mr. Irons, the truant officer, walked through the checkstand where Javier bagged for the manager.

"This boy here is not like those pachuco gangsters from Simons. I know those boys well. I arrest about half a dozen of them every day. Truancy, believe you me, is the least of their offenses," Mr. Irons said, reaching for his wallet. "I know Mexicans. This boy here can be saved."

Through the long, rectangular, heavy glass windows of the holding bus door, the Anglo-American driver observed Javier with his books and white apron in hand. The driver put the magazine down and threw the switch. Javier withdrew from his pocket a nickel which he dropped into the coin box. He moved to a spot at the back of the empty bus. In five minutes the driver would guide the transportation machine through its zigzaggy twenty-minute route to almost the end of the line in south Montebello.

To the Anglo population, Simons was the end of the line, at the extreme southeastern border, on the other side and out of town. Javier knew of many colonias, but none were like Simons. Most of these barrios were situated on the other side of some physical marker: a railroad track, a bridge, a river, a highway. Simons was not only on the other side, but it was also constructed in a hole, "El Hoyo," dug by its own residents. Walter Simons had chosen the site because nobody wanted that parcel of undesirable land, but he had recognized the excellent red clay earth needed for brick. The land, located in an isolated area, was perfect to keep low-wage Mexican labor in cheap dilapidated housing close to the work site and protected from the prejudicial attitudes of the City of Montebello. Most of the barrios were not planned but were outgrowths of labor camps, while others were merely accidental occurrences of nature and demographics. One such area was Barrio Cantaranas, the singing frogs.

In 1931 an Anglo-American populated area was invaded by millions of giant frogs that emerged from the San Gabriel River and covered every space inside and out of the homes. The frogs were everywhere. A plague had surely struck. The people fought the frogs with chemicals, fire and sticks but failed to scare away the ugly beasts. The frogs kept coming, and for every one killed, two or three appeared. The residents struggled for days to end the plague. Finally the homeowners decided to bring in help, the cheapest they could find, and so hundreds of Mexicans were brought early in the morning to battle the frogs. The people toiled throughout the day. By nightfall both Anglos and Mexicans were exhausted. The Anglos could only hope that the frogs would leave by morning. When darkness finally overcame the last ray of the sun and as the moon rose, there was heard a humming followed by singing. As the chorus grew louder the Anglos became frightened, for they could not understand any of the lyrics. The frogs sang in Spanish. The Anglo residents gathered their families and ordered the Mexicans to lead them out of the amphibious net. The

Anglos abandoned the area to the Mexicans who began to serenade the frogs with a few tunes of their own, and by daybreak the horrible frogs had disappeared. Some returned to the river, but thousands more followed the running Anglo-American homeowners. The Mexicans remained, inherited the abandoned land and homes, and renamed the area Barrio Cantaranas.

Javier smiled as he looked at the dissected frog in his science text. The engine started and the driver pulled away from the curb. The driver's attentive eyes moved in the long rearview mirror and stared into the night on the advancing street. In contrast to the Cantaranas story that everyone knew, Javier thought of Simons as a colonia with an important history, with a logical explanation for its existence, a premeditated, organized colonia. . . . Mr. Simons made it happen. Everything is his. The store, pool hall, post office, movie show, bachelors' cabins, Vail School, the library, the church, the water tower, the electricity, the clinic, the trains, the machines, the lots. The houses, unpainted and battered by the weather, the walls of scrap lumber, barely standing together, all the same, two, maybe three bedrooms, a kitchen and small living room, no bath, no toilet. Some have been there for thirty, forty years, but they're clean on the inside and the outside, pretty garden, lots of plants, it's not too bad, it's not too good. It was planned by Mr. Simons and the City. . .

Simons was built at just the correct distance from Montebello to discourage the Mexicans from going into town. It was logical to have a separate school, church and other conveniences. The Simons Mexicans were to live, work, play, worship and trade apart, at a safe distance from Montebello. When Simons was established it was never proposed that the company town be a part of Montebello, or for that matter any city. It was understood that the Mexicans were to remain apart in every way.

The bus turned right on Carmelita Street and headed west to Greenwood where it would make a left turn into the agricultural fields. The Japanese used to own or rent practically all the farm areas. Javier and Arturo had worked picking peppers, cauliflower, melons, tomatoes. They liked the Japanese. However, there were no Japanese left in the area; after Pearl Harbor they were herded into trucks and taken away to concentration camps.

The bus stopped in front of Greenwood Elementary. A large woman with two shopping bags leaned against the driver's seat as she secured a nickel for the coin box. She put the change purse in her bag and with the two shopping bags in hand turned toward the back of the bus. She stopped suddenly, startled to see Javier in the back seat smiling at her and her heavy red and green Pendelton jacket buttoned to the neck. Her black pants just covered the tops of her heavy brown boots. She situated her bags on the window side and as she sat a word formed clearly and silently on her lips: Pachuco. Javier looked to the side. . . . The riots, sell me to the Atchison, Topeka and the Santa Fe Railroad for fifty-eight and one-half cents per hour. They're not going to forget and we're not either, lady. . .

The bus drove faster. In a few minutes he would arrive at his stop. Javier's right eye, then his left, caught a glow in the sky above Simons. The bus driver and woman seemed to be hypnotized by the soft roar of the motor, the floating of the bus over the consistent waves in the road and the growing light to the south. The brightness was more intense than usual. Perhaps they're burning more kilns tonight. . .

As Javier walked to the front of the bus he stooped over to see the eerie half-globe of yellow illumination broken up by the bus windows into squares near where he lived. The door opened. Javier looked at the woman. She had a yellow moustache and long hairs around the mouth. Her lips, puckered with hate now, silently formed two words: Mexican Pachuco. Javier stepped into the darkness of Date Street. He noticed that the drizzle had stopped and the sky was clearing. The yellow-orange glow now had an odor of oil, tar smoke. He took one step toward home. Simons is burning. As his steps turned into a fast run he saw the progress of physical matter, the scientific advances, the blinding flash over Hiroshima. He ran faster, perspiration running down from his temples. He saw the flashing lights of the fire trucks stationed on the bluff. He felt the heat of the nuclear age, which produced in him a sensation, a feeling which he believed resided in the heart of every man, woman and child. It was the fear that something altogether unearthly and beyond the range of human experience, understanding and control had occurred and was happening now. His clothes were soaked when he got to the edge. He looked down at where he lived. . . . Oh no . . . His eyes swelled. He knew. Javier realized it was not the end of the world, but he felt that he witnessed a kind of minute preview of the end of all things in the world of his childhood.

While Javier stared at the fire, his older brother Arturo was being driven home from the Palladium. During the hour drive, Arturo rubbed and scrubbed at the five spots on his white shirt sleeve. He turned several times to look at the stains, the red wine drops, which seemed to bother him intensely. Alberto shook his head in disbelief at his cousin's annoyance. . . . Esta loco el Arturo . . . He drove on through the wet clearing night. Next to Alberto, Mike listened to Johnny Magnus' rhythm-and-blues sounds blaring in the 1944 Ford. Mike sat against the right front door from where he could see Alberto drive and Arturo rub his shirt sleeve.

Because of the mishap, the spilled wine, they had left early, a little after one in the morning. Arturo had reacted strangely to the stains on the shirt and to the man who had spilled the wine. He had grabbed his arm and contemplated the red whiteness as if he had been wounded with shotgun pellets. After a while he yelled at the man to get him some water. The gentleman declared that certainly he would; he was expecting much worse but decided to go along with the absurd request. He never returned. The restrooms had long lines, the bar was impossible to get near enough to yell at the bartender, and the kitchen was closed. The only two water fountains were out of order and there was not one glass of water on the tables.

"I got water . . . to get some. Let's go, Alberto!" Arturo held his arm high, demonstrating to everyone the tragedy of his sleeve. The red spots threatened to ruin the harmony of color, material and creation that he alone understood. Urgently he moved to leave. His face filled with hatred and potential power of explosive violence. Arturo screamed at the crowd to open a path.

"The son-of-a-bitch never water came back with!" he yelled in his scrambled way.

Women moved away, men stepped aside, others clenched their hands. Hundreds of eyes followed Arturo rush his wine-stained shirt to the now appearing stars of the night.

"The guy got shotgunned!" someone shouted.

A deep, fast-moving murmur competed with the music. Alberto and Mike caught up with him at the door. They turned to see faces of anger, sadness and terror. They made a dash for the car into the sudden silence of the night.

"Raining it isn't!" Arturo held his sleeve up above his head, enraged, and screamed at the sky.

Mike opened the door. "Get in. Your mother will wash it."

Arturo shook his head as he maneuvered into the back seat and began to rub the stains. He would refuse to allow his mother to wash the new shirt. He would take it to the cleaners, although, in his eyes the shirt was ruined. As they drove, the street lights illuminated a series of film frames housing the sleeve. The red stains did a dance for Arturo. They moved, formed patterns, created innovative designs, suggested new perfections. His artistic paradigms multiplied into countless more abstractions. The process was simple but he could never verbally communicate his knowledge, his aesthetic conceptions. These reamined forever locked in his mind. The people who dealt with Arturo on an intellectual plane were confused and perplexed by his perception of the world.

Alberto downshifted to make a right turn off Washington onto Vail. A strange smell infiltrated the car.

"Smells like rubber." Mike took a whiff with his big hair-filled nostrils.

"Hope it's not the brakes." Alberto lowered the window.

"Not tonight. It's coming from the outside." Mike stared through the windshield.

"Tar or tarpaper burning." Arturo's vision and mind caught the glow from the lights at Vail School.

Ever since Arturo was five years old, people had noticed his extreme neatness and cleanliness. When he was only seven, he organized the corner of Micaela's and Flor's bedroom where he and Javier kept their clothes chest. Arturo's two drawers were locked to insure that every object, article of clothing and toy be kept in its place. As he grew older he accepted responsibility willingly and manifested great satisfaction in helping his mother and father. By the time he was twelve he was in charge of the garden and he swept and maintained the yard. He kept the fences, grounds and walls of the house immaculate. He never feared work but welcomed it as a privilege. On his arrival home from school, he would ask his mother what was for dinner, grab some fruit, check his corner of the house and sit and stare into the pages of his books. After an hour he would go out to the garden where he would spend the rest of the afternoon and early evening rearranging, sweeping, watering and cleaning. His friends would come to invite him out, but he would usually refuse them, preferring to stay by himself.

In his teenage years Arturo acquired even more friends. Both his peers and older people were attracted to him. His handsomeness, cleanliness and unique understanding of the world brought forth admiration. Octavio and Nana were often complimented about their oldest son. However, they realized something was wrong with him. They could never resolve the puzzle.

"Arturo works hard, Octavio. We don't have to insist," Nana said.

"Yes, but he doesn't learn anything," Octavio replied, annoyed.

"Perhaps it's us." Nana sat at the edge of the bed and removed her slippers.

"That can't be it if the others are learning. At least read, write, add, subtract. The basics. He should learn the basics. Even I who never went to school know the basics. I don't understand him, Nana. I don't understand!" Octavio slipped under the covers.

Arturo rapidly fell back in his academic achievement in the second grade. The teacher sent a letter to his mother explaining that Arturo needed special attention, that he was not learning the letters and numbers and purposely wrote backwards after he was shown the correct way. This learning situation became worse in the third, fourth and fifth grades. Arturo continued to fall behind and gradually lost interest in what the school provided. What he wrote was misspelled; letters and sometimes whole words were written backwards or upside down. He could not read and had a hard time pronouncing words and forming sentences. He said things jumbled. By the fifth grade, he could neither spell nor write his own name. In November, Nana was called for a conference with the teacher, Miss Singer.

"Mrs. Revueltas, your boy is unmotivated, has a short attention span and lacks the ability to concentrate. He cannot read, add or subtract. His penmanship is poor. He doesn't seem to recognize letters. I believe that Arturo is retarded, possibly brain damaged. Did he ever have a serious illness when he was younger? Did he ever fall or injure his head? In junior high school Arturo might attend a special education program where he will learn a simple trade until his sixteenth birthday when he can leave school to work and help you." Miss Singer smiled and patted Nana's hand. "Thank you for coming."

Nana did not move. She sat confused and perplexed by what she had heard. "But Arturo is a smart boy," she said as she watched Miss Singer walk to a table and return with a stack of papers.

"Here! Look at your son's work. There are first graders doing better work. They need our attention, Mrs. Revueltas, more than your son. Wouldn't you agree? Look at Arturo's work. It's terrible! This is not the work of an intelligent boy, but the work of a retarded child! I have been teaching for twenty-five years. I know! Mrs. Revueltas, you must understand; we'll do what we can. We'll try and keep him entertained here. Once he's in junior high the program might help him." Miss Singer stood up.

"Arturo trabaja mucho. He works hard!" Nana was not convinced and remained seated.

"Of course he does, Mrs. Revueltas. He's also neat and clean. You should be proud of that. His obsession with cleanliness and neatness makes him do his work over and over again. He takes too much time to do a simple assignment. I'm sorry to say this, but that's a sure symptom of a retarded person." Miss Singer walked to her desk, sat down and began to work.

Nana returned home late that warm spring afternoon in early May. She often took long walks to defray her tiredness, the monotony of housework, the anger toward Octavio; to see other men and women living; to take deep breaths and smell the world beyond her house; to rest; to attain, even for an instant, peace and tranquility. Today Nana had spiritually walked and talked with her son, but the questions she asked he could not answer.

"What's wrong with Arturo?" Nana asked herself, bewildered.

She opened the front gate and noticed that Arturo had watered her favorite plants, beautiful lavender hortensias. He too loved to nurture flowers by the doorsteps. She found him sitting in a corner staring into his book. Nana loved her son and knew he was intelligent.

"Arturo, bring your books. Let's sit in the garden. It's a nice afternoon."

Arturo smiled, picked up the books and went out through the kitchen to the table and benches his grandfather had made for the family. The afternoon became a warm light over the table. He waited for his mother. Nana sat at his right. He touched her hand with his left and noticed her natural perfume. How sweet it was to him. Finally she spoke.

"Arturo, show me your reading book."

The child placed the book in front of his mother.

"What are you reading?" Nana asked.

"Here." Arturo pointed to the first page of a second grade reader. He smiled with pride.

Suddenly Nana felt a rush of energy move to her heart and eyes. She caught, blinked the tears away and embraced her second-born. She realized for the first time the level at which he was reading. She felt herself the failure; she was to blame. She had allowed him to fall into this deep pit of darkness.

"Now, how can we get you out of this deep black well?" Nana whispered in a breath. "Arturo, read."

He looked into the page and began to read slowly. "Dick and Jane, nar . . . ran up the hill. Spot nar aterf them," he said haltingly.

"Faster, hijo."

He did not want to undestand what Nana said.

"Dick acht sot nur, said Jane. Run, nur psot, said Dick." Arturo read faster.

Nana heard sounds which did not represent the words on the page. Arturo read nonsense. A fear, a panic for her son began to overcome her. She would not permit this to happen; she would not lose control for his sake. She smiled and looked into his eyes.

"Arturo, I want you to write this." Nana pointed to the last sentence he had read. She waited while he copied the words.

"Arturo, don't you see the words? Look carefully at the letters."

"Yes, Mama." Arturo's eyes filled with tears that fell on the words he had written.

"Write this one." Nana pointed to *brown* and Arturo wrote *nword*.
She placed her finger under *boy* and Arturo wrote *yob*.

"Look at the letters."

"I see them, Mama. I see them!" Arturo cried and hid his face from his mother.

He turned away, feeling that he had repeatedly disappointed her. Now everyone, his teachers, friends, his father, and even his mother had told him to see the words, to pay close attention to the letters, to concentrate on the signs. Arturo did exactly what he was told. He saw the words and he wrote what he saw as well as read what he saw. But he was always wrong and he did not understand why. At times he considered himself the most stupid person in the world. He understood the concepts, numbers, letters, words and sentences communciated to him but he could not intelligibly express the signs, meanings, or relationships to other people. Arturo could feel with his mind what he saw, but he could not describe what he felt in an understandable manner. It was if a playful transparent mirror had been placed between his brain and the world. What he perceived was decoded differently from what others saw.

As he grew older, more frustrated and battered psychologically by the constant negative belittling feedback from his teachers, counselors, friends and the ever-present worried glance of his parents, he began a process of falling into himself, into a deep resentment and bitterness for those who criticized him. He fell into an intellectual hatred, for he considered himself far more intelligent than his detractors. Some time after the examination, Arturo made an effort to explain the idea of purity to his mother: "The colored ink breaks off the paper its purity."

Arturo believed that putting ink on paper invaded the nothing, pure color of the paper. He believed that words should be warehoused in a form other than paper and books. Words to him manifested themselves into pictures and images, and these entities that he saw should be expanded and not locked in words, in sentences, on pages, in books. Ink violates a space; words imprison themselves in themselves and red wine ruined the nothing of his shirt sleeve and he was angered that it had stopped raining.

The smell of burnt wood permeated the air. As Alberto made the turn onto Southworth, the smell was explained.

"What the hell happened?" Alberto said softly to himself as he slowed the car to a stop in front of Arturo's grandparents' house. Mike opened the door and placed one foot in the mud and stood to look at the devastated street.

"Looks like they dropped the bomb, Arturo!"

Arturo stared at the roof of what used to be his house. It seemed that the walls had collapsed and the fire had engulfed all the material objects inside but had not burnt the roof. The crown, the head of the house, was whole. He thought of his mother.

The debris among nine or so piles of charcoal smoldered as he walked around to the back yard. An outhouse was the only human-built wooden object left standing on his side of the street. Water dripped from the fountain his father had built. Arturo observed the car disappear onto Vail. Only the rumbling sound of the engine persisted for a moment longer, and then there was silence, interrupted by an occasional crackle of a burning dream that lay decomposing on a bed of ashes.

Arturo believed his father saw him as a failure, and he would work for the rest of his life, if necessary, to eradicate this image. He turned to find the person whom he loved, respected and feared, and as he moved toward him Arturo realized that he had been holding his right stained sleeve. He laughed a half-cry and separated his arms. . . . And I wanted water . . . Arturo looked into his father's eyes under the bill of a grey English sports cap. Amidst disaster, the boy with the infinite configurations of the world found his father and felt himself for the first time in his life as a man equal to him.

"Papa!"

Octavio, as if he had held his breath for some time, exhaled a cry that was toned not with anger but with anguish, a desire for help: "Arturo!"

Father and son stood together. Nothing of the past mattered, only this place, condition, disaster, moment in which they walked over the still hot ashes. Arturo would assist his father who accepted with pride his son's help.

"Where are we going?"

"To your Uncle Asuncion's house. We are all there."

"Will they give us another house?" Arturo asked, half knowing the answer.

"It will be difficult. They have black-balled me, son. They don't want me in Simons."

They walked toward Vail Street, neither man realizing how much one supported the other. Octavio continued to explain his condemnation by the Simons Brickyard administration.

"I left the brickyard, and after I supported the union I don't think that Mr. Simons will give me a house."

"Papa, what now? What are we going to do?"

Upon hearing the questions, Octavio recognized the great improvement in communication that Arturo had made. Part of the world was destroyed by fire, and in that part Octavio discovered that his son could communicate intelligibly. Confidence swelled in an instant of happiness for his son's accomplishment. The litany of denials and insults for trying to buy a home in Montebello rushed to his brain. For his family and for Arturo, who walked proudly next to him, Octavio made a decision he had thought about for over a year that would affect Nana and the family.

"What are we going to do?" Octavio repeated. He rested before guiding his son across Vail Street to the Vail Airport side, where Lindbergh had once landed. "Well, we are going to buy property and build our own home. Our own home!" Octavio shouted into the dark morning.

"And I'll help, Papa." Arturo joined his father's enthusiasm.

For Arturo there would be no more fear now. He felt comfortable walking with his father and shared the excitement of helping with the plans for their new house. . . . Nuestra casa . . . Finally a light from his Uncle Asuncion's kitchen broke the joyful reverie. Octavio knew that Nana waited. She met them at the door. Arturo embraced her and did not try to restrain the tears caused by love and the idea of the new house. . . . For her, all for her, he thought as he let her go. Nana smiled and turned toward the living room.

"Go to sleep next to Javier," Nana whispered.

Before going to his brother's side, Arturo reconfirmed his promise to Octavio: "I'll help you, Papa."

Moments later Nana and Octavio stood alone feeling the psychological wounds the fire had opened. Suddenly they embraced and cried softly. With Nana's heart pounding against his, Octavio, relieved that his family was alive and safe, began to sense a sharp urgency, a desperation that would affect his health and would not cease until he drove the last nail for the completion of a house or his coffin.

Chapter 21

Nana dragged a piece of tarpaper that had collapsed on her beautiful yellow wood-burning stove. "Oh, look at the stove!" she cried, disappointed and heartbroken.

All day the family worked sifting through the carcass of the house. Every room had been gutted and every article of furniture and clothing was ruined by the fire or smoke. Not much was salvageable. Physically and emotionally the family was devastated. That morning Nana had arrived first and for about an hour stared at what remained of her house.

When Micaela came, Nana was able to break the spell that the charred and burnt wood placed on her. She didn't know where to start. Micaela suggested the kitchen. At nine-thirty Octavio started clearing what used to be the living room area. Nana had told him to try to sleep, but Octavio could not. He claimed he was never more full of energy. Soon after, Arturo and Javier parked the car and began working in the bedrooms. At about noon, Flor, with the baby bundled up in her arms, brought lunch. She went to the center of the ashes, put the shopping bag down, adjusted Gregorio on her shoulder, and for an instant saw her family in a ridiculous light trying to save what was not there amongst the ashes.

"Mama, Papa, it's time to eat," Flor called.

Everyone stopped and looked at Flor standing with Gregorio who peered out from the blankets and searched for his mother. From where Flor waited, the family appeared framed in grey and black ash. Nana cleaned the ruined stove. Octavio pulled at a small coffee table, Micaela piled damaged clothes near the water pump, and Arturo and Javier emptied the contents of charred drawers from the bedrooms. All except Flor and Gregorio were squatting or kneeling. When they heard her voice, the family rose. Each member, almost simultaneously, dropped whatever object he held and went to the center of what yesterday was home. Gregorio toured in the arms of his brothers and sisters and finally was content with Nana. Flor distributed sandwiches, burritos, soft drinks and beer for Octavio. As they ate, the sky grew clearer and the sun shone through the thinning clouds. They sat in the middle of the ashes and talked.

"Mama, I don't think we can use those clothes. They smell terrible!" Micaela said to her mother.

"We're not taking our clothes," Arturo added.

Nana did not say a word. She ate in silence. Suddenly she sobbed, breathed deeply, cried and hugged her baby. "Forgive me, son! I don't want to upset you with this accident that you don't understand."

"Papa, what are we going to do?" Javier asked the necessary question.

"Look for a house," Octavio reassured the family. "But for now," he continued, "we must leave all this. It's ruined. The refrigerator and bicycle were the only things saved. We'll take those, nothing else."

The warm sun lighted the Revueltas' as they rose from what for twenty-five years had been their safe zone. Together they walked away. They thought of the change that would come in the new home. Octavio, Nana, Micaela, Arturo, Javier, and Flor had confidence in themselves, and each in his own mysterious way was confident that the family would survive. Nana held the baby against her heart. She sat with Micaela in the back seat of Arturo's immaculate car. Octavio quietly sat in front with his oldest son. They drove off and left Javier and Flor to ride the bicycle back to Uncle Asuncion's, where the family would stay until Octavio found a permanent home. None of the other families who had lost their homes were faced with the urgency of shelter as Octavio's was. Within three days of the fire all the victims were housed in permanent or temporary Simons Company dwellings.

Damian and Milagros were one of the first couples to receive temporary housing. After four days with Uncle Asuncion, Octavio moved Nana and the children to Damian and Milagros' house. Octavio hoped that after his father and mother were given a permanent home, he would be allowed to stay in the house he presently shared with them. Octavio and Nana understood that only luck would let them stay. Octavio's future in Simons was all but over; he, Nana and the children were living there on borrowed time. The administration had warned him, black-balled him, and identified him as a union supporter and as a man not willing to cooperate. Octavio and Nana stalled for enough time to locate an acceptable home. They had searched in different places in the surrounding communities, but the response was always the same: "We don't sell to Mexicans!"

Octavio and Nana inquired about the terms of purchase of several homes east of Whittier Boulevard, in Montebello. As soon as they entered the open house or met the salesman they were simply ignored or told directly, "We don't want Mexicans here."

There was no place near the center of Montebello or east of Washington Boulevard, what some people considered north Montebello, where Mexicans could purchase or rent a house or apartment. Perhaps Octavio's aggressive stare from in between heavy eyebrows bothered the salesmen. Perhaps Octavio was too Mexican to be allowed in the Anglo areas of Montebello. Octavio and Nana tried to buy in Anglo Montebello because some of their relatives and acquaintances had bought houses in the forbidden white garden. Octavio asked rhetorically why they were accepted into the gringo neighborhoods. These Mexicans were gringophiles who thought like, acted like, and wanted to be gringos. They didn't question the cost of their gringophilia. They didn't care. They would live in gringo Montebello regardless of the consequences. The few families that moved to the northern section were lighter complexioned than the Mexicans who resided in Simons.

As for Octavio and Nana, words and glares of rejection fell on them continuously. The Anglo world did not reject his labor or the blood of his relatives or neighbors. For work or war, the Anglo world needed him, but it refused to allow him to live among its citizens. Mexicans had to be pushed away and kept at the periphery of Anglo-American society, of Montebello society. Although bitter, Octavio never mentioned his sentiments to his wife, his sons, or his daughters. Instead, his attitude was manifested in a quietness, a coldness toward his family. Nana sensed the hatred even in the tranquility of night when he slept or in the excitement of his desire for her, and although their bodies met sweetly, a great distance pulsated between their minds. Octavio disliked gringos. They denied him shelter that he deserved, had earned, and could afford for his family. He felt less a man, a father, a husband; less in the eyes of his wife, children and friends. Octavio did not possess the power to overcome the gringo adversaries.

Damian and Milagros sent most of their belongings to their new company home on Rivera Road in front of the railroad tracks near the general store. For two weeks they had shared their old house with Octavio, Nana and family. The fire had not kept Octavio from work. He did not miss one day, nor did Damian who continued his job as a kiln firer. One afternoon after Octavio said goodbye to his father and mother and left for work, Nana helped Milagros pack the few articles of clothing which remained. Arturo and Javier took several boxes and furniture to their grandfather's new house. One by one Nana and her children embraced grandfather and grandmother who moved less than a mile away.

"Nana, if you need anything, let me know," Milagros called from the small front porch of the house.

Nana, concerned with her children, was left alone again in the night, in that borrowed Simons Company house. Ever since the fire she had felt vulnerable and afraid. How perishable those material objects accumulated over the years had been. Her dreams of the future had melted into the ashes of what was once her home. Nana, horribly afraid and shocked, worried where her family would live. She hated the fact that Octavio had been blackballed by the Simons foremen. At times hate was the only reaction that rose in her heart. She blamed Octavio for causing this strange and mortal anxiety and for bringing her to this condition of homelessness. Yet Octavio was obviously suffering as much as she was. Although he ate well, Nana noticed that in proportion to the food he consumed, he slimmed down.

"Octavio, como estas perdiendo peso." Nana served a late breakfast especially for him.

Octavio would seldom answer. As days passed he became sullen. His eyes seemed to look far away beyond the objects and the people of the present. When he communicated, he spoke softly and stared through the person he addressed. He refused to recognize the condition of the house in which the family slept and ate on the floor. The Revueltas family lived like insects of the dirt. There was little furniture and clothing and only a few blankets. Never in his life had he dreamed that he and his family would suffer this fate. A bitterness palpitated in his heart and throbbed in his mind, but he blamed no one, only himself. He condemned himself for bringing his wife and children to living like cockroaches of the earth.

Nana's sister Paquita and her three daughters came to see the family and to invite Flor to stay with them for a few days. Flor begged her mother to let her go and Nana agreed. When Paquita left, she gave Nana one hundred dollars to help buy clothes. A few days later, Flor returned home with new clothes that her aunt and cousins had enjoyed buying for her.

"It is the least I can do, sister," Paquita said as she opened the door to the family's 1940 Ford pick-up truck. The three girls sat in the back and waved goodbye as the sound of the motor thinned away.

Gradually the Revueltas family accumulated the basic material objects needed for them to function once more in society. Every day each member of the family returned to the temporary shelter with the hope that their father had found a permanent home. On his free time Octavio searched for a house. Arturo or a friend drove Octavio through the surrounding neighborhoods and cities chasing down friendly tips, addresses in the newspaper, and for-rent and for-sale signs. Octavio wanted a home near his work and near Simons. However, the homes that were available to him were not what he wanted for his wife and children. He preferred a home in north Montebello but the owners would not sell to a Mexican like Octavio.

Discouragement and anger consumed his life. When he returned from a day's search he prepared silently for work. Octavio changed clothes, ate quietly, put on his work hat and looked at Nana. . . . I will go out tomorrow to search again . . . She understood, and not a word was spoken between them.

One day Octavio returned home at seven in the morning. He drank a glass of warm milk, ate a slice of Mexican sweet bread and lay down to sleep. Nana lay next to her husband to embrace his slimming body. She encouraged him but there was no response. Octavio, with eyes opened wide, stared up at the ceiling, resting, waiting for the moment to start the search again. Nana cried in silence and held his head on her bosom. Octavio was like a worried, obsessed and terrified child.

"Octavio, leave this. Don't worry anymore. We will find a place. You'll see, we'll find one," she said, trying to comfort him.

Octavio was gone and she was alone with the children who would be hungry soon. Micaela and Arturo arrived from work at four; Javier and Flor got home about three. In the kitchen Gregorio cried in a large toilet tissue box that Javier had brought home from work.

"Let's go to the living room," Nana said, picking the child up. She kissed him and placed him on a blanket in the center. In those moments she forgot everything and life seemed almost normal. She listened to the voices that filled the house, voices that in their particular way demanded of her to be an all-working, knowing, understanding, loving mother. Nana did not move. Lost in her thoughts and dreams of a normal life, she was interrupted by a feminine figure at the front door. Gregorio was at her feet. Nana caringly looked at her son and moved to the door where a woman leaned forward and peered through the screen.

"Nana, it's Mrs. Cushner," the figure said, almost whispering.

Nana recognized the face which spoke through the grey woven wired veil. One by one, as they heard the voice, the children entered the living room. Flor went to the baby and held him. Six inquisitive and annoyed faces made contact with the woman. An awkward tension held all seven together as Nana invited Mrs. Cushner in without saying a word. Both women moved to the kitchen and sat on two of the four chairs that were around the only table in the house. Mrs. Cushner ignored the young eyes that rested upon her. Urgently, nervously she spoke to Nana who felt surprised and ashamed. Under these conditions, Nana did not want to receive a friend. Nonetheless she did, for Mrs. Cushner, who recognized Nana as a dignified woman, sat at her table. They had known each other since Nana's first child. Dr. Harold Cushner had delivered her second baby at home. Gregorio was the only child who was born in the antiseptic delivery room of Montebello's Beverly Hospital. The two women had socialized only during the visits to the doctor's office and at times when they ran into one another at the market. Still, they felt an unexplainable bond which made them feel like sisters.

"Some coffee, tea?" Nana asked.

"Tea, thank you."

Mrs. Cushner took a deep breath. The tension had subsided. She smiled at the children waiting in the living room. Each one had a particular analysis of the situation, an answer for her visit. Both women peered down into their empty cups and watched the circular motion of the spoon as Nana prepared the tea.

"I read about it. I told Dr. Cushner it might be your house. I'm sorry, Nana." Mrs. Cushner's voice communicated a genuine concern.

"Thank you," Nana said, lowering the cup onto the table.

"Well," Mrs. Cushner began with a little excitement in her voice, as if what she was about to say was an excellent thought, an idea that she had conceived that would make her listener happy. "I said to Dr. Cushner that we should help Nana and her family. And so I went out and I found a house for you. It's very clean and nice, perfect for you. The schools are close by. It's two blocks from where we live. And it's furnished, every room."

Nana's lips shaped a smile which she held while images of the perfect house, the dream come true, the object of Octavio's search projected onto her mind. She wanted that house.

"Nana, I've told you many times that I don't think you should live like this. You just don't belong here. And your children don't belong here." Mrs. Cushner's words cut deeply into Nana's heart. Nana wanted to believe them.

"You can move in tonight. I'll send for you and the children and the few things you might want to take. Or if you like, tomorrow morning." Mrs. Cushner waited. "What do you say? I've reserved the house for a week. It's there waiting for you. Nana, please tell me you'll take it."

Micaela, Javier and Flor heard the offer. They knew what Nana's response would be, word for word, in Spanish or English, and in their hearts they silently repeated it.

"I have to tell Octavio," Nana said.

In the children pessimism prevailed and shattered the outside chance, the hope of hearing something new, at least different. For it was always the same words, the punitive verb "tell," not "consider," "talk," or "discuss." The children immediately forgot Mrs. Cushner's news. It was something that had been said willy-nilly and could not be taken seriously because it was not of the real world.

"Talk to him. You have a week to decide." Mrs. Cushner attempted to hide her disappointment. She finished her tea and looked around once more. "You just shouldn't be here, Nana."

Nana offered her more tea and then filled her own cup. She stared into the boiling water. The steam caressed and followed the contours of her mestizo face. A soft tranquil shine made up her cheeks and nose. Her brow wrinkled a little when she looked up.

"Thank you, Mrs. Cushner. I'll tell Octavio when he gets home."

That evening Octavio arrived tired and irritable. It had been days since he had gotten any proper sleep. Although Nana did not want to tell him about Mrs. Cushner's surprise visit and offer, she felt compelled to do so. Her description of the house and conditions for renting it lasted just about the time it took Octavio to eat one pan dulce and drink one cup of hot chocolate. He listened carefully to what his wife had said. An offer had been made and he would respond, but not tonight.

"We'll see tomorrow," Octavio said and went to bed and slept.

Nana cleared the table and put the milk in the ice chest. If he loses more weight he must go to a doctor, she thought. She recalled Maximiliano. How quickly he withered away to death. She would not allow that to happen to Octavio.

The sun shone in the cool morning the day after Mrs. Cushner's visit. The briskness woke the family and made everyone arise from bed earlier. Arturo and Micaela went off to work. Javier and Flor had just finished breakfast and were preparing to leave for school when a voice outside called their father's name. Nana walked to the door and saw that it was El Placatelas, a new assistant to William Melone. He stood exactly in the place where Mrs. Cushner had been.

"Buenos dias. I want to speak with Octavio," El Placatelas said.

"He's sleeping. . ."

"It's urgent that I speak with him. Please tell him that I am here." El Placatelas stepped forward against the screen door. His physical posture indicated that he would not leave. His tone of voice revealed anger and that he would not deal with a woman.

"Here I am, Placatelas. What do you want?" Octavio responded as he tucked in his shirt.

El Placatelas did not waste any time. "Mr. Melone sent me to tell you that this house will be taken by a new worker. Mr. Melone wants it empty by early tomorrow morning."

Octavio had expected this news but not this soon. He was not ready. "Hey, please tell Mr. Melone that I need a week to find a house for the family."

"Mr. Melone anticipated that. He said that you cannot stay one day more after today. He wants it empty by early tomorrow. If you want to complain, go over there with them. That's all." El Placatelas finished his job. He walked away silently, stopped, leaned forward and to the side and cleared his nose. He wiped his fingers on his pants as he moved on.

Nana moved to a chair and collapsed her tired body.

"Why can't we move to Mrs. Cushner's house?" Nana queried.

"We can't take Mrs. Cushner's house," Octavio said. "We don't want to go where the gringos don't want us. Don't worry. Get the kids off to school. I'll be right back."

She hurried Javier and Flor out the door. Nana did not want them to be late for school. She moved around the kitchen automatically, preparing food for Gregorio whom she heard stirring in the bedroom. The fruit and cereal were ready, the milk warmed and poured into a plastic-covered cup. Gregorio was the only one of her children who had begun to drink from a cup so early. She sat with her son, helped him eat and imagined about the faraway places she heard described on the radio. Nana went to the door and searched the street for Octavio. The baby played at the table while she folded clean clothes. When Octavio returned, he sat next to Gregorio. She turned towards him with a blank expression. In seconds Octavio knew he would feel worse, for what he had to tell her would not change their housing situation.

"I want you to start taking our belongings to Uncle Elias' house. He doesn't have room in the house but he lent us his garage. When the boys return they will carry over what is left," Octavio said, hoping for a sign on Nana's face, but no expression of emotion registered. "Tonight I'm working two shifts, until eight. That way I will have Saturday and Sunday off. This weekend we will find a house," he promised.

Octavio sat at the table and played with Gregorio's hands while Nana placed his lunch in a brown paper bag. Still there were no emotional clues on her face. Octavio, embraced and kissed her.

Nana nodded and meant to say, "Go on now. That's fine." But instead of her wonderful voice, cold silence filled the kitchen. As soon as Octavio was out of sight Nana sat in front of Gregorio and cried. With clenched fists she sobbed and at that moment she hated El Placatelas, Mr. Melone and Mr. Simons and understood that now more than ever Octavio would not capitulate to the enemy.

"After almost twenty-five years, Gregorio, what we have is a loaned dirty garage. I know they could have let us have this house for a couple more weeks. But they didn't. They want to punish your father because he was a member of the labor union. That's why they don't want to help us. Oh son, you can't imagine how much I hate Mr. Melone and Mr. Simons. They forgave and did not harass other workers who were involved with the union, but not your father. They made him a target, an example." She ran her tongue over her lips to catch the tears. She picked up Gregorio and hoped that somehow he would remember her anger.

After Nana changed Gregorio and placed him in the living room to play, she began to gather clothes and kitchen utensils. She wanted everything prepared so that when the children returned they could move the household to Uncle Elias' garage. Flor arrived and immediately took bags to the garage. When Micaela walked into the kitchen she thought for an instant that her father had found a house, but one look at her mother told her the move was temporary again.

"Where are we going now, Mama?" Micaela asked angrily.

"Don't ask. Help your sister and you'll soon see," Nana said as she continued preparing the evening meal.

Arturo walked in about five, understood what was happening and did not say a word. He ate quietly and when finished went outside and took the spare tire out of the car trunk.

"Boxes here, clothes there," Arturo showed his two sisters. He wanted boxes in the trunk and the clothes in the back seat. He was afraid the boxes might scratch or rip the upholstery.

With Arturo's help, by six the Revueltas household had moved from a Simons temporary house to a Simons dilapidated garage. After the family was installed, Arturo went for Javier who worked at the market until seven in the evening. Uncle Elias brought extra blankets and two lanterns and explained to Nana that the family could use the outhouse. He demonstrated the water pump and told Micaela and Flor to collect bricks to build a small comal for cooking. About the time Uncle Elias finished with the pit, Arturo and Javier arrived. Javier went to his mother and put his arm on her shoulders and listened to Uncle Elias.

"You can use as much wood as you need. Good night," he said.

"Gracias, don Elias," Nana replied.

By eight the family was settled in the garage. Wrapped in blankets they lay or sat in a circle around a lamp hanging from a beam. Micaela and Flor talked softly, Javier did homework and Arturo sat cross-legged with Gregorio on his lap. He gazed out into the night in wonder of the mighty stars. Gregorio observed his brothers and sisters and his mother sitting in a chair above them dressed in a plain blue dress. Her hair was down, not in the usual molote but straight and with a touch of silver. Her eyes were blurred and her cheeks shone with silent tears. Gregorio followed one drop to the dirt floor on which the other children waited.

To Nana, sleep came periodically throughout the night. In the early morning she crawled in next to Flor and slept for two hours until five thirty when her eyes opened automatically. She went outside to the comal and started a fire. At nine, Octavio would be back hungry. She checked to see what food there was in the makeshift icebox. Plenty for breakfast but she would have to shop that day. While she prepared a cup of coffee, a familiar voice called her name. Nana turned to find Milagros standing before her in black against the greyness of the morning sky. Nana sobbed.

"Get your kids up and come with me. I don't want to see you living here," Milagros said, taking her daughter-in-law by the arm and walking her toward the garage. "Don't cry anymore. Don't let them see you this way."

They both entered and hurried the boys up. Milagros got the girls to dress Gregorio. In less than half an hour the family left. As Arturo put the last of the boxes in the trunk of the car and tied down the open trunk door, Uncle Elias appeared.

"You're going, Arturito?" he asked.

"Mama Milagros," Arturo answered, proud and happy to tell him who had come for them.

"Milagros," Uncle Elias repeated. He walked slowly, placing his large body in front of the garage. Milagros came out with Gregorio in her arms.

"Buenos dias, Elias," Milagros greeted him and turned toward the children. "Well, what are you waiting for? Let's go now." She led and they followed.

"Wait a minute. That bicycle and refrigerator stay here. For the use of the garage, well, for the night," Elias called out as Nana passed him.

"Of course, don Elias, you're absolutely correct, for the use of the garage. They'll stay with you. What do we need them for?" Nana bit her lip. "Thank you for everything, don Elias," she called out, not turning to look back.

That morning the Octavio Revueltas family went to live once again with Milagros and Damian. Milagros had declared her wishes in such a tone that Nana could not have argued with her. Nana accepted with the condition that she would cook, help with the chores and supply the food for the household. She would have preferred a different arrangement, but under the circumstances no other choice was avilable in Simons.

In the backyard of Damian and Milagros' house on Iowa Street a huge apricot tree shaded four benches around its trunk. Often Milagros sat underneath the tree and thought about her life and her son Maximiliano. After his death her health declined. She grew heavier and walking became difficult. As a result of Nana's presence Milagros was able to make time for quiet moments of rest. Her daughter-in-law assumed the daily tasks of the woman of the house. She cooked, cleaned house and washed clothes. She cared for her children, her husband and made sure that her father-in-law had what he needed, for it became clear that Milagros could no longer do the housework.

One week after Octavio's family had moved in with his parents, the Simons Brickyard situation had changed radically and its future was in question. Octavio asked Nana to sit with him outside under the apricot tree. They sat on the bench and for a time listened to the sounds of the birds, the children playing in the street, a young neighbor couple conversing about their child, people hammering on a fence, a roof, a piece of furniture, the great machines of the brickyard and the trucks transporting brick. Octavio and Nana listened to Simons, a place teeming with builders' activity and with life. At that instant a brown insect scurried past them.

"Oh how ugly! Squash it, Octavio," Nana pleaded.

"No, that one's going to visit. Let it get to where it's going," Octavio smiled.

"I can't stand you, Octavio," Nana said, her upset face on the verge of laughter.

Octavio smiled and picked up a long stick and began to trace a house on the ground. "Nana, we have three thousand dollars saved. With that we can buy a lot and build our own house."

"Octavio, your mother has been wonderful to us, but we are not comfortable living here. When will you buy the lot?"

"Don Sebastian has two lots on Español Street for sale. I have told him I want one. I'll speak with him this afternoon," he answered.

"I like the idea, Octavio." Nana allowed her voice to trail off into silence.

"Don't you want to see them?" Octavio enthusiastically suggested, hoping to excite her about selecting the lot.

As they sat under the apricot tree listening to the living music of Simons, he considered the amount of money needed to purchase the lot and the material and labor to construct the house. He was prepared to work as much as he could, but he could not take time off from Phelps Dodge. He had planned for Arturo and Javier to work on the house along with the men he would hire to help in the main construction. The money worried Octavio. He did not want to spend the family's entire savings. He had considered getting another job, but that demanded too much of his free time. At that moment, sitting with his wife under his mother's apricot tree, Octavio decided that he would return to gambling after his regular work hours in order to build a house for his family.

Nana picked up a twig and began to add flowers and trees to the drawing Octavio had started. "How will you pay for the house?" she asked, placing a hand on Octavio's right knee.

"We'll pay for it. Don't worry. Look, Sebastian wants three hundred for the lot. The material we'll pay for on delivery. Labor we'll pay every two weeks. We can do it," Octavio said, placing his hand over Nana's.

"Then let's do it!" Nana stood. Octavio still held her hand. They kissed.

"Will you go with me to see the lots this afternoon?" Octavio asked softly.

"Yes. The children don't know about this, do they?"

"No, no one knows. Why not tell them right now? And my mother too. Maybe the kids will want to go."

Octavio could not restrain his enthusiasm and happiness, that at least he would build his own house. As he walked toward the entrance of his parents' home, he sensed that the family had stepped in a new direction and that within a year they would not have to depend on company housing. Rumor had it that the Simons Brickyard was in danger of folding. While traveling in Europe with his wife, Walter Robey Simons had choked to death by a plague of brown insects that had inundated his mouth while he was calmly sleeping in his bed in a hotel in Paris. That morning the workers heard the news unperturbed, for after all Walter Robey Simons had been just another patron.

Chapter 22

The family, once told of the building of the house, became active in the planning and gathering of materials. Every member wanted to participate, to contribute labor, thought or money. The Revueltas family manifested the general national spirit of rebuilding a new world after the war. The Mexicans were builders who felt quite comfortable with the new spirit of rebirth. To create a new world from one that had been destroyed was not a new task for them. Their history demonstrated that they had successfully confronted this kind of challenge several times before.

When Octavio raised the pick over his head, he and his family and the men he contracted had begun to answer the challenge of rebuilding and starting a new life. After Octavio had swung the pick down to split and shatter the earth he paused to smile at Nana and the children. As the family proudly awaited the next swing, Octavio removed his shirt and started to dig the foundation of their new home.

Arturo, Javier, Felipe Franco and Benjamin Basurto grabbed shovels and picks and followed the trench formation marked by stakes and heavy white string. Gregorio touched the string and drew a warning from his father; nonetheless, he continued to play with the footings. Flor measured the perimeters and discovered that the future house was designed in a perfect square. She frowned at the shape from the corner where she had begun. Flor preferred the architectural design of the houses in Simons. She objected to the idea of living in a square box. The rectangular houses of Simons had added-on rooms that made the structure an adventure to walk through. She took Gregorio and walked away from the unbeautiful corner.

Micaela and Nana contemplated the men working. Both women looked closely at one man: Octavio. In that instant the flesh, cartilage and bones of his neck, back and arms appeared skinless and exaggerated. Amazed by the strength and sinuous profile of the male body before her, Micaela thought that someday she would meet and love a man like her father. Octavio stopped, leaned on the pick and rested while Micaela's reverie melted into her father's glimmering perspiration. Octavio smiled at Nana and his daughter and swung the pick again. Happy and satisfied with what he built, his body did not hurt.

Nana was concerned about Octavio's constant, slow weight loss. The image of the slim, deteriorated, infected body of Maximiliano, who had died of leukemia two years after she and Octavio were married, lay below the surface of Octavio's strong body. Octavio seemed to work faster, as if he expected to finish the digging for the foundation in one day. His lean beautiful animalness was not the body of the boy she had married twenty years ago; instead it was the body of the man to whom she was still sensually attracted. But Octavio's slow, unnatural weight loss bothered her and made her uncomfortable amidst her children. Octavio slung the pick to the earth. At the point of penetration his arms and back tensed. . . . He must be as beautiful when he finishes in me . . . Nana faded as the frame transformed into a voice.

"Please go and prepare some tacos for later. Send one of the girls," Octavio said and wiped his brow.

"I want a ham and cheese sandwich, Mama," Javier called out from the other side of the square.

"Sodas, some sodas," Arturo added to the order.

Nana heard but did not respond. She knew what they wanted. Her concentration was focused on Octavio's health. . . . Don't work so much, Octavio . . . Nana could predict his reaction. She remained silent.

At five in the morning Octavio opened his eyes. He had had a restless night. Today, after two weeks of digging trenches, mixing, pouring cement and dealing with the building inspectors from the city of Montebello who had delayed the construction because of the negative statements made about the fire department, Octavio and his crew would begin the framing of the house. In a week he had finished the necessary work on the foundation. The inspectors had finally given Octavio the go-ahead. The framing materials had arrived, were paid for and waited at the site. At last he and his family would see their house begin to take shape.

He blinked his eyes repeatedly, chasing the sleep away. He rubbed and opened them wide. Under the covers he reached to touch the small of Nana's back, her buttocks. He turned toward her. She assumed the natal position. He maneuvered his left hand and arm under her pillow, around her neck and down her shoulder to hold and caress her left breast. With his right hand he held her other full bosom. Nana murmured sleepy complaints and held his hands still. He kissed and inhaled her fragrance. He pushed his penis against her rump and cuddled her. In that wonderful warmth he dozed off. Still early in the morning he opened his eyes again. His left arm had fallen asleep. He lay on his back and listened to the movement in the kitchen. . . . My mother never seems to sleep . . . He imagined Milagros brewing coffee and preparing breakfast for Damian. In a few minutes Nana would take over and feed the entire family.

Damian was a man who seemed to eat privately even when surrounded by his family. That morning the children hurried through breakfast. Their conversation was centered on the house and they decided to check the status of the construction. Micaela and Arturo went to work, Javier and Flor to school. Gregorio lay in his bed traveling through the great mountain ranges and deep valleys of the ceiling. Milagros washed dishes. Octavio sipped coffee and Nana made lunches. As Damian rose from the table and took his lunch from his daughter-in-law, he paused and watched Octavio motion for more coffee. There were no words, only the sound of sudsy water, clinking dishes and glasses. Today Damian left later than usual. Nana found Damian's vacillation strange. She saw him stare lovingly at his oldest son. The crusty, strong, sixty-six-year-old moved toward Milagros and touched her shoulder. She froze, surprised by the rare caress. Milagros dried the last dish and concluded that his concern was not for her but for Octavio. Damian moved to the door and nodded at the man he had conceived and for whom he would willingly die to save from death. He recognized Maximiliano's symptoms and watched the infected, decayed body float through the memory fluids in his brain. Nana observed the drama created before her. Something odd and unique about the morning, perhaps magical, was on the edge of occurrence.

"Adios, Papa," Octavio smiled at his father. No matter what his father had done, Octavio never lost respect for him.

"Have a good day, son." Damian left, wishing that Octavio had kissed his hand. But that custom was practiced only with the old generation, not with the young people, he mused as he went to fire up one of the huge brick kilns not far from the house.

In the kitchen three were left: Milagros who knew exactly what would occur; Nana who had an idea and would not be surprised; and Octavio who made ready to begin the framing of the house which at that moment was all that he had on his mind.

Milagros thought about her friend doña Marcelina Trujillo Benidorm, the great curandera, and the narratives of their life that they had often repeated to each other. Octavio walked alongside his mother, partly angry that the work on the house had been interrupted and partly relieved that his mother had finally forced him to visit doña Marcelina. He never expected it to happen that morning. At first he had resisted, but upon Nana's insistence and Milagros' glare he began to walk out towards the church north of Vail, on Rivera Road across from the American Foundry, to doña

Marcelina's domicile. Mother and son advanced carefully and silently on Vail Street, passing workers on their way to their daily labor. The people who greeted Milagros and Octavio asked about the construction of the house.

"Good morning, señora. How's the building, Octavio?"

"How are you, doña Milagros? And the project, Octavio?"

Everybody in the neighborhood was interested in the progress of the Revueltas house. A change of attitude toward the family was implied in the casual conversation. In some, a shade of jealousy, envy and hope of failure belied the external ritual. As Octavio's answer, "Bien, gracias," was always constant and as the house rose, feelings became harder to disguise. The neighbors now considered the Revueltas family different. In their view the Revueltas' were no longer poor but had become "los ricos que construyen una casa sobre la barranca." The effect of this change of opinion built pride within the Revueltas family. They became aware that Octavio was accomplishing a task that at the time not many families dared to dream about and even fewer were capable of doing.

To the outside world the Revueltas' home indicated a success, but within the family it caused some tension between sister and brother. Aunt Felicitas and Aunt Rogaciana felt antagonistic toward Octavio's wife and children. His two younger sisters seemed to interpret all discussion about the house as an ostentatious show of uppitiness and money.

In them, jealousy and envy were the result of what Octavio built. Their husbands, they complained, had never thought of leaving Simons. The men had never expressed the idea of independence. When the women brought the subject up, their husbands' response was not original.

"It can't be done," the men would say.

"Too expensive."

"Where does Octavio get so much money?" Aunt Felicitas and Aunt Rogaciana wanted to know.

"God knows," the men replied.

"They pay him very well at Phelps Dodge. Why don't you get a job there?" the aunts demanded of their husbands.

"He also wins a lot at gambling."

"It was the fire. We don't need to move. We are fine here."

"But I don't want to live in this shack forever. We deserve something better!" Aunt Felicitas and Aunt Rogaciana cried out in disgust.

Milagros sighed at the results of success. This family friction preoccupied her. Nonetheless she supported Octavio. She felt his actions would serve as a model for her family. They were builders. They should build again.

For a while Octavio walked behind Milagros. She stopped to wait for her son.

"There's the house," Milagros announced, standing perfectly still and slightly raising her chin. Milagros stood strong. A breeze played in her black hair. Beyond her face Octavio looked at the house. He felt that he was about to step into a photograph.

The greeting was short. They knew what had to be done. Marcelina Trujillo Benidorm seemed to Octavio to be one hundred years old and yet he saw her as a beautiful young woman. She opened the door and bade them enter into an immaculately bright white room. The room was large, higher than what the exterior revealed. On the wooden floor stood no furniture. On the walls, evenly spaced, were images of the passion of Christ. The entrance to the house was located in a truncated corner where Octavio waited. To his left, in the center of the wall, was a passage to another space to which he was being led by the two women. As he was guided into the area he heard his mother bid him farewell. In front of him on the wall hung a painting of two praying figures: a man sitting on a wheelbarrow and a woman sitting in front of him. The painting was dark; storm clouds dominated the distant sky on the horizon. Situated under the canvas was a wheelbarrow; in front of it was a black block. Octavio discovered a cross standing diagonal to the corner on his right.

"Octavio, sit here."

He obeyed and while he listened he saw his mother observing from the centered opening in the wall. A quilted, multicolored jacket and black skirt covered his vision when doña Marcelina, with her fingers intertwined on her lap, sat on the black block. She smiled and initiated an ongoing litany of prayers, declarations and demands, all the time describing the contents of each potion she mixed for him.

"El susto is always black. It is a black veil that covers the brain and the eyes. It came upon you in the form of a great shock the night of the fire." She made the sign of the cross. "Drink these ground white spiders in manzanilla tea so that they can take us to where the black susto has hold of you."

Doña Marcelina complimented Octavio on his fine cooperation as a patient. She stirred up another potion. "Drink this ground octopus in yerba buena tea so that the black susto will take its form. Yes, I'm beginning to see. Soon I will be close enough to ingest it," she said in a serious tone.

"It is huge. Help me. Strength, spirits of my ancestors, accompany me now." Doña Marcelina battled to gain control and dominate her foe.

Fascinated, Milagros intently witnessed the struggle. As the battle evolved it seemed as if Octavio took on doña Marcelina's physical characteristics. A transfiguration had occurred. Octavio was physically her. In this way she was able to explore his/her body readily and locate her enemy. From where Milagros stood she saw that the face of her son reflected the image of doña Marcelina. After some time a large grotesque form on the right buttock and lower back of the curandera began to appear. The shape grew distinctly into a strong octopus with powerful tentacles that wrapped around doña Marcelina's waist. At times the beast pulsated. The susto was alive, parasitic, sucking the life of Milagros' son, but now doña Marcelina had traveled through the physical body of Octavio and had taken the susto out. It now clung to her. It wanted to live on, but the curandera knew how to control and consume it.

Gradually Octavio reappeared in his own body and face. His heart no longer heavy and tired, his spirit bright and free, his eyes sparkled once more. Hours had passed without his realizing the passage of time or what he had done. When he began to focus on the objects of this world, he was startled to find that he wore a replica of doña Marcelina's jacket. Octavio smiled over to his mother, took off the jacket and placed it over the wheelbarrow. He never asked where the jacket had come from. He went to his mother. Some time later doña Marcelina gave Milagros nine small pouches.

"Give him one pack each day. There are nine. He cannot miss one day." Doña Marcelina implied a danger if Octavio interrupted the nine-day treatment. "El Susto is clawed deep in your right hip. It's large and strong. It already has eight thick tentacles. You should have come earlier. But I ingested it. With my treatment I will cut its eight tentacles and the beast will dissolve in nine days. One day for each tentacle and the ninth for the spider body of the susto." Doña Marcelina calmly escorted the patient and the guardian to the opening of life on earth.

"Gracias, may God repay you," Milagros whispered.

Doña Marcelina discreetly took the money in Milagros' right hand. Octavio waited at the center of the white room for the ritual to end. He glanced toward the painting on the wall in the room where he had been cured. Carefully he studied the painting and discovered to his astonishment that the composition had been altered. The man who prayed had been taken out of the painting. Everything else remained the same. As doña Marcelina Trujillo Benidorm waved goodbye, he found himself waiting for his mother to open the door to their house.

Arturo drove his car under the carport he had built. He turned off the engine and sat comfortably listening to the radio. Through the windshield to the left he could see his Aunt Felicitas washing clothes in a large aluminum tub and hanging the garments on the clothesline. While she washed and hung, Arturo noticed that her lips never ceased moving. A chuckle came to him as he imagined the dastardly words and comments that the hard work evoked from his aunt's bad-tempered mind.

Aunt Felicitas distorted her mouth in disgust when she realized her nephew stared at her from his immaculate car. Whenever Aunt Felicitas and Arturo moved into a space together, a strong tension grew. Their extreme dislike for each other was not a family secret. There had been minor confrontations, stopped and controlled by Milagros. The family tried to steer them apart but as Arturo became more independent the disharmony between aunt and nephew became more critical and overt. The cause of the rift was known only to Aunt Felicitas and Arturo. The terrible secret affected both so strongly that one could not incriminate the other without suffering psychological damage. Every member of the family had a theory, but each kept silent for they feared the vulgar vocal wrath of Aunt Felicitas. In fact she had alienated many of the neighbors. Anyone who complained about her children or stood in her way was verbally attacked. Her mouth was feared not only by the neighbors but by her family as well. Francisco Tibor, her husband, was often the target of verbal abuse. Her yells often shattered the tranquility of the street.

Arturo turned the radio off, closed the door and entered the house. He found his mother, as he expected, preparing dinner for the nine who lived in the house. He understood it was part of the agreement that his father, mother and grandparents had arranged until the house was finished. Nonetheless, Arturo did not like his mother working so hard for all of them. Nana's face reflected a stone tiredness. Tortillas and meat with chile warmed on the stove.

"What time do we eat today, Mama?" He picked up a tortilla and a small piece of meat.

"In half an hour, son," Nana answered and continued her work.

"Wash car, Mama." Arturo chewed on the tasty morsel of tortilla, meat and chile as he went out.

Nana listened to her son's scrambled words. He was improving, but she wondered when he would translate the world into a language that was always understandable to other people. Tears came to her eyes and she fought back a sob. She heard Micaela's voice. The family was reentering the safe zone of Simons and the house. Except for Octavio, who would return at one in the morning, or the next day if he played cards. She hated his gambling; she hated cooking for the family; she hated being where she was.

The inside of the car carefully cleaned, Arturo started to wash the body. As he progressed, his Aunt Felicitas sneered at the way he pampered the automobile. Their eyes met once. A frozen silence and pause bridged the wooden fence. She screamed at her youngest son. He cried. She slapped. He wailed. She dragged him into the house.

Arturo washed the tires. His thoughts wandered through the day to the dance he planned to attend. Saturday and Sunday he planned to work on the house, for the sooner it was completed the sooner he would be out of his grandparents' house and away from their next-door neighbor, his Aunt Felicitas. Living crowded made him feel unclean. With a soft white cloth Arturo rubbed the car toward perfection. In forty-five minutes he finished. He proudly contemplated his magnificent machine. Aunt Felicitas, angered at what she interpreted as arrogance, furiously snapped the wet clothes before hanging them on the line. Arturo smiled, never noticed his aunt and walked into the kitchen where the family sat to dinner.

Nana moved around the table serving everyone. Damian and Milagros sat at opposite ends as patriarch and matriarch as well as an estranged couple, ex-lovers, silently nursing and maintaining past wounds. Micaela and Arturo discussed the dance. Javier asked if he could study in Nana's room. Flor offered pieces of meat to Gregorio, who threw them on the floor.

"Don't do that, Gregorio," came a soft reprimand from his grandfather.

"Eat, don't play," Nana scolded, stooping for the meat on the floor.

Flor placed more meat on Gregorio's plate. He flung three pieces toward his grandfather, Micaela and Arturo. One piece fell into Micaela's bowl, splashing chile onto her blouse and into her eye. She lifted her head, her left eye closed, stinging. She desperately reached for a towel. Arturo, Javier, and Flor laughed.

"Bull's eye!" Javier yelled. The laughter continued at Micaela's burning eye. Milagros smiled and wagged a finger at Gregorio.

"This little devil will pay for it if he doesn't behave," Milagros admonished Gregorio who seemed to listen. He placed the meat in his mouth and ate satisfied. His brown eyes moved from face to face.

Damian rose, thanked his daughter-in-law and walked out. Milagros silently contemplated the empty space which he left. Gregorio was on the left of Milagros and saw the others, one by one, leave the table. Nana washed the dishes while Gregorio and his grandmother sat at the table. Nana dried her hands and threw the towel over her shoulder.

"Do you want anything else, doña Milagros?" Nana reached for the plate.

Arturo walked into the warmth of the kitchen and went to the door.

"Be very careful, Arturo," Nana called to him as the door closed.

At last she was able to make a cup of tea and sit down. Gregorio continued contentedly entertaining himself with pieces of tortilla. Milagros stared into nothing. These trances which she fell into were bothersome to Nana. It was as if her mother-in-law's brain had disconnected itself from the rest of the body, incapacitating it for physical motion and feeling. Milagros' pupils would become intensely black, seeing beyond what surrounded her. Nana touched Milagros' hand. No response.

"Did you like the dinner?" Nana spoke almost into Milagros' ear.

The matriarch in black turned her head slightly. She was coming back from the place she contemplated.

"How about some tea?" Nana touched her hand again.

"Damian will not come home tonight," Milagros said softly.

Anger and a feeling of being dirty came over Nana. She regarded Milagros' aggrieved face. What was it that made her endure? Why was Damian the way he was? Why did Octavio do the things he did? Nana was convinced it was because they were owners of nothing, as her father used to say. Suddenly the house became silent as if some horrible, unexpected, faraway cry insisted on complete attention. Loud unintelligible voices now dominated the outside.

"What's happening?" Nana moved to the door.

"¡Ay Dios, Felicitas!"

Milagros recognized Arturo's voice as she rushed outside after Nana. Arturo raved, standing next to his car, wiping the mud spots which had splattered on it when Aunt Felicitas had thrown away several tubs of wash water. She was screaming insults to him as she and her older son were returning to spill another tub of wash water.

"No, ya!" Arturo screamed.

"Son-of-a-bitch, you are retarded! Go to hell!" Felicitas' tongue lashed out.

The tub was swung back and this time the water splashed onto Arturo and the car. He turned desperately toward the automobile, trying to protect it from the dirty water.

"Stupid fucker! What do you think, that you own this place?" Aunt Felicitas warmed up.

"Fuck you!" Arturo, infuriated, lashed out in her terms.

"Your mother! Fuck your mother! And I hope she teaches you to speak, idiot! Intruders! All of you are a bunch of intruders!" Aunt Felicitas shouted before the neighbors and family.

At that instant Arturo saw his mother standing near the apricot tree. Next to her were his brothers and sisters.

"Fuck yours! You whoring aunt!"

Aunt Felicitas, frenzied by the grave words, squatted and picked up a rock. Arturo rose with two bricks in hand. The combatants were only five feet apart.

"Oh, no!" Nana stepped between them. Milagros came to her side. The two gravely hurt mothers stood daring their children. Aunt Felicitas ran to her house still shouting insults.

"You should have allowed the boy to break her mouth! Someone has to shut that snake up!" a man yelled from another yard.

Arturo dropped the bricks and sobbed. Nana embraced and held him as if he were a child. Javier and Micaela took Arturo into the house. Milagros sat under the apricot tree and stared towards the dairy. Nana approached and saw that her eyes were as black as obsidian. Nana said nothing. Terrible, deep-seated emotions had been expressed. Ugliness had smeared their life and at that moment they both realized that they had been damned by their own. Two women: one sat and waited and the other went into the house to do what was necessary. Nana knew she would never forget that evening. She would urge Octavio to finish quickly. She could not last in Damian and Milagros' house much longer.

Octavio arrived home at about one in the morning and found Nana waiting under the apricot tree.

"You should have taken us to another place, Octavio. You always want to stay here. When something happens, you bring me to your mother's house. When we were married you brought me here. Until I insisted on getting a house. And now here we are again," she grumbled.

"It's not so bad. There was no other convenient choice," Octavio said under countless stars.

"We are tired of living in a corner. And with what happened today with your malicious sister! Your children and I saw what she did to Arturo. She threw crap on us. You must finish as soon as possible!" Nana continued.

"It will be months before we finish. We're hurrying. You must bear with this a little while longer."

Octavio stood and waited for her. They walked into the small room where they slept. She checked Gregorio who slept on Nana's side of the bedroom on the floor on three folded blankets. Gregorio slept peacefully.

The next morning Arturo did not speak to anyone. While Nana finished making breakfast, Octavio looked at the dirt on Arturo's car and told him that he would wash it at the building site. An hour later, Arturo had the car flirting with perfection. He looked for his father who nailed two-by-fours between eight-foot studs. Octavio gestured his approval and then pointed to a stack of short four-foot scraps.

"Bring those over here and we'll cut them," Octavio shouted.

Arturo reached for the bundle of wood tied with rope and flung it over his shoulder. He slowly carried the heavy bundle to his father who waited with a saw. As Arturo approached, the early morning sunlight darkened his crouched body into an anonymous silhouette. Octavio stared into the image and recognized himself thirty years earlier carrying wood for his mother's comal. With each step Arturo took, Octavio journeyed from a building site in the present to a place in the past. He did this almost at will, controlling the images and visions of the journey.

Chapter 23

. . . When I brought wood for my mama I was younger than Arturo. I worked like a mule. I walked along with my load of wood on my back, my body covered with mud. I would jump in the river, dive into the deepest part, against the strongest currents, to get branches and trunks that the river dragged downstream. I would take them to my mama and she would be very happy. I liked to see her smile. She had a round face, full of life. She worked a lot. My papa was hardly ever at home. He worked, but he was also enviciado with gambling and women. I being the oldest helped my mother the most. When my papa disappeared and would not return home for days, sometimes weeks, I found ways of getting food for my brothers and sisters. My mama was pregnant many times, but she lost some; some were born dead and others did not survive the year. When we came to this country my brothers were four: Federico, who followed me; Maximiliano, may he rest in peace; Jose and the child Julio, may he be with God. My sisters were two: Rogaciana, who followed Jose, and Felicitas, the youngest of all of us. My grandparents, uncles and aunts on the side of my mother and father were already in Simons. They came under contract in 1907 and 1908. Because of the Revolution in Mexico, we had to come.

Many incidents occurred that even now I cannot explain. First they killed my Uncle Cipriano and then they were saying that they wanted to kill my papa because he had shot at el Coyote, a bandit who wanted to take advantage of the rancho. My papa ran him off the ranch. Later we learned that government troops captured him. El Coyote's family blamed my papa. The rumor was that they were planning to kill him.

Soon after, another incident happened that mortified our family. This occurred when my grandparents and uncles still lived on the ranch. My Uncle Asuncion had married a girl from the ranch. Erlinda was her name. A few days after the wedding my uncle contracted to go north. He came to Simons to earn money to send to Erlinda so that she could join him. It happened that my uncle worked for more than a year. Erlinda lived in my grandmother Carmela's house patiently waiting for my Uncle Asuncion. One day my grandmother Tiburcia came to visit. My grandmother Tiburcia noticed Erlinda's waist and back and told my grandmother Carmela that her daughter-in-law was pregnant.

"That cannot be," responded my grandmother Carmela.

My grandmother Tiburcia insisted and they spoke with Erlinda who confessed that it was true. My grandmother Carmela found a switch and hit Erlinda until she told her the father's name. Upon hearing his name, my grandmother Carmela became infuriated and grabbed Erlinda by the hair and threw her out, clothes and all, to the street.

"Take her, comadre," she told my grandmother Tiburcia who answered that she never wanted to see Erlinda again and least of all anywhere near her house.

Well, the two grandmothers condemned Erlinda. My mama suffered greatly when she found out about the affair. My papa disappeared for several months. He returned home and began to leave very late at night, at times at one or two in the morning. He would say that he had to guard the sugarcane. I remember that once my mama followed him, and without anyone realizing, I also went out after the both of them. It was a night with a lot of light from the moon which illuminated the road. My mama saw my papa go to a shack about two miles from our house. A woman came out and embraced my papa. They both entered very happy into the shack. Upon seeing my mama wrapped in her shawl, wailing along that lighted road toward our house, I cried.

All of us, my parents, brothers and sisters had to abandon the ranch. We had a lot of family living in Simons and because my grandfather Alvaro sent money to my mama to bring us over here, we decided to come. Then from the ranch we went to Quiseo de Abasolo and to Irapuato. This was at the beginning of 1918. We remained there almost seven months. My papa became ill with influenza. He was very grave, but little by little he became better. That disease infected everyone and we encountered corpses everywhere we went. Wherever we walked, death was our companion.

During this time no tickets to travel by train from Irapuato to Torreon were sold. They said that there were no more tickets because Pancho Villa had destroyed the tracks to the north. He had destroyed and burned rails throughout a large area. There were no more tickets. We stayed there in Irapuato. Our money ran out. We had to work in whatever job we found. The day came when we could not wait any longer and we took the road toward Torreon. Wherever we found work we stayed for a few days. We even picked cotton. At day's end we would go to the nearest town to see what we could find to eat. I worked a lot on the railroad and my papa worked in what he could, but I worked more. We advanced all along the tracks or on roads near the tracks in case they needed workers. My papa was still sick. Others began to get sick. The influenza epidemic got worse and smallpox attacked two of my brothers.

In two months we reached Torreon. All of the family was sick except for myself and my mama. We didn't know anyone and there were no hotels. We had money to eat but there was no place to stay. We huddled under a water tank there. It began to rain. My papa and I looked for a place to escape from the water above. We found a camp of workers, railroad people, and we crawled under the railroad cars. The water fell in torrents. There we slept that night, wet, cold, hungry and sick. In the morning we discovered that Julio was burning with fever. My papa and I went in search of a doctor. We found no one. About three in the afternoon the clouds in the sky struck each other. It was going to rain again and we ran to where our family was. I noticed that my papa still suffered from weakness. Upon seeing the railroad cars at a distance we started to run with all the strength we had left. In that instant the sky opened. I saw my papa face a fear of not wanting to arrive where my mama was with the sick child. That foreboding came true because when we neared the railroad car where the family was we saw my mama sitting crosslegged. In her lap and arms she rocked my brother Julio.

We prepared a grave as best we could because the rain would not stop. When we went for him, my mama did not resist. She cleaned his face, combed his hair, buttoned his jacket and gave him up to my papa. We placed him in a hole lined with rocks. When we were burying him, my mama prayed the rosary, and with each rock my eight-year-old brother disappeared. If we cried, no one could tell because the rain drenched us and cleaned our faces. Together we were a flood of tears united by the anguish of death. In those moments I hated but I did not know at whom my hatred was directed. I crawled shivering underneath the railroad car until I finally fell asleep and in my dreams I swore to Julio that all the family would make it to Simons. I knew that was what Julio wanted the most—to reach Simons. . .

Octavio watched Arturo struggle step by step with the bundle of wood . . . . After we buried Julio, we followed the tracks north. We worked on them until we arrived at a station called Ortiz near Chihuahua. It took a month on the road. My papa and brothers were still traveling sick. On moving further to the north we found more dead. Hanged men abandoned for weeks. Many times we would rest under a tree only to look up and find the bare feet of a hanged man. And then one could explain the foul smell that one became accustomed to from miles away. I think that all of the north smelled of rotting corpses. Villa had rebelled again and was recruiting men, gathering arms and executing those who resisted him. A carrancista was pursuing him, a General Francisco Murgia who got great pleasure out of hanging any Villa sympathizers. This Murgia was in the habit of taking a town and hanging all the Villa sympathizers he found from all the posts on the main street leading to the plaza. There was much killing and fear during this time. And death appeared everywhere.

It began to rain again when we arrived at Ortiz. Along the tracks were five railroad cars. We went there and went underneath the cars. We lived there for more than a month. We slept there also. One day a lot of government troops came near and began to shoot near the edges of the city of Chihuahua. Then a corporal from the troops that were stationed there came to us. He knew me. He told us that we should leave because Villa's troops would be coming soon. We gathered our belongings and fled toward the north.

Faraway from the city of Chihuahua the sky ripped open again. In the distance we saw a small ranch and we approached it. We were huddled against a wall when two older girls walked by. They asked my mama what happened and why we were huddled against the wall. I remember very clearly what my mama told them. She told them that it was because we did not have a place to live. One of the girls understood and told us to wait and she ran to a house nearby. There were about fifteen houses there in all. The girl went and she called the woman with whom she lived. She was the goddaughter of that woman and she went and called her and the woman came immediately.

"What are you doing here? It's pouring rain and this man is sick," the woman said. She checked Rogaciana and Federico and she told my mama that the children were sick with smallpox. They had been reinfected.

The woman took my mama by the arm and took us to her house. And when we arrived we found out that the woman was a guest of her comadre. After a short while both of them stood before us and the woman asked her comadre, "Well, how are we going to do it?"

"Let them come in and I will give them my room," answered the comadre.

"But where will you sleep?" asked the woman.

"In the kitchen," answered the comadre.

And that night for the first time in months we slept under a roof. The comadre gave us her room. We slept well that night, dry on that soft earth. Thank God and those women.

Mrs. Fulgencia Camilo had many goats and donkeys. In the morning she would get up around four. She would milk a goat and she would take milk to my papa. After a few days Mrs. Camilo told me, "I will teach you how to make money here. Look, take a pick, an ax and a donkey. I will take another donkey to bring a load of firewood to the house, and you sell your firewood near the track or the town."

We went and later arrived at a parcel of land. I looked about and saw nothing. "Well, where is the wood around here?" I asked. In Guanajuato there were large trees where I lived. From them I got firewood, but here nothing.

Mrs. Camilo told me, "Look, just pay attention to the earth and you can see that the earth rises. Dig there."

I listened carefully and I did what she told me. I began to dig and dry roots came out and I cut them. In a little while I gathered a load, and she did also. And I went off and sold my wood for three-fifty. I did that for about a month.

One day by the tracks where we had been a workers' camp was set up. I spoke with the foreman about a job. He told me, "Yes, yes, come to the railroad car, I will give you a car for all of your family. But there is one thing. If the train goes south, you have to go with it."

"No," I told him. "We are going to the north."

"Well," he said, "that's the thing. It is not convenient for you, but work is. Come tomorrow."

The next day I went with him to work at the Cañon del Diablo to dig up tracks that the water had buried. When we finished we went to the Ortiz station. One day in the afternoon I was working near the station when the governor of Chihuahua pulled in with a trainload of soldiers and cavalry. Within half an hour, up ahead from where I was, they started shooting.

"Here come the Villistas!" they shouted.

I found out later that General Murgia accompanied the governor and they were searching for Villa because Villa had kidnapped a Mr. Knotts, a rich gringo miner. Villa asked for fifty thous and American pesos and he wanted them in gold because he hated the gringo faces on the American bills. Murgia and the governor were savagely killing anyone they suspected was a Villista. I saw that a bridge to the north started to burn. At that hour General Murgia ordered his soldiers to gather all the residents in the area and put them to work. Screaming, Murgia ordered the foreman, "I swear to you, that if I cannot pass by two in the morning, I will execute every one of you."

I worked at the bottom of the bridge. We were scared to death because we knew that Murgia would keep his word. I looked up. The bridge was still burning and we were at the bottom planting wooden pillars and nailing crossbeams so that we could lay track on the top to allow the general to pass. Before two in the morning the general crossed. When I was resting, the foreman told me, "You know what, my job is to go in front of the train, five, ten meters ahead, inspecting the rails. If you want to, go. You are strong and a good worker."

"No," I said, "I will stay here."

Then he gave me a paper. He told me, "When the paymaster comes, he stops at the station. Give him this paper and he will pay you."

That is the way it was. I gathered and sold firewood when there was no work at the station. I waited for my family to get well, to get stronger, so that we could forge ahead. It happened that in a moment of carelessness the Villistas burned the bridge again and I worked again on the railroad track. I worked a little less than a year for the railroad.

My mama and my brothers and sisters went to stay in Chihuahua. When the train would go to the city, my mama would send us tortillas and she would send my papa tobacco or cigarettes. What we would ask for, my mama would send. My papa and I stayed in a boxcar in the outskirts of the city. We heard much about the Revolution: that they killed Zapata, that they executed Felipe Angeles in Chihuahua, that Villa's army was destroyed, that Villa still roamed the area avenging the death of his friend Felipe Angeles. Suddenly one day the Revolution calmed down. We found out that the train traveled to Ciudad Juarez, to El Paso. We arrived at the border on the first train that passed through Chihuahua.

We stayed in Chihuahua for about two weeks. My grandfather sent a message to an uncle of mine who lived near Texas that we were there, that he should go see us. He went and he told my father, "Well, get ready, I will come for you soon, but I am going to take you across through the river."

My papa said that was fine. The next day my papa received a telegram from my grandfather who had sent some money. That morning the owner of the place we were staying in came over. "Let's go," he said. "I will take you to change the money."

The man, his son, my papa and I went to El Paso to change money. In Ciudad Juarez a man approached us and asked if we wanted to work.

"No," my papa said. "We are on business."

"I want you to help me," the man said, "only for a day or two. I need help."

"I told my father to go on, that I would go work with the man. My papa said that was fine and I went. The man took me to a place full of adobe houses on the very edge of Ciudad Juarez. Further on were fields and beyond, desert. There were two houses with doors of the same color and we went inside and I started working. It was only making mud for adobe blocks. At two o'clock the man said, "Let's go eat."

When we finished eating, I returned to the house where I was working. But when we left the house I was working in I did not pay attention to the number. There were two very similar doors, exactly the same color but I did not know which was mine. I did not remember if it was the first or the second. I went ahead and slightly opened one. I quickly realized that that was not mine because there was a cow and a saddled horse inside. Suddenly I heard a woman scream.

"Oh! A thief!" she yelled to a man there. "A thief!"

The man, half-naked, ran out with a gun and shot at me. I screamed and raised my hands that I was not a thief, but he still fired at me. Nearby stood a woman with her daughters and they began to shout that he better not shoot me and they verbally attacked him because perhaps they did not like him. The cantina was nearby and the man for whom I was working came out and asked the aggressor, "Well, what is happening?"

I told him that the man wanted to shoot, that he accused me of being a thief. My boss went to the man and insulted him and told him, "What do you accuse him of? Show me, show us what he stole from you."

The man went away. And we entered the house we were working at. There was a bucket of water, muddy water that we washed our hands with. That muddy water appeared crystal clear to me. I grabbed the bucket and drank and drank.

"No!" the man yelled at me. "Wait. I will be right back."

He came back with a glass of whiskey and sugar. I felt better with that. After a few days I did not return to work, for the work had finished there.

At last my uncle came with the man who was going to help us cross. We crossed the river when the current was not strong, when the water was waist deep. I carried Felicitas on my shoulders; Federico carried Rogaciana. After the crossing the coyote took us to his house where we rested and ate. My uncle had gone ahead and returned the next morning and took us to his house that he had nearby. All the family arrived there and we stayed a few months. My brothers and I often talked about the trip and remembered Julio. We were five brothers but Julio died; now we were four.

Octavio observed Arturo set the bundle of wood on the ground. Arturo glanced up and smiled.

While we were at my uncle's house, it so happened that some neighborhood boys came by and invited us to go swimming. The water was very near. "Well, let's go swimming," I remember them saying.

We all went. There was beautiful shade. Maximiliano and Jose swam in a ditch. After a while two more boys arrived. They began to break bottles.

I told my brothers to get out of the water for they might cut themselves. But my brothers refused because the water was very cool. It was very hot. When those boys came they began to call us names. They said that we were Germans. What are they? I wondered. Finally I told them that we were not, that we were Mexicans, the same as them.

"Oh! You didn't like what I said?" one of them replied.

"No, I'm just letting you know that we are Mexicans like you," I said.

With that he jumped me and the other boy jumped my brother Maximiliano and we started to fight. It happened that I cut the boy's face, his nose and his cheek very badly. I split his face in half. He ran away to the police and accused me of being a smuggler and that we crossed without paying. Two policemen came with my uncle. One policeman waited until his partner tired of trying to scare us. He came close to us and told us not to be afraid, that those boys were a bunch of troublemakers and they had many complaints against them. He advised us to cross where we were supposed to.

"Arrange your documents," he told us, "and come across the right way."

In the morning the family returned to Mexico, to Ciudad Juarez, to arrange our papers. My papa and I were the first to get our legal papers and then the rest of the family. Then the family went to El Paso where my papa and I waited. A few days after, my papa and I went to a labor contracting office where they signed people on for work across the country. There were plenty of contracts for everywhere. They asked the group of men where they wanted to go. Some said California, others said different destinations, but most people wanted to go to California. In a short while a contractor came.

"You want to go to California, don't you?" he asked.

We were about seventy men who were under contract with that individual. But he forced groups of men to stay at places all along the way. About forty men arrived late at night in Los Angeles and complained that they were hungry.

"Well, you must wait until we buy some food," the contractor said. He asked my papa, "Have you been here before?"

"No," my papa answered.

"Let's go then, come and help me with the provisions," and he got two other men to go. I spoke up and said that I too would go with them. The contractor ordered me to stay. But I insisted.

"I will go also," I told my papa.

"Alright, you can help in something," the contractor told me.

As soon as we began to unload the provisions, the hungry men bunched up and grabbed food. Then my papa told me, "Let's go."

We left the camp. We traveled, hiding from everyone, and we walked through the night and we arrived in Long Beach. A heavy fog came in and we could barely see. My papa was not familiar with these places. The signs were not what we were accustomed to so we asked, but no one could help us because we asked for "Simones" and here they know the place as "Simons." We walked and walked until we found a man who told us that we were far from our destination. He told us to go to a movie house nearby and talk with a man who knew how to get to Simons. We found that man and my father asked him for Simons. And the man thought for a moment.

"Oh, yes," he said. "I believe I know where. I'm not sure but I think it's in that direction. Follow the tracks, the railroad tracks in that direction. Follow them and where you see the houses from where you stand on the tracks, that will be Laguna Road. When you are there, walk on and look to the right. The houses are painted white."

Yes, they were whitewashed with lime. As we approached Simons from afar you could see the houses shine white from the morning sun. Right away my papa ran into a cousin. "Come on, cousin. Come on in," she said and she invited us to her house and we ate.

Her husband who was also a relative had a horse and buggy. They were ranchers; they planted many vegetables. He told us, "I am going to take you to my uncle."

He took us to my grandfather who gave us a room and in about three weeks my papa and I started working at the brickyard. After five weeks we sent money to El Paso where the family waited. We sent money each week so that my mother, brothers and sisters could come. They sent us telegrams saying that they were on the way and that we should go for them at the central train station in Los Angeles. We received a second telegram indicating the time and date of arrival of the train. My papa and I went to meet them in Los Angeles. When they got off the train we all embraced and I thought of Julio. We had finally made it to Simons.

Arturo had untied the bundle of wood and separated it by lengths. He stood proudly before his father, silently telling him that the wood was ready for cutting and that they should begin building their new home.

The Brick People is a work of fiction. Any similarity between the characters and people, living or dead, is coincidental.